BEFORE SUNRISE

Bryan T. Clark

This work of fiction is just that, a work of fiction. Any similarities or references to real people, events, establishments, organizations, or locations are intended only to give this fictional work a sense of reality and authenticity. Names, characters, and situations are the product of the author's imagination and used fictitiously, as are those fictionalized events and incidents.

BEFORE SUNRISE

DEDICATION

Life Lessons within the Game

My dearest husband, thank you for the countless hours you have spent reading every single draft or change I sent your way. Your honest and not-always-so positive feedback is what made this manuscript become a novel. I love you with all my heart and soul.

To my high school swim coach: Even though I had never swum on an organized swim team until high school, you believed in me enough not to cut me. You taught me how to win, how to accept losing, what it means to make personal sacrifices, and how to give mutual support to others. Most importantly, you helped me find my swagger. Even though I had the biggest crush on you, I swear this book is not based on you.

To the supporters who purchased and read my first book, *Ancient House of Cards*: Thank you for the honest reviews. Just like my swim coach, you too have taught me something in this life. Through your honesty, I have learned what a conjunctive verb and dangling modifier is, and most importantly, what you, the reader, expect.

Last but not least, a big thank you to my beta readers, Alma C., Amy R., Brian I., Brian R., Erin H., and Israel S. You did exactly what I asked and needed, holding nothing back. The genuine feedback you provided on the manuscript was invaluable.

Don't Choose Darkness When You Can See the Light

Bryan T. Clark

ABOUT *BEFORE SUNRISE*

Just **Before Sunrise,** as the fog lifts from the pool, the light reveals the tapered backs of male swimmers in Speedos concluding their morning workout.

Nicky O'Hare, a promising freshman recruited to the Tampa Bay University swim team, shows promise both in and out of the pool. The lean Irish kid with the boy-next-door good looks from Brandy, South Dakota, is likely the most talented swimmer on the team. Ready to experience all that college life has to offer, Nicky has even put finding a boyfriend on his wish list.

Coach Philip Silva, a former Olympic swimmer with a once-impressive swimming career, has recruited Nicky as part of his mission to rebuild the University's failing swim program. Focused on the upcoming season, Philip's real challenge will be keeping his secrets and demons submerged below the surface.

All seems well until one night when Nicky and Philip end up at the same Fourth of July celebration. With fireworks in the sky, the hot and humid night reveals the attraction between the two. But can these boundaries be crossed? Suddenly forced to reevaluate his life, Philip is met with the moral dilemma of discovering true love with the University's rising star.

Before Sunrise presents a story of friendships, love, complicated relationships, and deception, woven into an unexpected ending.

1

The screaming was deafening as it reverberated from the walls. The crowd was on their feet, stomping and shouting as they witnessed what could only be called a phenomenon. Nicky O'Hare was having one of the best swims of his life. With each stroke, he felt his fingers stretching his arms further forward. Tilting his head slightly when he took a breath, he saw his teammates walking alongside the pool, jumping and screaming "NIC-KY, NIC-KY, NIC-KY," as they clapped in unison.

Nicky increased his lead with every stroke; his teammate Connor pushed to regain his lead, but he was no match for Nicky. This finish by Tampa Bay's newest recruit had been predicted by no one.

When Nicky hit the wall first, he hit it with such force that even the coach was concerned. Ripping his goggles and cap off, Nicky held on to the red and yellow plastic floating rope that divided the lanes. Looking up at the scoreboard to check his time, he then scanned the pool deck looking for Coach Silva. Seeing his entire team and the crowd erupting into mass euphoria over what just occurred, Nicky couldn't help but smile, knowing his time had to surely please his coach, the only person that mattered. The freshman from Brandy, South Dakota, population seven thousand, just showed everyone at his first college-level meet—including Connor Moretti—that he was here to win.

As Nicky pulled himself out of the pool, Coach Silva was right there, first giving him a double high-five, followed with a hug and a light pat on his wet ass. To the spectators watching, the hug was nothing, but for Nicky, that hug was worth all the effort. It was also a scene, a feeling he knew he would play over and over in his head later.

The electrifying energy from the win continued into the visitors' locker room as everyone high-fived and congratulated Nicky on the amazing race. The kid who had only joined the team six weeks ago was an instant phenom. During a team meeting prior to hitting the showers, it took several minutes to quiet the group before the coaches spoke. As everyone settled in a tight cluster, Nicky noticed Connor was missing.

"Okay, okay, give me a minute!" Coach Silva, the team's head coach said as he held up his clipboard trying to get their attention. "Quiet for a minute."

Coach Silva stood with a grin across his face as he waited a few seconds more for the guys to stop laughing and chattering. "That was an excellent start to what is going to be a goddamn good season for us—" Not letting the coach finish, the group of half-naked bodies again broke out in cheer, high-fiving and snapping each other with their towels.

"Guys, I'm not finished," Coach Silva yelled and then rolled his eyes, conceding to having lost control of his swimmers again. Nicky, the only person in the locker room who had the coach's complete attention, stood gazing at him. The shy introvert was anything but shy when it came to his lascivious thoughts of Coach Silva.

Nicky was shocked when the coach made direct eye contact with him with that thousand-watt smile. There was something about the way Coach Silva stared at him that knocked him slightly off balance. Mesmerized by his new coach, he would do anything to please him—anything.

Lost in his fantasy, Nicky was caught off guard when hoisted by his teammates as the celebrity of the hour, and was lifted up by one of the guys and thrown over his shoulder. With his wet bottom exposed to everyone, several of the guys slapped at his ass through his wet Speedo. At five-ten, Nicky was shorter than most of his teammates, with the exception of the guy on the team everyone called Squirrel. Like a rag doll, Nicky was swung around as beaming faces chanted, "NIC-KY, NIC-KY."

When the coach was finally able to speak again, he made it short, congratulating the team on their win and ordering them to get cleaned up and return to the bus so they could get on the road.

Heading to his locker after the team meeting, Nicky caught a glimpse of Coach Silva and his two assistants as they took to a corner of the locker room facing one another in a huddle. Nicky still couldn't believe he was here, eighteen hundred miles from home, swimming for Coach Silva. From the first day that the coach showed up at their doorstep ready to deliver his recruitment spiel, Nicky was infatuated with him. Since then, Nicky had countless dreams of the coach. Each dream was the same: *It was early morning, and Nicky was awakened by a loud bang. As his eyes adjusted to the dark, he saw the coach coming toward him and taking a seat next to him. The room was unfamiliar to Nicky and exposed for all to see, yet no one paid them any mind. Almost as if it was outside, there were no walls, and they were elevated above the world. Nicky lay his head on the coach's lap, and the coach stroked his hair. Each time, when Nicky looked up at him, the coach would smile at him and then gently kiss him on his forehead. The tender strokes of his hands soothed Nicky back to sleep.*

Coach Silva stood with his back to Nicky and never saw his admirer as Nicky walked by. The coach, standing at six feet and two hundred and ten pounds, was engrossed in his conversation and unware that his ass was being admired by his new star swimmer.

Locating his locker, Nicky dialed in the combination and popped the old metal door open. Standing next to Nicky, Connor was the first to broadcast that he needed a hot shower as he slipped off his Speedo in one swoop. Connor left his damp bathing suit on the floor as he grabbed his towel. He forcefully bumped Nicky as he passed behind him, causing Nicky to brace himself against the locker in front of him to steady himself.

"What a punk."

"Huh?" Nicky turned around to see his teammate Tyler Peterson, the other new freshman, staring up at him from the wooden bench between the rows of lockers.

"He's mad that you buried him out there in the 400. He's a punk."

Connor was a year ahead of Nicky and also swam on the school's water polo team. Over the summer, his parents had shelled out big bucks for him to train with an Olympic coach on the West Coast. Though he wanted to believe there was no bad will in Connor's shove, Nicky couldn't discount the negative vibes he had felt from the guy from day one. Slipping off his wet suit, Nicky tossed it up into his locker on top of his gym bag before turning to address Tyler. "Are you hitting the shower?"

Tyler, who was tapping out a text to someone on his phone, shook his head without looking up. "Naw, I'm heading back to the bus. Save you a seat?"

"Yeah, thanks." Nicky wrapped his towel around his small waist and tucked the end against his flat stomach as he made his way toward the familiar smell of sweat, urine, and steam emanating from the shower room. With ten shower heads in the dated communal shower room, Nicky waited at the entrance for the next available shower.

Noticing his teammate J. B. standing at the far end of the shower, Nicky looked away. Embarrassed, yet awestruck at the sight of his glistening dark skin, Nicky couldn't stop himself from taking several more uncomfortable glances at the six-foot-one, lean hundred-and-ninety-five-pound sophomore sculpture. Covered in soap, J. B. was in his own world as he stood under the hot water with his back facing his teammates. As the hot water ran down his neck and back, his mocha chocolate skin was being revealed to Nicky.

Captivated, Nicky waited his turn against the wall, sizing himself up to those in the shower. In high school, only being one hundred and fifty pounds was about average for those on the team, and he shared the same ordinary sandy brown hair and ruddy skin tone as everyone else in the neighborhood. The only things that set him apart from most of his friends were his light green eyes and long lashes, which were not a big deal to anyone in the small town of Brandy.

When Bryson, one of the senior varsity swimmers, walked out and ran a towel through his golden highlighted hair, he left his tanned body exposed as he gave Nicky a nod, signaling it was his turn. Half smiling back at Bryson, Nicky rolled his eyes. *Jesus, is everyone a fucking God around here?* he thought. Stepping into the shower, Nicky took the shower head next to J. B.

Nicky adjusted the water temperature and then pumped a heap of soap from the dispenser into the palm of his hand. With a few more glances, Nicky covertly stared at his teammate through the steam, taking in his broad back, massive thighs, and butt.

J. B.'s skin tone reminded him of a cup of silky hot chocolate, the water running down his beautiful back and legs. Growing up in the Midwest, Nicky had never seen a nude black man.

Even though Nicky had seen J. B. over the last several weeks in his Speedo during practice, this was the first time he had seen him in the buff. Nicky had wondered several times if the rumor was true about black men. He was sure J. B. was stacked just based on what he had been able to see in the tiny Speedo. When J. B. turned around and faced him, Nicky, gasping, knew it was true. It was darker than the rest of him as it dangled down between his legs like a horse's dick, muscular and thick, hanging straight down toward the floor. It took everything in Nicky not to stare and to look away.

J. B. gave Nicky a casual nod as Nicky forced his eyes to look at the aqua green tile behind J. B. "Dude, I'm sorry for making you swim so hard. My legs started cramping up again, and I just couldn't do it. You saved our ass in that relay," J. B. said as he raised his arm to the shower head, rinsing what little soap that remained in his shaved armpits.

"Yeah, um, thanks," Nicky replied, adjusting the temperature of the water that kept changing on him and not wanting to look at J. B. Nicky reflected on the last race. Despite J. B.'s poor performance swimming the third leg before him, which almost cost them the race, Nicky was able to make up the distance and pull out a win for the team. Nicky concentrated on keeping his eyes up. "You need to eat more bananas to take care of that cramping; your body is telling you that it needs more—"

"Man, don't ever tell a brother to eat a banana!" J. B. interrupted Nicky in mid-sentence.

Nicky froze, not understanding the sudden aggressive tone in J. B.'s voice. It took him a second to connect the racial implications of what he had just said, causing his cheeks to turn an instant rose as he watched J. B. for whatever was coming next. J. B. starting laughing as a wide grin swept across his face. Nicky was even more confused.

"I'm sorry. I didn't mean anything by it," Nicky said, embarrassed before realizing that J. B. was playing with him.

Moving closer into Nicky's personal space and towering over him, J. B. leaned in and chuckled, "I'm just fucking with you, dude. "

In that moment, inches apart, J. B. seemed massive. His beautiful brown biceps and massive chest were unlike anything Nicky had ever seen. J. B.'s dark brown eyes stared intensely into Nicky's, adding to the tension that rose in Nicky's belly and lower extremities. Nicky broke the stare, reaching for more of the cheap soap. Dumping a fair amount of soap into the palm of his hand, he focused down at his feet as he vigorously scrubbed his scalp.

After finishing up his shower and getting dressed, Nicky dashed out to the waiting bus. He couldn't wait to board the bus so he could call his parents with the news about the meet. Scanning the full bus, he saw Tyler about five rows back and made his way to the empty seat next to him. Removing his earphones from his ears, Tyler smiled. "Where've you been?"

"I had to get dressed." Nicky flashed back to J. B.'s beautiful wet body standing next to him in the shower as he waited for Tyler to stand up, offering him the window seat. Bursting with energy, Nicky moved into his seat and settled in. As promised, Tyler had taped Nicky's races today so he could load them onto YouTube for his parents to see. It was his mom, sitting in the bleachers during his high-school meets, who was his number-one fan. Even on days when he wasn't as good as he wanted, she had a magical way of making it all better by the end of the day. He knew his dad was supportive as well, but he worked long hours as an accountant, so most of the time, it was just Nicky and his devoted mom at the meets.

Growing up as an only child, Nicky had never spent much time away from his parents, and going away to college was a big deal to the whole family. Other than the occasional summer camp or a week-long stay with his grandparents, who lived two hours away from the house he grew up in, it was always just the three of them.

The bus rocked as the driver disengaged the brakes, and the big red and gold bus that bore the school's mascot, *Tampa Bay Red Devils,* started to move. Making its way out of the parking lot, they were heading back to campus. Pulling out his phone, Nicky placed his call to his mother, instantly hearing her excitement on the other end. After twenty minutes of filling her in on the high points of the meet, he asked how everything was going at home. Learning that very little had changed at home, they said their good-byes. Nicky sunk down into his seat as he remembered the days when it was just him and his mom in her Buick heading home after a meet. Although that was just last year, it seemed like a lifetime ago.

Settling into the long bus ride, one by one, his teammates around him dozed off. Staring out the window, Nicky sat in his seat, listening to Kelli Pickler sing his favorite song, "Best Days of Your Life," on his iPod.

As the bus rolled along, the sun set, and the inside of the bus grew dark. Nicky sat silently for the last hour as the reverberation of the engine soothed him before adjusting himself—there was something about after a swim meet, when the work was done, that made him horny. For the tenth time, Nicky called up the feeling of the coach congratulating him on his win earlier, the physical contact, the feel of the coach's hand on his ass. Lightly rubbing his hand against the soft nylon sweatpants that housed his growing woody, Nicky glanced over to see if Tyler was asleep.

Just as Nicky looked at Tyler, Tyler nodded toward the front of the bus. Nicky looked up, first laying eyes on Coach Silva and then seeing that the other two assistant coaches, Dean and Paul, were talking to J. B. in the first two rows.

Coach Silva and Paul were sitting in their seats directly behind the driver, and Dean and J. B. were standing in the aisle next to them. As most of the twenty-four swimmers that made up the team slept, Nicky watched as they whispered to each other, all with serious looks on their faces.

Nicky focused for some reason on the back of J. B.'s head, staring at the short curly hair that faded down his neckline. The thought occurred to Nicky that he didn't know any of the African Americans that lived in his hometown. There were a few African Americans in his school, but he didn't know any of them. He liked J. B., although his massive size intimidated him just a little. He chuckled to himself, thinking about how Tyler—a flamboyant blond-hair, blue-eyed gay guy—and J. B.—an African American—were the two people he had hit it off with. Nicky snickered again, recalling what his mom told him when they checked him into the dorms prior to the start of the semester: *"Behave yourself and study hard, but remember to have fun and enjoy the experience."*

When the bus pulled into the campus parking lot just after ten o'clock, the team sluggishly stirred about the cabin. Nicky had gathered up his duffel bag from the overhead bin when he realized Squirrel was standing behind him. Squirrel was the shortest swimmer by far on the team, with reddish brown hair that matched his unibrow. Standing at five-eight, Squirrel was a little chunky for a swimmer, but he had one of the best butterfly strokes on the team.

"We're heading to The Harbor to shoot some pool. You want to join us?" Squirrel asked in a horrible mock British accent.

The Harbor was ten minutes from the university on Bay Shore Boulevard. Several blocks of expensive clothing boutiques, restaurants, craft stores, and unique home interior shops ran along the harbor. The area was popular at night, when young adults congregated in the small five blocks that hosted the Bay's nightlife. Nestled between two of the hottest night clubs was Art's Pool Hall, a favorite amongst the Tampa Bay University swimmers. The Harbor and Art's were nothing like Nicky had ever seen. In fact, he had never ever been to a pool hall, if you didn't count Jeff's Liquor Mart on the corner of Main and Chestnut back home. With two pool tables in a back room, it was a hangout spot for the less amiable people in town.

Wavering on his answer, Nicky heard his mother's voice: *Now, Nicky, make sure you study every night, but don't forget to have fun.* "Naw, I think I'll pass tonight," Nicky responded as everyone started moving forward.

Nicky filed off the bus behind his teammates, trading the freezing air-conditioned bus for the thick, humid nighttime air that Tampa was known for. The high humidity made him think it was going to rain, causing him to eye the dark grey clouds that shadowed the moon.

Glancing over, Nicky saw Coach Silva and Coach Paul talking off to the side of the bus. Coach Silva glanced over at Nicky, which captivated every cell in Nicky's being. Nicky again was immediately frozen in the moment. He had to physically remind himself to move his feet and not to stare. It was another four or five steps before Nicky heard Coach Silva call out to him, "Hey, Nick. Good job today. Practice before sunrise tomorrow!"

Nicky knew that meant five-thirty, which was going to hurt. "Okay, Coach," he said, swinging his backpack over his shoulder; butterflies leaped in his stomach that Coach Silva had noticed him.

Across the parking lot, Nicky saw J. B. jumping into an old car driven by a young woman. Looking too young to be his mother, Nicky figured she must have been his girlfriend, whom he had only heard about. Nicky watched as J. B. leaned in to kiss her before the dome light faded out.

As a couple of more car doors slammed around him and the sounds of people greeting loved ones floated by, Nicky watched the cars as they drove out of the lit parking lot. Suddenly homesick, Nicky released a heavy sigh before starting his trip up the hill to his dorm. Clear across campus, the walk about ten minutes to his dorm took him to the far south end of the campus.

Tampa Bay University was built originally as an all-boys school in the early 1950s. After the State of Florida took it over, converting it to a university, it was pieced together over the years to make a full-fledged campus. In general, the campus was landscaped with dog-wood trees and thick vines of wisteria. The scent of wisteria floated throughout the campus at night, becoming a favorite of Nicky's. Prior to moving here, he had never seen the cool-looking vine that hung from trellises flanking the walkways throughout the campus. The old multi-level brick building that housed some of the older classrooms intrigued him the most. He once told his mom over the phone that he felt like he was at Harvard because of all the old brick buildings, and she had laughed at him. Although thousands of students were on campus every day, the flower gardens and small patches of lawn that doubled as the perfect spot for students to study or sit with friends created a tranquil and picturesque atmosphere.

The newest addition, built five years ago, was the sports complex. It included a ten-thousand-seat football stadium, an indoor basketball arena, and a state-of-the-art outdoor aquatic center. The massive pool, built to Olympic specifications, had twelve lanes divided in the school colors of red and gold. A floating divider in the middle separated the men's team from the women's team during practices. The school insignia of a bright red devil was tiled at the bottom of the pool on both sides as well as in the diving pool adjacent to the main pool. Permanent concrete bleachers bordered both sides of the pool. At the far end of the pool was the only grass area, with a couple of small trees and a snack shop on wheels that was run by the booster club.

The campus was usually sleepy by seven in the evening, with the exception of the area around the Walter Einstein Center, which housed the bookstore, food services, and student lounge. With the average daily temperatures around seventy-five degrees in Tampa, most students congregated out in front of the center, meeting up with one another, tossing Frisbees around, or studying in small groups for hours under the dogwood trees.

Nicky was assigned to Hayden Hall, the noisiest dorm on campus. Mostly comprising freshman and sophomores, the building had a reputation as one big frat house. His building sat at the end of a row of three that were each four stories in height. After the sun went down, Hayden Hall was the darkest as it sat farthest away from the lit parking lot. Approaching his building, Nicky heard the sound of students laughing and screaming and music coming from the open windows in the building. He was so glad that his parents had never seen this on their two visits.

Nicky made his way up through the narrow walkway, battling the humid air as it pierced his lungs. When Nicky entered room 371, his roommate, Juan Carlos, was sitting at his desk. The desk, which had replaced the lower bunk, was lit by an emerald green reading lamp. In addition to the small lamp, Juan had a noisy black fan going, and his oversized laptop took up most of the desktop. Nicky had the same unit on the opposite side of the room. The room was tiny, with barely enough room to house the two pieces of large furniture, leaving little space between the two. When they both sat at their desk at the same time, their backs were almost touching.

Lit only by his roommate's lamp, the room was dim as Nicky entered. Enrique Iglesias Jr. was blasting from two tiny speakers buried somewhere in Juan's mess. Juan was from Monterey Bay, California, and believed he was the greatest soccer player that TBU had ever recruited. Born in the United States to parents from Spain, his family owned several car dealerships on the West Coast. The five-eleven, one-hundred-seventy-five-pound freshman was good looking, wealthy, and cocky.

Juan had taken over what little wall space they had, filling it with posters of his two man crushes, David Beckham and Cristiano Ronaldo. Although Juan was straight, he idolized the two soccer players—and who was Nicky to deny him?

Nicky and Juan's dorm room overlooked the practice soccer field. From their third-story window, it was a shouting distance down to the large spans of lawn. Because the field was not lit at night, it wasn't unusual to catch a whiff of weed drifting up from the field after dark.

"Hey, what's up? How'd it go?" Juan asked, never taking his eyes off the game he was playing on his laptop.

Tossing his backpack onto his bunk, Nicky's eyes adjusted to the low light in the room. "It was good." Pulling his chair out next to Juan, Nicky flopped down onto it. "How was your night?" Nicky could smell the beer and weed emanating from Juan.

"Hung out with my boys down in Kenny's room," Juan answered as he twisted and turned his body, struggling to kill whatever it was he was shooting at on the screen.

"Who was there?" Nicky asked, thinking that he wouldn't know any of Juan's friends by name anyways.

Juan continued to focus on the screen as he ducked at something before flames lit up the screen. "Huh?"

Without the energy to hold up a conversation, Nicky gave up. Standing up, there was one thing Nicky needed to do before calling it a night. "I'm tired; I'm going to grab a shower."

Nicky walked over to his tiny closet next to his bunk and grabbed his shower caddy. The sexual tension was still racing through his body, which was not unusual for him after a meet. At home, he would sometimes masturbate twice in a day for the first few days following a meet. Tearing off his socks, he slipped into his flip flops and headed to the men's showers down the hall.

In the month they had been living together, Nicky saw little of Juan and knew less about the people he was hanging out with. They were hardly in their room at the same time, which allowed Nicky plenty of time to take care of his sexual tension. Nicky was up and out of the room before sunrise every morning for practice, followed by classes and then a second workout in the afternoon. Juan's classes didn't start until the afternoon, and then he was gone to wherever he hung out until nine or ten every night.

Walking into the shower, Nicky let out a sigh of relief when he saw he had the communal showers all to himself. He found that, by ten o'clock, he could count on being the only one in there most of the time, which worked out perfectly since he preferred taking his showers at the end of the day as opposed to in the morning. Stripping off his red and gold sweats, he settled under the hot flow of water. As the heat of the water soothed his aching back and arms, Coach Silva popped into his head, which made his dick come alive. He imagined the coach's smell as he was drawn into his arms for the celebratory hug on the pool deck earlier today. He could feel the strength of the coach's arms, if even only for a brief second. He could see the warmth in his eyes, feeling once again the coach's hand on his butt cheek. Nicky poured a fair amount of soap into the palm of his hand and glanced around, ensuring he was alone. Reaching down, he took hold of himself and relieved the last bit of tension he had in his aching body.

2

As he pulled into the driveway of the home he had purchased three years ago when he relocated to Tampa, Coach Phillip Silva was pleased with the performance of his team this evening, especially his newest recruit Nicky O'Hare. He knew there was something special about the kid from South Dakota, but he got the feeling he hadn't even scratched the surface of his potential. So talented, eager, and beautiful, he had to admit. Way too young, but definitely beautiful. He recalled his own behavior moments after that great swim by O'Hare today, him hugging and slapping the kid's ass. His intention was professional, but he couldn't deny he secretly enjoyed the feeling of that perfect wet cheek. The coach laughed at himself admiring such a baby—he was turning into an old troll, he thought to himself, shaking his head.

Coach Silva's 1,800-square-foot Spanish Colonial was located in the quaint and affluent Old Hyde Park neighborhood. The three-bedroom, two-bath house had been restored just prior to him finding it. It sat on a narrow street lit by historical street lamps, which lay between countless homes with well-manicured lawns and trees. The home, like many of the homes on the street, was built with deep burgundy brown bricks and was slightly elevated above the street. What caught Phillip's eye when he first saw the house was the beautiful picture window facing the street.

The house was dark and humid as he entered through the garage door into the kitchen. Turning on the kitchen light, he was met by Emily, his two-year-old black and white Harlequin Great Dane. Her head at his waist, she waited for the signal to stand on her hind legs and place her front paws on his shoulders, the two of them staring eye to eye while Phillip massaged the back of her floppy ears. Although her weight strained his aching back, he allowed her this pleasure.

Looking at her pink and black food bowl, he saw that the bowl was almost full, which was not unusual for her. Whenever Phillip was gone overnight on a trip, even though his best friend, Steven, looked in on her, she rarely ate anything, only snacking until he returned.

More than ready for a glass of wine from the bottle of Staggs Leap that was sitting on the counter, Phillip prompted Emily to get down. Conveying how much she missed her daddy, she gently fell to the floor and then went to her food dish to eat her long-overdue dinner. With one eye on him, Emily watched as Phillip leaned against the counter and hit the play button on the recorder that hung on the wall.

Pouring the Cab into a wine glass, he listened to the first of two messages that had been left in his absence.

"Hi, Phillip; it's Mom. Call me when you get in. Your aunt and I will be in Florida next month for a few days, and we would love to see you that weekend if you're in town and not busy." He smiled at the sound of her voice. He had been missing his mother since she moved to California to be close to her only sister. The move came shortly after Phillip's dad died three years ago.

Phillip remembered when he got the call that his father had passed away. He had just moved to Tampa when his mother, Maria, called him and told him the news. She said he had just come in from tending to a young calf born without eyes. He was looking tired when he came in, so she told him to go wash up before dinner. When Phillip's father, Victor, never returned, she stood at the bottom of the steps and called for him several times. When he didn't answer, she went up the stairs and found him dead on the bathroom floor. The doctors said it was a massive heart attack, and he most likely felt nothing other than a single sharp pain in his chest.

Phillip pushed the button to play his next call. "Hey, Phillip, this is Steven. Wanted to see if you want to meet up later for drinks. Martin and I are going to be down at the Cotton Club around eleven if you are interested."

"End of calls," the computer-generated voice announced.

Phillip knew he had to return Steven's call tonight, but it was going to have to wait until his shower. He had met Steven and Martin two and a half years ago when he first moved to Tampa. Phillip was exploring the bars during his first few months in town before realizing it was not his scene. The night they met, he was sitting at the bar talking to the bartender when this five-foot-seven, roly-poly man appeared, ordering two Coco Cabanas, requesting extra piles of fruit in the glass. He introduced himself as Martin Hunter III. When he held out his hand for Phillip to either kiss or shake, Phillip did neither; he threw his head to the side and huffed.

Initially, Phillip thought Martin was hitting on him, until Steven appeared several minutes later, looking for his husband who was apparently taking too long with the drinks. Steven apologized to Phillip for Martin bothering him, and the rest was history: a friendship was made.

With Emily tailing him, Phillip walked back to his bedroom with his glass of wine in hand, ready for his shower. He turned on the shower and adjusted both knobs, searching for the right temperature. While the water warmed, Phillip stripped his clothes off, leaving them on the bathroom floor. After popping open the medicine cabinet in search of some relief, he grabbed the bottle of Oxycodone and washed two pills down with a healthy swig of wine. When he turned around to grab a towel out of the linen closet, Phillip caught a glimpse of his body in the full-length mirror in the bathroom before looking away.

At thirty-four years old, Phillip's body was toned—more so than most of his friends, even those a few years younger than he. But he hated his body, remembering how he used to look in his twenties. He would have never guessed that his V-shaped swimmer's build would have disappeared so fast when he stopped competitive swimming after the accident. Somehow, Nicky floated across his mind again. Imagining Nicky being disgusted at seeing him naked and out of shape, time had marked the years past. Phillip remembered when he was Nicky's age.

In the mirror, Phillip no longer saw that lean kid with abs of steel and a booty that everyone wanted. This person was older and a little thicker than he liked to admit. Discounting his poor eating habits, Phillip blamed most of it on the accident and the years of pain meds that followed. To soften the truth in the mirror, over the years, Phillip had intentionally allowed his body hair to grow out, which now lightly covered his chest, arms, and legs with coarse black hair.

After a relaxing hot shower, he wrapped a towel around his naked waist and walked out of the spacious en suite that the previous own-ers had converted from an existing bedroom. After dialing Steven's number, it was picked up on the second ring. "Welcome back," Steven said, sounding a bit tired.

"Hey there. What's going on?"

"Sooo…how did you guys do?"

"Good. This looks to be a promising year. We have a couple of good freshmen on the team this year. It came down to the end, and for a moment I thought we were going to lose. Some small adjust-ments in the lineup, and we should be good. Good to see how my guys perform under pressure." Phillip sighed as his body relaxed into several pillows against his headboard. "I just got in. Six hours on a bus is hard on an old man's ass these days," Phillip said as he slid his towel out from underneath him, tossing it over onto the chair next to the bed. Emily had hopped onto the queen size bed as well and took her usual spot next to him, laying her head on one of the decorative chocolate and blue pillows. "So what did I miss?" Phillip took a sip of his wine. *Mmm, that's good,* he thought to himself as he stared at the glass.

"For some reason, all of us old timers were out last night. It was a bar full of us from the old to the cranky. Alex, Kenny and Rick, and Dewayne and Peter were all out. Martin and I got there around ten-thirty."

"Wow, I haven't seen Kenny and Rick in about a year. How are they doing?" Phillip asked as he rubbed Emily on her belly and watched as she kicked her legs when he hit her ticklish spot. Steven and Martin, and Kenny and Rick were the only two gay couples he knew, combined with one or two other friends. Phillip had managed to barely make a handful of friends since his arrival in Tampa.

"Well, Rick is still traveling a lot, and Kenny looks like he is getting old."

"Aren't we all?" Just thinking about it made Phillip take another sip from his glass. "What else is going on?"

Steven was silent for a second or two. "Well…Martin and I did meet someone that would be—"

"—Steven, I told you stay out of my private life. I don't need the two of you picking out who I am going to date."

"Some of us disagree with you! After that last—"

"—Steven!"

"Okay, okay. But can I at least tell you about him?"

"No!" Phillip held the phone to his ear as he rose from the bed and walked down the hall to the kitchen to refill his glass. "I told you guys: I'm not looking to have a relationship with anyone." A relationship was the last thing in the world Phillip was looking for. Every relationship he had ever had was enough proof that he was not relationship material.

"I didn't say you had to marry the guy. Just have dinner with him, or just drinks. What harm can that do?"

"Goodbye, Steven. I'm hanging up now." Although Phillip's tone was light, he meant every word of it.

"Oh, all right. I'll leave the next piece of shit for you to find since you attract them like bees to honey. It's your life."

Phillip leaned over his granite countertop as if he wanted to smash his face down on it. "I'm not sure if I should say 'Thank you' or just hang up."

Steven's tone was softer, "Good night, sweetie."

"Night." Phillip knew that his best friend meant no harm, but another try at a boyfriend was not on his agenda. He grabbed the half-empty bottle of wine and headed back down to his bedroom, where he found that Emily had not moved from her spot on the bed. Phillip was tired and just wanted to unwind for a while before going to sleep. He settled down next to Emily, and with his remote found the eleven o'clock news.

Two hours later and a bottle of wine finished, his pain meds kicked in enough that he could attempt to sleep, even if it was for only a few hours. He pushed Emily back over to her side of the bed, turned out the light, and sank his naked body down deep into the posh bedding, hoping for a good night's sleep. As he drifted off to sleep, his last thought was the same as any other night, plummeting off the cliff; his body jerked one last time.

Waking up after three hours of sleep, Phillip rolled over to look at the clock on his nightstand. His back was killing him, and without hesitation, he took another Oxycodone.

Drifting back to sleep, Phillip saw himself around age nine or ten. He was playing on the dairy back in Imperial, Texas, where he grew up. The son of a Portuguese dairy farmer, Phillip had never expressed an interest in the family business. His mother would fondly tell the story of Phillip at age three, sitting in an empty bathtub, crying for her to fill it with water. As he grew older, he swam in the nearby lake every day instead of completing his chores around the farm. When his parents accepted the fact that they couldn't keep him on the dairy, they let him join the local swim team.

Phillip was the fastest kid within a hundred miles of the small farming community of Imperial. By his freshman year in high school, it was apparent to his coach that he was Olympic bound. His high-school coach sat his parents down and explained to them just how talented their kid was. Initially, his father rejected any thought that Phillip was not going to be part of the family dairy or that college was not going to be a part of the plan. Simple people, Phillip's parents in particular didn't understand the athletic world their son was about to be submerged in. They couldn't understand the fascination surrounding someone swimming, and they didn't see how it had any value.

Phillip trained day and night and rose to the top of the ranks as someone to watch during high school. After high school, he moved away to train one-on-one with a trainer in Roswell, New Mexico. His new trainer, Marcus Jobert, a Frenchman, had two Olympics under his belt. If not for a short visit in New Mexico's Department of Corrections for a DUI accident that killed his female passenger, he would have had three. Now out of prison, the "Danny DeVito" of the swimming world was rebuilding his name in the U.S. swimming community.

Making the U.S. Olympic Swim Team was both Phillip's and Marcus' goal. Phillip lived, ate, and trained with Marcus. The combination of the two of them was as perfect as it could have been. Marcus was like another father, but one who understood Phillip and his passion for swimming.

Phillip's training left little time for a social life. On those rare occasions when he had a moment and was able to get away, he was as normal as any eighteen-year-old, with sex on the brain and a perpetual hard-on to prove it. Unfortunately, once Phillip realized that it was the same sex that he was attracted to, a small town like Roswell left little for a young gay man to satisfy his needs.

It was at a little bookstore in town called Virginia's New and Used Books that Phillip's sexual needs were satisfied. For some odd reason, Virginia had a small section in the back of the store where gay and lesbian books and magazines were kept. Initially, Phillip thought he struck gold when he stumbled upon it. He frequented the bookstore for his supply of adult magazines, but one night, he accidently discovered that what was in his magazines was also taking place in real life right out in the back alley in the middle of the night.

Down the dark alley, the world had no limits: men-on-men sex, blow jobs, and whatever else you were willing to do between trash bins. Initially, Phillip walked through the alley in disbelief that men were having sex out in the open with only trash cans and the night sky concealing their acts. With each visit, his disbelief in what he was seeing was over taken with an eagerness to participate.

It was rumored that some of the younger men asked for payment for their services, but most men were there to satisfy a need their wives couldn't. At times, Phillip thought he recognized a man who worked at the bank, the principal from the local junior high school, or the man who delivered their propane once a month.

With almost no body fat and a beautifully tanned body, unbeknownst to Phillip, he was becoming a popular figure in that alley. Men were known to wait hours hoping this would be the night that Phillip showed up. It was almost always that younger males had the pleasure of being with him, leaving the old men content with just the opportunity to watch two young studs in action. Over the next four years, anonymous sex in the back of the store and in his car was Phillip's existence. It was his striking good looks that made him unforgettable, which over time worked against him. With time, those in that tiny back-alley circle pieced together little bits of who he was, and he started to become recognized for his skills outside of the pool.

One day prior to practice, Marcus surprised him at the breakfast table. Up to this point, Phillip thought he had been outsmarting Marcus and concealing his trips to the alley.

"Good morning," Phillip said as he sat his milk, cereal, and mixing bowl on the small kitchen table.

All Phillip got in return was a mumble, the old man never looking up over the newspaper that blocked his face. Phillip poured himself almost a half a box of Captain Crunch into a mixing bowl and then drowned it in milk. He proceeded to eat as he read the back of the cereal box.

After several minutes of silence that had gone unnoticed by Phillip, Marcus spoke. "So, what's important to you?"

"Huh?" Phillip asked with a mouth full of cereal.

"What is important to you?" Marcus repeated as he laid down his paper.

Phillip caught the tone but was unsure of what he had done, or if there was an answer that Marcus had already decided and he was supposed to guess what it was. "What do you mean, what is important to me?"

"You're not going to waste my time. If swimming is not important to you, then say so. You can pack your bags, and I will put you on a bus back to mommy and daddy."

"What are you talking about?" Phillip replayed yesterday's work-out in his head. He swam his ass off yesterday. Marcus even high-fived him when he climbed out of the pool after almost two and half hours of swimming. Everything was fine yesterday—at least he thought it was.

Marcus stared at Phillip. "Is any of this shit important to you, or do you want to be known for sucking cock in the alley behind the bookstore?"

Phillip was shocked at the direct hit he had just taken. Feeling like a kid who was in trouble, he just stared at Marcus, waiting for whatever was to come next. He was stunned and embarrassed that his dark-alley behavior had been discovered. Up until that point, the consequences had never once crossed his mind.

"Well? What is it?"

"I…I want to swim. I want to go to the Olympics."

"Really?"

"Yes, sir." Phillip had nothing else to say, racking his brain for something more convincing. Denial was too late at this point. *How did he know? What does he know?* Phillip asked himself. Scared, Phillip put down his spoon as he waited for Marcus to say something. *Anything, just say something,* he thought.

"Then we swim." Picking up his paper, Marcus went back to reading the morning's headlines.

Although Marcus had been a man of few words, there was no mistaking what he meant. From that morning on, Phillip never went back to Virginia's bookstore again and concentrated solely on swimming.

By the age of twenty-four, Phillip had become a two-time gold medalist in the World Championships and had been chosen to represent the United States Swim Team in the 2000 Summer Olympic Games in Sydney, Australia.

Before the start of the games, Phillip and Marcus flew over a week early to acclimate to the change in weather. Phillip's parents were scheduled to fly in the day before the race. They were all on top of the world. All the hard work and the plan had come together just how it was supposed to.

The morning Phillip was scheduled to swim his first race, he was to meet Marcus at the pool at six o'clock that morning. The trip to the aquatic center from the Olympic Village was supposed to take about an hour by van. As the twelve-passenger van made its way toward the aquatic center on a narrow highway, a semi-truck carrying a load of melons traveling too fast was approaching from the opposite direction. Phillip never saw it coming. The truck sustained a blow out and crossed over the center divider, hitting the van head on. As the van plunged two hundred feet over a cliff, Phillip, the only survivor, was ejected from the van just before it exploded into a ball of flames. Phillip was found halfway down the mountain with a broken back and leg, ending his swimming career and Olympic dreams.

3

J. B. squeezed his large frame down into Desiree's burnt-orange Honda Civic and then gently leaned over and gave his girl a kiss on her cheek. At six foot one and as dark as a coffee bean, Jeremy Ronald Breedlove was known to all his friends and family as the smart, yet handsome J. B.

"How'd it go, baby?" Desiree asked. She had been waiting in the parking lot only a moment or two before the bus rolled in. Desiree was a beautiful, big-boned girl with flawless skin the color of brown cocoa. She and J. B. met in high school, and it was then that J. B. told her that he was going to marry her someday. She was attending Tampa Bay Community College, studying to be a Registered Nurse.

"All right, I guess. You been by Momma's house yet? What she got to eat on the stove?" he asked as he settled down in the car and exhaled a deep breath.

J. B. was a local boy, growing up twenty minutes away from the university in one of the poorest Tampa neighborhoods, known as Junk Town. It got its name as it was where everybody discarded old couches, broken washing machines, refrigerators, and anything else that was no longer of any value. The saying "One man's junk is another man's treasure" held true in Junk Town.

Raised by a single mother that everyone called Momma B., J. B. didn't know much about the loser he identified as his dad, other than

J. B.'s two older brothers, who shared the same DNA. He also knew that he lived in the same city, and despite not having any kind of a real job, managed to keep nice cars and rings on his fingers. From time to time, J. B. would see his dad around, but he was nothing to J. B.

Now in his sophomore year at TBU, other than school, J. B.'s only other responsibility was to look after his three little sisters while Momma B. worked her two jobs. J. B. was determined to make something of his life, to make his momma proud. He studied hard, and Desiree was by his side every step of the way. At school, it was rumored that J. B. was the recipient of a big cash donation from Bill Gates given to inner-city kids.

Built more like a football player than a swimmer, he chose to swim in high school for the same reason he joined the debate team and ran for prom king. He believed that if he assimilated himself within the white culture, he would have the exact opposite outcome of what he saw happen to others in the black community. J. B. believed that the white community had some sort of secret on how to succeed and was purposely keeping it to themselves.

J. B. wore his hair short, clipped close to his scalp. He was well dressed, attempting to mimic the white kids in school, wearing one of the four classic button-down shirts he owned, along with khakis and Dockers.

Desiree pulled the car up to the curb of the salmon-colored, two-bedroom rental that J. B. had grown up in. The house hadn't changed much in the seventeen years Momma B. had been renting it. Bushes and grass had been replaced with gravel for a makeshift driveway for the car that Momma B. once had. Bars covered the front windows and the cheap screen door that barely kept any bugs out. For what Momma B. had paid in rent over the years, she could have owned the house by now.

Desiree looked over at the four punks hanging out across the street, smoking cheap weed. It was dark, but she knew that it was Ray-Ray, Tiny, Jamal, and Lil' Kev.

"What up, gangster," Jamal hollered to J. B. across the dark street.

"What up, man," J. B. replied back as he started across the street toward the four thugs.

"J. B., I'll see you inside. Don't be out here all night!" Desiree told him as she hit the alarm on her car, looking right at Lil' Kev. "Keep your black hands off my car, Lil' Kev. I ain't playin' with you." Lil' Kev acknowledged Desiree's warning with a slight nod upward, but his facial expression told her to go to hell.

J. B. was outside about ten minutes before coming inside the house. "J. B.!" his little sister Penny, who was turning ten, whined the minute he entered. When J. B. looked up, he saw Tina, the oldest of his three sisters, standing behind Penny, looking stern. The house was simple; the living room was the first room coming into the house, with a small dining room toward the back. Around the corner from the dining room, out of sight, was a U-shaped kitchen, with the original appliances tucked along the walls.

"I told her to clean up the dishes an hour ago," Tina snapped as she walked across to Penny. "He ain't goin' to save you, 'cause he ain't doing no dishes either!" she said, yanking Penny up by her arm and escorting her little sister into the kitchen.

Tina was eighteen and the oldest of the three girls, with his sister Dee-Dee just eleven months younger than her. The two could be twins, both plump around the waist, with big eyes and a flat nose. God had compassion on Penny. Although they had different fathers, she shared J. B.'s skin tone and was gifted with beautiful hair.

"Did Momma leave anything on the stove before going to work?" J. B. asked to anyone who would answer.

Dee-Dee, who was sitting on the couch getting help from Desiree with her math homework, spoke up. "Yeah, Momma cooked some greens, and there are two pork chops in foil that she left for you guys." Dee-Dee was the talker of the three girls.

"Des, you going to eat a chop?" J. B. asked.

"No baby, I ate at my mom's. Go ahead," Desiree replied.

"Can I have your pork chop if you ain't eating it?" Dee-Dee asked Desiree.

Before Desiree could answer, J. B. spoke up. "Hell no, you ain't getting that chop! I ain't ate all day," J. B. told her as he turned his back on them and walked into the kitchen.

As much as his sisters drove him crazy, he loved them, and they were the reason he chose to stay local and go to TBU. Now, his brothers were a different story. The oldest of the three boys was Clifford, who was currently serving a life sentence in the penitentiary for a bad drug deal that had left one man dead. J. B.'s other brother, Maurice, was two years older than J. B. Maurice was in and out of the county jail and working his way up to the penitentiary to spend his days and nights with Clifford. At the moment, Maurice was out and currently living in Atlanta with his baby's momma and their two kids. He worked as a carpenter on occasion, and when times were good, he sent money home to help his momma raise his siblings.

The next morning when J. B. woke up, he heard his mother cooking breakfast in the kitchen. He threw the blanket off and rose from the couch, which doubled as his bed at night. "Hey momma, how was work?" he asked her as he walked into the kitchen and poured himself a cup of coffee. He knew that his mother had just gotten home, as she was still in her red 7-11 shirt.

"Just another night," she replied as she flipped over several pieces of bacon. "Baby, why ain't you at practice this morning?"

J. B. rolled his eyes at her question. "Wasn't sure what time you were coming in. I didn't want to leave the girls alone."

"Yeah, I tried to leave on time, but Sheri was running late this morning and didn't show up 'til after six." Momma B. removed several strips of bacon from the heavy cast-iron skillet. "Can you wake the girls? I'm almost done here, and I got a four-hour shift at Sears this morning."

"I'll take care of them," he replied, grabbing a piece of bacon that was already cooked and laying on a plate.

"Desiree called for you about twenty minutes ago, sweetie. She said she was on her way over and would drop off Tina and Dee-Dee at school. God knows that girl is a saint... Ain't like her no-good momma." Moving more cooked bacon onto the plate in the middle of the stove, Momma B. shook her head as she turned over the last of the bacon still in the skillet. "In school, I done whipped that woman's ass enough to last her a lifetime... Can you walk Penny to school this morning?"

As he was walking out of the kitchen with a mouth full of bacon and another piece in his hand, J. B. heard his mother call out, "How was your swim thing the other day?"

"Good, momma," he replied as he kept walking toward the girls' room.

"That's all you got to say is..." he heard her yell as he entered the girls' room.

By the time J. B. had the girls up and moving, he heard his mother in the other room and knew she was rushing. "I'm leaving; breakfast is on the stove. I'll be home by one. Ya'll hear me?"

From one of the bedroom windows, J. B. watched as one of his mother's coworkers from Sears pulled up at the curb and Momma B. jumped in the old, ratty black Pontiac Grand Am. No sooner had they pulled away when Desiree pulled up to the house. J. B. saw her from the window as she exited the car, wearing a bright pink fitted blouse, white Capri pants, and sandals. As she made her way to the front door, J. B. stared at her large breasts as they bounced around in her top. Although a large girl, Desiree walked with an air in her step, carrying her head high, comfortable as a woman with curves.

When Desiree came in, she gave J. B. a kiss on his cheek, knowing he hadn't brushed his teeth yet. "You got practice this morning?" she asked.

"Yeah, but I missed most of it already. I have to walk Penny to school. Momma's gone already. What time did you leave last night?"

"I don't know. I helped Dee-Dee with her math. You were asleep, maybe eleven or so. I would take care of Penny for you, but I have class this morning at seven forty-five. Are the girls ready to go?"

Within minutes, the house was empty, with everyone on the move, starting their day. J. B. made his way down to the city bus stop after dropping Penny off at Hoover Elementary.

4

S tanding next to his locker, Nicky dropped his towel and slid on his sweatpants over his bare skin. Nothing felt better than going commando, allowing the boys to hang free after wearing a wet tight-fitting Speedo for hours. Just as he tied the drawstring, Coach Silva rounded the corner. Nicky followed his eyes as the coach stared intently at him as he moved into Nicky's personal space. When the coach grabbed him and pulled him even closer, he felt as if his legs were no long able to hold him up; the rush was enough to cause him to pass out. He would have surely collapsed if not for the coach holding him up.

Lifting Nicky's polo shirt up over his head, the coach cast it to the ground. Bare-chested, he lightly touched Nicky's nipples, causing him to shudder and suck in air. Slowly he ran his hand down Nicky's flat belly, his abs reacting to the touch as they tightened inward. Reaching the elastic, the coach gently tugged on Nicky's drawstring and allowed gravity to drop his sweats, exposing all of him. Standing completely naked in the locker room, his skin was still cool from his shower.

The coach smiled at the sight of the beautiful naked body. Nicky stepped out of his sweats, ready for whatever the coach had in store for him. His breathing picked up, again drawing attention to his flat stomach.

"Let's go into my office," the coach whispered to him.

The office was too far away, and Nicky knew it. "No, just fuck me."

"Dude, wake up... Get up... It's after five... What time are you supposed to be at practice?" Nicky woke up with Juan standing over him. When it clicked that he was dreaming and had overslept, Nicky jumped up and out of bed. His erect penis was fully exposed as he scrambled around, looking for his sweats. He grabbed a pair of sweatpants from the floor and a clean t-shirt from his drawer. Nicky knew he was late as he skipped brushing his teeth in the room sink and thanked Juan for having his back. Grabbing his duffle bag from the night before, Nicky was out the door in a matter of a minute and a half.

Nicky felt his heart pounding as he ran through the cool, sleepy campus all the way to the aquatic center. When he hit the locker room, it was already empty; the team was in the water. He grabbed a dry pair of Speedos from his locker and carefully tucked himself into the front of them before running out to the pool.

The morning had a slight chill in the air, and Nicky saw steam rising from the pool that was heated anywhere between seventy-six and seventy-nine degrees. Coming through the gates, Nicky saw his teammates were already warming up and heard Coach Silva yell, "Good morning, Nicholas! Glad you made it," sounding quite angry.

"Sorry, coach," Nicky mumbled.

"Don't tell me you're sorry! You should be apologizing to your teammates as you're the reason we're warming up this morning with a 4000!"

Nicky groaned, throwing himself into the pool. Hitting the water, he knew he was going to catch hell from the guys after practice. Falling in sync with his teammates, Nicky fell into a relaxed state of mind, his arms, legs, and feet now mechanically moving and performing their part in keeping this machine above water.

Practice was grueling. They were exhausted from the day before, and the coach was hitting them hard. Nicky didn't think it was ever going to end, as the laps were nonstop all morning. With the morning sun now shining down on him, his legs and arms were mush. Just when he had nothing left, he heard Coach Dean, the assistant, blow the whistle twice, signaling that practice was over.

Slowing to a float, Nicky rolled over onto his back, out of the corner of his eye catching Coach Dean glaring at him. Nicky had never gotten a good feel from Coach Dean; no matter what he did, it wasn't enough for the guy. Working with mostly the varsity swimmers, Coach Dean was also the full-time water polo coach. The guy was probably in his late forties, short and full of testosterone. The rumor was that at one time he was an exceptional water polo player in college, but now he was just a fat slob. He had heard that he wasn't married and had no kids. Nicky guessed him to be at least ten years older than Coach Silva.

As Nicky was pulling himself out of the water, his teammates Squirrel, Connor, and Dutch were walking by him, heading to the locker room. Out of nowhere, the massive six-three, two-hundred-and-twenty-pound Connor reached out and pushed Nicky backwards, sending him into the pool. Nicky resurfaced as they were walking through the gates toward the locker room. He knew they were pissed at him for that huge warm-up at the beginning of practice, and he wondered if the feeling was shared by the rest of the team as well.

"That's messed up!" he heard Tyler say as he extended his long, tanned arm out to lift Nicky out of the water. "I'm just as tired as they are, and I'm not acting like an ass. What happened to you this morning? How come you're late?"

"Overslept," Nicky mumbled as he fought to catch his breath.

Nicky and Tyler walked into the locker room. As the two freshmen on the team, their lockers were next to each other. Nicky sat on the bench between the rows of lockers, stretching his neck, still trying to catch his breath after the brutal workout.

Tyler, standing at six-two, stripped off his Speedo and stood naked next to Nicky. In his effeminate voice, Tyler was going on about something to do with Dutch and his girlfriend, but Nicky had tuned out the first part of whatever occurred and was now lost in the conversation.

"Man, she was so drunk; I thought Dutch was going to kill her. That bitch is nasty. I don't see what Dutch sees in her, but then again, I don't see what anybody sees in females." Pausing for a slight second, Tyler looked around the room. "Are you hitting the showers?"

Nicky nodded his head without making eye contact with Tyler. "Yeah, I'll be there in a minute."

When Tyler walked away toward the showers, Nicky glanced up, ensuring he was gone. He smiled as he watched Tyler saunter straight through the locker room butt naked, head held high, and towel in his hand instead of around his waist. His bare ass was white as snow. As flamboyant as Tyler was, the girls adored him, and the guys were not threatened by him for some reason. With blond curly hair with streaks of copper from the chlorinated water, coupled with his golden brown tan, Tyler was beautiful by anybody's standards.

Although Nicky was not sexually attracted to Tyler, he did find him fascinating. Admiring not just his ass but his confidence, Nicky found him to be eccentric from the first day he met him. He had never seen a guy walk around every day in a sport coat and a different fedora for every day of the week. Drawn to him, Nicky was sure he had to have been the son of some wealthy aristocrat or politician.

The two swimmers met during Freshman Orientation Week after Tyler had been stalking Nicky for a half hour or so, then "accidentally" bumped into him at a booth for the Latin American club. Tyler wasted little time hitting on him. Although Nicky rejected his advances, they became friends immediately.

By the end of the day, since neither of their roommates had checked in yet, they went to Housing trying to have their dorm assignment changed, but were told it was too late.

It wasn't until later that Nicky discovered that Tyler was a party animal and way more promiscuous than him. Tyler considered two weeks a long-term relationship and avoided relationships altogether when he could. The life of the party, everybody loved Tyler. Tyler didn't talk much about his childhood, but through conversation Nicky had pieced together that he was from Utah, had been adopted, and his parents were elderly.

Nicky, still sitting on the bench, heard Tyler shouting and cussing at someone in the showers. Nicky chuckled to himself, knowing the guys just didn't know when to leave their new teammate alone until it was too late.

"Nicky, I need to see you in my office before you leave."

Flinching at the unexpected voice, Nicky was pulled from his thoughts. By the time Nicky turned around, he only caught a glimpse of Coach Silva as he was walking back toward his office. By the sound of the coach's gruff voice, Nicky knew it was probably about being late. His mind went to the worst-case scenario of being kicked off the team or suspended as he played the command back several times in his head. Nicky told himself that he would never be late again and knew he had to convince the coach of the same when he went in.

After showering, Nicky made his way over to the coach's office, where the door was open. Coaches Silva, Dean, and Paul were inside at their desks, talking. The office was small for three coaches, with all four walls made of glass looking out into the locker room and toward the showers. Piles of paper and gym equipment lay on each of their desks, and the smell of dust, dirt, and mildew lingered in the air.

"Come on in. We wanted to discuss the meet with Florida State this week," Coach Dean announced.

Nicky sighed in relief as he glanced over at Coach Silva and then back at Coach Dean. Nicky felt his nervous stomach relaxing just a little.

"The Gators are tough. Finished number two last year and are looking for the number-one spot," Coach Silva said as he leaned back in the tattered desk chair.

"Well, sir...look at some of their swimmers this year: they lost Graham, Chandler, and Chavez, their three sprinters." Nicky's eyes darted back and forth between the three coaches trying to give them equal attention. "That's where their strength was. Fast and furious. They don't have it this year," he replied as he stared at the coach's rose-colored lips and beautiful white teeth. He knew he should be listening, but just as fast as he told himself to stop, thoughts of kissing those full lips collided with any logic.

"You're right; that's what Paul said a minute ago as well. We're putting you, Ron, Dutch, and Squirrel in the 400-yard medley relay... J. B.'s out. It's going to be a hard meet for you; you also got the 200 freestyle, 200-yard backstroke, and the 100 butterfly. That's a lot to swim."

"Thanks, Coach. I'll be ready." Nicky hesitated for a second debating on whether to ask, "Where are you putting J. B.?"

"We haven't got that far yet," Dean answered sharply.

Nicky again cut his eyes over to Coach Silva, staring at his thick, wavy black hair and five o'clock shadow. His olive complexion and brown eyes—*shit, he's looking right at me.* Embarrassed, Nicky looked down at the floor as he took in a large breath.

"You can go. Thanks, Nicolas," Nicky heard one of them say. He couldn't believe he got caught ogling his coach. Mortified, he backed up and then exited the office. He knew they knew and they were probably laughing at him as soon as he left. Playing the whole moment back in his head, Nicky wondered how he could have been so stupid.

Letting out a sigh once he had taken a couple of steps away from the office, he bolted past the showers, hurrying to get outside. His chest was tightening up, and everything around him was in a blur; he needed fresh air—and fast.

Once outside, the morning air rushed into his lungs, causing his whole body to tingle. He placed his hands on his knees as he bent over. After a few seconds, Nicky pulled it together as he stood up. Looking at his watch, he saw that he had just enough time for some oatmeal in the dining hall before chemistry, his first class of the day. He knew he had to eat something.

Later that day, Nicky, J. B., and Dutch met up at Taco Joe's, their favorite fast-food dive, which probably once was a Taco Bell at one time. Nicky reflected back on Connor, pushing him back into the water after practice. "Dutch, what's up with Connor? Does he have a beef with me?" Nicky asked.

Dutch paused for a minute, frowning, wrinkling up his forehead. "What do you mean?" he asked.

"You want me to beat that white boy down for you?" J. B. interjected.

"Naw, he's all right," Dutch replied, paying J. B. no attention. "It just takes time to get to know him is all." Dutch turned to J. B., "Anyways, he's got thirty pounds on you, and he's two feet taller; good luck taking him down."

J. B.'s eyes grew wide at Dutch's jab. "That corn-fed fucker couldn't take me. I'd drop him like a penny in the collection pot." J. B. puffed his chest out and held up a fist before finishing off his taco.

The three were silent as they all reached for another taco from the shared pile in the middle of the table. Nicky looked at the two as they continued bantering back and forth. He couldn't help but smile, as he enjoyed just hanging out with his new friends.

"By the way, Dutch, what was up with your girl Peggy last week? You need to put that shit in check. If Desiree pulled some shit like that, her ass would be sitting on the curb!" J. B. said.

Dutch, who was now a sophomore, had met Peggy at a party during his freshman year. Dating on and off ever since, she was hot headed and loud, while Dutch was passive and quiet.

Dutch shook his head as he shoved the last of a taco in his mouth. "Naw, man, it's all good. She was horny and wanted to leave. I should have taken her Puerto Rican ass home when she asked me to. She's just hot blooded, that Latina shit."

J. B. shook his head. "You better reel that shit in, or you're going to have one hot mess."

The guys were carrying on over lunch for an hour before J. B. noticed the time and realized that he had to head on over to his chemistry class. Nicky thought about his one last class of the day as well and how much he hated math. He knew it was going to be hard in college, but not this hard.

5

On Friday morning, as the team loaded on the bus for the hour-long drive to Florida State, the guys were excited, and their energy level was on high. Squirrel, Connor, and Dutch were all sitting in the back row. They were known as Coach Dean's water polo kids, as they were also on the water polo team and were always together. All three were sophomores, and Squirrel and Connor were best friends. Dutch, the smartest of the three, acted as the middleman whenever the other two disagreed about anything and was skilled at defusing even the worst problems. In front of them were the two seniors, Bryson and Ron, the quiet ones on the team. The two were both left over from the previous coach and losing team.

As the bus rolled down the two-lane highway, Tyler yelled from the front of the bus, "Hey, Squirrel, where did the name 'Squirrel' come from?"

Before Squirrel could answer, J. B. yelled, "His ass is so scary that if you look at him wrong, he's going up a tree or in a hole." The whole bus started laughing, except the trio.

Few knew that Squirrel was born Nathaniel Levi III and came from a close-knit Mormon family. His father was a two-time Olympian for the U.S. Diving Team, and his brother was a U.S. world gold medalist in diving as well. Nathaniel somehow was born afraid of heights and was done growing at around five-six. He suffered from ADHD, and anything that involved standing around, like diving, wasn't for him. In junior high, because he scurried everywhere instead of walking, someone started calling him Squirrel, and the name stuck.

That day at the meet, TBU hit the Florida State Gators with everything they had. By midway, they had finished virtually every race with a one–two finish. Connor swam his all-time best in the 200 butterfly and set a new conference record. Nicky had placed first in his 100 butterfly and 200 free.

In the 400 medley relay, by the time Dutch reached Nicky, they had fallen into third place. Nicky again had to regain their lead in the last 25 yards to secure the win for the team. At the end of the relay, Nicky had just pulled himself from the pool and was still fighting to catch his breath when Coach Paul approached him. "Hey Nicky, there's a news crew over there that wants a quick interview with you."

Nicky looked over and saw the reporter and cameraman standing off to the side. Butterflies leaped in his stomach, knowing he was going to have to talk to someone with a microphone; Nicky would rather swim another race instead of talking to a reporter.

Walking over to the reporter, Nicky saw the cameraman turn on a light at the top of his camera. Holding up her microphone, the petite ginger reporter began her interview. "Nicky O'Hare, we've been watching you this season, and the crowd seems to love you. What does that feel like?"

Nicky looked up into the crowd and then back into the camera as he continued to fight to regulate his breathing. "I love swimming, and the crowd and the excitement they bring to the sport."

"Congratulations on the exciting win. How proud are you of that win just now?" she asked.

Nicky took in a whiff of onions on her breath as she leaned into him. "Um…thank you." Taking a slight step back, he went on, "I don't think about the win; I'm thinking about how I swam the race."

"You showed a great deal of patience. How much of that was your strategy?"

Remembering to smile into the camera that was just inches from his face, Nicky said, "It was a good race. Give me the challenge, and I'll give you all that I have. If I'm in a good position, I'm generally confident that I can bring it home."

"Tell us about that last twenty-five yards?"

"It hurt like crazy."

"Do you feel the pressure of swimming the last leg of the relay without any type of a lead?"

"I knew I had the finishing power to get it done, and we're swimming great as a team. We're all happy with that win."

"You're the most impressive freshman we have seen at TBU in years. Are we watching the next Michael Phelps?"

"I think it will be many years before we see the next Michael Phelps," Nicky answered, laughing uncomfortably at the question.

"You and your teammate Connor Moretti battled it out until the end in the freestyle; does it matter in the long run who gets first?"

"You have a personal goal, but the main goal is that our team gets the points for taking first."

"Congratulations again on a great swim," she said as she smiled and turned toward the camera.

"Thank you." Nicky glanced at the cameraman and was taken aback by his grin, which was clearly expressing that he liked what he was looking at. Self-conscious at the sudden attention, Nicky awkwardly ran his fingers through his long bangs, brushing his hair back—really in an effort to hide his face behind his hand before looking away.

Noticing that the next race had already started and that his teammates were cheering on their mates in the water, Nicky saw that Tyler was in the water with an enormous lead against three Gators and Squirrel had a solid fifth. Nicky took a place along the deck of the pool with the others, and several of his mates patted him on the back in congratulations. Out the corner of his eye, he caught Connor with his arms folded across his chest, glaring in his direction. When Nicky looked at him, Connor rolled his eyes before turning his back to him. As uneasy as the reporter and cameraman made Nicky, it was being snubbed by Connor and his posse that skewed his sense of confidence.

6

Steven had already ordered a glass of Chardonnay by the time Phillip arrived at the Rio Grande Brazilian Steakhouse for lunch. Frazzled by the morning, Phillip was ready for a cocktail.

"I hate these tropical storms in the middle of the day," Phillip proclaimed as he removed his light rain jacket and wrapped it around the back of his chair. "Sorry I'm late. Where's Martin?" Phillip asked, taking a seat in his chair and unfolding his napkin, laying it carefully across his lap. The dining room at the Rio Grande was small, with just a few small tables in the center of the room and high-back booths along the walls.

"He's a little under the weather, so I left him at home with a cup of tea and the remote," Steven answered.

"The place is empty," Phillip said as he looked around for the waiter to take his drink order. There were two other tables occupied, one with a young couple and the other with a family with three little children, the mother fighting to keep the youngest one in her booster chair as the dad played on his phone.

Phillip put down the extensive wine list just as the waiter returned. "Can I start you two off with some drinks and appetizers, or are you ready to order?" he asked, pouring each of them a glass of water.

"Let's see... I think I'll have a glass of your house Cabernet," Phillip answered.

Once the waiter was out of earshot, Steven asked, "So how have you been?"

"Good; it's been a busy season, and I'm tired. Even though it looks like we're going to finish this season fifth in the conference, our athletic director is pushing to bring our aquatic program to the attention of the sports world faster than I may be able to produce. After football, basketball, and baseball, he's fourth on the list when it comes to money, and to move up that ladder, he's got to produce a quality program that attracts the top in swimming, diving, and water polo."

"Fifth doesn't sound so bad. You were like eighth last year, weren't you?" Steven asked.

The waiter reappeared with Phillip's wine. "Are you two ready to order?" he asked.

After placing their orders, Phillip started again. "Well, not only am I competing with the other sports, but we compete with the other aquatic programs as well." Phillip stopped for a taste of his wine.

"I'm not sure I get what you mean."

"It's about the money. The better your program does—meaning winning championships—the more athletes become attracted to your program, attracting bigger and better players."

"Well, since you've been there, you've been consistent in ranking the team higher each year, right?"

"So far. I'm just now starting to get swimmers interested in swimming with me because of what we're doing, not because the top schools won't take them."

Steven lay his fork down. "I've lived here for thirty-five years, and I've never seen the type of coverage your boys are getting from the media these days. That kid, Connor something or another, is blowing up the pool this season. Any chance of him ever making the Olympics?"

"Oh, sure, but I have this new recruit that's already challenging him in almost every stroke. This kid O'Hare is like nothing I've ever seen. He's hungry for it and is already laying down some remarkable times. I found him in this little backwoods town up in South Dakota a couple of years ago and have been watching him develop over the last two years. Just the sweetest kid, but when he's in the water, he turns into this killer dolphin. He's amazing."

"Oh really. How amazing?" Steven raised an eyebrow.

"No, I don't mean like that." Phillip hated when Steven did that.

"Like what?"

Phillip knew Steven was playing with him, but he didn't like it. "I can hear it in your voice. I know what you're thinking."

"Yeah I can hear it in *your* voice when you're talking about him. You can't fool me, *Coach Silva.*"

"I'm not trying to fool anyone. He's just a nice kid." Phillip could feel his heart rate increase, and it was over this whole conversation. Rubbing his thumb up and down his empty wine glass, he looked around the room to avoid eye contact with Steven.

Phillip knew from his own past experience how sexually charged all the training made him. He also knew how available sex was in the dorms, now that these kids were away from their parents' eyes. Not seeing Nicky as that type, his other new freshman, Tyler Peterson came to mind. Maybe the two of them *were* having sex—with each other. Why he was thinking this, he didn't know, but it was an unsettling thought for him.

As the dining room started filling in around them with the lunch crowd, Phillip's parmesan-crusted pork loin was served along with a second glass of wine. Phillip made a nearly inaudible sound, shifting his body weight off of one butt cheek on to the other, looking for a comfortable spot.

"Are you hurting?" Steven watched Phillip take a pill, swallowing it down with a sip of his wine. He had gotten familiar with his friend's chronic pain early in their friendship. "I have the cutest chiropractor. You need to see him!"

"Trust me, Steven, this is way beyond a chiropractor." Phillip's brows were furrowed, and the color had drained from his face. He took another sip of his wine and lowered his head.

"You be surprised what a chiropractor can do." Steven sounded off, slightly annoyed. "Can I get you something? Do something?"

"No. Just give me a minute. I just took something," Phillip mumbled as he let out a large sigh. "I just have to wait for this muscle relaxer to kick in. I'll be fine."

The two sat in silence for the remainder of their meal, Phillip barely touching his food. When the waiter appeared, offering to clear their plates, the two sat back, giving him room to gather everything up in one pass. Phillip watched as the waiter cleared the table and then left.

"So...do you like that?" Steven asked.

"Who? The waiter?" Phillip shouldn't have been surprised by the question. Steven rarely missed anything with a penis and had obviously caught Phillip eyeing the waiter as he cleared their table. "He's all right, I guess." Phillip tried to play it off. He knew that his best friend always had sex on the brain and would fuck anything single.

"Well, do you have anything better that the rest of us don't know about?" Steven narrowed his eyes to a squint as he waited for his answer. "I'll take my answer off the air if it makes it easier for you."

"Yeah, and I'll plead the fifth."

Across town, Nicky and Tyler prepared to take the drive up I-60 to Clearwater Beach. Tyler had just found out that Nicky had never seen the beach, and proclaiming himself as Nicky's new best friend, he was bent on driving out there so Nicky could see the sun set on the sea. They threw a blanket and a twelve-pack of beer in Tyler's white Range Rover and within thirty minutes arrived at the beach.

Nicky was in awe as he saw the ocean. For the first time seeing water as far as his eyes could see, he couldn't help but wonder where all the water came from. Marveling in the moment, Nicky caught a whiff of the salt in the air as he waited for Tyler to unload the car.

"It smells fishy," he told Tyler as he kicked off his flip flops and headed toward the white sandy beach, which was mostly empty, save for a few people walking along the shore. They had about twenty minutes before the sun set down on the water, and the sky was turning a burnt orange across the water's surface.

"The sand looks like sugar," Nicky cried out to Tyler, who was still sitting on his tailgate removing his shoes and rolling up his pant legs.

"I can't believe you've never seen the ocean," Tyler said.

"Yeah, well, we don't have beaches in South Dakota."

The two walked down the shore until they were stopped by large rocks that cut them off from the other side of the beach.

"The tide is in, so we have to climb over," Tyler announced as they both stood looking at the rocks.

"Climb over?" Nicky asked, unsure if it was safe to do so.

"Yeah, there's no one on the other side. It's the gay side of the beach. Watch your step; it can be slippery," Tyler said as he started up the side of the rock.

"What's the gay side?" Nicky hollered to the back of Tyler's head before following him.

As the waves came in and crashed up against the rocks, it sprayed the salty water up into the air, which fell down on them like rain. By the time they reached the other side, they were both drenched. They picked out a place on the sandy beach a few feet up from where the tide had reached its final point before retreating to the ocean.

"This is cool. What makes it the gay side?" Nicky said, staring out onto the ocean, still not believing what he was seeing. With Maroon Five playing from Tyler's iPhone, Nicky grabbed a beer from Tyler's backpack and took a seat on the blanket Tyler had unpacked.

"I don't know, but sometimes guys are out here naked tanning. It's a good place to cruise."

Nicky wondered if Tyler had ever cruised here and how that all worked.

Quietly, Tyler said, "I can't believe you've never seen the sun set on the ocean."

"It's beautiful." Nicky never took his eyes off the orange sky as he gently shook his head. "So that means it's rising on the other side of world, right?"

"Yeah, like in Australia."

Nicky was silent for a minute before asking, "Have you ever been to Australia?"

"Once, when I was a kid. I don't remember it, though." Tyler's voice suddenly boomed, "Have you ever had Sex on the Beach?"

"What?" Nicky had never been around someone so direct.

"Calm down," Tyler laughed, "I'm not asking you if you want to have sex with me on the beach. It's a drink: orange juice, peach schnapps, and vodka, or something like that. I forget."

Tyler was not at all his type, but with just one beer in him, Nicky was already relaxed. Tyler continued going on about different cocktails as Nicky's mind drifted off to thinking about letting Tyler be his first. *He could... But not here, in public,* he thought to himself as Tyler continued to chatter.

"—oh and the Buttery Nipple and one called the Silk Panty Martini." Tyler starting laughing as he reached down into his backpack and handed Nicky another beer.

Missing some of what Tyler was talking about, he assumed those were drinks as well. "I have a question for you," Nicky said before Tyler could say something else. "Have you ever had sex on the beach—I mean, real sex?"

"No, but I would," Tyler responded.

Surprised by Tyler's answer, Nicky felt a tightening in his shorts, having to adjust his cross-legged position. Nicky turned to face Tyler. "But you've had sex before?"

Laughing, Tyler smacked him lightly on the back of his head, "Yeah."

Nicky shifted again and self-consciously tugged at his now fully engorged crotch that was bound and begging to be freed from confinement. He felt his face growing flush and the relaxed state from the beer disappearing. After asking the question, he hoped

Tyler would not ask him it in return. He thought of the few times he had fooled around with a neighbor years ago. That was the extent of Nicky's sexual activity, and he was still a virgin at eighteen. He wondered if he was the only virgin on the team.

"Who have you had sex with?" Tyler asked.

There it was. The question. Nicky's gut wrenched as his initial impulse was to lie to his friend. He wanted to lie. It would be easier than facing the humiliation that was sure to come if he didn't. His mind raced for something, anything to say.

"You're not a virgin, are you?" Tyler asked. "You are! You've never had sex!"

"Yes—I mean no." Nicky scrambled for his words. "No, I've never had sex." There, the truth was said as he waited for the laughter, which didn't come. Nicky eyed Tyler several times, trying to get a read on what his friend might be thinking. Sitting in silence, the two stared out toward the sea.

Between the squawk of the seagulls returning from a day at sea and the tide as it broke one hundred feet out, there was no other place Nicky wanted to be. The raw honesty, free of judgement, he was overtaken with a sense of calm that washed over him, releasing his insecurities into the sea.

Lost in his own world, Nicky heard the song "My Heart Skips a Beat" coming from the phone lying between them. Nicky let out a snicker, breaking their silence.

"What? What's so funny?" Tyler asked.

Sheepishly, Nicky's smile swept across his face. "Nothing," he laughed.

"Nothing, my ass. What's so funny?" Tyler demanded.

"You better not laugh... But I think of Coach Silva every time this song comes on."

Tyler cocked his head slightly toward the music. "No way! Would you do him?"

"Yeah, I think so. He's my type," Nicky muttered.

"How do you know what your type is if you've never had sex?" Tyler leaned into his friend, knocking him backwards onto the blanket.

Nicky lay on his back staring upwards. "I'm not dumb, just a virgin. I know what I like."

"So are you a Top or Bottom?" Tyler teased.

Nicky grew silent as he thought about it. In truth, he didn't know the answer to Tyler's question. "If I say a Bottom, does that make me the girl?" Nicky asked.

Tyler, bursting into a louder laugh, fell across Nicky's chest. "No, you dimwit. It means you're a *Bottom*." Their faces inches apart, Tyler poked at Nicky several times. "Do I look like a girl to you?"

Nicky's cheeks flushed red as he stared into Tyler's blue eyes. Overwhelmed with a sense that Tyler was about to kiss him, Nicky pushed Tyler off him. "So, what do you think about the coach?" Nicky asked as he put a little room between them.

Tyler grumbled as he too sat up. "He's not my type at all. He's too old and straight-looking for me. Is he even gay?"

Nicky's secret was out; he had been crushing on the coach ever since that first afternoon he'd walked into Nicky's house to recruit him to TBU. Nicky remembered sitting in their kitchen while his mother and dad listened to Coach Silva deliver his speech on why they should choose TBU. Since that day, Nicky had never stopped thinking of Coach Silva.

Even when Nicky toured the campus on two separate occasions, it was just to see the coach, hoping he was still the vision of the man in his head. When he talked to the coach on the phone prepping for the actual move, Nicky found that he was more excited about the prospect of being in the presence of the coach every day than about going away to college. Now since being here, he felt as if the coach hardly looked at him.

The moon now towering over the ocean, Nicky's knees were curled up into his chest as he watched the moon rise. With a heavy sigh, Nicky gently tugged at his friend who had fallen asleep. "Wake up. We need to head back."

When swim season was over, Nicky was ready for a break from the grueling twice-a-day practices. Although his first season at the college level was more than he dreamed, he felt as if his studies had suffered. Always being just a C average student in high school, he was barely passing any of his courses now. With his scholarship dependent on his grades, Nicky was not that confident that he could pull his grades up to a C in any of his classes, even if he buckled down now that practice was out of the way.

Nicky wasn't sure how Tyler was balancing it all, as he never heard him talk about studying. Nicky found it all-consuming at times, trying to balance swim practices, classes, and his studies, all the while still making sure he was enjoying his first year of college. The last thing he wanted to do was embarrass or disappoint his parents by flunking out during his freshman year.

Nicky had been overwhelmed with college from the first day, especially by his English literature class, which required twice the amount of papers of the other classes. The only class he enjoyed was his medieval culture class on Wednesdays, which he shared with Tyler. Nicky wasn't sure if he liked the class because Tyler was there, or if it was because of the various other school jocks who were also there looking for an easy grade.

7

After wrapping up the season, J. B. planned on taking a break from the pool to concentrate on his studies. He told himself that once the semester was over in June, he would start his off-season training. Knowing the season didn't start again until September, he had plenty of time to get back into swim shape. He also knew most of his teammates were going to take a break as well. Since the water polo team was using the aquatic center over the summer, the swimmers would switch their off-season training to the city pool to train until the season started.

It was late afternoon, and J. B. was done with his last class. He walked through the campus, heading toward the bus stop. With a smile on his face, he realized that for the first time in his entire life, he felt that he could do this, that he could be something more than what his dad had amounted to. When his cell phone buzzed in his pocket, J. B. looked at it, seeing it was Nicky. With a swipe of his finger across the screen, he answered the call. "Wha's up, Nick, my man. You missing me?"

"Something like that," Nicky laughed. "A couple of us are playing pool down at Art's later on; you want to meet us?"

"Yeah, what time?" J. B. asked.

"Ten."

"All right, see you then. Later." J. B. hit the call end button and dropped his phone back down into his pants pocket. Continuing toward the bus stop, J. B. daydreamed of what his life was going to look like five years from now when he and Desiree were done with school. He would be married to her, and with the money they would be making, they would buy his mother her own place, perhaps something nice like Desiree's parents had bought a couple years ago. He envisioned his momma living good, driving a new Lincoln or a Jaguar.

Majoring in business administration, J. B.'s plan had been to build a family catering business with his mother and brother Maurice, if Maurice stayed out of jail, that is. His mother had been doing it on her days off for years, and her Southern soul food cooking had the reputation for being the best in town.

J. B. knew that with what he was learning in school, coupled with his mother's recipes, they could make it work. Maurice was a master at construction and could repair or build anything, so J. B. was looking past the catering business and had been talking to his mother about an actual restaurant. J. B. had dreams, big dreams, for his family.

At Art's that evening, Nicky, J. B., Tyler, and Dutch were shooting pool, laughing, and joking in the dimly lit pool hall. Tyler was lining up his shot as he stood over the table, considering his options. Dutch was in his usual good mood and had been teasing Tyler all evening.

Dutch smiled as he stood right behind Tyler and asked, "So what's up with this Gay Pride shit next month? Why do you get a Gay Pride Month to celebrate? Parades and parties—what the hell do I get?"

Nicky and J. B. both shook their heads as they smiled and waited for Tyler to react, which happened right after Tyler missed his shot and sunk the eight ball.

Rising up from the table, Tyler spun around on Dutch. "What do you get? Your big butch ass gets to come out of the closet in June. That's what you get!" Nicky and J. B. were in hysterics in the corner as

Tyler continued to let Dutch have it. "And when you come out, don't think anybody will be attracted to that little dick of yours!" With both hands, Tyler scattered the remaining balls across the table. "Keep messing with me, and *your* balls are next!"

The guys were all laughing wildly at Tyler's performance, and if not for Dutch's phone ringing, Tyler would have continued.

Trying to compose himself, Dutch signaled for the guys to be quiet as he answered his phone, "What's up."

Dutch mouthed that it was Connor and again signaled them to shut up. "Huh... No. Shooting pool with the boys." Tyler, Nicky, and J. B. sat in silence as Dutch moved to the other side of the pool table. "Why don't you come over...? Nicky, J. B., and Tyler."

Tyler, Nicky, and J. B. simultaneously exploded into hand gestures, indicating "Hell no" as they jumped to their feet, ensuring Dutch saw them. Dutch made a sour face as he waved them off, again telling them to shut up.

"Oh, right. Catch you later." Dutch tried to play off the call as he casually put his phone back into his jeans.

"Homey, don't want to play with us, I take it?" J. B. asked.

"Naw, it ain't that. You know Connor. He's just a good ol' Southern boy, and there's no changing that," Dutch replied.

"What does being a good ol' Southern boy have to do with it?" Tyler piped in, "What, Southern boys don't like blacks or fags?"

Dutch didn't want to have this conversation because in his heart he knew Connor didn't like any of them. "Whose turn is it?" Dutch asked, manipulating the conversation.

It was almost one in the morning when Nicky glanced at his watch—the guys had been playing pool for about three hours. Realizing he still had a couple of hours of studying and reading to get through, he announced he was quitting, and the rest of them followed suit.

Walking out of Art's, the sticky, humid air hit Nicky in the face, causing him to take a deep breath. Having only dropped a degree or two, the air was oppressive, something Nicky would never get used to.

"You guys want a lift back to campus?" Tyler asked as he checked his pockets for his keys.

The three looked at each other before Nicky answered, "We're good. I'm sure you have a booty call that you have to get to anyways."

"Well, as a matter of fact, I do. Which is the other way, but I don't mind," Tyler replied unconvincingly.

The three waved him on as they declined again, said their good-byes, and walked toward campus.

"What are you doing tomorrow?" Nicky asked J. B. as the three of them headed down the deserted street.

J. B. shrugged, indicating nothing, waiting for Nicky to go on.

"Well, I was thinking of buying a used motorcycle. I know you had one a couple years ago. Maybe we can go look at a few?"

"What are you looking at getting?" asked J. B.

"I've looked at a couple of Ninjas."

"What are you looking to spend?" Dutch asked.

Nicky thought about the money he received from his grandparents when he graduated last year. He had banked it, knowing once he was in school his cash flow would be limited. "I don't know, maybe seven or eight hundred."

"I didn't know you rode," Dutch said.

"Yeah, I suppose I have to teach you to ride that mofo too," said J. B.

Nicky chuckled, "Yeah, and in trade, I'll teach you how to swim. How's that?"

As they crossed the street, Dutch was quiet as J. B. and Nicky continued talking about bikes. When they reached the corner, Dutch announced, "Boys, this is where we part. I'm heading over to Peggy's apartment," pointing to the opposite direction of the campus. "I promised her I would come over when we were done."

"Don't sound too excited," Nicky said as he extended his right fist to bump fists with Dutch.

"Yeah, we had a fight earlier. I wish I could just head back to the dorm and crash. I hate drama."

Once Dutch was gone, the two continued down Robinson Boulevard, which would take them to J. B.'s bus stop. "So how are your little sisters?" Nicky asked, more to make polite conversation than a need to know. If J. B. was going to talk about anything, it was about his little sisters, who were in the fourth, eleventh, and twelfth grade. Nicky knew J. B. loved his sisters and watched over them like a hawk.

Nicky didn't know much about his new friend other than he was sophomore carrying eighteen units. He knew that J. B. missed a lot of practice because he was taking care of his sisters and that he was only an adequate swimmer at best. In quiet chatter, no one was sure just how he made the team. The running joke was that the girls in the bleachers came to see J. B.'s massive bulge packed into his tiny red and gold Speedo, and the guys came to see how cheated they were. There was nothing J. B. could do to hide it, and in truth, he didn't care.

When they approached the bus stop across the street from the main entrance of the university, Nicky asked J. B. if he wanted him to hang out until the bus arrived.

"Naw, man, it should be here any minute," J. B. said, reaching out and giving his boy a hug. Agreeing to meet up in the morning, Nicky gave J. B. a second hug before heading across the street and into the dark and sleepy campus.

8

With Nicky's freshman year coming to an end, Nicky and J. B. were thankful that Desiree was able to help both of them with their studies when she could. Nicky was impressed with how smart Desiree was. He liked her the most out of all of his friends' girlfriends. Every time Nicky saw her, she reminded him of Mo'Nique, a female comedian he had seen on TV. He often kidded with J. B. that he was going to steal her away from him.

Now that it was June, Nicky was excited about heading home for a couple of weeks and being in his old bed before he had to start up his summer training. He wasn't able to go home back in April for spring break because he had qualified for the NCAA Regional Championships, and he hadn't seen his parents since Christmas. At the championships, which were held in Atlanta, neither he nor Connor's times were fast enough to qualify for the nationals.

He packed his duffle bag onto his new motorcycle and was looking forward to his four-day trip across the country. Nicky knew his mother wasn't going to like him buying the motorcycle, but it was his money and what's done was done, he told himself. He planned on taking his time, enjoying the different states. It was all going to be unfamiliar to him, and he was looking forward to the experience.

The second day into his trip, Nicky needed an early break off the bike, so he pulled into a small, cheap motel outside of Nashville. After checking in, he drove around and parked the bike in front of his room so he could keep an eye on his prize possession. After getting off the bike, Nicky looked up, making eye contact with a tall, slender man. The man, who appeared to be in his late thirties, was walking toward him carrying a bucket of ice. "Hey there; it looks like we're neighbors. I'm Mike," the stranger called out from a couple of feet away. "Where you from?"

"Tampa—I mean, South Dakota." Scanning the man over, Nicky thought to himself, *Why are you asking, and what do you want?*

When Mike stopped in front of him, Nicky noticed his dirty cowboy boots and tight Wranglers, which screamed, *Look at me. I'm from Nashville.* Fumbling with the card key, Nicky couldn't get his door to open fast enough.

"Here, let me try," Mike offered.

"Thanks, I got it." Nicky again pushed the card key in a third time and again got a flashing red light.

Mike took the card key from Nicky, nudging him to the side. "It's in the motion. Like a woman. If you just shove it in, they ain't going to give you nothing. Slow, like this." Two flashing green lights appeared, and the door popped open.

"Thanks." Nicky smiled at the lanky cowboy as he took his card key back.

Standing at the doorway, Nicky scanned the depressing-looking room. There was a desk and chair next to the door under the window and an old TV mounted on the wall facing a double bed against the back of the room. The corn-yellow-colored carpet reminded Nicky of his grandmother's house.

Seeing from the corner of his eye that Mike was walking away, Nicky closed the door. Laying his duffle bag down, Nicky walked into the tiny bathroom and scanned the sink and toilet. Staring at the sea-foam-colored shower curtain and missing tiles above the shower head, Nicky welcomed the sense of relief as he emptied his bladder into the rust-stained toilet.

That night, as Nicky was laying on his bed watching TV, he was feeling relaxed and ready for an early night when he heard a knock at the door. Looking out the window, he saw it was Mike at the door, holding a twelve-pack of beer. Seeing the beer, Nicky gave little thought to opening the door and inviting the guy, whom he had re-named Cowboy Mike, into his room.

After popping a beer open, Nicky lay on his bed with Mike across from him in the dirty blue desk chair. Cowboy Mike did most of the talking as Nicky listened and drank. Within a couple of hours, Cowboy Mike had drunk most of the twelve pack. In a relaxed mood, Nicky was working on his third, which was about his limit. Sensing he had to go pee, he felt more of the buzz once he stood up.

Nicky stumbled to the bathroom and stood over the toilet as he released his bladder. Not only was Nicky more drunk then he initially thought, he was horny as well. He grinned, thinking that he was sure he caught Mike a couple of times staring at his crotch. Nicky tugged at his now semi-erect penis a couple of times, shaking it dry before shoving it back down in his pants.

Nicky wished it was Coach Silva in the other room and not Cowboy Mike. He sighed. He was missing not seeing his coach every day. Nicky pulled out his phone to send the coach a text saying hi. Holding his phone in his hand, Nicky paused, unsure what to text without sounding dumb. After thinking about it for a couple of seconds, Nicky texted, *Hey did U catch the nationals on ESPN?*

Nicky leaned against the wall, staring at the screen, waiting for a reply. When none came, Nicky slipped his phone back down into his jeans and returned to the room. He noticed that Mike hadn't moved out of the chair and was reading one of the motel pamphlets. Nicky sat on the corner of the bed next to him and resumed watching TV.

"You all right?" Cowboy Mike asked, breaking up the silence between them.

Nicky wondered if Mike had sensed his boredom with his company. "Yeah, just trying to reach a friend. He hasn't texted me back." Nicky glanced again at his phone.

Within a couple of minutes, Nicky felt his phone buzz. Sure that it was Coach, Nicky anxiously removed his phone, looking at the message and seeing that it was from him: *Yeah, caught it. Where R U?*

In some shitty motel, Nicky replied.

Nicky's phone buzzed again: *No. What state?*

Looking at Cowboy Mike, Nicky typed back: *Nashville.*

Nashville's not a state, the message read.

Nicky snorted as his thumb worked the tiny keys: *WTF????*

Nicky watched his screen, waiting for a reply, and could see out the corner of his eye that Cowboy Mike was staring at him. It was a couple of moments before his phone buzzed again: *Have U been drinking?*

Alarmed by the text, Nicky scrolled up to see the whole thread, wondering what he typed to make Coach ask that. Seeing nothing, Nicky texted back: *No.*

K. B safe, appeared across Nicky's screen.

K, Nicky typed back

Good night ☺

Staring down at his phone, Nicky grinned at the smiley face Coach had added. Mike paid no attention to the fact that Nicky was focused more on his phone than whatever he was talking about. When Nicky did look over, Mike was staring at Nicky's semi-erect cock, which was wedged tightly in his jeans.

Feeling an extreme horniness induced by the brief text messages to the coach, Nicky watched Mike's eyes as they darted between his crotch and eyes. If Mike was going to look, Nicky was going to give him something to look at, purposely stretching his upper body across the bed, exposing his lean body. Within seconds, Mike took the bait, locking his eyes onto Nicky's crotch. Seeing Mike's response gave Nicky an adrenaline rush. Feeling mischievous and naughty, Nicky continued to tease the cowboy as he lay flat on his back on the bed. Rubbing his hand across his stomach, causing his t-shirt to rise, Nicky exposed his flat abs and navel. This got an instant reaction from Cowboy Mike, which also pleased Nicky. Nicky continued to play with

Cowboy Mike, growing hornier with each act. Nicky hadn't jacked off in the past two days and could probably cum just thinking about it.

Over the next thirty minutes, Nicky waited for Mike to make some kind of move on him. He thought he had made it clear in his actions that he wanted to play, but Cowboy Mike stayed fast in his chair. Nicky wondered whether he had misread Mike and was ready to ask him to leave if something didn't happen soon.

"You look tense," Mike said.

"I do?" With his buzz, Nicky was feeling anything but tense. "Yeah, well, it's probably from being on the bike for two days," Nicky lied.

"Do you want a massage? I'm told I'm good with my hands," Mike said, staring hungrily at Nicky.

Nicky felt his heart flutter at the offer, followed by a sinking feeling in his stomach. "O…okay." Nicky was nervous. His lack of experience now taking a backseat to his desire, Nicky anxiously glanced at the window, ensuring the curtains were closed. He took off his shirt and laid across the bed in front of Mike.

"I need some oil or lotion," Mike stated as he moistened his bottom lip with his tongue.

Nicky dug down in his bag until he found something. "Will this work?" Nicky asked as he held up a small tube of lotion he had just picked up from Walgreens.

"Yeah, that's perfect. Do you mind if I get comfortable too?" Mike asked as he kicked off his boots.

"No, that's fine," Nicky murmured as he watched Mike remove his boots. Mike climbed onto the bed and straddled Nicky just below his buttocks, shifting his body weight a couple of times until he found a comfortable spot to sit in. He worked on Nicky's shoulders, neck, and then upper back. Nicky laid there, and initially his pulse raced, but then the massage became more pleasurable as Mike's hands were replaced with the coach's. Attacking the aches and pains hidden within Nicky's muscles, he fantasized that it was the coach tenderly making love to him. Mike's hands were strong as they squeezed and worked the tension out of Nicky's shoulders and upper neck.

Nicky fell into a hypnotic state as Mike worked his way down to the small of Nicky's back, where his pants stopped him from going any further. Pressing deep into the muscle, several times, Nicky let out a light moan and gasp when Mike would hit certain spots in the small of his back. Nicky had never experienced such pleasure as Mike applied pressure and held it for a few minutes before moving on.

"If you slip off your pants, I can work your thighs and legs," Mike whispered into Nicky's right ear with a definite promise of more.

Without verbally acknowledging his request, Nicky hesitated for a second before pushing his hips and ass up, and with one hand loosening his belt and then unsnapping the button on his jeans. Mike tugged on Nicky's jeans, slipping them down and over his feet, revealing Nicky's creamy white swimmer's butt. With his jeans removed, Nicky lay naked on the bed, somewhat regretting having gone commando this morning. Initially uncomfortable about being nude, the excitement of the situation overtook his discomfort. Hearing Mike let out a groan, he began caressing Nicky's ass more than the intended thighs and legs.

"Is your ass shaved? It's so smooth, like a baby's," Mike whispered.

"I swim…on a team… We shave everything," Nicky said, enjoying every bit of the attention Mike was giving to his sore muscles.

With Mike still straddling his body, Nicky felt Mike moving about behind him before dismounting off the bed. Then, from the corner of his eye, Nicky saw Mike's shirt fly over his head and onto the floor.

"It's getting hot in here," Mike muttered as he stared at Nicky. "Do you mind?" Not waiting for a response, Mike then removed his jeans, stripping down to his boxers. "Now that's better," Mike announced as he climbed back onto the bed.

Going back to work on Nicky's thigh, the sound of Mike's breathing increased, with an occasional groan as his kneading grew deeper and longer, pressing Nicky's small frame deep into the mattress. With each squeeze, Mike lowered his body down closer over Nicky's entire naked body, reaching and massaging Nicky's shoulders and arms.

"Roll over," Mike whispered into Nicky's ear.

Unaware that his penis was fully erect until he obeyed Mike's request, Nicky laid on his back, still nervous. Within seconds, Mike's hands massaged Nicky's pelvis, pushing against Nicky's cock lightly as if accidently.

Nicky sensed Mike was about to kiss him just as it happened. The pungent odor of stale beer and cigarettes on Mike's breath came with the kiss. Nicky gently pulled back, offering up the side of his neck. He wasn't sure if Mike caught it, as Mike was all too willing to move to whatever was offered to him.

Within minutes, Mike whisked his own boxers off and stretched his body out on top of Nicky, pressing his erect penis against Nicky's. With their naked bodies rubbing against one another, Nicky's thoughts again went to the coach making love to him, which caused his body to respond positively to the sensations.

Kissing Nicky on the neck, Mike whispered into Nicky's ear, "I want to fuck you. Would you like that?"

At nineteen years old, Nicky had never had actual intercourse, and his heart nearly stopped at Mike's request. He didn't know what to say and questioned if he was supposed to say anything at all. He had masturbated in the past while thinking of giving himself to someone, and he'd even experimented with his fingers to see how it would feel. Intercourse was not out of the question for Nicky; he just didn't know the first thing about how to do it.

When he didn't respond to Mike's request, Mike gently rolled Nicky back onto his stomach and massaged his lower back again. Nicky felt his heart pounding against his chest as he watched, via the closet mirror, Mike reach for the tube of lotion. After a couple of squeezes to the tube, Nicky felt Mike's hands on his ass, followed by a finger as it slipped down in between his two small buttock cheeks. There was no denying that it felt good as Nicky groaned into the pillow.

With slick fingers, Nicky felt Mike slide a finger down into him. Initially tight, Mike gently worked one finger, and then two, and then a third finger into Nicky's ass. Nicky felt Mike reposition his body over his, and then with unexpected pain, Mike entered him. Nicky jerked in response, frantically sucking in air. Fighting to breathe, Nicky wanted to shout, scream—anything—as Mike held still over him. Just as Nicky was about to plead to be let up, his body yielded to the invasion.

Nicky knew it could not have been more than a minute or two when Mike frantically thrust, two maybe three more times, as he let out a vulgar moan in Nicky's ear. With his hot breath hitting the back of Nicky's neck, Nicky lay there wondering if he was done and if that was all it was.

Lying there, Nicky's attention was soon drawn to what sounded like several car doors closing and a man and woman talking to each other outside. Nicky listened as it sounded like they were coming into the room next to him. Wondering who they were and what they looked like, his mind created a vision. After several minutes, Mike slid to one side of Nicky and then rolled over onto his back.

"Do you mind if I smoke?" Mike asked as he lit up a cigarette and repositioned himself with his back against the headboard. Realizing that his ass was covered with something wet, Nicky grabbed his t-shirt and wiped his backside. Not wanting to make eye contact with Mike, Nicky shut his eyes and drifted off to sleep.

Feeling as if he had just closed his eyes, Nicky awoke in a panic, unsure just how long he had been sleeping. Having a sensation that he needed to go to the bathroom—and now—he jumped to his feet, sprinting to the bathroom. While sitting on the toilet, Nicky felt nauseous, a flash of heat overtaking his body causing him to be light-headed and dizzy. Nicky felt like his insides had been shredded as his stomach cramped. He struggled to catch his breath as he emptied his bowels in the toilet.

After a couple of minutes, there was a knock on the door, "Hey, are you okay?" Mike asked.

"Mmm-hmm, just stomach cramps. It's fine," Nicky murmured. It was several minutes more of just sitting there before Nicky felt his stomach settling down and felt safe enough to return to bed. Nicky again heard his new neighbors through the walls, although he couldn't make out exactly what was being said. Nicky was startled when he heard another knock on the bathroom door. "Hey, I got to go," Mike shouted through the door.

"Okay."

"Are you going to drink theses beers? I'll take them if not," Mike asked.

"That's fine; take them. You bought them. They're yours," Nicky replied as he rolled his eyes.

Regretting the last couple of hours, Nicky sat on the toilet until he heard the door close and the room was quiet.

The next morning, as Nicky was preparing to leave, he looked down the row of motel rooms and noticed Mike's mini-blinds were still closed. Nicky straddled his motorcycle and rode out of the parking lot onto the street, where he hit the throttle.

Heading into Iowa, Nicky stopped for a late lunch in a local coffee shop just across the state line. Inside the small diner, it was mostly empty, with the exception of an elderly couple and several young African-American women in a large booth in the corner. All dressed in similar black dresses, one of the girls turned and smiled at him.

Taking a table across from them, Nicky watched them as they squabbled and laughed at one another until one of them caught him staring. She smiled at Nicky as they both looked away from each other promptly.

Nicky got a sense they were talking about him when one of the girls stood up and approached his table, laying a flyer in front of him. The young girl was beautiful, with skin the color of wheat. Her eyes, a dark brown, matched her long, crimped hair.

"Hey there," the girl said, "I'm with the Harlem Hymns. We're performing tonight at the African Methodist Episcopal Church down on Sixteenth Street." She turned her head slightly back toward her friends clarifying the "we."

"Oh," was Nicky's only response, as he wasn't even sure what an African-something church was. "What…what kind of music?"

"We sing everything. 'How Great Thou Art,' 'A Change Is Gonna Come,' 'I Am Redeemed.' I think you'll enjoy it."

Nicky had never heard of any of the songs, and his expression clearly reflected so. Another one of the young ladies had stepped up next to her friend and offered her hand out to Nicky. "Hi! My name's Regina. You know songs like 'Amazing Grace,' 'I Can Only Imagine,' 'Oh Happy Day'… Do you like R&B? You know Boyz II Men, Whitney Houston, Mary J?"

Nicky's expression perked up when he heard Whitney Houston. "Oh, I know Whitney Houston!"

The first girl chimed back in, "Okay then, music like what she sings. We want to pack the church, and it's free."

By this time, four of the six young ladies were standing around Nicky's table, energetically trying to persuade him to come see them. They made him think of J. B., and he wondered if his sisters were like these girls.

"Do you live here?" Regina asked.

"No. I'm just passing through," Nicky responded.

"Well, so are we, so you need to come see us."

Nicky examined the flyer more closely and saw the girls were part of a choir out of New York. He thought he had heard of the choir and may have seen them on TV. With the smiles and the pleading, Nicky knew they were not going to settle for a no.

"I'll come," he told them, making eye contact with each of them, hoping they believed him.

Once the group left the diner, it grew quiet, as if the life had just left it. Nicky finished his meal and after paying the check headed out to find another cheap motel for the night since he was staying to see the performance.

Locating a small inn, Nicky checked in and made his way to his room on the second floor. Realizing that he didn't have anything to do for the rest of the day, Nicky pulled out the flier from his jean pocket and looked at it. Again he thought of J. B. and wondered if he went to church, which stimulated his curiosity. The performance didn't start until seven this evening, which was almost two hours from now. Making up his mind that he would go, he lay on the bed, hoping for a short nap before the performance.

When Nicky woke up, he knew he had been sleeping a while as the room was now dark, with the exception of the light shining in from the red neon *No Vacancy* sign. Exhausted, he pulled himself up off the bed and made his way into the tiny shower. Within a half hour, Nicky was showered and out the door to find the African Methodist Episcopal Church.

Maneuvering his motorcycle across the dirt parking lot, Nicky was surprised with the amount of cars there. The lot was full, and everyone seemed to already be inside. Trying to make the least noise possible, Nicky idled his bike as close to the church as he could.

After shutting down his bike, Nicky heard the music coming from inside the massive white church. He strapped his helmet to his bike and then made his way up the five stone steps, past the white pillars, and approached the ten-foot-high wooden doors, which were closed. He could now feel the foot-stomping vibration under his feet as he inched closer to the door. When a dark-skinned elderly man peeked through the little window carved in the ornate wooden door and saw Nicky approaching, the man's face lit up. He opened the door, welcoming Nicky inside. Stepping inside the sanctuary, Nicky smiled at the old man, who was wearing a dark burgundy suit and shiny white patent-leather shoes.

Scanning the sanctuary, Nicky's mouth fell open, letting out a slight gasp when he realized he was the only white person in the chapel. Although he could still hear the music, everything else in the room went to slow motion as he took it all in. The thought never even occurred to him that it was going to be in an all-black church as he mumbled "African Methodist Episcopal Church" several times to himself. A couple of women in the back pews, wearing large beautiful colored hats, turned around to see who was late. Nicky's feet were heavy, and there was no turning back as he looked around the sanctuary for a place to sit.

The church was packed with men and women of all ages and children dressed in little suits and dresses. Everyone was standing as they clapped their hands and sang with the choir. Nicky was halfway down the aisle when the old man with the burgundy suit tapped him on his shoulder and pointed to the row of pews Nicky was about to pass by. Without question, everyone in the row automatically shifted slightly to the left, allowing for Nicky to squeeze in on the end. Nicky watched as the man returned to the front entrance.

He pinched his body into the end of the pew, not wanting to take away more room from the elderly lady who had just moved her purse to the floor to allow space for him. Peeking over the woman's enormous peacock-blue hat, Nicky focused on the choir on stage.

Nicky focused up toward the altar, looking for Regina and the other girls he had met in the diner. Seeing the first girl who approached him, he realized he never got her name. The only name he got was Regina's. Searching across the five rows of choir members, he saw Regina.

As the angelic voices filled the church, Nicky found himself fully engaged in the music as the fifty-plus choir members sang "This Little Light of Mine," which his mother used to sing to him as a child. For the first time, now hearing the choir sing it, he understood it was a gospel song. The soulful voices echoed off the gigantic walls as the choir members snapped their fingers and swayed to the music in their ruby-colored choir robes. Occasionally, the elderly woman next to him turned and smiled at him with a slightly curious look on her face. Her smile was warm, and her perfume smelled of his grandmother. Checking out everyone in his pew, Nicky thought that the old lady was perhaps with the couple on the other side of her, he surmised, and the children next to them were her grandkids. Mesmerized by the all-black choir as they sang, Nicky knew many of the pop ballads and sang along with the entire assembly.

Everyone sang with the choir for the next hour as they went through a variety of music from slave songs to Broadway. When the lights were dimmed and the stage lighting behind the choir warmed to a beautiful neon blue, Nicky knew the performance was coming to an end. As the choir started their rendition of "Amazing Grace," he felt the elderly woman softly take his hand. Seeing everyone in front and across from him holding hands as well, Nicky flashed on the night before, feeling dirty about having sex with Cowboy Mike. A tingling sensation flowed through him as shouts of "Amen" and "Praise Jesus" were being cried out around him. Nicky felt at peace and closer to God than he had in many years.

When the magical concert came to an end and the lights were brought back up, Nicky filed behind everyone else as they made their way out of the large church. Entering the narthex, Nicky saw the elderly man who had seated him standing by the exit. "Thank you for coming," the man said as he extended his hand to shake Nicky's.

"Thank you," Nicky replied as he made eye contact with the gentleman and shook his hand back.

"I'm Pastor Clive Washington," he said, letting go of Nicky's hand. "It's nice to see the young people worshiping with us. The good Lord works in extraordinary ways."

"Thank you. It's nice to meet you." Nicky's hand was pulsating from the strong grip the little guy had. "I enjoyed the music, sir. They were great."

Making his way down the steps, he reached his motorcycle, pausing before picking up his helmet; he had an idea. He removed his phone from his inside jacket pocket, and with his back facing the church, Nicky snapped a selfie with the big church behind him.

9

A
rriving at his parents' house just after five o'clock, Nicky saw that his dad's car was not in the driveway. Realizing that today was Monday, he remembered Monday was his father's late night catching up from the weekend. His father had been an accountant for twenty-some years and worked long hours in a tiny office in a local strip mall. His income was moderate, and it hadn't changed much over the years, which kept Nicky's mother on a tight budget.

Nicky certainly never thought of himself as poor, but knew little about the family finances other than that they lived within their means. Growing up in the same house his entire life, they had one car because his mother didn't drive, and clothes shopping was reserved for back-to-school shopping only; all of which Nicky now better understood.

As Nicky strapped his helmet on the back of his motorcycle, his mother came out of the house to greet him. Standing at five-four, Mrs. O'Hare was a chunky woman. His mother was wearing the same tattered apron that she wore faithfully from the time she started supper until the dishes were washed, dried, and put away. Mrs. O'Hare brushed her hands clean as she waited for him to finish up. Nicky saw eyes watering up at the sight of her only son home for summer. When she was able to hug him, she held him tightly for several seconds before releasing him, wiping her eyes with the end of her apron.

"Your father hasn't come in yet," Mrs. O'Hare announced as she reached down and took the duffle bag full of dirty clothes at Nicky's feet. "Are you thirsty?" she asked, ushering him through the kitchen door into the house. The three-bedroom, one-bathroom home was the only house Nicky had ever lived in.

"Want some iced tea?" She didn't wait for an answer before she retrieved a glass from the dish rack sitting on the counter next to the sink. Nicky took his usual seat at the small kitchen table, facing his mother as she poured his tea and sat it next to him. He knew she saw the motorcycle parked under the kitchen window, but she didn't acknowledge it. Back when he told them over the phone that he was planning on purchasing it, his mother went quiet. Her refusal to acknowledge it now was proof that she objected to the purchase.

"What time is dad coming in?" Nicky asked, knowing that it was usually around seven o'clock on his late night.

"Oh, I don't know. I suspect he will be here around seven-ish." Sitting down next to him, Mrs. O'Hare couldn't stop looking and smiling at her boy. "So how are your classes?"

Taking in a whiff, Nicky caught the scent of pot roast cooking in the oven. It was his favorite, and he knew that there was also probably a cherry pie in the refrigerator for him too. He pondered her question, as his father would be asking it as well. "They're good."

"What does *good* mean? How are you doing in your classes?" she asked more directly.

"Good," Nicky repeated, trying not to sound irritated. "I passed everything; I think I told you that I got a B in my medieval culture class the first semester, right?" Nicky cut eye contact, knowing he barely got a C in all of his classes this last semester. Wanting to change the subject, Nicky tried to sound excited. "Oh, I forgot to tell you! You know my friend Tyler, who's on the team with me? We're sharing a room in the fall."

"What happened with Juan? Why aren't you going to live with him again?"

"Juan's a nice guy, but it would be nice to have someone from the team with me in my room. Besides, Juan and I have nothing in common."

"Where is he from?"

"Who?"

"Tyler."

"Oh, from Utah."

"Is he Mormon?" she asked with concern in her voice.

"I don't think so. He has never said anything about being a Mormon."

"Did you ask?"

"Ask what?"

"If he's Mormon," she asked, now sounding exasperated.

"No. Why would I?" Nicky replied, growing annoyed as well at the conversation. Nicky had come to realize many years ago if he humored her with her twenty questions, she would get tired of pulling teeth to get answers.

"Then how do you know?" Mrs. O'Hare asked. Nicky stopped to take another drink of his iced tea.

"I don't mom, but Squirrel—you know the little guy I told you about—he's Mormon, and Tyler doesn't practice the same stuff he does." What Nicky meant was that Tyler drank, had sex, and was gay, all the things that would make a bad Mormon.

Seeing that his glass was almost empty, Mrs. O'Hare retrieved the tea jug from the counter and refilled Nicky's glass.

"Thanks." In the still of the conversation, there was a moment when Nicky thought of Coach Silva. He had never fantasized about anyone like he did the coach. He wanted to talk about it. Maybe this was as good a time as any to come out to her. He was not sure why, but it felt right. As an only child, he was close to his mom. Although they never specifically talked about sex, nor would they, Nicky was able to always beat around the bush enough that she would eventually catch on to whatever it was.

"I hope you and dad will get a chance to come to one of my meets next season. We have some incredible swimmers. Coach Silva..." Hearing the front door open, Nicky stopped at the sound of his father coming in.

"Where's my boy?" Mr. O'Hare called out from the other room.

"We're in here, dear," Mrs. O'Hare answered for the both of them.

"Hey there, son!" his father cheerfully greeted him as he entered the kitchen.

"Hi, dad." Nicky stood up to give his father a hug.

"When did you get in?"

"Just a little while ago."

"So that must be your motorcycle out front that your mother yelled at me for you buying."

Nicky looked at his mother and then back as his dad. "Sorry; was it in your way?" Nicky mumbled.

Tucking his briefcase behind the kitchen door, Mr. O'Hare took his place at the table as Mrs. O'Hare kicked into action, setting their place settings and bringing the food to the table.

As soon as she sat the pot roast down, Nicky dug into the chunk of meat, not waiting for his dad. "So how was work?" Nicky continued to fill the rest of his plate with mashed potatoes and boiled string beans. Nicky listened as his father hinted for the millionth time about what it would be like if Nicky came to work for the business after graduating.

Finishing up the last bit of pot roast and potatoes, Nicky dabbed his white bread into the remaining gravy on his plate, occasionally looking up at his dad with an "Uh-huh." When Nicky was finished, he excused himself from the table, taking his iced tea out into the living room, where the only TV in the house was. He looked at his watch as he parked himself on the couch, wondering where the remote control was these days.

Later that evening, the three sat in the living room, watching TV like any other night in Nicky's childhood until Nicky decided to retire to his room. His parents normally outlasted him another hour, just until after the eleven o'clock news.

The next morning Nicky was up early, wishing he would have slept in longer. Having adjusted to the early mornings due to school and practice, it became natural for his body to rise with the sun these days. Stumbling into the kitchen, he was surprised to see his father still there, finishing up the last of his cup of coffee and the morning newspaper. Nicky didn't know anyone who read the paper other than his dad.

"Good morning," Mr. O'Hare greeted Nicky, watching his shirtless, tired son pass by him, walking toward the coffee pot on the counter next to the stove.

"Hey," Nicky grumbled as he rubbed his eyes. Nicky pulled down a mug from the cabinet above the coffee pot and poured himself a cup. He only needed coffee during his off-season, as the cool water of the pool usually did the trick in waking him up.

"So who helped you pick out the bike?"

"J. B.," Nicky mumbled, taking his seat next to his father.

"Is he the black kid on your team?"

Nicky knew his father meant no harm in his reference to J. B. as "the black kid," and a year ago, Nicky himself probably would have used the same descriptive word. But now he knew better and wouldn't refer to one of the white kids as "the white kid." Nicky started to call this out to his father, but decided against it, not wanting to overstep his role in the father–son dynamic.

"How do you like it?" his father asked.

"It's nice. Runs good."

"How much did you pay for it?"

Nicky knew this question was coming. He felt that J. B. had worked him a good deal and the bike was worth what he paid. The fact that he hadn't spent all of his graduation money would also soften the blow. "Seven-fifty."

Closing up the paper, his father took a final sip of his coffee and let out a satisfied sigh. "I've got to run. I'll see you tonight, son." Mr. O'Hare lightly kissed Nicky on the forehead and left for the office.

After Nicky took his shower, he located his mother in the garage, starting his laundry that she had hauled in yesterday.

"Hey, Mom, I'm going over to the pool for a workout," he said, referring to the pool that he swam at during high school. During the summer months, the city used it as the city pool, opening it up to everyone for recreation. From six until eleven in the morning, the pool was open for laps before the kids took it over at noon.

"Dinner is at five," she told him, as if it ever changed.

Nicky hopped on his motorcycle, and after backing it out of the driveway, he was on his way toward his old high school, which was only about five blocks from the house.

After an easy workout in the old familiar pool, Nicky continued on toward the Mobil gas station his best friend's parents owned. Both loners, Spencer had been Nicky's best friend since ninth grade, and the two swam on the swim team together. Nicky saw Spencer's car parked out front of the station and was relieved he was there. He had seen Spencer a couple of times over the Christmas holidays, but now with the warmer weather, Nicky was hoping they could go floating down on the river like they did in summers past.

He found Spencer and his dad in the parking bay working on an old 1965 Corvette the two had been restoring for as long as Nicky knew them.

"Hey! How's school going? When did you get home?" Spencer hollered when he saw Nicky walk into the bay. In his blue overalls and grease-covered hands, Spencer hugged Nicky, trying not to get grease all over him. "Hey, Dad, look who's here," Spencer called out to his father, who was continuing to work on the car.

Nicky politely waved to Spencer's dad, but barely got a response back as the man continued what he was doing under the hood.

"What's going on, dude?" Nicky asked, clearly seeing that at least Spencer was glad to see him. Spencer looked as if he had put on a few pounds, most likely because he no longer swam and was now working full time with his dad at the station.

"I came by to see if you wanted to go floating," Nicky asked quietly, not sure if his dad would approve.

"When?"

"Today. I don't have anything going on," Nicky replied.

"Aww, man, I can't. My dad is leaving early today. My grandma is in the hospital, and he has to take mom over there to see her."

"What about tomorrow?" Nicky asked.

"No, I can't. My brother is coming in to help dad and I drop the engine in the 'vet tomorrow."

Hearing the bell that triggered when a car pulled in for fuel, both Nicky and Spencer looked toward the fuel pumps. Feeling slightly rejected by Spencer, Nicky was at a loss. "Well, I'm home for a couple of weeks. Call me so we can float and catch up."

"K. I will," Spencer told him, his body language signaling to Nicky that he had to go take care of their customer. Nicky walked out of the bay feeling as if something had changed between them since the last time they had hung out. The vibe was off; he felt it.

As Nicky strapped his helmet on, Spencer called out, "Nicky! It was nice seeing you." Nicky nodded as he watched Spencer glance back at his dad.

Over the next couple of weeks, other than maintaining a light swimming routine at the pool, at the request of his father, Nicky had rebuilt a section of the backyard fence and cut the lawn each week. Nicky also helped his mother out by cleaning out both the attic and garage on two of the hottest summer days.

After not hearing from Spencer for several weeks, it was apparent to Nicky that he wasn't going to call. He was saddened that he would never be able to tell Spencer all the cool stuff he was doing at school. Other than hanging out with a few other friends from high school, Nicky's summer passed like any other summer. He was bored before the end of June and missing his new campus life and friends.

After talking to Tyler one night on the phone, he had been convinced to cut his dull getaway by two weeks and return to Tampa early. Tyler had already checked into their dorm room in Hayden

Hall and talked about the fun Nicky was missing out on by not being there. With no better offers, Nicky accepted the invite and broke the news to his parents that he was heading back earlier than planned. Although he could see the hurt on his mother's face, he raced back to Tampa to join up with his friend and the possibility of seeing his coach.

When Nicky made it back to the university, the campus was quiet, with just a few students that were attending the summer session. There were also a few students on campus who were playing sports and enrolled in other summer programs.

Surprised that Tyler had their room set up, the first thing Nicky noticed was the 40" flat screen sitting on one of the desks. This meant no more having to visit the student lounge at the end of the hall just to watch TV. Although the lounges were nicely furnished in school colors, with red couches and gold-painted coffee tables, the rooms were often noisy, and little TV watching went on in there.

"Hey, I hope you don't mind the curtains and the matching bedding. It was my mom," Tyler said as he shook his head in embarrassment. Although Nicky enjoyed the privacy that rooming with Juan had afforded him, Tyler was everything that Nicky wanted to be: fun, loud, and scared of nothing. It was nice seeing and hearing Tyler's loud voice. Staring at Tyler's golden brown hair with the copper highlights in it, his light blue eyes really stood out. Tyler was easy on the eyes, and Nicky saw what others found attractive about the guy. He was already glad to be back, and ready to laugh again.

Tyler had lined up their first party to attend on the Fourth of July. The party was in Fort Lauderdale, and Tyler offered to drive the four hours and pay for a motel room to stay the night. Nicky originally didn't want to go, instead hoping to return to the pool and to a routine that was familiar to him. Just being out of a consistent daily workout made Nicky edgy. He needed to burn that energy off every day rather than store it inside. The rumor was that Coach Silva had recruited the Quintero twins from California; they would definitely add strength to the team, but this also worried Nicky a little. He had looked up Austin, the faster of the two freshman twins, and saw that he had finishing times that rivaled some of his best. The last thing Nicky wanted to do was give up several days of practice for a party. It was at the last minute, with a great deal of begging from Tyler, Nicky caved in and agreed to go.

Sunroof open, windows down, the two headed down US-27 on their weekend road trip to Fort Lauderdale. Nicky sat in the passenger seat of Tyler's Range Rover Googling the city, seeing that it was famous for its beaches, art, and culture. The more time he was spending around Tyler, the more he liked him and his knowledge of the world. Thinking of their dorm room compared to last year, Nicky was loving having their own TV, mini refrigerator, and endless snacks right in the room.

"That was nice of your mom to buy us all that stuff for our room," Nicky said.

"Yeah…I guess." Half grinning, Tyler gave a glance over at Nicky as his head thumped to the music playing.

"How come you never talk about your mom or dad?" Nicky asked. With nothing but silence from Tyler, Nicky turned to look at him, and for a minute he thought Tyler may not have heard him. Seeing the muscles tighten in Tyler's face, Nicky hoped it wasn't his question causing such a strained look on his friend's face.

Tyler cleared his throat, "Well, I never met my biological dad, and my mom was a junkie."

"Are you kidding?" Lost for words, Nicky could tell by Tyler's expression that he wasn't.

"No. She's probably dead by now. I was adopted when I was seven," Tyler added. Silence again filled the air for a brief moment. "My adopted parents, well… they're older. We don't have much of a relationship these days."

Tyler went silent. His brows narrowing together, he gripped the steering wheel and focused on the road. The conversation ended there.

The rest of the road trip was uneventful, with Nicky keeping the conversation much lighter. Nicky picked up on the ocean scent as they reached Fort Lauderdale. Nicky now understood why they made air fresheners called Ocean Breeze, even though the scents weren't even close to being the same.

Tyler had rented a room across the street from Hollywood Beach. Their room overlooked the white sandy beach and emerald-green ocean. After checking into their room and showering, Tyler suggested they go out for a bite to eat prior to heading over to the party. He explained to Nicky that it was good for them to have something in their bellies and not drink on an empty stomach.

Along the beach strip, they found a small mom-and-pop diner, complete with the round red vinyl booths, plate glass windows, bar stools, and a fifties-style short order counter. After seating themselves, the waiter dropped off two waters at their table. Tyler was the first to look up, and his expression caused Nicky to look up as well. The waiter, who could have been a double for Zac Efron, was standing ready to take their order.

Tyler leaned forward as he ran a finger across his lower lip. "Hello there," Tyler said, smiling up at the young waiter.

"Would you like to hear the specials, or do you know what you want?" Either oblivious to Tyler's awful advances or not interested, the waiter took out his pad, ready to take their orders.

"Well, what's the special?" Tyler asked with a much softer tone in his voice.

Nicky was surprised at Tyler's directness toward the waiter. There was a part of him that wanted to crawl under the table and hide, yet he envied Tyler's ability to be smooth and confident.

"Tonight, my mom has prepared meatloaf and mashed potatoes with a white cream gravy. You get two biscuits and a slice of your choice of pie for $8.99."

"Does it come with a drink?" Tyler asked.

"No…*it's only* $8.99," the waiter snapped, never even looking at Tyler.

Catching Nicky off guard, Nicky spat out his water onto the table as he exploded into laughter at the remark. This broke the tension as the waiter looked at Nicky and smiled.

"I'll give you a drink if you want one," he then told Tyler in a lighter tone.

A little put out that he was the butt of the joke, Tyler told him that his water would be just fine.

"And what can I get you?" the waiter sweetly asked Nicky.

"I think I'll have the bacon cheeseburger, with the seasoned fries instead of the steak fries, and a 7 Up," Nicky announced as he closed his menu and smiled.

"Good choice," the waiter said. "It'll be right out."

After the waiter left, Tyler fanned himself pretending to be hot. "Now that was fine. He was totally hitting on you."

"No, he wasn't. He was just being nice," Nicky replied.

"You're not for real. Before I realized he was into you and not me, I was ready to butter his biscuit with a little of my own gravy. It too is homemade."

"Tyler, don't be nasty," Nicky pleaded as he crossed his arms against his chest.

"He all but pushed my ass out of the booth just to smile at you. You didn't see that?" Tyler squawked back.

Uncomfortable, Nicky rolled his eyes at Tyler, as he thought of something to say to change the subject to anything other than him and the waiter.

Throughout the meal, not only was the waiter attentive, specifically to Nicky, but was seen several times staring at them from across the diner. At the end of the meal, the waiter reminded Tyler that he had a slice of pie with his dinner.

"Wow, I am stuffed. What kind do you want, Nicky? We can split it."

"Peach," Nicky stated.

"No, I hate peach pie."

"Get the apple then," Nicky said.

When the waiter returned, he sat a piece of apple pie in front of Tyler and then a piece of peach pie in front of Nicky. "Here you go, since you wanted the peach." The waiter handed each of them a spoon for their dessert, and then placed the bill at the end of the table next to Tyler. "Are you guys in town for the weekend?" he asked Nicky.

"Yeah, we're here for a party," Nicky responded.

"Oh, who's having the party?" the waiter asked, his focus still directed on Nicky.

Nicky looked at Tyler for an answer, realizing he didn't know the guy's name. Tyler had told him on the drive down, but Nicky had forgotten the name already.

"Jerry Castro. Do you know him?" Tyler asked in a slightly bitchy tone.

"Yes, as a matter of fact, I do. He owns the art gallery down the street and eats in here a couple of times a week. He has some great parties. I didn't know he was in town this weekend. If the party is slow, which I doubt, Rubies down the street picks up after ten and has a good vibe on the weekends. You should check it out while you're here."

"We're leaving in the morning, but thanks." Tyler snatched the bill from the table and examined it. Pulling out a twenty, he handed the black tray back to him. "Keep the change."

The waiter winked at Nicky before turning and walking away.

"See. Now do you believe me?" Tyler said as he stood up ready to leave. Nicky rolled his eyes without answering, realizing that Tyler was right.

Tyler's GPS led them down to North Atlantic Drive and chimed when they reached their destination. Stopping in front of a huge, three-story glass-front Mediterranean house, Nicky couldn't imagine that it was just one home. The circular driveway was already crammed with parked cars, which forced Tyler to park on the street.

"So who is this guy?" Nicky asked as the two of them walked up the driveway. Nicky had never seen a house this huge. Glancing up, he saw several guests on the second story through the massive window and a guest standing out on the balcony looking down at them. Although most people were inside, to the left of the property was a large grassy area with tables and chairs that looked out to the ocean. Nicky knew it wouldn't be long before the sun was going to set. He wouldn't mind coming back out and watching it, he thought as they reached the front door.

"He's a friend of the family," Tyler answered.

"I thought he was a painter?"

"He is. Relax, it's going to be fine."

When Nicky thought of a painter, he thought of the guy who sold his work at flea markets, fairgrounds, and local art shows. This was not one of those guys. Nicky tensed as his walk slowed. Glancing again at the people up on the balcony, he was definitely regretting the decision to come.

Nicky was surprised when they reached the front door and Tyler walked in without knocking. Nicky followed closely as the two made their way through the house. No one had stopped them, nor did anyone seem to care they were there. The crowd was much younger than what Nicky had first seen on his way in. Between their early twenties and thirties, the attire ranged from shorts to sport coats and everything in between.

"What do you want to drink?" Tyler asked as they stopped in front of a long table with two bartenders in black vests. The bartenders stood with their hands behind their backs, waiting to serve them.

"I don't know. What do they have?" Nicky scanned the additional tables behind the bartender, looking for something familiar to him. There were bottles and bottles of what Nicky assumed was various liquor. "I guess a Coke."

"He'll have a rum and Coke, and I'll take a Red Bull and vodka," Tyler said to one of the bartenders. Nicky watched as he made the drinks and then handed each of them their drink. Tyler turned to walk away.

"Don't we have to pay for them?" Nicky couldn't avoid the panic in his voice.

Tyler chuckled at his friend as he shushed him, then explained it was called an open bar. Following Tyler, the two made their way down into a large living room full of people. "Relax. I'll introduce you to Jerry as soon as I see him."

"Do you know anyone else here?" Nicky's voice cracked. He wanted to flee and would be willing to hang out in the car and wait if Tyler insisted on staying.

"Nope, but I see a few I wouldn't mind getting to know." Nicky followed Tyler's gaze toward three young guys standing next to a large piano. All three were cute and about their age. One of the three caught them looking and politely smiled back at them before casually turning away. Nicky was amazed at the amount of windows in the room giving way to Florida coastline. He wouldn't even have to go outside to see the sunset.

As the night went on, the crowd continued to grow, and the house was overflowing with young partygoers. After their third drink, Tyler had parked Nicky in front of the swimming pool with the promise of being right back with more drinks, but that was forty minutes ago. Nicky had devoured a bowl of chips on the table as he watched everyone in the pool flirt and make out with one another. He was needing to go to the restroom but didn't want to not be there when Tyler returned. The pool was filled with mostly men, who were also the majority of the guests in the house. It was like watching a movie as they became increasingly more sexual with one another. When it became too much for him, with several of them now skinny dipping, he knew it was time to leave.

Standing up, Nicky looked around for an escape route. He was going to find Tyler and get the keys for the car from him. Nicky figured that his phone could keep him entertained in the car for hours while he waited. Covering the entire downstairs area, Tyler was nowhere to be found, which meant he was most likely upstairs. Nicky started toward the steps when he saw a lady come out of a small bath-room off to the side of the grand staircase. There was no line, so he dashed across the marble floor toward the bathroom before anyone else could get in.

Nicky stalled inside the tiny powder room, admiring the glass bowl sink that sat on a lit countertop that looked like the ocean. It was the coolest thing he had ever seen. If nothing else, the night was an experience, to say the least.

Opening the door, there was a man standing off to the side, wait-ing his turn. Not wanting to make eye contact with anyone, Nicky looked down and passed the man.

"Nicky!"

Initially thinking it was Tyler who called him, Nicky looked be-hind him at the man. Stopping in mid-stride, Nicky gasped as he saw that it was Coach Silva.

"Co...Coach Silva? What are you doing here?" Nicky was stum-bling for words.

"I'm surprised to see you too." Coach Silva's eyes moved up and down Nicky's body before he took a step back.

Nicky saw that his coach was just as surprised as he was as the two stood there fumbling between hugging and shaking hands. Nicky's brain shutting down, he just stared into the coach's beautiful brown eyes. "I'm leaving. I mean, I'm here with Tyler. We're leaving...when I find him."

Phillip laughed as he lightly touched Nicky's shoulder. "Relax. It's okay. How was your summer?"

"Good. I was able to make it home for a few weeks. That was nice." Nicky was able to control his breathing a little.

"So who do you know here?" Phillip asked.

"Um...no one. I came with Tyler, who knows the owner, I guess. He's somewhere around here too. Who do you know here?" Standing face to face, his coach seemed so tall, his shoulders and chest stand-ing out in his plain white dress shirt. Nicky focused on the slivers of dark chest hairs sticking out of the top of his shirt.

"Jerry," the coach answered.

"Yeah, I didn't know him until tonight. Tyler introduced me to him a couple of hours ago."

"He's a good friend of mine. We met years ago through some mutual friends. He owns an art gallery in Tampa, one here, and a couple on the West Coast."

"Oh wow. So his paintings are in *his* galleries?" It was half a question, half an *Oh-I-get-it moment* for Nicky when he realized the connection. "I get it. So people go to his gallery to buy his paintings." Nicky smiled at the revelation.

It wasn't long before two drunk brunettes stumbled up on them, asking if they were in line. Phillip politely signaled that it was okay and to go ahead.

"So you're here with Tyler?"

Tyler, that's right, Nicky remembered he was looking for Tyler to get out of here. "Yeah, he's somewhere around here. I was about to check upstairs for him."

"Well, he'll show up, I'm sure." Phillip smiled at Nicky, which calmed him slightly. "Come on, I'm heading over to the bar for a drink," he said, gesturing for Nicky to follow him.

When they arrived at the bar, the one bartender took the coach's order. "Would you like another, sir?" Looking at Nicky, the bartender held up a Coke can.

"Oh yeah, please," Nicky answered, paying more attention to the jet-black hair that tapered down his coach's neckline. When Nicky received his drink, he realized the bartender had given him another rum and Coke.

"Let's find a place to chat and catch up." Phillip directed him toward another room across from where they were standing.

Entering the room, it looked to be a library or study of some kind. There were wall-to-wall bookcases, two couches, and a large desk in the middle of the room. Both taking a seat on the same couch, Phillip smiled again.

Initially, the conversation was light, with Phillip doing most of the talking. After getting the coach filled in on Nicky's summer adventures, Nicky relaxed.

"You know, I see you in the water, and I can't believe you didn't start swimming until high school. I will never admit to saying this, but you're probably the best swimmer I have out there."

Nicky blushed at the compliment, turning away not to show his embarrassment.

"I embarrassed you. I'm sorry." Phillip paused. "You don't know how talented you are."

Nicky took a bigger than normal drink from his glass. "Thank you," he muttered, not believing it could be true. For some reason, Connor flashed in his head. Imagining him training with a professional trainer made Nicky envious. "Do you think I could make nationals if I trained harder?" Nicky asked shyly.

"I believe you could." Phillip smiled, looking warmly into Nicky's eyes. "I think you could even win nationals, with the right trainer."

"How about a gold at the Olympics?" Nicky asked, half laughing.

Phillip laughed, "A gold? Not a silver or bronze, but a gold. I like the way you think."

After about an hour of the two of them talking on the couch, Nicky saw Tyler through the double doors, holding a guy's hand as the two came down the steps. Initially, Nicky's impulse was to get up, but then decided that he was good and wanted to stay right where he was. He had forgotten he had even been looking for Tyler so he could leave.

The coach noticed that Nicky was looking over his shoulder and turned around to see what Nicky was looking at. "What is it?"

"Oh, it was Tyler. I just saw him coming down the steps," Nicky said as he sucked the last of the ice out of his glass.

Phillip looked at his watch. "Oh, it's almost midnight. Fireworks! Let's go!" He waited for Nicky to stand up before leading them out to the back yard. There were at least a hundred people gathered out on the lawn looking up to the sky. The show had just begun, lighting up the sky in purple, gold, and red. The sonic booms were loud, as the rockets were launched over the ocean one right after another. With glittering stars raining down over the water, Nicky stood in awe at the pageant of lights.

Within minutes, a waiter with a tray of champagne appeared, offering them a glass to enjoy with the show. Nicky hesitated, but Phillip took two glasses from the man's tray, handing one of them to Nicky.

"So is everyone supposed to kiss at midnight?" Nicky shouted over the constant booms over their heads.

Phillip laughed. "No. That's New Year's. Tonight, we just enjoy the show."

With the fireworks casting a twinkle in Phillip's eyes, Nicky couldn't stop smiling, wishing it was New Year's Eve so he could get that kiss. Feeling his heart beat against his chest, Nicky wanted that kiss. He would, right here in public if the coach asked. Not even after a race did Nicky's heart pound like it was pounding right now.

At one point during the show, they were standing side by side, and Nicky's hand lightly brushed against Phillip's pant leg. It was like a charge of electricity. Holding his hand within inches of Phillip's leg, Nicky did it again. He had lost focus on the show, as a burning desire to be closer to Phillip over took him.

After about twenty minutes of continuous thundering booms came a mass of hissing and uninterrupted crackling. *This must be the grand finale,* Nicky thought as the blasts vibrated through his body.

Lights showering down all around them, the entire coastline was lit up. Spectacular colors filled the sky, a grand ending to an unbelievable show. With no breeze, the gunpowder and smoke lingered in the air around, causing everyone to retreat to the house.

Turning to follow the crowd, they were met by another waiter with a champagne bottle in hand asking if they wanted more.

"Sure, thanks." Nicky said as he extended the bottle outward. Nicky observed the coach watching him. Wondering if the coach was going to say anything, Nicky second-guessed his actions.

After two sips from the second glass, Nicky started to become lightheaded, with a good buzz going.

"Are you okay?" Phillip asked as he reached out and grabbed Nicky by the arm, stabilizing him.

"Yeah, I probably need to find Tyler, though."

"Tell you what. Why don't you have a seat, and I'll find him?" Phillip chuckled at Nicky as he guided him over to a chair.

After about twenty minutes, Phillip returned to find Nicky passed out in his chair with his head folded in his lap. Phillip gently nudged Nicky awake. "Hey, I couldn't find Tyler. Do you think he left?"

Too drunk to reply, Nicky tried to focus his eyes on his surroundings.

"Come on, I'll give you a ride back to your hotel." Helping Nicky up, Phillip led him around the side of the house to his car.

Settling Nicky into his car, Phillip paused after he started the engine. "Where are you guys staying?" But it was too late: Nicky had already passed out again.

"Well, it would have been nice to know where I was taking you," Phillip mumbled aloud as he cranked over the engine.

With no alternative, Phillip put the car into drive. "No worries, I'll take you back to my room, and you can call Tyler in the morning."

A light snore was coming from Nicky when they reached Phillip's hotel. Walking Nicky into the room, he stood him next to the bed and laid him down on it. The coach removed Nicky's flip flops and after working a little was able to get his jeans and shirt off. Leaving his underwear and t-shirt on, he tucked Nicky into bed. With a spontaneous laugh, Phillip shook his head, thinking, *I can't believe this is happening to me.*

Staring down at Nicky's half-naked body, Phillip wanted so much to touch him, brush his hand across his angelic face. He told himself how wrong that would be and retreated immediately to the bathroom.

With the bathroom door locked, Phillip could feel his heartbeat racing as he brushed his teeth and washed his face. With a heavy sigh, he returned to the bedroom and joined Nicky in the only bed in the room.

Waking up a couple of hours later, Nicky went to reposition himself when he realized someone was in bed with him. The last thing he remembered was watching fireworks at the party. Looking around the room, he tried to figure out where he was. Nothing looked familiar until his eyes adjusted to the dark, and he saw that he was in bed with Coach Silva. His head continued to spin as he remembered that they were together at the party. *This has to be the coach's room, but how did I get here, in his bed?* Nicky asked himself, trying to call on what little brainpower he had. Adjusting his body again, Nicky's leg rubbed against the coach's, touching bare skin. He reached down and felt the coach's bare, cool skin, confirming what he was hoping. He was still drunk, no doubt about it, but now he was drunk and horny as he lay perfectly still next to the coach, fantasizing.

Nicky lay in bed, listening to the coach's deep breathing. Now fully awake, his heart pounded as he stared at his coach, wanting to touch his face. Nicky's penis swelled with each tantalizing thought. Nicky lay on his back as close as he could next to the coach, thigh touching thigh. Fully erect, Nicky gently played with himself, lightly touching his balls, then thighs, and then back to his balls before working up the nerve to brush his hand over the coach's chest, feeling the hairs that made him so sexy.

Thinking he felt the coach move, Nicky pulled his hand back next to him and pretended to be asleep. Within a couple of minutes, Nicky again touched himself, feeling the soft, slippery fluid that was now leaking from his cock and fighting the urge to stroke it. Nicky had been awake for almost an hour now and wanted the coach more than anything, working up his nerve to touch him again. This time, he slid his hand down across the coach's massive thigh, moving upwards towards his boxers and down again. He felt the coarse hairs that covered the rock-hard thighs that he'd dreamed of for so many nights. Nicky then brushed his hand over the front of Phillip's boxers, imagining how close he was to his cock.

Nicky again lightly rolled his hand over the coach's thigh, feeling the tightness of the muscle—perhaps it was the alcohol, but they felt massive. There was no stopping Nicky now: he was drunk, horny, and had the restraint of a six-year-old.

With little movement, Nicky used one hand to slip his underwear down far enough that he could use his toes to hook the tiny piece of fabric that connected them to his body and pull them off, leaving them under the sheets at the foot of the bed. Naked, Nicky straddled the coach's stomach, lightly sitting on his waist. As the coach lay sleeping, Nicky stroked his own cock, making use of the oozing precum. Kissing the coach's neck and cheeks, Nicky rubbed the coach's hairy chest.

Nicky kissed the coach on the lips, taking in the musky smell coming from his neckline. Nicky filled his lungs with the scent, *his* scent. Lost in the moment, Nicky suddenly felt the coach's head sharply move and then jolt backwards. Surprised at first, the coach pulled back, and Nicky knew he was awake... But then the coach lifted his head as he grabbed Nicky's head and returned the kiss.

With Nicky still straddling the coach, they kissed feverishly. Their kiss was forceful, tongues finding one another as their heads twisted from side to side. Coming up for air, Nicky reached down between them and freed the coach's cock from his boxers. Feeling the coach under him, Nicky took hold of his own cock again and stroked himself. The sensation of the coach's hands when he took a firm grip of Nicky's ass caused his body to respond, and with just a couple of pulls, Nicky came in his hand, pumping his seed over the top of his hand and all over the coach's chest. Nicky collapsed, leaning his head next to the coach's as he fought to restore his breathing.

With his face lying on the coach's chest, Nicky felt the coach's heart pounding. The rapid beat of his heart echoed in Nicky's ear, soothing and further connecting him to his coach. They lay silent, as Nicky's head rose up and down with each breath the coach took. In total nirvana, Nicky's breathing slowed, and he soon slipped back into an alcohol-induced deep sleep.

10

S tanding in the shorter of the two lines, Phillip stared aimlessly up at the coffee shop's menu board. He must have read it at least three times, yet all he could think about was last night and that Nicky was still back at the hotel, in his bed, naked. When he left the room, Nicky was sound asleep. In order to slip out from underneath him, Phillip had to move slowly, with the goal of getting out of that room. He needed air.

There was a pit in his stomach for not stopping what had occurred. Nicky's actions were clearly due to the alcohol, and he allowed it to happen regardless. The incident played over and over in his head, allowing Nicky to crawl on him, pretending like he was asleep while Nicky ran his hands up and down his body. He could have stopped it long before the kiss, but he didn't.

Phillip inched up closer to the front of the line. Two people now in front of him and he still didn't know what he wanted. That wasn't true. He did know, and it was Nicky. Phillip had been attracted to his star swimmer long before he was willing to admit it to himself, but now, there was no amount of denial that could allow him to overlook the truth. A year of purposely keeping his distance from the nineteen-year-old had been for naught. Did Nicky somehow see through his avoidance and have some idea about his feelings?

Thinking about Nicky's naked body on top of him, he remembered how Nicky's beautiful ass felt in his hands. He imagined what Nicky's ass would have looked like if he could have seen it in the mirror or if there was more light in the room. Each time that Nicky let his hips arch against his body, Phillip remembered feeling Nicky's soft round balls touching down on his abdomen.

It was the bathroom light—which Phillip had left on in case Nicky woke up in the middle of the night—that provided just enough light to see when Nicky brought himself to a climax, cords of cum shooting all over him.

The dark circles under Phillip's eyes were a dead giveaway that he hadn't slept. Phillip was exhausted; he hadn't slept a wink after Nicky collapsed onto his chest. He enfolded Nicky's body into the pit of his arms and held him all night. Listening to the sounds of Nicky's breathing, an occasional sweet snore, Phillip struggled to make some sense out of what just happened. Nicky hardly moved, other than the periodic rubbing of his face. Phillip wanted to believe it was the champagne, but was Nicky really this brazen? Was he not the sweet, competitive young man that went out of his way to please others?

Phillip thought about his own actions when he was Nicky's age, how sexual encounters meant nothing to him. It was all about getting off, and at times, it didn't matter who was in that alley behind the bookstore long ago back in New Mexico.

Feeling the crotch in his pants tighten, Phillip re-experienced the moment Nicky spilled his seed all over him. It took everything Phillip had to not roll him over last night and make love to him.

"What can I get you, sir?" the young woman asked, giving Phillip a sincere smile and waiting for his response.

"I guess… I'll just have two coffees, please." It didn't matter what the specials were or what was on the board; his brain was unable to process anything other than what had happened last night.

Staring at the barista, he knew something was off as she stared back at him. Then he heard her say, "Sir…would you like cream or sugar in those?"

"Oh, no, thank you. Just black." Coming from out of nowhere, Phillip thought about what his old coach Marcus said to him, *Is any of this shit important to you, or do you want to be known for sucking cock in the alley behind the bookstore?* Marcus's voice was as plain as day, as if he were standing right in front of him speaking. Phillip was forced to make a choice that day. Right then and there, he had to profess his commitment to his coach to never return to that alley again.

Last night most likely meant nothing to Nicky. He was a horny, drunk nineteen-year-old who did the same dumb-ass shit that Phillip had done at his age. Phillip was mortified that he allowed this to happen, and even more so that he wanted it to happen. His stomach was tied in knots, and there was no way he would be able to drink this coffee. Tiny beads of sweat formed across his forehead under the hairline as he struggled with regret, knowing he could lose his job if word got out.

Thinking back to when he first arrived at TBU four years ago, he dated a student on campus for a short while, but that guy was only six years younger than he was. Could he really justify a sixteen-year age difference? Society, his friends, colleagues, would they think of him as a perv for dating students? Oh sure, professors on campus a lot older than him went out with their female students all the time, and everyone turned a blind eye to that. Phillip knew this would be perceived differently, right or wrong.

There was no denying that Nicky reminded him of himself at that age, quiet and shy as he took in the world around him. Modest in his values and honest and pure in his actions, there was a sweetness about the young man. He loved how he could be so laid-back, but in the water, he became this beast with a strong desire to crush everyone. Yeah, Phillip couldn't deny that he was also physically attracted to Nicky. The possibilities, the excitement, the potential of having a relationship with another person excited Phillip. He knew he was crazy to think that could be with Nicky. Phillip laughed at himself. *Why would a nineteen-year-old want me?*

Taking a deep breath in an effort to calm himself, Phillip picked up his two cups of coffee. He knew it was time to head back and face the music, whatever that was.

With a sharp ray of sunlight creeping in through a tiny slit in the curtain, Nicky tried to swallow, but his throat felt as if it had been packed with cotton. He glanced around the room, having no idea where he was. Tilting his head slightly relieved the pressure for a second or two before the pounding returned.

Nicky slid his legs across the bed, causing his feet to hit something soft. Reaching under the covers to retrieve whatever it was, he realized he was naked just as he brought his underwear from under the sheet. Launching into a sudden flurry of thoughts, his mind was racing as he searched for answers as to what had happened. He was in the bed alone, and there was no sign of anyone else in the room. He tried to sit up, but the throbbing in the front of his head was too intense.

Nicky closed his eyes as he fought to remember something, anything. He remembered he and Tyler went to a party last night. *Where is Tyler?* he wondered. *Tyler, Tyler, Tyler,* he kept repeating, trying to jog his memory. The fireworks came to him. In a panic, he remembered he was with the coach. *The coach! Did I dream it? Did I have sex with the coach?* Nicky's body temperature rose, forcing him to kick the covers off of him. "Shit, I'm naked," he mumbled, pulling just a sheet over him. *Where is he?* Nicky looked around the room, seeing that the bathroom door was open and the light was turned off.

His chest tightened as he scanned the room, looking for anything to tell him he was confused, that he was wrong about what he thought he remembered. *I was dreaming,* he told himself. There was a small suitcase on the chair across from him. Just as Nicky was about to search through it for clues, he heard the door lock click. *Shit, someone's coming in.* Leaping back into the bed just as the door opened, he saw that it was the coach. He was in the fucking coach's room, just as he suspected.

"Good morning. I thought you might need a cup of coffee." The coach extended a cup to him. "It's black. Drink it. It'll help your head."

Nicky tried to say something, but nothing came out. His throat was dry, and no matter how many times he tried to swallow, it didn't help. Taking the coffee, Nicky couldn't look at him.

"Trust me, you'll thank me later." His tone was uncertain. *Later? Later? What did he mean by "later"?* Taking a sip of coffee, a rush of oxygen to the brain caused Nicky to release a sigh. Sitting up in bed, he watched the coach as he moved about the room, packing his toiletries away in his bag.

Nicky heard his phone buzz and looked around, wondering where it was. Realizing that the phone was still in his jeans, which were on top of the desk, Nicky started to reach for them before remembering he was still naked. Scurrying to put his underwear on first, Nicky got to his jeans and pulled out his room key and phone. Seeing that he'd gotten five text messages from Tyler last night, he scrolled through them, occasionally taking sips of his coffee.

1:48 am: I cant find u. where r u?

2:15 am: Dude r u still here?

2:20 am: I am leaving. Hope u r at the room.

4:03 am: Went to Rubies and met someone see u in the morning.

7:37 am: just going to sleep. I will be back at the hotel to pick u up later. Will call u. Dont worry about checkin out.

Nicky looked at the time and saw that it was just a little after nine. He shot a text back to Tyler. *Call me when u wake up.* He glanced up at the coach, whose back was now to him.

"I think I'm sick." Nicky got out of the bed.

"I suspect you're hung over. You only had two glasses of champagne; you're definitely a lightweight."

Nicky thought about the four, or was it five, rum and Cokes he also had, but decided it was probably not a good idea to let his coach know that.

The coach disappeared into the bathroom, shutting the door behind him. When he came out of the bathroom, it was the first time the two made eye contact.

"If you get dressed, I can drop you off wherever you're staying." The coach's voice was flat.

"'Kay..." Nicky looked at his hotel key card. "We're at the Lighthouse Inn. Do you know where it is?"

"No, but I'm sure I can find it."

The five-minute ride to Nicky's hotel was quiet. Nicky was unsure of what to say and waited for the coach to say something—*anything*, Nicky thought—but it never happened. When they arrived at the Lighthouse Inn, the tension between them was thick. Embarrassed by his behavior, Nicky couldn't be more relieved to get out of that car. Hurrying up to his room, he was sweating profusely and felt as if he was going to vomit any second.

Nicky hadn't been able to eat anything all day. That night, as he lay on his bed in his dorm room, he was uncertain about his future: Would the coach kick him off the team? Would he be kicked out of school? What would he tell his mother? In a daze, Nicky heard his phone buzz. He looked at the screen, which read *P Silva*.

Nicky hesitated for several rings and picked it up right before it was about to go to voice mail. "Hello," Nicky said.

The other end of the phone was silent for several seconds before Nicky heard a throat clear. "Can you talk?" the voice asked as it cracked into Nicky's ear. By the coach's tone, Nicky knew it wasn't good.

"Yeah, I'm in my room by myself. How are you?"

"Good, but I am calling to see how you're doing. Are you okay, I mean about with what happened?" Phillip asked.

Nicky's mind kept telling him that he was about to be kicked off the team. He had overstepped his bounds, to say the least, putting at risk his education, the coach's job, and the whole team's dreams, just because he was drunk. He knew, though, that was a lie; it wasn't because he was drunk. It was because he had wanted it for so long.

Nicky overheard his schoolmates on the other side of his door as their voices made their way down the hall and into the room next to him. In a whisper, as if they could hear him, Nicky replied, "Yeah. I'm okay. I'm sorry about last night."

"I know. You were drunk."

Nicky moved onto his side and repositioned himself up onto his right arm as he fought back tears. "Well...not that drunk." He was stammering.

"What do you mean?"

"I wasn't that drunk. I knew what I was doing. I'm sorry. I swear I won't say anything to anybody. It was my fault—all of it," Nicky said as a tear fell from his eye. He gently wiped the next one that followed as his throat went dry. He didn't want his coach to hear him crying as he fought to hold it back. "I...I wanted it. I wanted you." Nicky covered his mouth as he sobbed, not wanting to make a sound.

"So you're not regretting it?" Phillip asked tenderly.

"No...I've been thinking about you all day. I wanted it. I've wanted to kiss you since the day that I met you," Nicky stammered.

They were both silent on the line. The extra-long pause was acceptable, as long as his coach didn't want to hang up. Nicky sat up in his bed, drying his eyes with his shirt. He had been wondering what it was going to be like when they were again face to face. "I've been freaked out all day," Nicky said.

"You're a brave one, aren't you?" Phillip responded.

"Not really. I just really wanted you... I..." Nicky stopped himself from saying that he loved him. There was a pause on the coach's end, long enough that Nicky questioned whether he should have said as much as he did. "Are you still there?" Nicky asked.

"Yeah, I'm here... You know that I'm damn near old enough to be your father?"

Nicky thought he heard the coach take in a deep sigh. Their conversation stalled again; this time, Nicky was unsure if he should say something or just wait for the coach to say something first. Nicky held the phone to his ear as he waited. The only sound was the muffled voices coming through the walls from the room next door, and he could smell the faint odor of marijuana coming in through his window. He didn't know what to say as he waited for the coach to say something.

After a couple of minutes, Nicky heard the door handle jiggle and knew that it was Tyler coming in. Within seconds, the door blasted open, slamming into Nicky's bunk.

"Are you on the phone? Hang up! Hang up, I got something to tell you," Tyler whispered, demanding Nicky's attention. Nicky had grown accustomed to Tyler's theatrical and flamboyant behavior and found that it was usually easier to just accommodate him, but he wasn't ready to get off the phone just yet.

"Is someone there?" Phillip asked.

"Yeah, Tyler just walked in." Nicky tried to shoo Tyler away, but Tyler kept signaling him to hang up the phone.

"Oh. We better say good night."

Nicky sighed, mad that Tyler didn't know how to let up. Was this the end? Did they just hang up? Nicky pushed his sandy blond hair out of his face, staring at the dingy beige wall across from him. "Okay." He knew he couldn't hang up first; his heart pounded as he envisioned the coach on the other end of the phone. *What was he wearing? Was he sitting or lying down in his bed? What was his house like?* Nicky thought about taking the phone out to the hall until he heard the coach speak again.

"Good night."

Nicky listened as his phone went dead. The coach had hung up.

Seeing that Nicky was off the phone, Tyler approached his bunk. It was clear to Nicky that Tyler was charged up about something. "I met this cute guy down at Chicago Coffee House," Tyler started in. "As soon as I walked in, our eyes locked. I was going to get my coffee to go because I was supposed to meet Charlie at the library. He was so cute, though, that I changed my plans. I sat at the table next to him and pretended to read the newspaper. Every time I looked up, he was staring and didn't care that I was catching him, so I stared back."

Tyler was being animated, flashing his hands about as he told his story. "So I just got up and introduced myself. Turns out his name is Richard, and you know what that stands for!"

Puffing out his bottom lip, visibly not following his friend, Nicky asked, "What does it stand for?"

"Uh…dick!" Tyler replied as he pointed to his own.

Still not understanding the connection from Richard to Dick, he asked again, "How do you get Dick from Richard?"

"You have to ask nicely." Tyler erupted into laughter at his own joke. "I'm going to call him right now and see if this number is any good. It better be his number."

Not in the same playful mood as Tyler, Nicky rolled his eyes at Tyler's little joke. "Call him, but keep it down. I'm going to sleep," Nicky said as he rolled over, trying to recapture his thoughts of the coach. Hearing the numbers being pressed on Tyler's phone, Nicky closed his eyes.

"Hello, is this Dick? I mean, Richard. It's not too late, is it?"

The next morning, Nicky and Tyler were up early with plans to train at the city pool. When they reached the pool, they did their separate workouts. Nicky had a specific training regimen that few of his swimmates could keep up with. Nicky warmed up with fifty laps, alternating between the freestyle, backstroke, and the breaststroke every couple of laps. He swam for a solid hour before taking his first break. As he lightly paddled in the water, cooling down, he saw Tyler standing next to the edge of the pool talking to Dutch. He took a second to look at Dutch, noticing the heavy muscle tone that water polo players had, quite unlike the build of a swimmer. As Tyler and Dutch turned and looked at Nicky, he shot them a slight nod, acknowledging them before resuming his workout.

When Nicky was done with his workout, he saw that Tyler was back in the pool and still working out. A little less socializing and a little more swimming and Tyler too could have been done, but his friend loved to talk. Nicky located his towel and flip-flops next to the chair where he had stripped off his sweats. After towel-drying his body, Nicky gave Tyler a wave, letting him know he was taking off.

It felt good to be back in the water again, feeling so alive after a tough workout, the smell of chlorine on his skin, the pink hues in the sky lit up by the morning sun that rose sometime during his workout. He breathed in the morning air and let out a big sigh. Instead of waiting for Tyler, Nicky decided it was a great morning to walk the mile and a half back to the campus. Feeling his phone buzz in his sweatpants, Nicky looked at it and noticed he had two missed calls from Phillip. Nicky smiled as he stared at the number.

When Nicky was back in his dorm room, he nervously called Phillip back. The phone rang twice before Phillip picked up. "Hello."

"Hey, Coach, it's Nicky. Did you call?"

The coach was silent for a minute, "Yeah. I did. I'm sorry for calling so much... I wanted to see what you were doing later... Would you like to have dinner?"

Nicky was surprised by the question. "Yeah...what time?"

"Just be at my place by six. I'll take care of the rest."

"'Kay, text me your address," Nicky said as he fought to hold his excitement back.

After hanging up the phone, Nicky checked his screen three times before the text with the coach's address appeared. Exhausted from a lack of sleep the last two nights and his workout, Nicky lay across his bed and within seconds fell into a deep sleep.

He had been sleeping for hours when Tyler rushed into the room, waking him up with all the noise.

"Guess who's pregnant?" Tyler screeched.

"You?" Nicky teased as he rubbed his face, trying to open his eyes and adjust to the flurry in the room.

"Uh, no. You're a fuck head… Dutch told me at the pool this morning that Peggy's pregnant. Don't say anything to anyone, but he's not sure it's his and he's pissed. You know they broke up last month for two weeks, and she was off whoring her shit. Nasty doesn't change," Tyler said as he stripped off his clothes to take a shower.

"So that's what you guys were talking about. I could tell something was up." Nicky moved from his bed down into his desk chair.

"I'm going down to the Harbor to meet a friend," Tyler declared.

"A friend, or a friend friend?" Nicky asked, arching one eyebrow.

"No. Just a friend. You wanna go?"

"Naw, I can't." Nicky hoped his simple decline would satisfy his friend.

"Why? What do you have to do? You've been in this room all day. Come on," Tyler jabbed.

"Yeah, well… I'm going out this evening too. So don't freak out if I'm not here when you come in." Nicky waited for the response that was sure to come with his announcement.

Just as anticipated, Tyler whipped around toward Nicky as he grinned. "Where are you going? Don't tell me you got a date. Do I know him? Who is it?"

Nicky's eyes dropped down at Tyler's naked body standing in the middle of the room, as casual as if he was fully dressed. "None of your business. None of your business and none of your business. Put a towel on!" Nicky shouted.

Smirking, Tyler gyrated his hips, causing his penis to spin as he moved closer to Nicky.

"Ew, don't touch me with that thing!" Nicky chuckled as he jumped from his chair onto his bed.

"Tell me. Do you have a date or not?" Tyler hooted.

"Yes, it's a date, but that's all I'm telling you." Trying to hold back a smile at the sound of the word *date,* Nicky looked down at Tyler from his bunk and waited for his reaction.

Tyler's eyebrows rose. "Well, good for you. It's about time you got laid." The two smiled at each other, silently communicating to one another the possibilities that might be in store for Nicky this evening.

"I have to go grab a shower, and I'll be right back. We have to talk game plan for you." Tyler winked at him before spinning on his heels and grabbing his towel, which was draped over the back of his study chair.

11

Prior to Nicky's arrival, Phillip went back and forth several times in his head whether to call the date off. Phillip had planned to stay in and cook a dinner for the two of them. They could talk and feel out the evening without distractions or the fear of being seen in public. Between the heart palpitations and overthinking, he had to talk to someone, and who else to call but Steven, the one person that he could trust to give it to him straight without condemning him.

Hesitating to make the call, Phillip remembered what Steven had said to him when he had called him on the way home from Fort Lauderdale and told him what happened. *"Relax, you didn't do anything wrong other than put a drunk stud in your bed. I think you're overthinking this. He was drunk."* But inviting the young swimmer over for dinner was a game changer.

Picking up on the third ring, Steven answered his phone playfully. "Hey there, dolphin man."

"Oh boy, guess what I just did," Phillip said, trying to sound as playful. "I just invited Nicky over for dinner."

"Okay," Steven responded with concern in his voice.

"I don't know what I'm doing. Am I nuts? He's nineteen years old," Phillip asked while Steven remained silent. "Say something... Did I fuck up?" Phillip pleaded, wanting to hear something, anything, good or bad; he just wanted someone to tell him what he should be doing.

"I'm listening to you. It's just…ever since I've known you, you've never had a boyfriend. You don't even date. So why him?" Steven asked.

Phillip thought about his short relationship with Rory several years back, which had ended before he could even tell Steven. Steven was right. At thirty-five years old, he'd never had an honest relationship with any man. Coach Marcus first put an end to any kind of male companionship, and then his accident cemented the deal. Phillip wished he could say that it didn't concern him, the fact he might grow old and never experience love. Phillip was silent as he thought about Steven's question. *Why Nicky?*

Without answering Steven's question, Phillip asked, "Look, let me ask you. Do you think I should?"

"Truthfully…no, it's not a good idea, but hell, you've already invited him over and professed your undying love to him!" Steven responded.

"So what do I do?" Phillip pleaded.

"You're not calling me for advice; you're calling me for permission," Steven told him.

Phillip was quiet. He knew Steven was right. Rory would have been the closest thing to a relationship, and even Phillip knew that was just a couple of months of good sex with the same person for once. Phillip was no stranger to sex, but that was not what this was about. He wasn't just thinking about having sex with Nicky; he wanted to be next to him. Over the last year, he'd all but completely ignored the guy, trying to erase the strong feelings he was having for him. He even had dreams about him, and his heart hurt when he spent more than five minutes around him.

"Phillip, are you there?"

"Yeah, I'm here. I want to explore this, I guess. I wanna see him. I'm not obsessed with wanting a relationship with someone. This is not what this is about. No one has ever affected me the way this guy does."

"Okay, then—"

"No, wait, let me finish." Phillip cleared his throat. "I've never been in love, but if this is just a taste of what you and Martin have, if Martin thinks about you the way I think about Nicky, then I want in. Do I need the unnecessary stress that this could bring me? My whole life was about chasing a dream, and when that was taken away, I think I just stopped dreaming." Phillip paused for a second to think. "I fucking get up in the morning knowing I'm going to see him. Sometimes we don't say two words to each other all day, but I got to see him and that was enough for me. But now...but now, it's not enough. Today, on the phone, you know what he told me?" Not waiting for an answer from Steven, Phillip continued, "He told me that he knew what he was doing in that hotel room. That he likes me. He said that he's liked me since he first saw me. No one has ever said that to me. No one, Steven!"

Steven took in a large breath. "So what about Nicky? You talked about you, but what about Nicky if this all goes sour?"

Phillip took a moment to think about what his friend was asking him. He watched as Emily strode down the hall and into the bedroom. She had a concerned look on her face as she laid her head in Phillip's lap. "If anything, I've put his needs ahead of any of mine. He's nineteen years old. Why would he want to be in a relationship with me? He's got his whole life ahead of him to find love. Of course, I've told myself that if it didn't work out, I could be man enough to continue coaching him." Phillip lightly patted the bed and Emily took his cue, jumping onto the bed and nesting down next to him. "He's an amazing swimmer, and there's a lot of potential there that he hasn't even tapped into yet."

"That's all fine, but what about any legal ramifications? Could he be in any trouble with the school? I don't know how he's paying for his college, but could any scholarships be in jeopardy?" Steven asked.

"It's not against the law. It's against the university's policy. So, yeah, there is some threat there. It's very much frowned upon. I'm not going to lie: Even I've judged other professors I heard were dating their students." Phillip glanced at his watch, seeing that he had an hour before Nicky arrived. "I appreciate you talking to me. Trust me, I heard you." Phillip scratched at his light five o'clock shadow, realizing that he also had to shave before Nicky got there.

Phillip shifted his body on the bed before leaning back, placing his head on Emily's ribcage. "Even with everything saying, 'No, don't do it,' I can't stop thinking about him. I get a flutter in my stomach. I feel like I'm tongue tied when I do talk to him. Like he knows I'm staring at him. I feel like a little schoolgirl with a crush on a boy in her class. He makes my heart skip a beat."

Steven snickered on the other end of the phone.

Phillip waited for his friend to stop laughing at him. "Don't laugh. I feel like that actress in that movie. What was it—?"

"—*Basic Instinct*?" Steven chimed in.

"No. You're an ass. I was going to say *Steel Magnolias*. You know, Julia Roberts." Phillip pulled the phone away from his ear at the sound of Steven bursting into laughter.

"You mean Shelby," Steven was barely able to get it out between spurts of laughter.

"It's not that funny, *Clairee*."

"I know. I know. Well, there you go. I think you've answered your own questions. Baby, it sounds like you've been hit by Cupid. Go cook a glorious meal for him, and call me with the details in the morning."

Several times on the drive over to Phillip's house, Nicky found himself checking his mirrors looking for Tyler. With a grin, he chuckled each time that he did it, thinking about how Tyler was more consumed with his own life and wouldn't put in the extra energy to be that nosy.

Nicky cruised the neighborhood, reading off the addresses on the curb until he found 574 Morrison Drive. The coach's house was a lot closer to the university than he thought—he could have walked it in about ten minutes.

With the motorcycle idling between his legs, Nicky debated on whether to park in the driveway or on the curb. After thinking about the narrow streets and the possibility of someone hitting his bike, Nicky kicked it into first gear and crept up the driveway.

Letting out a heavy sigh, Nicky eyed the upscale neighborhood. Unsure if his palms were sweaty from his riding gloves or because he was nervous, Nicky wiped them a couple of times down the side of his black slacks, the nicest pair of pants he owned. Sighing again, he tried to gain control of his breathing as he looked at his watch and saw that he was ten minutes early.

It was clear that Nicky had gone out of his way to look presentable. This was only the second time he'd worn slacks since leaving home, and the button-down light-blue shirt was a going-away gift from his parents. With fresh helmet hair and the click of his heels on his dress shoes, Nicky started up the walkway.

After knocking, Nicky ran his hands through his hair, trying to loosen the matted spots. Hearing the handle twist, he blew into the palm of his hand and then smelled, ensuring his breath was okay. When Phillip opened the door, Nicky felt overdressed, seeing that Phillip was barefoot, in jeans and a white V-neck t-shirt.

"You look nice. I guess I should have told you that I was cooking and to come casual. Come in." Phillip flashed a warm smile at Nicky as he stepped aside to allow him in.

Nicky stepped into the grey marble-tiled foyer and was immediately greeted by Emily, who stopped him in his tracks. "Who is this?" Nicky asked as he gently held out his hand for Emily to sniff.

"This is Emily, my pride and joy."

"Damn, she's big. How old is she?" Nicky bent down onto one knee as he took hold of Emily's face and begin massaging behind her big floppy ears. "Oh, you like this, don't you?" Nicky asked sweetly.

"She's two." Phillip took hold of Emily's collar, pulling her back away from his company. "That's enough. Let Nicky come in before you cover him in dog hair."

Following Phillip out of the entrance way and into the living room, Nicky scanned the interior of the house, trying not to look nervous. The living room was large, with a massive sectional in the middle facing a large flat screen mounted on the wall.

Just a few steps in front of Nicky, Phillip talked without turning around. "It's not as nice as Jerry's in Fort Lauderdale, but it's home."

The navy-blue sectional had grey and blue pillows, which for the most part were the only colors in the room, making it appear warm and inviting. Nicky trailed the coach, listening to him as he stole several brief looks at how Phillip's ass moved in his jeans.

"Do you recognize this?" the coach asked, stopping in front of a large painting on the back wall of the room.

Nicky stared at the painted canvas showing the backs of several nude male silhouettes. They were all standing on a white sandy beach, staring out into an incoming storm. The artist had captured the masculinity of the male form, made evident by their broad shoulders, narrow waists, and muscular butts and thighs.

Studying the painting, Nicky knew that he liked it. At first, he thought maybe it was the coach with friends. Glancing down, he then saw the scribbled signature in the lower-left corner. *J Castro.*

"This is a painting from Jerry Castro. Now, I remember. He had several of these hanging in his house." Nicky recalled seeing several paintings similar to this one in the house, each piece being slightly different, whether it was the position of the dark clouds, the lighting, or the angle of the silhouettes. "Is it a collection?" Nicky turned to look at Philip.

"Well, yes and no. This is the only one that sold. He had it in his gallery here, and I fell in love with it and had to have it. The others in his house are all the ones he did first, trying to capture this." Phillip extended his hand, showing Nicky the clouds forming over the ocean. "He was never satisfied and just kept repainting the same scene until he got it right. Or at least what he thought was right. "

"Yeah, I heard most artists are crazy." As soon as the words came out of his mouth, Nicky wished he hadn't said them, thinking that he just insulted Phillip's friend.

Walking into the kitchen, Nicky noticed it was much lighter, thanks to the windows and sliding-glass door leading out to a patio. Nicky first noticed there was no table for eating in the kitchen. There was a large center island in the middle of the room. On one side sat four barstools, and on the other side, a large stove and the rest of the appliances. Staring at the massive stove, Nicky saw that it had twice the number of burners of his mother's stove. The countertops were a grey granite, and the cabinets looked to have been painted a flat black.

Phillip pointed to the stools, gesturing for Nicky to take a seat as he moved around to the other side of the counter and in front of the stove. Phillip twisted numerous knobs, and then Nicky heard several loud clicking noises before a flame shot up on one of the burners. Phillip moved a pot over the flame before lighting another one. Sitting on his bar stool, Nicky watched as Phillip removed the lid from another pot and stirred something down in it.

"Can I get you something to drink? Sorry, but I'm out of champagne at the moment."

"Ha, ha, you're funny. For the record, I didn't even like it." Making eye contact with the coach, the two held their stares before Phillip smiled and turned his back to Nicky, heading toward the refrigerator. Nicky felt as if butterflies were in his stomach, dancing and flying about. Smelling whatever was cooking, Nicky's appetite reappeared for the first time since the incident in the hotel room. "Do you have soda?"

"No soda, but I have lemonade, iced tea, and cranberry juice."

"I'll take iced tea." With Phillip's back to Nicky as he retrieved the iced tea, Nicky stole several more glances at Phillip's ass through his worn jeans. *He has a great ass*, Nicky thought as he remembered the feel of his thighs. He couldn't believe he was sitting in the coach's kitchen and there weren't a bunch of other swimmers or staff around.

It was just the two of them, and the coach was cooking him dinner. Nicky let his eyes wander up from the coach's ass to his back and on up to his hairline. He adored his jet-black hair. The wavy curls had a shine to them. When Phillip turned to the side, Nicky noticed that he was cleanly shaved. Nicky loved that sexy dark stubble that appeared on his face typically in the late afternoon.

Phillip slid a glass with iced tea across the raised part of the center island, where Nicky was sitting. "There's no sugar in it. Tell me if it's okay."

Nicky took a sip, "It's good. What is it?" Whatever it was, it didn't taste like any iced tea his mother had ever brewed.

"It's peach mango." Phillip moved back in front of the stove and stirred the contents in one of his simmering pots. He then shifted over to the side countertop and started chopping what looked to Nicky to be the start of a salad. This was the first time Nicky had seen a man in the kitchen move with such grace and aptitude, producing wonderful aromas. Nicky could count on one hand how many times he had seen his dad prepare a meal: twice, his mother had been sick and one weekend when she went to visit his grandparents. All three times, the meal was a wreck.

Phillip was sautéing mushrooms in butter, and in another pan, he was stirring something that Nicky couldn't make out. "What's in that pan?" he asked as he pointed to the pan.

"This, my specialty, a rosemary Cabernet reduction."

Nicky moaned with delight, wondering if he had ever had a reduction.

Phillip sipped on a glass of red wine as he moved about the kitchen. Nicky liked watching him, as he looked as if he was having fun bringing it all together. Nicky noticed there were a lot of pots and pans being used, as well as something cooking in the oven. It seemed like it was going to be a lot of food, but he was starving.

"What's your favorite thing to eat? If you had to eat one thing for the rest of your life, what would it be?" Phillip asked.

"Oh, gosh, I don't know. I think maybe pizza. Or spaghetti. What about you?"

"Mine would definitely be salad... I don't want to get fat."

Nicky chuckled, "Yeah, I can't see you fat. We could have salad one day and pizza the next. The best of both worlds." Nicky caught a gleam in Phillip's eye as he stared back at him.

"But no onions on the pizza," Phillip replied as he stepped over Emily, who was stretched out across the kitchen floor.

"Deal." Nicky felt that nervous pit again in his stomach as he watched the coach's six-foot frame move around him in the kitchen. Nicky wanted to kiss him, touch his face, and have those strong arms around him. The combination of excitement and trepidation took Nicky from being in the moment as his thoughts bounced from running out the front door to hot and heavy sex with his coach.

Other than Cowboy Mike, Nicky's sexual experience was next to nothing. He thought about that night in the motel. It was anything but good. Looking at Phillip, Nicky had no doubt that tonight would be better. Just the thought of making love to Phillip made his empty stomach flutter.

"—on your salad?" Phillip was staring at Nicky, holding a bottle of Italian dressing. "Hello, in there." Phillip waved the bottle in front of Nicky's face.

"Huh. What?" Nicky asked.

"Where did you go on me? I asked if Italian dressing was okay on your salad."

"Oh, yeah. My mom makes that."

Phillip smiled at Nicky. "Well, I'm sorry to say this is not homemade."

"That's fine." Nicky returned the grin that the coach was flashing at him.

"Look, I'm a good cook, but I'm not your momma, so don't expect any of this to taste like your momma's." Phillip laughed as he carried the dressing and the salad bowl to the dining room table and returned. "We're almost ready. Can you take these into the dining room?" Phillip handed Nicky a covered serving dish as well as the butter tray. When Nicky went to take them out of Phillip's hand, it was the closest they had been to each other all evening. Their faces less than a foot apart, Nicky wanted to kiss him, but came to his senses—he could never be as bold as he was the other night without being drunk again.

Nicky entered the dining room and saw that Phillip had lit several candles around the room. Smelling the scent of vanilla, Nicky looked around the room, taking note of another painting of several dogs at a table playing poker. He wondered if it, too, was one of Jerry Castro's. Phillip had the lights turned down over the table, with a long table runner down the middle. There were eight chairs around the massive table, but only the two end chairs had place settings in front of them. Nicky looked at the distance between the two settings, not liking that he would be so far from Phillip. Nicky grabbed the place setting and eating utensils from one end and moved them down to the opposite end, next to the other setting. Smiling to himself, he returned to the kitchen.

"I think I'm ready. Here, take this." Phillip gave Nicky another covered dish as he grabbed a glass casserole dish that he had removed from the oven a few minutes prior.

Nicky followed Phillip through the swinging door into the dining room. When Phillip saw that Nicky had moved his place setting, his right eyebrow arched as he flashed a huge smile. Seeing the coach's beautiful long eyelashes and cute dimples when he smiled, Nicky was overcome with the desire to move closer, to touch him. Nicky stepped into Phillip's personal space and went for it, kissing the coach on his lips. Although fast, Nicky savored what he thought was probably cherry-flavored lip balm. Although it was nothing more than a peck, Nicky felt his legs turn to jelly and his heart skip a beat.

"Well, that was unexpected, but nice," Phillip said as he stared into Nicky's light green eyes. With both their hands full, the moment was over.

Sitting down to eat, Phillip had prepared a homemade salad, braised lamb chops with the reduction sauce, mushroom risotto, broiled asparagus, seasoned lightly with olive oil, sea salt, and cracked pepper, and garlic bread.

Nicky was so hungry that he didn't realize that he was eating at lightning speed as he moved through the salad portion of the meal in half the time as Phillip. Sitting in the small, candle-lit dining room with a table spread with gourmet food, Nicky imagined that this was what it would feel like if they were in a restaurant.

The room was initially quiet as they ate. Occasionally, Nicky attempted to steal glances when Phillip wasn't looking. Each time, he was caught by Phillip, who sent him a smile that said, "Take as much time as you want; it's okay to look."

"You don't mind me looking at you?" Nicky asked timidly, but holding his stare.

"No. I like it." Phillip broke the stare first by looking at his plate and then back at Nicky. "I do wonder what you see, though. I'm not beautiful like you."

Nicky felt his heart skip. "You think I'm beautiful?" Nicky was confused; women are beautiful, and men are handsome. *So am I the girl?* Nicky thought to himself, unsure what to make of that, if that were indeed true. He did let Cowboy Mike fuck him, and he wanted the same from Phillip.

"What's wrong with being beautiful?" Phillip asked as he took a sip of his wine.

"I've never heard of a guy being called beautiful, that's all."

Phillip let out a tiny snort, then wiped his mouth with his hand. Smiling at his date, Phillip leaned back in his chair. "It's not about how you look. When I call you beautiful, I'm talking about you. Your heart, your soul, the being that makes you who you are. It's sweet and kind. It's what makes you beautiful. Of course, you're handsome too, but that's the outside of you. The beauty is deep, much deeper. I didn't mean to embarrass you." Phillip placed his hand over Nicky's.

Nicky looked at the hand that just covered his, the hand that just caused his entire body to quiver. He had never heard anyone talk like that, much less about him. He didn't know what to say. This whole evening, he had been outside his comfort zone, starting with the moment Phillip opened the front door and smiled at him. Outside of a silly crush on someone, he had never had such a strong attraction to anyone. He'd not even had a single date in high school, though he'd been okay with that because he had his swimming. Now, sitting in someone's candlelit dining room with unbelievable food seemed like someone else's life, nothing remotely like his own.

Phillip had completely thrown Nicky off his game over the course of the evening. Fearing that he would say the wrong thing or screw up, Nicky started overthinking everything. Watching to see how Phillip held his fork and drank from his glass and even how he chewed his food, it all seemed so grown up, sophisticated, suddenly.

"So do you like wine?" Nicky struggled for something to say, trying not to seem like some dumb kid from the Dakotas. *Of course, he likes wine, he's drinking it. Why did I say that?*

"I do. Sometimes, on a super-hot day a cold beer is nice, or if I'm on the water, whether it's skiing or fishing. But for the most part, I do like my wine."

Cowboy Mike flashed in Nicky's head, as he recalled how much he had drank that night in the motel room. From Cowboy Mike, his brain went to sex. Remembering the pain when Cowboy Mike first entered him, he wondered if Phillip would hurt, too. Then a bigger thought formed in his brain: What if Phillip would want him to be the top? He didn't know if he even knew what to do, if there was even something to know. The thought never occurred to him that he would have to do that. How would he even know if that would be something Phillip wanted? Should they talk about it? Surely not.

"Are you even listening to me?" Phillip asked in a joking tone.

To answer Phillip's question, no, he wasn't. He was panicking, completely in his head. "Oh, yeah. No, I mean. I'm sorry. I was thinking about something." Nicky's brain was firing rapid thoughts one right after the next. *Do I tell him what I was thinking? No, yes, no.* "I'm sorry," Nicky stuttered.

"It's okay. I wasn't saying anything important. How's your dinner?" Phillip again smiled, allowing Nicky to look into the most beautiful copper-brown eyes he had ever seen.

After a long dinner, Nicky was more than ready to leave the table. Although he had calmed down a touch, most of his thoughts were still sexual ones about the man sitting next to him. Several times over the course of the dinner, Nicky felt the swelling in his crotch. Experienced or not, the anxiety running through Nicky's body coupled with sexual tension had him ready to explode.

"Should we retreat to the living room?" Phillip asked. Leaving their plates on the table, the two walked into the living room on the other side of the dining room wall. Phillip waited for Nicky to take a seat on the couch and then took a seat next to him. The two fell back into the large grey pillows, both groaning as Nicky rubbed his belly in a circular motion with his hand.

"I ate too much," Nicky admitted as he stuck his belly out as far as it would go.

"Me too."

Turning to Phillip, Nicky asked, "Can I help you with the dishes?"

"Good lord, no. Those dishes are going to have to wait. I'm too full to even think about doing them." Nicky felt Phillip lock his eyes on him, and the two stared at one another for several seconds. "You know, I can't believe you're here," Phillip whispered.

"I know... Coach, not that it matters, but how old are you?" Nicky asked as he stared at the fine lines that ran across Phillip's forehead and at the corner of his eyes. Everything about him was sexy: the lines on his face, his thick brows that perfectly matched his hair, even his brown nose with the slight bump on it. Nicky also couldn't help but notice how white the coach's teeth were every time he smiled at him.

"Probably old enough to be your father." Phillip replied.

"No, really. I... I've been crushing on you since the first day I saw you. I bet you didn't know that, during practice, sometimes I lose count of my laps because I'm watching you on the deck." Nicky stared, waiting for a response to his bombshell revelation.

Phillip smiled, not knowing that his smile made Nicky's heart stammer. "Well, that explains the five or six extra laps you sometimes do. I thought you were just showing off." Phillip guffawed as he took another sip of wine. "I'm thirty-five, if you just have to know."

Silence filled the room. Nicky felt the desire to kiss him again and was wishing for the courage that he had in Fort Lauderdale. The two had been inching their way closer and closer to each other all night, and now their legs were touching as they were mere inches apart from the other. *Just do it,* Nicky told himself. But he couldn't.

"I want to kiss you," Phillip said softy, followed by a second of silence between them before Nicky felt Phillip's hand as it was laid gently on his cheek. Nicky stared into the center of Phillip's eyes, which were gazing softly back at him. He could smell the coach's breath, an indescribable sweet scent that lingered between them as their lips met. Nicky felt the coach's soft lips as he kissed him, lightly touching his chin and tilting his head to one side.

Nicky's lips parted as Phillip kissed him. He felt the coach's tongue for the first time as it lightly brushed against his own. His heart was racing, and he couldn't breathe as the coach continued to kiss him. *Breathe through your nose,* he told himself, *breathe through your nose.* Nicky felt the coach's hand as it ran up the back of his neck, softly brushing through his hair. Welcoming the coach's masculine hands and velvety lips, Nicky's body went limp, allowing the coach full access to his mouth. It was as if the coach was controlling Nicky's own lips as they moved in sync.

Nicky's nervous energy was released at once, surrendering to the sweetness of the moment as the intensity built between them. Nicky's hand skimmed across Phillip's crotch, and he felt the stiffness in Phillip's pants. Nicky too was hard, feeling his own cock compacted down in his underwear. The two positioned their bodies long ways on the couch, Phillip's body over Nicky's.

Lying on the couch, the two explored each other's mouths over the next hour, stopping sometimes to catch their breath. When they weren't kissing, they were touching each other's face as they stared in each other's eyes. These moments only lasted a short time before their tongues were together, madly kissing the other again.

Time completely lost, Nicky reached for Phillip's belt, attempting to undo his pants. He felt Phillip's hand cup his, stopping him.

Raising up, Phillip looked down at Nicky, his chest heaving from the heavy kissing. "We have to stop," Phillip murmured.

"Huh, why?" Nicky stared into Phillip's eyes, looking for a clue as to what just happened. He tasted Phillip as he licked his swollen lips. The body contact, Phillip lying on top of him, the friction: All were almost unbearable as Nicky pressed his hips up into Phillip's own body. He was ready to cum, on the edge of producing a big mess right in his own pants. He didn't want to stop. He wanted more of Phillip, to feel his naked body. Nicky wanted to be naked against it. He wanted all of it.

Phillip fought to catch his breath, "Because—"

"But I want you." Nicky cut him off.

"I want you too. Not just sexually. I want you."

"But—" Nicky started to say.

"Shhh... No," Phillip whispered as he reached down for a light kiss. Nicky took in Phillip's breath as he pulled him back down on top of him, the two madly kissing each other again.

"Get naked," Nicky mumbled as he exhaled a breath.

Phillip gently pulled away again. "Nicky, we have to stop." The ticking of the wall clock fell between them as Nicky lay there, attempting to catch his breath. "I need to know what you want. We need to talk about what it is that we're doing, what *we* want."

"I want you," Nicky whimpered as he tried to pull Phillip down again, begging to be kissed.

Phillip resisted the force. "I want you too, Nicolas. That's why you need to go. Before it's too late and we do something that we can't take back."

Nicky let out a faint giggle. "You mean like me climbing on top of you and jacking off?"

"Yeah, exactly." Phillip smiled as he sat up more, leaning back into his couch pillows. Nicky sat up as well. Phillip stared, gazing at him before taking his finger and lightly brushing the blond highlights out of Nicky's face. "God, I would love to make love to you tonight. But you're too important to me to not try to get this right. Do you get what I'm saying?"

He didn't like what he was hearing, but Nicky got it. They had to talk first. About what, he was unsure, but it sounded important.

"Go home. I'll call you in the morning, I promise." Phillip sat all the way up as he shot Nicky a pouty smile.

Nicky glanced at his watch; it was after eleven. Rubbing his face, Nicky contemplated the only option he was given.

12

As the sun crept into Phillip's bedroom, he felt a body pressed against his. He knew it was Emily, but his heart wished it was Nicky. Phillip had slept little the last couple of hours. Every waking thought was of last night. He was in euphoria as he thought about touching Nicky's soft, creamy white skin. He was finally able to look deep into Nicky's sweet green eyes without fear of his affection being revealed by a gaze held too long. Last night was everything he wanted. He had no idea how he was ever able to resist him. Denying it for so many months, he reflected back on the night in the hotel. Remembering the moment Nicky pulled his naked body onto his stomach, he had been awake long before Nicky climbed on him, immobilized and stunned at what was happening. He would never forget the feeling of Nicky's small buttocks in his hands that night. His ass was hairless and cool to the touch. Each cheek fit perfectly in Phillip's large hands as he took hold of them, keeping Nicky in place over him. Had Phillip moved his hands off of Nicky's ass, it would have been over—Phillip would have never been able to resist making love to him.

Phillip heard the sound of his phone buzzing, signaling that he had a text. Phillip stretched his arms as far as he could, just barely reaching the phone on his nightstand, where it always was. Seeing that he had a text from Nicky, Phillip smiled at the message: *Thinking of U.*

Phillip saw that Nicky had just sent it ten minutes ago. Phillip lay in bed, thinking about what he wanted to send back. First typing *Good morning,* Phillip erased it as he snickered at the thought of Nicky lying in bed, just waking up as well.

Thinking of U 2. Phillip hit "send."

Almost immediately, a reply appeared on Phillip's phone: *I'm thinking of you more.*

How do you know?

Because I am touching myself as we speak, and yes I am thinking about U.

Phillip felt a surge under the sheets as his cock liked what he had just read. Phone sex had never been his thing, and sexting was definitely not something he had even ever thought about doing.

U R a naughty boy. Why arent u in the pool? Phillip really did hate texting.

Meeting Tyler and JB later.

Phillip had his phone in his hand, thinking of something silly to text back to Nicky, when his phoned buzzed.

Can I come over after???

Phillip's heart instantly accelerated, and his chest tightened as he re-read the text. Every bit of him wanted to see Nicky, but he hadn't formulated a plan on how all of this was going to work. He shifted around, trying to get up; his back was killing him, having been on the couch for hours last night. Phillip headed to the bathroom to pee and take his morning dose of pain meds. After peeing, he snapped open the mirror on the wall, revealing the small medicine cabinet behind it. There were several orange pill bottles, but Phillip reached instead to a box labeled Fentanyl 50 mcg.

Phillip knew he had to answer Nicky's text, and he already knew that he was going to say, *Yes, yes, yes come over.*

Applying the Fentanyl pain patch to his shoulder, Phillip knew that by saying yes, there was no turning back. He was committing to exploring a relationship with one of his swimmers, an act that could get him fired. He couldn't wait to see Nicky again, but he couldn't let things go as far as last night without first having a discussion with him about what he wanted. If Nicky was just looking to hook up, or as they called it now, friends with benefits, he was not interested.

Yes. What time? Phillip replied to Nicky's text.

Finally. I was starting to get nervous. Around 3?

Don't be worried. I have a conference call at 3.

K 4?

Phillip didn't mean to tell Nicky not to come; he only meant that he would be on the conference call with his two assistant coaches. He hated texting, knowing that this whole conversation would have taken two minutes or less over the phone.

No, three is ok just let yourself in and be quiet.

U take 2 long 2 text back lol. This time, Nicky also added a smiley face with sunglasses at the end of the text.

Three o'clock, Phillip thought as he looked at his watch. This didn't leave much time for the things he had planned on getting done today. Originally, the plan was to go to the office and study a couple of hours of video that had been sent to him. But he'd downloaded the videos to a zip drive for Dean, which was still in his bag, so he could watch them here at the house. Then he remembered Emily had a vet appointment this morning as well.

R U even still there? Hello? Phillip read.

Realizing he was supposed to have responded, he re-read the last message he sent to Nicky before replying: *I cant wait to see you. I suppose you want pizza?* Phillip typed as fast as he could.

Yup u know me already.

Phillip took his shower while his coffee was still brewing. With a full cup of coffee in hand, he and Emily set out on their morning walk around the same two blocks they walked every morning. Once back at the house, he took a seat on one of the bar stools in the kitchen for his second cup of coffee, a yogurt, and his PowerBar while Emily munched down her bowl of dry Science Diet.

When Phillip was done with breakfast, he started in on the dishes from last night as he played it over in his head. Although pleased with his dinner, it was not his focus as he moistened his lips just thinking of kissing Nicky. The thought of last night made Phillip breathless as he remembered the feel of Nicky in his arms.

With fleeting thoughts bouncing everywhere, Phillip's brain stopped on all the what-ifs. Thinking about his own body, the scarring from the accident, and the extra weight, compared to Nicky's slim, tight body, he was embarrassed at the thought of Nicky seeing it. Playing the night of the fourth over in his head, when they were sitting in Jerry's library talking, he got no vibes from the swimmer at all. But then, waking up with him rubbing and gliding his hands up and down his thighs—to this day, that was a wonder of disbelief.

Phillip wanted a relationship; it was what he always wanted, someone to share his life with. Besides Steven, Marcus was probably the closest friend Phillip had, and they hadn't talked in three years. Yeah, Steven was his good friend, but he had Martin. Most of his acquaintances were all married or in committed relationships.

What Phillip wanted was way beyond sex. If sex was what he wanted, he knew how to get that; he had years of practice obtaining that. The moment Phillip saw Nicky, he convinced himself that he had to have him in his lineup because of what he brought to the team. No doubt about it, Nicky was one hell of a swimmer, but he was also a thief—he stole his heart without him even knowing it. But what did Nicky want?

Should he even expect that, at nineteen, Nicky would know what he wanted? *Damn nineteen,* Phillip said to himself. How could this work? Phillip's stomach churned.

After finishing the dishes, he and Emily were back out the door, heading to the vet, farmers' market, car wash, and the cleaners to pick up this week's laundry. While waiting for his car at the car wash, Phillip took this time to call Steven to fill him in on the details of last night. He had been putting off calling him all morning for fear of all the questions Steven was going to fire at him. Phillip had no answers, and that was what really scared him.

"So, do tell. It's almost noon. Please tell me he didn't just leave?" Steven joked.

"No, he didn't just leave. In fact, I kicked him out last night," Phillip answered.

"Dear God, that bad already?"

"On the contrary. That good." Phillip smiled at the thought of Nicky under him as the two lay on the couch exploring one another. If he closed his eyes, he could smell Nicky. A soapy, clean scent filtered through his nose as he thought about it. "We had a great dinner and conversation, and then afterwards we went into the living room. He's sweet."

Phillip tugged on Emily's leash to get her attention and to get her to stop pulling in an effort to go play with the kids just out of her reach. Having a Great Dane was a conversation starter, but with him on the phone, she was left to find her own entertainment. Lowering his tone, Phillip stood up to move down to the corner of the building.

"One thing led to another, and we started making out. Damn, he's a good kisser." Steven's breathing intensified. "This went on for a couple of hours. My God, it was like we were in heat. My back is paying the price for it now, though."

"Paying the price for what? What happened?" Steven howled.

Phillip laughed into the phone. "Nothing. Nothing happened. There we were, getting all hot and heavy, and I had to stop it before it happened."

"Before what happened?" Steven's voice was escalating to a shriek.

Phillip knowingly toyed with his friend. "You know…it."

"What the fuck is *it*?" Steven demanded.

"Seriously. There we were making out and ready to take it to the next level. And that wasn't what I wanted. I mean, I did—I mean I do, but not yet. I want to take things slow. I want to make sure this is something we both want."

"Jesus Christ, Phillip, he's nineteen, and you sent him home with blue balls. Oh, you're cruel."

"What about me? I was just as worked up." Phillip looked around to see if anyone was within earshot of him. "I want to make sure this is the right thing."

"He's nineteen! He needs to get off!" Steven cried.

"You don't know Nicky. I'm sure he isn't just looking for sex. You know, like we were at nineteen. He's quiet, shy, and a little backwards. An only child. He's from South Dakota."

"You mean like, 'Yes, ma'am, yes, sir, pecan pie country?'"

"No, like he is sweet and not mean and bitchy," Phillip jokingly fired back. "Look, my car's ready, and I've got a shitload of things to do today before he comes over." Phillip waited for a response to that last part.

"He's coming over again? What happened to taking it slow?"

"Goodbye, Steven," Phillip said as he hung up the phone.

Phillip had been on his conference call with his two assistant coaches for about ten minutes when he heard Nicky's motorcycle pull up. Within a couple of minutes, he heard the front door open and shut, and moments later, Nicky appeared at the doorway of Phillip's home office. Nicky mouthed as he demonstrated that he had to go pee. Phillip smiled as he resumed listening to Coach Dean discuss times and schedules for the upcoming season. Coach Paul wanted to get the swimmers practicing earlier this year, which meant working with Coach Dean on scheduling around the water polo players' time in the pool.

When Nicky returned, he had a glass of water in hand and moved about the small office, looking at all of Phillip's trophies and medals on display around the room. On the wall were pictures of Phillip all over the world: the US Invitational, the Tokyo Games, the World Cup, and at least a dozen from various NCAA championships. Phillip heard Nicky chuckle and looked over to see him staring at an old photo of him. The photo was taken at least ten years ago, judging by how skinny the coach was back then. Looking at another photo on the wall, Nicky stopped again. Phillip saw that he was staring at an old picture of him standing on the podium, smiling from ear to ear. Nicky turned around, catching Phillip staring at him. While pointing at the photo, Nicky mouthed, "You?" and then started laughing.

Phillip rolled his eyes, being overdramatic as he flipped Nicky off before refocusing on his call. Occasionally glancing up at Nicky, Phillip looked at his adorable tiny ass in his jeans that barely hung off his thirty-inch waist. In his faded jeans and black V-neck t-shirt, Nicky made laid-back look very sexy.

Nicky made his way around the room until he was behind Phillip. Looking over Phillip's shoulders, Nicky took a minute to watch the video that was playing on Phillip's computer. Trying to get it all done, Phillip was watching videos of several high school juniors during his conference call.

Nicky soon settled into an empty chair on the other side of the coach's desk. As soon as Phillip was able to make eye contact, he motioned to Nicky as if he was eating something with a utensil and then chewing. Nicky smiled, nodding, so Phillip held up five fingers.

Phillip held the receiver between his ear and shoulder as he stopped the video and ran a search of pizza parlors in the neighborhood. Locating Pizza My Heart, Phillip signaled for Nicky to come around and look at the monitor. Nicky took a seat on the edge of Phillip's chair and scrolled through the menu.

Once Phillip got a nod of approval from Nicky, he placed an online order for a large pizza, half combination, and half ham and pineapple. Nicky slid back into Phillip's lap, and Phillip, liking how well he fit there, gently kissed him on the forehead as he switched the receiver to the other ear. Nicky leaned back and snuggled into Phillip's shoulder, nestling his head into Phillip's chest.

When Phillip ended the call with his two assistants, Nicky had dozed off in his lap. Phillip stroked Nicky's silky hair back as he lightly rocked his small frame until he woke up. Startled, Nicky raised his head, looking around the room before realizing that he was in Phillip's lap.

"Did you go to sleep on me?" Phillip asked as he nudged Nicky to stand up.

"I did. I can't believe it. I like sleeping on you, I guess."

Phillip laughed, thinking that was the second time Nicky had fallen asleep on him. "I like you sleeping on me as well."

Stretching on his tippy toes and his arms reaching for the ceiling, Nicky let out a booming yawn.

"Really?" Phillip asked as he stared at Nicky, who was now rubbing his face, still trying to wake up.

"Wow, I really fell asleep, didn't I?" Nicky moved sluggishly over to the wall of medals opposite them. "It's a trip, just how good you were. I can't believe you almost swam at the Olympics." Nicky bent over to examine some of the medals in a lower cabinet. "I see you keep these under lock and key," Nicky said, pointing to several gold medals.

"So you don't think that picture looks like me?" Phillip pointed to the old picture that Nicky was laughing at earlier.

"Well, yeah, it kind of does. How old were you?"

"I think around twenty-two, twenty-three. That was the games in Sydney." Phillip saw that Nicky wanted to ask or say something. "What? Just ask," Phillip said, causing Nicky to look at him.

"So what happened? I mean, the accident?" Nicky sat back down in the empty chair across from Phillip.

"I haven't told this story in a while." Phillip cleared his throat as he positioned his body to get comfortable. "Well…the morning of the accident, a bunch of us athletes were all waiting to load into the buses at the Olympic Village. They had several shuttles running back and forth all day, taking athletes to the various event centers. The bus I was waiting on was going to the aquatic center and a couple of other places. The bus was full before I could even board." Phillip paused as he envisioned that morning. It was one of the last few memories he had of the day.

"Me, six divers from the Venezuela team, and a French diver took an overflow van that was going to follow the bus. The trip to the aquatic center was supposed to take us about an hour. I remember the van was hot, with little air circulation. The last thing I remember was sitting in my seat, listening to music on my headphones."

Phillip continued, "To this day, I don't remember anything about the accident. I remember waking up in the hospital with my parents beside my bed and my mom crying. The accident scene was broadcast non-stop, and we watched the horrific thing over and over while in the hospital. The reports said that the van was hit by a semi-truck and plunged two hundred feet over a cliff. Everyone else in the van was killed, burned beyond recognition. I was ejected before the fire, and they found me halfway down the mountain. My back was broken in two places, as was my right leg, and that, my friend, was the end of my swimming career and my Olympics."

Nicky stood up and walked over to Phillip's chair. Before Phillip knew what was happening, Nicky plopped back down in Phillip's lap and was about to kiss him when Phillip felt a sharp pain bolt through his back. It took everything Phillip had not to make a sound as he nudged Nicky to get up.

"Oh, my God, I knew you were in that accident! You were in *Sports Illustrated*. I mean, the accident was. When you were coming to visit my parents on that scout trip, I Googled you and read the article." Nicky stared at Phillip's bare right leg. "So is that where you got that big scar on your leg?"

"Yeah," Phillip said as he took Nicky by his hips and moved him off of his lap, wincing in pain and regretting that he was wearing shorts. Now on his feet, Phillip excused himself and retreated into his bathroom for pain meds.

As Phillip exited the bathroom, he heard the doorbell ring, followed by Emily's roar of a bark and nails scratching across the tile floor as she charged the front door. Phillip picked up the pace down the hall back toward the front door as he yelled at Emily to shush.

Once dinner was handed over by the delivery driver, Phillip carried the pizza into the living room, where Nicky was standing. "Are you hungry?" Phillip asked, sitting the box on the coffee table.

"Oh, yeah. I haven't eaten all day."

"What do you want to drink?" Phillip asked as he moved toward the kitchen. "Go ahead and start. I'll get it."

"Can I have some cranberry juice?" Nicky asked.

"Sure, one cranberry coming up." Phillip was in and out of the kitchen within minutes, returning with napkins, a couple of plates, one glass of cranberry juice on the rocks, and a glass of wine for himself.

Sitting side by side, the two ate as they talked about the high school swimmer Nicky had viewed on the coach's computer. Phillip took note that Nicky was clearly in a more playful mood and appeared relaxed. Nicky ate two slices of pizza to every one Phillip ate.

Licking the grease from his fingers, Nicky smiled at Phillip. "Thank you for inviting me back over."

"I think you invited yourself, if I recall." Phillip took a sip of his wine and then placed it back on the coffee table.

Nicky again smiled as he grabbed Phillip's glass of wine and took a sip.

"You're a brave little shit." Phillip chuckled, causing Nicky to giggle as he reached for his sixth slice of pie.

"For the record, I don't like it." Nicky stated as he made a sour face.

"The wine? Good," Phillip told him in a not-so-joking manner. Phillip wanted to talk; he wanted so much to know where this was going, if anywhere. He couldn't hold back any longer. "I had a good time last night."

"So did I...until you told me to leave." Nicky flashed Phillip a cute grin as he stuffed the last of the piece of pizza he was working on into his mouth.

"Yeah, well, about that. Be honest. What exactly are you looking for? I mean, are you just looking to get laid?" *I wonder if that was too blunt,* he thought. "Last night, you were ready to go for it. Are you usually that aggressive? Not that aggressive is a bad thing. The night at the hotel, then last night, you were pretty forward."

Nicky's facial expression turned to a look of embarrassment as his eyes cast down to the floor between them. He sat in silence for several seconds before looking up. "Truthfully...I'm not aggressive. Not at all. At least, I don't think so."

Phillip lost eye contact with Nicky again. Clearly, Nicky didn't want to look at him. Phillip thought for a minute, realizing this conversation was not going be so straightforward. "Tell me about your other boyfriends, people you usually date," Phillip asked, then sensing something was wrong. "Are you all right?"

Nicky looked up at Phillip. "This is embarrassing."

"What? That I called you aggressive?"

"No. That I've never had a boyfriend. I've never even dated."

Phillip gasped as he swallowed hard. *Are you fucking kidding me? You're a virgin?* "You've never dated anyone?"

"Nope." Nicky grabbed Phillip's wine glass from the table and swallowed the remaining wine in it.

"Whoa, slow down, Betty!" he said, seizing the empty glass from Nicky. He never saw this one coming.

"Who's Betty?" Nicky wiped his mouth with the back of his hand as he stared at Phillip.

"No one...it's not important." Phillip paused as he thought for a minute. He never thought the conversation would go like this. Now he understood that, because of Nicky's lack of experience, he probably had no idea what he wanted. Without thinking, Phillip went into coach mode. "Let me tell you what I want... Not just sexually, but I want to be with you. I've never had a real boyfriend either, although I'm nowhere close to being a virgin."

Phillip paused for a minute to gauge how much Nicky was comprehending and if he had to slow down. Seeing that Nicky was clearly listening and holding eye contact, Philip continued, "I'm looking for something more. Someone to spend my life with. I have to be honest with you. I've liked you for a long time. It started sometime last year. You were in the office with me and Dean and Paul. There was something that happened that day. Like a switch was turned on. I know it'll sound like I'm crazy. I think," Phillip laid his ring finger on Nicky's lower lip and lightly traced it with his finger, "I think I fell in love with you that day."

Phillip's heart was pounding in his chest. He couldn't believe he just told Nicky O'Hare that he loved him. There was no way a nineteen-year-old could be ready for all of this. Phillip was ready to backtrack, to give Nicky an out, when Nicky's smile grew across his face.

"That day I was in your office—I know what day you're talking about. It was the day I was late for practice. I thought you caught me staring at you, but it was me who caught you staring at me. That whole moment was weird, and I didn't know what to make of it."

"I don't remember what happened, but since you left that day, I haven't been able to stop thinking about you." Phillip moved a little closer into Nicky's space.

Nicky smiled as he stared into Phillip's eyes. Phillip leaned in and gently kissed Nicky's lower lip once, and then again, the second time pulling back as he looked into Nicky's eyes.

"Do we have to figure it all out today?" Nicky murmured.

"No. We don't. But I do need to know that you want more than just sex," Phillip said.

"I want you. Whatever that is, I'm in."

Phillip leaned in again and kissed Nicky. He then stood up and extended his hand to Nicky. Nicky took his hand, and Phillip led him down the hall to the master bedroom.

Setting Nicky gently down at the edge of the bed, Phillip began to undress himself as he stood over Nicky. Undoing his shirt, he allowed it to drop to the floor. Without taking his eyes off Nicky, Phillip unsnapped his belt and undid his pants, grinning slightly as the button popped. Stepping out of his pants, he was left in his boxers.

Phillip walked over to the bathroom and switched the light off, and the room went dark. With just a light shining from down the hall, Phillip returned to the bed and saw Nicky's eyes as they moved up and down his body. Phillip feared what Nicky was thinking about his body, yet the wanting glimmer in Nicky's eyes told him his reservations were in vain. Standing Nicky up, Phillip undid his jeans first and had Nicky step out of them.

Pleased to see that Nicky had gone commando, Phillip lifted Nicky's t-shirt over his head and tossed it by the clothes already on the floor. Nicky stood naked, waiting for Phillip, staring, waiting for his lover to show him the way.

Phillip pulled back the sheets, and without a word, Nicky's small frame slipped into the bed. Removing his boxers, now both naked, Phillip followed, pulling the covers up over their bodies as he gently rolled on top of Nicky.

He gently kissed Nicky up his neck, nibbling at his skin as he made his way up to his mouth. Nicky let out a light moan, and he surrendered his entire neck, tilting it to one side. Phillip ran his hands up against Nicky's shoulders—his skin was soft and delicate as only young skin can be. He felt Nicky's cock stiffen between them as their bodies rubbed against each other.

Phillip's mind was racing, not believing this was happening. This was so different than the night in the hotel room. This time, he was an active participant, making love to the man he had for so long dreamed about.

Nicky's lips were like kissing satin, Phillip thought as he gently tugged and bit his lover's lower lip. Willfully, Phillip drank in the warmth of Nicky's breath each time he exhaled, as if taking in a part of Nicky's being. Feeling Nicky's heart beat as it pounded against his own chest, their two hearts thumped in sync. Moving his hand up the inside of Nicky's thigh, he felt that swimmer's thigh, muscular, strong, and solid. *This is really happening*, he thought as he caught a whisper of his name being uttered by Nicky.

The scent of Nicky's skin was intoxicating, driving Phillip's heart rate up exponentially as their bodies rubbed together. Phillip knew that he wasn't going to last long. Skin on skin, their bodies moved against one another, causing a gratifying friction for the both of them. As their thrust intensified, almost violent, Nicky wrapped his arms around Phillip's head, trying to hold on.

"Mmm," Nicky purred, followed by another moan, and Phillip sensed Nicky was getting close. Nicky stretched his arms to the far corners of the bed, grabbing as much sheet as he could as he let out a cry, his back arching up off the bed. "Oh God, I'm gonna—!" he cried as his body thrashed about, the back of his head repeatedly slamming back and forth against the pillow.

The sound of Nicky's cries brought Phillip to climax as well, his own body tightening, sending volleys of white lights behind his eyelids.

Laying on top of Nicky, Phillip was unsure whose heart he was feeling that was pounding so fiercely. *It's going to explode,* he thought as it vibrated through his whole body. Lifting up slightly, Phillip stared at his young lover and saw his eyes closed, fluttering beneath his eyelids, lost in the moment.

They lay not speaking for several minutes until Nicky cleared his throat. Gently sliding out from under Phillip, Nicky murmured, "That was amazing." He repositioned his body, bringing one leg over Phillip's lower body, snuggling the rest of his body as close as he could to Phillip.

Well, so much for taking it slow. Phillip chuckled to himself as he wrapped his arms around Nicky's shoulders and held him until they both fell asleep.

13

At 5:38 am, two nude bodies stirred about in the bed.

"Good morning," Nicky said as he awoke to Phillip stroking his hair lightly. Rubbing his eyes, he took in the unfamiliar bedroom, seeing it in a new light. Not believing he was in bed with his coach, Nicky peeked under the sheets, seeing their naked bodies inches apart from one another.

"What are you looking at?" Phillip asked.

"I can't believe I'm here. Here with you." Nicky's dick stiffened again as his naked body brushed against Phillip's warm one. Thinking about last night, Nicky threw the covers back, exposing a full woody throbbing against his flat abs.

"Oh, good lord. I forgot how it is to be nineteen." Phillip smiled as he lifted Nicky's cock up and then let it spring back against his stomach.

"Ouch. You fucker!" Nicky cried as he curled his body into a ball and laughed.

Phillip rolled over onto his side of the bed. "I need to go pee, and you need to brush your teeth first." Phillip eased up out of the bed. Walking into the bathroom, he shut the door behind him.

Nicky watched as Phillip's naked body moved across the room, disappearing behind the closed door. The coach's body was thick and muscular, his bubble butt white and furry compared to the rest of his olive complexion. Nicky was surprised to see the contrast, thinking his russet color was his natural skin tone. It never dawned on him it was a tan from being out in the sun all day.

Nicky especially liked the coach's furry behind. It was the complete opposite of his small, smooth ass, which probably didn't have a single strand of hair on it. Phillip's was round and high, which reminded him of J. B.'s ass, but furrier. He rubbed his hands across the beautiful bedding all around him as he listened to the sounds coming from the bathroom. Smelling the sheets and then Phillip's pillow, he thought that he had never laid on anything as soft and luxurious as this bedding.

Running his hand lightly up and down the sheets, Nicky wondered what the fabric was; he didn't know the difference, but he thought it was either satin or silk. Nicky again held up the comforter to his nose to smell it once more as he sat up and leaned against the headboard. His eyes danced around the room, taking in the large space. The massive eight-drawer dresser adjacent to the bed had a jewelry box, a couple of books, and a single picture frame sitting atop it. Stretching over to get a closer look at the picture, he figured that the man and woman in the picture were most likely Phillip's parents. He wasn't sure who the other elderly woman was standing next to them, but she looked a lot like the other woman. Could they be twins?

Hearing the bathroom door unlock, Nicky leaned back as he watched the door. Phillip reemerged, now wearing a robe.

"Do you want a cup of coffee?" Phillip asked, walking toward the hall. "I need coffee."

"Yes, please." Nicky was a little disappointed that the coach wasn't returning to bed. "Hey, can I use your toothbrush since I *have* to brush my teeth?"

"Yeah. It's in there on the counter." Phillip smiled as he left the bedroom.

Nicky jumped out of the bed and took his turn in the bathroom, first peeing and then brushing his teeth with the wet toothbrush Phillip must have just used. Nicky was about to head down the hall toward the kitchen when Phillip returned into the room with two cups of coffee.

"You drink your coffee black, right?" Phillip asked as he handed Nicky a cup.

When Nicky went to reach for it, Phillip raised it up. "Not so fast. A kiss first."

Smiling, Nicky swung his naked body into Phillip's robe as he went in for his kiss, nearly spilling both cups of coffee.

"Easy now. Do you do anything slowly?" Phillip laughed. "Crawl back up onto that bed."

Nicky took his cup of coffee and returned to the bed as ordered. He watched as Phillip disrobed and joined him. Wrapped in Phillip arms, they sat in the bed, drinking their coffee as they finished waking up. Catching Phillip looking at him made Nicky feel desired. There was a sweetness in the way Phillip looked at him that made him feel wanted but also protected.

"So, how was last night for you?" Phillip asked as he shifted his shoulder to better accommodate Nicky under his arm.

"It was amazing. I felt like I was going to explode." Nicky closed his eyes and let out a sigh, revisiting last night in his head.

"You did explode. All over the place." Phillip ran his free hand across the sheets and then his chest. "Look at me. And we're going to have to wash these sheets today."

Nicky stroked Phillip's chest. His chest was nice, lightly covered with black hair with a tiny bit of grey woven throughout. Nicky saw his cum—or was it both of their cum?—crusted in the hairs. "That's gross. How come you didn't wash it?"

"I just saw it." Phillip laughed. "Do you want me to wash it off?" Phillip smiled at Nicky as he put his coffee on the nightstand.

"No, I want to add to it," Nicky smiled and turned to kiss Phillip. Putting his cup on the nightstand as well, Nicky rolled over and back into Phillip's arms. The two sunk down into the bed, kissing one another frantically as Phillip's arms wrapped around Nicky's body, holding him tightly. The two explored one other with their eyes, hands, and lips, kissing and caressing each other all over their bodies. Within a few breaths from each other, they both cried out, achieving orgasms simultaneously, mixing the results of their desire together once again.

Once they caught their breaths, Nicky dozed off, but barely, still able to sense Phillip moving about. "Don't fall asleep; we need to shower, baby." Phillip was gently nudging him. Nicky groaned, resisting; he didn't want to get up.

"What's on your agenda for today?" Phillip asked as he took Nicky's hand and led the way into the bathroom. First grabbing each of them a towel, he turned the shower on to let it warm up.

"Nothing, really. I'm meeting Tyler and J. B. at the pool in a little while. Afterwards, Tyler and I were going to go over to the Cultural Center Complex. The Latin American club is having a free event." Nicky gently touched Phillip's side, running his fingers lightly down his ribcage as he admired his lover's body.

"Let me guess: You two are going for the free tacos?" Phillip asked as he stepped into the shower.

"What about you?" Nicky asked, following Phillip into the warm water. He didn't want to leave. He was ready to blow off practice—Phillip just had to ask.

"I'm heading to the office. I have videos to screen and then a meeting at four with the aquatics director."

"What's the meeting about?" Nicky asked, watching Phillip squeeze a fair amount of soap onto a blue loofah and then offer it to him.

"Just going over this upcoming season, budget stuff, and some traveling I have on the calendar."

Nicky's eyes were closed, trying to avoid soap going into his eyes as he scrubbed his face with the sudsy loofah, "So that's your boss?"

"Yes. He's like the big boss over swimming, water polo, and diving."

Nicky was quiet for a minute as he rinsed the soap from his hair, face, and ears. Being able to open his eyes again, he focused them back on Phillip. Nicky observed that Phillip was now lathered entirely with soap. Nicky's stared at Phillip's body—oh, how much he loved that big, hairy chest and those large, brown nipples. To Nicky, everything about Phillip was sexy, and he was taking a shower with the sexiest man alive. Nicky continued looking at Phillip's naked body, studying it as if he would never see it again.

Phillip had turned his back away from Nicky and was under the showerhead as he rinsed the shampoo out of his hair. With Phillip's back to him, Nicky's dick swelled as his eyes dropped down to Phillip's furry butt. Watching the warm droplets of water run down Phillip's back, disappearing into the crack of his ass, Nicky couldn't resist lightly touching it.

Phillip responded to the touch, turning around and seeing Nicky's newly formed woody. "No. Not again. I need a minute." Phillip gently tugged on Nicky's wet slippery dick while telling him no, which was a mistake.

"Please. I've never done it in the shower," Nicky begged.

"No!" Phillip asserted firmly. "If you want it, then you have to come back tonight. How about dinner again?" Phillip flashed Nicky a naughty smirk as he bounced his eyebrows up several times.

"How 'bout I stay the weekend?" Nicky's grin was even bigger and naughtier.

That evening, as the two sat in Phillip's back patio having dinner, it was a perfect sixty-eight degrees. A slight breeze carried the fragrance of Phillip's rosebushes across the yard. Unknowingly, it was a scent that provoked in Nicky memories of him as a child, playing in his grandmother's yard. Now he felt grown up, sitting in the backyard, having dinner with his boyfriend. *Boyfriend? Is Phillip my boyfriend?* He would like to think so, although it had been only a couple of days, not even a week since the earth-shattering Fourth of July party that started all of this.

Nicky's entire body felt as it had been charged and weighted with energy, making him unable to focus on anything outside of wanting to be with Phillip. Since they hadn't gone on an official date, they weren't dating, or were they? All he knew was that he raced through his day and enjoyed none of it as he counted the hours until he could return to Phillip's home. This afternoon while he was away, sometime after his workout, he found himself thinking of actually being fucked by Phillip. Although the sex they were having was more than anything he could have ever imagined, he found himself thinking about going all the way with Phillip and what it would feel like with Phillip inside of him. Nicky really wanted to belong to Phillip fully and completely in this intimate way.

There was no doubt in Nicky's mind that it was not going to be the same as with Cowboy Mike. Since he and Phillip hadn't actually gone all the way, he wondered if it was his responsibility to somehow communicate that he wanted Phillip in this way. He played the night with Cowboy Mike in his head, looking for something that he could identify as a signal that he must have given Cowboy Mike.

Nicky's nervous energy was taking him on an emotional roller coaster in his own head, one minute just wanting to be next to the coach, laughing and teasing each other, to this weird silence between them as if they had nothing to say to each other.

"I…I love your yard." Nicky said in an attempt to make small talk. Looking around the greenery that encompassed the entire yard, he really did like it. Nicky shifted his attention between Phillip and the yard as he admired the tranquil space that had been created.

Just beyond the brick patio, there were pathways bordered with well-groomed boxwoods. On the other side of the boxwoods, Phillip had designed miniature gardens filled with beautifully colored roses. The back fence was lined with red camellias and lush green ferns.

"Thanks. I don't get out here nearly as much as I want to, though." Phillip cut a piece of his steak and popped it in his mouth. While chewing his steak, he cut into his baked potato, moving a small piece to the side. "I'm happy that anything grows back here."

Nicky, unable to contain his energy, felt as if he was failing miserably in conversation each time silence fell between them. Tonight was a lot more difficult than the previous two nights, and perhaps the coach had changed his mind about him.

"So...did you know I was gay when you recruited me? When did you know?" Nicky stammered, looking for something to say, yet feeling more nervous with every minute that passed.

"I don't know. I probably suspected it when I first met you." Phillip chuckled as he smiled at Nicky. "You were a cute kid back then. A little puny, but cute."

"Puny!" Nicky shrieked. "Why do you say that?"

Phillip continued to laugh at Nicky as he took his hand. "No, I'm just kidding. But seriously, when you showed up last year for your freshman year, I was surprised at the muscle mass you had put on since I had last seen you."

"Yeah, me and my best friend from back at home started going to this new gym in town. Before that, I had never trained with weights." Taking note of the compliment, Nicky couldn't help but wonder if saying he had a best friend sounded stupid.

"Weight training can be tricky for swimmers; you need that strength from lean muscle mass, but not the weight itself." Phillip glanced over at the edge of the table where Emily had just appeared.

Nicky watched as Phillip graciously fed her a piece of his steak. Unwilling to share, Emily promptly took it away from the patio to eat in peace. "I don't think I knew for a fact that you were gay until... let's see? I think we were at our first meet together. That was Georgia Tech. I overheard Tyler talking about something, and I remember saying to myself, 'They're both gay'. I think I even wondered if you guys were messing around with each other."

"Were you jealous?" Nicky smirked.

"Oh no. Not at all. It was more of a matter of the two of you becoming unfocused. Between being away at school for the first time, training at a college level, and Tyler being, well, you know, a bit on the wild side. It was a concern." Phillip wiped his mouth with his napkin. "How about me?"

"When you called me," Nicky answered.

Phillip raised his brows as he cocked his head to one side. "Called you when?"

"The other day. After we got back from Fort Lauderdale. I thought you were calling me to kick me off the team. You know, for jumping your bones and all."

Phillip let out a faint sound that sounded like it could have been a laugh.

"Then, when you didn't chew me out and you called the next day to invite me over for dinner, then I kind of knew." Nicky had cut up his steak at the beginning of the meal and was now eating the small pieces he had piled to one side.

"I still can't believe you've never dated or had a boyfriend. That's bizarre to me," Phillip stated.

"Why?" Nicky said, genuinely not understanding where Phillip was coming from. For Nicky, it wasn't until he arrived at TBU and met Tyler that he spent any time around someone who talked about being sexually active. Between his college swimmates and Tyler, Nicky heard more sex talk and thought about sex more than he ever had prior to TBU.

Feeling like he should bring up his experience with Cowboy Mike, Nicky thought of how to do it, of what he should say. Nicky's cheeks turned a light rose due to the lie he was digging for himself. He knew he should have said something the other night when Phillip first called him a virgin. Again, he weaved out of the present moment as he thought about how much it hurt when Cowboy Mike entered him and then how much he liked it once the initial pain was gone.

When the two finally made it into the bedroom, Nicky felt like he had been waiting to have sex all night, hoping that tonight would be the night they went all the way. He told himself that once he had Phillip completely, Cowboy Mike wouldn't matter, that he would go away forever and the truth would be what Phillip believed. But an hour later, as the two naked bodies lay side by side, breathless and covered in sweat, Nicky stared up at the ceiling fan, wondering if he was doing something wrong. For the first time since they got together, Nicky went to sleep less than satisfied with just an orgasm.

On Saturday morning when the two awoke, Nicky was tightly secured under Phillip's strong arms. Phillip's body was warm, with a scent of musk. Their naked bodies nestled under the heavy comforter, Phillip lightly stroked Nicky's hair. "What do you have to do today?"

Nicky shifted under Phillip's arms, lifting his face slightly up. "Nothin'." That was a lie; he was supposed to meet Tyler at the pool in forty minutes. He wasn't accustomed to blowing off his morning training, though he never had a reason to until now.

"Do you want to hang out here, maybe watch a movie? I don't think I have anything for breakfast, but I can run to the store while you take a shower." Phillip placed gentle kisses on the top of Nicky's head as he continued to stroke his hair.

"Do you have Netflix?" Nicky didn't want to remove himself from the arms of utopia, not for one second, but he also couldn't carry a conversation in that position. Rolling over onto his back, Nicky felt the mattress dip as Phillip switched his weight, moving to lay on his side facing him.

"What's Netflix? Is it like HBO or Showtime?"

"Kind of. It's—" Nicky was quieted by Phillip's lips as they gently touched his, followed by a longer kiss.

When Nicky was able to speak again, it took him a second to regain his train of thought. "Never mind, if you don't know what it is, then you don't have it. Do you at least have cable?"

"No, no cable either. I'm never here. I don't watch a lot of TV." Phillip moved his hand under the comforter and glided it across Nicky's chest. "You are so soft."

With the simple touch of a hand, Nicky's manhood sprang to life as his body stirred to the innocent stimulation. His heart rate increased, and he had to focus on his words. "Is there a video store around here? We can just rent a movie." Nicky lightly brushed his extending cock, then balls. Considering climbing up onto Phillip, he thought about what it would feel like with Phillip inside of him.

"I think there is one down on Brookside, across the street from the Chinese place." Phillip's hand leisurely moved down Nicky's stomach and across his hip before stopping on Nicky's groin. "What do we have here?" Phillip asked as he took hold of Nicky's hard cock.

"Well, you're touching me! What do you expect?" Nicky pushed his hip up into Phillip's hand and let out a light moan.

Phillip gave Nicky a mischievous grin before dipping his head under the comforter and taking Nicky into his mouth. Nicky let out a whimper as Phillip's warm mouth took him over the edge in a matter of minutes.

When Phillip resurfaced from under the covers, he was still wearing that mischievous grin as he looked into Nicky's eyes. "So, what was this about renting a movie?"

Nicky's breathing was rapid, his abdomen muscles flexing with each breath he took. He was certainly no longer thinking about movies.

After a shower, the two were about to walk out the door when Phillip stopped Nicky for one last kiss. The kiss initially was a peck, but when Phillip went in for a second kiss, he reached around and took ahold of Nicky's lower back and brought him up into his arms.

Stirring, Nicky wiggled out of his arms without thinking.

"Are you okay?" Phillip asked tenderly as he clipped Nicky's chin upward.

No, he wasn't okay. Nicky had suddenly been hit with a flood of emotions. He had fallen hard for this man. "Yeah, I guess so." Nicky muttered. He wanted to tell Phillip what he had done with Cowboy Mike; it was important that Phillip knew the truth.

Phillip looked into Nicky's eyes. "What does that mean?" Phillip took a slight step back as he surveyed Nicky's face.

"It's nothing. Let's go." Nicky nudged Phillip toward the door with a gently prod to his ribcage.

While in the video store, the two walked side by side as they examined the front and back covers of movies along the wall. Nicky, never letting Phillip from his sight, was euphoric every time Phillip returned the look, usually with a naughty smile that was a clear message of what he wanted.

"Have you seen this?" Phillip held up a box for one of the movies from the Twilight series. "It's the best one," Phillip added as he placed it back on the rack and then lightly ran his hand across Nicky's crotch when no one was looking. "Are you sure you're okay?" Phillip asked again.

Nicky felt as if he was acting childish but couldn't bring himself out of his own funk. About to answer Phillip, Nicky felt his phone buzz in his pocket. Taking the phone out, he saw that Tyler had sent him a text massage: *Where are u?*

With a friend.

What friend?

Ignoring the last message, Nicky put his phone back down into his pocket. Nicky looked at Phillip, who was staring at him.

"Nicky, are you sure you're all right? You're quiet." Phillip was no longer looking at box covers and had turned to face Nicky.

"Yeah, really. I'm okay."

"You're not having second thoughts about this, are you? If so, it's fine. We can take it slower. I know it's a lot," Phillip whispered. "We don't have to pick out a movie. If you want to go, I get it." Phillip's face was drawn and eyes narrowing downward.

Nicky felt Phillip's hand as it lightly brushed against his. He wasn't having second thoughts at all? "I think I'm just tired. That's all." Nicky picked up the movie box for *The Birdcage*. "Have you ever seen this?"

"Oh yeah. That's a good one. Have you seen it?" Phillip asked.

"No, but I've always wanted to."

"I could definitely watch it again. Let's get it." Phillip said.

From the video store to the grocery store, they were back at the house within the hour, managing not to run into anyone that they knew. Phillip put his pajamas back on and handed Nicky just a pajama top.

"Don't I get pants too?" Nicky asked as he took the shirt.

"That would be a 'no'. I want to see you." Phillip giggled.

Smiling at the nasty thoughts he was having, Nicky agreed and rolled up the sleeves to reveal his forearms. The pajama shirt, which came down just past Nicky's butt, exposed glimpses of his buttocks if he moved too fast. Catching Phillip looking at his backside made Nicky feel better, finally bringing him out of his funk.

Spending the afternoon and evening curled up in Phillip's arm watching their movie first and then a marathon of ESPN sports, the two sat on the couch all day talking, making out, and eating pizza.

When they went to bed that night, Nicky yearned for this to be the night that Phillip would take him completely. He thought about just saying it, telling him what he wanted, but it seemed so vulgar to say the words. So far, the sex they had been having was amazing, leaving him seeing stars and fighting for his next breath each time, but he wanted Phillip completely.

Fearful that maybe Phillip didn't want him in that way, Nicky's insecurities weighed on him. Was Phillip not wanting to have intercourse with him just a preference, or did it mean something else? Nicky closed his eyes as his breathing slowed. He heard a light snore from Phillip, who had fallen asleep with a smile on his face.

After the entire weekend being secluded in the house and disconnected from the world, by Sunday evening, they knew they couldn't neglect their responsibilities another day. Nicky needed to return to the pool, and Phillip had meetings with his two assistant coaches, and then a big meeting with his boss and the entire aquatic department first thing in the morning.

Nicky was slow packing his bag; he didn't want to go back to his dorm. "So if anybody were to ask, where should I say I've been?" He was mostly thinking about Tyler and the probing questions that he was sure to ask.

Phillip was silent for a moment. "I don't know; can we talk about it when you return tomorrow?"

"Oh, I am returning?" Nicky asked.

"Yes, and I'll even cook dinner again. There's a key under the planter next to the door. The big red one by the fountain. Use it to let yourself in if you get here before me."

When Nicky arrived back at his dorm room, the room felt strange, like it wasn't his space anymore. Though he wondered where Tyler was, he was thankful he was not around, which allowed him to avoid any questions about his whereabouts. With the fall semester not scheduled to start for another month, the building was relatively quiet most of the time. Having the room all to himself, with no class homework or studying to be done, Nicky took to his bunk in his corner of the room. Closing his eyes, Nicky slept for the next several hours.

The following morning, as he pulled the covers off his head, he saw the curled-up lump in Tyler's bed. Sleeping like a baby, Nicky never heard his roommate come in. Climbing down off his bunk, Nicky went for his shorts on the floor in front of his bunk. Without a bathroom in their room, Nicky had grown used to holding it all night, but by morning, he had to pee like a racehorse. Walking past Tyler's bunk, Nicky patted the lump covered under the thin sheet. "Hey, get up. It's almost nine o'clock."

"I'm awake," Tyler mumbled without ever moving.

Nicky waited to make sure his roommate was up before leaving the room. With two more additional prompts from Nicky, Tyler jerked the single sheet off from over his head. "Damn it, I'm up! Since when did you sleep here anyways?"

"It's nine o'clock, I'll meet you at the pool. I want to get started."

"What's the fucking rush? Hold on. Give me a minute, and I'll drive us."

That's exactly what Nicky didn't want. If he waited for him, Tyler would surely drill him about his whereabouts over the weekend.

"I texted you like a dozen times—where have you been?" Tyler was slowly coming alive.

"Dude, I got to go. I'll fill you in later." Nicky knew that was a lie, but he didn't want it to sound like some big secret either.

"I'm up." Tyler lifted his naked body from his twin bed, throwing the sheet toward the foot of the bed. Standing up, he gave little attention to the morning wood that he was sporting as he let out an over-the-top yawn and stretch toward the low ceiling.

Defeated, Nicky told him to hurry up and that he would be right back. Shuffling in his shorts and slippers down to the communal bathrooms, he relieved himself and then brushed his teeth. By the time he made it back to the room, Tyler was just slipping a pair of gold Red Devil sweatpants over his Speedo, followed by a red tank top.

Nicky slipped on an identical pair of sweatpants and then hooked his shorts to the back of the door before putting on a black V-neck t-shirt. The two were out the door in less than ten minutes.

Nicky was thankful that Tyler was clearly not awake and most likely hung over, as he said almost nothing on the short ten-minute drive over to the pool. When Nicky passed through the pool gates, he saw J. B. already in the water working out. Slipping off his flip flops and sweats, Nicky grabbed the lane next to J. B. and slid into the pool.

Nicky's workouts were consistent and allowed for no socializing with other people once he was in the zone. He trained hard and pushed himself. At the end of his workout, he still had an enormous amount of energy to burn from skipping his workout yesterday, so he continued to swim for an additional forty-five minutes.

When he stopped, he noticed that Tyler was gone already and J. B. was sitting on the bleachers talking on his phone. When Nicky climbed out of the pool, he walked over to J. B. and the two fist-bumped one another.

"What's happening, man? Whatcha you got going on later?" J. B. asked as Nicky sat down next to him.

"I got plans; what did you have in mind?" Nicky asked as he attempted to ring the water out of his ears by tilting his head sideways and jiggling his finger frantically into his ear.

"Thought maybe a movie or shooting some pool or something."

"Sorry, can't tonight. How about another time?" Nicky replied.

"Yeah, that's cool. Did you hear about Dutch?"

"Yeah, that sucks. Have you talked to him?" Nicky asked.

"Naw," J. B. mumbled as he climbed down off the bleachers. The two walked out together toward the parking lot.

"Can I ask you something?" Nicky mumbled.

"What?"

Nicky was losing his nerve and didn't even know how to ask J. B. his question. "Naw, never mind." Nicky couldn't.

"What. Just ax me. Whatcha want to know?"

Nicky took in a big breath and released his question at the same time as he exhaled, "When you and Des have sex, do you always fuck her?" Nicky couldn't believe he just said it. He wanted to crawl in a hole and hide somewhere, but he didn't want to ask Tyler. Tyler would be all over him for details, and Nicky was not ready for those questions.

"Damn, boy, I thought you were goin' to ax some bull-shit question, but you just straight up ax a mother-fucker the question don't you?"

Nicky laughed nervously. He just wanted him to answer the question.

"Whatcha mean, do I fuck her? Well, she ain't fucking me."

Nicky wished J. B. didn't have to be so loud. "No…I mean, do you always have intercourse?"

"Well, yeah, how else you goin' do it?" J. B. probed as he stared at his friend.

The two stood in the middle of the parking lot. "Just asking. That's all."

"Where's your bike?" J. B. asked as he looked around the parking lot.

"I drove over with Tyler." Nicky scanned the parking lot to ensure Tyler was gone and not just bullshitting with someone in the locker room.

As luck would have it, when Nicky returned to his dorm room, Tyler hadn't returned yet. After several hours of sitting in his room playing on Facebook, napping, and one call to his mother to check in, Nicky was bored and just wanted to be with Phillip. Grabbing his phone, he shot Phillip a text. *I'm bored, can I come over earlier than dinner?*

Almost immediately, Nicky's phone buzzed, and his screen lit up to reflect an incoming text from Phillip. *Of course.*

Shooting Tyler a text letting him know that he would be out again tonight and that he would see him at the pool tomorrow morning, Nicky put together an overnight bag, along with a couple extra shirts as he rushed around, trying to get out before Tyler came in.

When Nicky's phone rang, he glanced at the screen, already knowing it was most likely Tyler. Sending the call to voice mail, Nicky shoved the phone down into his backpack.

Grabbing the keys to his bike off his desk, Nicky was about to head out the door when he heard his phone chime, signaling that Tyler had left him a message. With no time to listen to it, Nicky was out the door and on his way back over to the one person he had been missing all day.

14

When Nicky arrived at Coach's house, he was unsure if he was supposed to ring the doorbell first or if it would be all right to just walk in. Unsure, Nicky rang the bell and took a step back as he waited. Not hearing Emily barking, his first thought was that the two of them were out on their walk.

Nicky was about to retrieve the hidden key when Phillip opened the door with a spatula in hand. Nicky's eyes shot up and down as he examined Phillip's physique before stepping into the foyer. Liking what he saw, Nicky couldn't help but smile.

"What's so funny?" Phillip asked as he shut the door and then tenderly took Nicky into his arms, kissing him several times with gentle pecks on his lips.

Each kiss was longer and longer before Phillip pulled away. "I'm glad you came over early. I was missing you too. Dinner's not quite ready," Phillip announced, breathing hard and licking his bottom lip dry.

Phillip led the way as the two cut through the living room to the kitchen. Walking past the couch, Nicky trailed Phillip, watching his ass as it moved up and down with each step. Dropping his backpack onto the couch as he walked by it, Nicky barely took his eyes off of Phillip's bubble butt and wide back as he envisioned him naked.

In the kitchen, Phillip finished putting his casserole together as he asked about Nicky's day. Once getting the casserole into the oven, Phillip set the timer for one hour.

"It has to cook for one hour and then cool for at least fifteen minutes after that. Let's go in the den and relax."

Nicky hoped by *relax* he meant kiss, make out, get naked, and have sex, smiling at the notion.

As they entered the den, Phillip stopped and smiled at Nicky. "Or would you like to move into the bedroom?" Phillip asked.

Nicky's face was flushed as he nodded his head. Phillip took Nicky's hand and slowly walked him down the hall.

Phillip pulled back the thick comforter and top sheet on the bed. Nicky unbuttoned his jeans, slipping them and his underwear off in one swoop. Both naked, Phillip pulled the covers up over them as he rested his body on top of Nicky. Feeling the coach's thick muscular arms, chest, and legs against his body caused Nicky to quiver and press his body closer into Phillip's.

Phillip's body was covered lightly in black hairs, revealing just enough of his skin tone that told Nicky that the white furry butt he was seeing was his true color.

The two naked bodies slowly and harmoniously explored each other with their eyes, hands, and lips, slowly kissing and caressing as the intensity grew between them. With time escaping both of them, within a few breaths from each other, they both cried out, achieving orgasms.

Laying there, Nicky wanted this moment to last forever, but it was quickly interrupted by the sound of the oven timer.

Phillip smiled at Nicky. "Are you hungry?"

"I'm starved. I haven't eaten since this morning," Nicky replied.

"Come on. Are you serious? You know you have to eat every few hours!" Phillip scolded.

"Yes, Dad," Nicky laughed.

Phillip rolled over towards Nicky and lightly kissed him. "You can call me Daddy, but not Dad."

"What's the difference?" Wondering what was wrong with Dad, Nicky took advantage of Phillip's close proximity, grabbing another kiss.

"I'll show you later," he said, raising his eyebrows and giving Nicky a naughty grin before exiting the bed.

Naked, the two entered the kitchen, where Phillip grabbed two oven mitts and removed the steaming casserole dish from the oven.

"God, does that smell good," Nicky said as he walked to the refrigerator and grabbed the tea jug from the top shelf.

"Well, it has to cool for a couple of minutes. Come on, let's take a quick shower." Phillip removed the mitts, tossing them onto the counter.

After their shower, the two slipped on their matching TBU sweats, laughing at the coincidence of their matching wardrobe selection.

The two fixed their plates and moved to the living room, where they sat next to each other on the couch.

"Now, if you don't like it, tell me." Phillip insisted as he leaned in for yet another kiss.

There was a tang of salt from the casserole on Phillip's lips as he lightly rubbed his own lips with his tongue. "It's good."

"Oh I forgot to ask 'bout Tyler? Was he in the room last night? Did he ask where you've been?" Phillip put down his fork as he turned towards Nicky.

Picking up on the pitch in Phillip's voice when he asked about Tyler, it reminded Nicky of the danger in what they were doing. "No, I was already asleep when he got in. This morning he asked a little, but I didn't say anything."

"I'm not worried about you saying anything. I know you wouldn't."

Nicky heard it again, the change in Phillip's speech pattern. He was worried, even if he said he wasn't.

They stayed on the couch, eating and talking while music softly played from built-in speakers above their heads. Nicky hadn't eaten this well since leaving home. He shoved fork after fork of the casserole into his mouth. He felt Phillip staring at him, and it was confirmed each time he looked up.

"So, tell me about your dad. When I was at your house recruiting you, I couldn't get a feel for him. Is he always that quiet?" Phillip asked.

"Yeah." Nicky had to clear his mouth of food as he took a large swallow and then a gulp of his iced tea. "He's an accountant. I think he sits in an office all day running numbers, nothing too exciting to run home and tell."

"What about your mom?" Phillip asked, "She seemed nice. Smart."

"My mom is kind of quiet, too. She never worked. She attended every one of my swim meets in high school. It's funny—she didn't even know I knew how to swim until high school."

"Really," Phillip responded. "How did that happen?"

"I wasn't much of a swimmer as a little kid. During the summer, I would sometimes go down to the high school where they opened the pool to the public, and I would swim with my friends. I guess I picked it up better than most. When I started high school, for some reason, I decided to try out for the swim team. No joking, I had never swum in a lane until that day. I kicked ass at tryouts. It was easy. I just thought my friends sucked at swimming; I didn't realize that I was just good at it."

"You're lying," Phillip said as he leaned into Nicky, asking for a kiss.

Coming up from their kiss, Nicky smacked his lips. "I swear!" Nicky loved kissing Phillip. The way Phillip's lips commanded control, it left Nicky light headed.

"Where was I?" Nicky paused for a second. "We're a typical Irish family, lots of stews, corned beef and cabbage, meat and potatoes, black pudding. St. Patty's was bigger than Christmas in our house. Although my parents weren't big green beer drinkers, we did the whole green decorations everywhere, the traditional dinner, and the parade."

"When did you know you were gay?" Phillip asked.

"I don't know. I'm not even sure it was a big realization for me. I just liked boys and was shocked when I found out that other boys didn't like boys too."

"Did you ever have a girlfriend?"

Nicky thought for a minute. "Yeah, I did. When I was in sixth and seventh grade, but by eighth grade, I knew I was gay. All you had to do was take one look at my bedroom walls. They were filled with posters of Justin Timberlake, Zac Efron, Maroon Five, and every Calvin Klein ad that had a guy in his underwear. I had a few encounters with a kid who lived across the street from us. His name was Ronnie. I think he was a senior in high school, or he had already graduated... Anyway, we messed around a couple of times until he joined the military and left.

"What about in high school? I can't believe you never had a boy-friend or anything," Phillip asked.

"No, not really. It was a small town. I had a crush on my best friend, Spencer, for a while, but he was straight. I didn't swim until I was in high school, and then I went crazy, masturbating a lot thinking about my teammates. I felt sorry for my mom; to this day, she prob-ably still wonders why, when she did the laundry, only one sock was hard and crusty," Nicky joked, half-kidding.

Nicky shared how it was his coach who realized that the short dirty-blond Irish kid from the small town of Brandy, South Dakota, was a diamond in the rough. He just had to teach him the proper way to breathe out, jump from the block, and how to do a proper flip-turn. Mind boggled initially, his high school coach quickly realized the kid was beyond anything they had ever seen at the high-school level. By his junior year, Nicky had every major college scout fighting for him, promising everything from his own apartment to a car if he would sign with their college.

"It was all the same story until you showed up at the door." Nicky stopped and held his stare into Phillip's eyes. *How is all this possible?* Nicky wondered as his eyes studied his lover's rose colored lips, his bright white teeth, the tiny dimple in the middle of his chin, and that perpetual five o'clock shadow. Nicky knew he had never felt this way about anybody. He gave Phillip a yearning look as his mind started to race with nasty thoughts.

"I remember that first day you came to our house. Everyone was sitting at the kitchen table, and you were talking about TBU. We had sat through so many pitches and heard so many promises, but for the first time, I knew my parents were really listening."

"Yeah, I remember. Your mom had a ton of questions."

"You were the first coach that ever stressed what the school could do for me academically," Nicky shared. "You talked about tutors, which caught my attention. In fact, you were the only one who ever questioned me as to what I wanted to do after college."

In an attempt to impersonate Phillip, Nicky bellowed, "*I promise you, Mr. and Mrs. O'Hare, I will take care of your son as if he was my own, and he will graduate and make you proud,*" Nicky mimicked as he laughed and grabbed his crotch. "Yeah, you're taking care of me, all right."

They both started laughing at Nicky's awful mimicry of Phillip. "But for real, I was drawn to you immediately, and now I know why. It was supposed to be. I remember looking at your face, your clothes, and even your lips when you talked. That night, I jacked off thinking about those brown eyes that just sucked me in," Nicky said as he smiled into the eyes he was talking about.

They had been talking for over three hours when Phillip brushed his hand over his watch. "Are you ready for bed?" he asked as he gazed into Nicky's eyes.

"Yeah, I guess so. I just want to take a shower. Don't fall asleep before I get out." Nicky pleaded.

Feeling clean and refreshed after a nice hot shower, Nicky wrapped his towel around his waist and set out to locate Phillip. Stepping out of the bathroom, he found Phillip already lying on the bed with a sheet lightly laid across him.

"Ow, sexy," Nicky commented as he drew closer. When Nicky reached the side of the bed, Phillip pulled the sheet off, exposing his naked body and semi-erect penis. Nicky loved the fact that his body was thick and no longer possessed that skinny swimmer's body like every other person around him. His chest was lightly covered with black hair; his thighs were large and muscular and covered in the same black, coarse hairs. Nicky's dick jumped as he reached for his towel and let it fall to the floor.

As soon as Nicky placed one knee on the mattress, Phillip pulled him in closer. "Mmm," Nicky moaned as their tongues met and Phillip's body brushed against his damp skin.

The sensual touch of the coach caused Nicky to collapse backwards onto the bed. Their naked bodies rolled from side to side across the bed as they hungrily kissed one another. Feeling lightheaded, Nicky just wanted to lay there and let Phillip make love to him. He lightly ran his hands up the inside of Phillip's thighs, feeling the hair as he brushed over the top of them. His hand came to a stop on Phillip's penis, and when he gave it a gentle squeeze, it pulsated inside of his grip.

Nicky's body was like Jell-O as Phillip rolled him onto his back. As Nicky lay motionless on his back, he watched as Phillip removed something from his nightstand. Phillip then positioned himself between Nicky's legs and applied a cool slippery ointment between his buttocks. Nicky lay still as Phillip pushed one finger inside of him, the ointment allowing his finger to slide effortless inside him. Nicky was both excited and afraid as Phillip slowly worked another finger in him and he loosened Nicky up with his fingers.

Nicky whimpered in ecstasy at the feel of his lover's fingers, which were about to drive him over the edge. Nicky attempted to lean up toward Phillip. He wanted his mouth on him, too. He wanted his lover's lips; he wanted Phillip to consume every inch of his body that was now on fire.

Unable to arch his body into an impossible position, Nicky leaned back into his pillow. Gazing up at his lover, Nicky watched as Phillip with one hand and his mouth removed a condom from its package and rolled it over his erection. Staring into Nicky's eyes, Phillip gently guided Nicky onto his stomach. Within seconds, Nicky felt Phillip rotate his pelvis down onto his buttocks as he gently pushed down into him.

As Phillip pushed deeper down inside of him, Nicky smashed his face into the pillow, trying to bear the pain as his body ignited into bliss. He would have come off the bed, if not for the weight of his lover on top of him. Fighting for control, Nicky let out a cry and then another as Phillip took over his body. He was no longer in control, burying his face deep into the pillow.

Phillip's thrust gradually picked up, and he drove himself deeper and faster into Nicky. "Oh God, oh God," they both cried out in unison, Nicky tossing his face from side to side on the pillow as his body was on the edge of releasing.

Overwhelmed and out of control, Nicky erupted into ecstasy all over the bed, his entire body trembling and bolts of light shooting all around him. For the first time in his entire life, Nicky was engulfed with shooting sensations throughout his whole body as Phillip came to a stop.

Once his breathing slowed, he lay under the coach, content to never move. Every so often, he felt Phillip's soft lips gently kiss him on the back of his neck, causing another bolt of electricity to surge through his body. Just before drifting into a light doze, Nicky felt Phillip gently lift up and pull out of him, causing a vacuum of air to rush into Nicky's lungs as he screamed once more in ecstasy. Hearing Phillip leave the room, he couldn't open his eyes. His body and soul satisfied, he was unable to move.

Soon, Phillip returned back into the room and sat at the end of the bed. Nicky felt the tender swab of a warm cloth as Phillip traced the curve of his ass, sliding the moist cloth softly between his cheeks and thighs several times. When finished, Phillip tossed the washcloth onto the floor next to the bed as he snuggled up next to Nicky.

The two lay in bed, drained of all energy. "Are you okay? I didn't hurt you, did I?"

"Nooo, I'm fine," Nicky murmured as he nestled up under the coach's armpit.

"Can I get you anything?" Phillip whispered.

"No," was all Nicky was able to muster.

Not sure if he had dozed off, Nicky felt Phillip's fingers as they delicately ran down his back, stopping on his ass. Nicky sighed, completely content. "Why didn't you try to have intercourse with me before tonight?" Nicky muttered, trying to get his voice.

"I knew you weren't ready until tonight. Your first time, it should be right." Philip gently ran a finger back up Nicky's back. "So, my little virgin, how was it?" Phillip asked.

Nicky paused for a second. How had his omission of Cowboy Mike somehow turned into this haunting lie? *I have to say something,* Nicky thought. But it felt wrong to say something now, right after they had made love. *Cowboy Mike, that was all wrong anyways and doesn't even really count,* Nicky reasoned. "I've wanted you for so long," were the only words Nicky was able to say.

15

In the morning, Nicky couldn't stop thinking about the lie between him and Phillip. It sat in his belly like a brick. There was no way around it: he was lying to Phillip, and he knew it. Coupled with the fact that they had the most amazing sex last night, evidenced by his ass still throbbing, Nicky was emotionally scattered. *I have to tell him the truth.*

Later that morning, Nicky watched as Phillip lathered up his body from head to toe and then started the rinsing process. Nicky knew he would start with his hair, face, and armpits before turning around and letting the water run down his back—and he did it on cue. Definitely Nicky's favorite part was watching as Phillip worked the soap out of the crack of his buttocks. Oh, how Nicky's own body responded to this show every time.

Phillip turned around, catching Nicky staring at him, and then looked down at Nicky's groin. He smiled at what he was able to do to his lover without even touching him. Caught, Nicky returned the smile before continuing to roam his eyes over Phillip's entire body. When Phillip turned around again for one final rinse, Nicky was surprised at the massive scar running down the backside of Phillip's back. With all the times he had seen Phillip naked, how could he have missed it? No doubt it must have been a painful break.

Drying off side by side at the counter, Phillip caught Nicky staring over at his naked body through the reflection of the mirror. "What? Why are you looking at me?" Phillip asked.

"No reason. I just like looking at you. All of you." Nicky produced a fake smile as thoughts of Cowboy Mike crept in.

"I have to head over to the campus this morning. What do you have planned since you don't have classes yet?" Phillip asked as he hung his towel on a towel rack behind Nicky.

"Meeting the guys at the pool later. Tyler wants to go over to the mall. Really nothing. Why?" Nicky watched as Phillip hung his towel up and casually walked over to his dresser. Even watching him put on a pair of boxers was sexy. *I'll wait until he turns around, then I'll say something,* Nicky said to himself.

Phillip turned around and smiled. "Because I want to see you again."

Nicky chickened out; he couldn't tell him right now. "You mean you're not tired of me yet?" After watching Phillip walk away and into his closet, Nicky retrieved a clean pair of sweats out of his bag.

"Do you ever wear underwear?" Phillip asked as Nicky slipped his sweatpants over his bare skin.

"Not if I don't have to. I'm in a tight-ass Speedo for hours. The last thing I want on is underwear. Anyway, the boys like to roam free." Nicky shook his pelvis, causing his dick and balls to bounce against the fabric of his sweats.

"Come on. I'm going to make sure you eat. I don't want you starving." Phillip put his arm around Nicky's neck and led him out of the bedroom.

"What are you cooking?" Nicky asked as he gave Phillip a kiss.

"Some of my mother's famous pancakes. Are you hungry?"

"Always."

After cooking several large pancakes, Phillip slid a stack of four over to Nicky, who was sitting with a cup of coffee at the bar. Drowning them in syrup, Nicky didn't wait as he tore into his breakfast. It was several minutes before Phillip joined him at the bar with his plate. With a full mouth, Nicky nodded in approval.

"So what happened? How come you didn't return to swimming after your leg healed?" Nicky asked after he was able to swallow.

"Oh God, are you kidding?" Phillip responded. "I told you about the accident, right? I spent months in the hospital and then almost a year in rehab just to walk again. The doctors said that, had I not been in the shape I was in, I would have most likely died from my internal injuries. Once I was stable, I was flown back to the States and eventually moved back into my parents' house on the dairy. While in rehab, there were staff everywhere to help me, but once I got home, my poor mother had to do everything." Phillip poured himself another cup of coffee and held out what little was still in the pot, offering it to Nicky.

"No, I'm good." Nicky replied, putting his hand over his cup.

"So by then, I was able to walk again—barely. I remember sitting in the living room all day. I wasn't exercising or doing anything to get any better. I fell into a deep, deep depression. I even thought about killing myself. Sometimes I wished I would have died in that accident because it seemed like it would have been better than where I was, mentally, that is."

Phillip paused long enough to take a sip of his coffee. "Over the next year, my mom watched me deteriorate. I was devastated that I would never swim again. My whole life had been about training, and it was taken away from me. I didn't have any friends. I never had time to have any, and now I was slipping into this really dark place. One day, I heard my mom talking to someone in the kitchen. I knew it wasn't my dad. You could set your watch by what time he came in. Anyway, I hadn't heard any car come down the dirt driveway, either. I remember trying to make out the low whispers, and then my coach, Marcus, walked into the living room. He scared me to death. I had no idea he was coming. He was looking at me like he was pissed off."

"Oh shit, did your mom call him?" Nicky asked.

"Yeah. She didn't know what else to do. Marcus just looked at me and said, 'Can you walk?' I told him that I could, and he stood at the doorway and told me to get up. I saw my mother standing in the kitchen behind Marcus when he said, 'Let's go. Your mom already packed your things.' I asked where we were going, but I knew. That day, Marcus drove me back to Roswell; driving straight through, we arrived late that night. I had slept most of the way, and the bastard put me in the pool that evening. He worked me that night until I had nothing left to give."

"Oh my God, you should write a book!" Nicky said.

Phillip laughed as he checked his watch. "I remember Marcus looking at me and telling me that as long as I was still breathing, there was a plan for me. He held me in that lap pool as I broke down and cried in his arms. After that day, I was ready to fight for it. I wanted my life back. We spent months in and out of the pool, training, reconditioning, and rebuilding my muscles." Phillip stopped, looking at his watch again. "I got to get running. Can you take care of walking Emily so she can poop before you leave?"

"Yeah, I got her. I'll knock out the dishes too."

"Ah you're a saint," Phillip said as he reached in for a kiss.

Phillip was not as late he as was pretending. He just didn't want to go into the details of what came next. After recovering from his injuries, but never reaching the condition he once was in, it was apparent to both Phillip and Marcus that his old life was never coming back. Phillip turned to coaching and was sought after by several major universities in the United States when the news broke that he might be shopping for a position. He was originally hired by Penn State as their head coach for the men's swim team, only to be fired a year and a half later when the school discovered his addiction to pain medication.

All the physiotherapy in the world couldn't fix his chronic pain, and over the years, unbeknownst to anyone, he had become a functioning addict. Phillip entered drug rehab for his addiction after being fired from Penn State. Once completed, he was hired by Tampa

Bay University as the assistant coach. It soon became obvious to TBU administration that he knew more than their current head coach, and Phillip was promoted into the position with the stipulation that he had to stay clean.

A life of coaching was not the life Phillip had dreamed of, but it was the life that was chosen for him. Now three years into this position, Nicky O'Hare was the most promising athlete he had recruited to date. His mission in life was to recruit the best swimmers and rebuild a failed swimming program at TBU, or so he thought.

16

Phillip and Nicky were inseparable over the next two weeks, shut up in Phillip's house every chance they had to be together. During the day, Nicky trained with Tyler and then hurried back to the house. The coach, in turn, cut out every meeting that wasn't important so he too could race back to Nicky.

One morning during the first week of August, Tyler caught Nicky alone in the locker room at the city pool before their workout. "Where the hell have you been at night? Don't bullshit me, either!" Trying to be serious, but flashing a grin from ear to ear, Tyler pushed Nicky against a locker.

With classes yet to start, the truth was that Tyler was spending less time in their room than Nicky. Nicky just didn't know it. It was on those rare occasions when he did show up and there was no sign of Nicky that Tyler wondered who was dominating his friend's time. "Is it a woman? Goddamn it, tell me it's not a woman! Oh lord, it better not be a woman." Tyler fanned himself as if he was going to pass out.

"Tyler, Tyler, knock it off. It's not a girl." Pushing Tyler off of him, Nicky walked away. "I'm not ready to divulge anything just yet. Come on, stop asking. You'll be the first to know when I go public. It's just too soon," Nicky pleaded.

"Just tell me: Do I know him?" Tyler asked as he caught up to his friend.

"Tyler! Stop!"

After practice, Nicky was a little nervous that Tyler might actually follow him this time. Nicky carefully watched the traffic behind him until he arrived at Phillip's house. It was a beautiful evening, and Phillip was standing out front with Emily, talking with one of his neighbors. Nicky knew that the neighbor must have caught Phillip and Emily while they were out for their walk. For a split second, Nicky thought about continuing to drive by and circle around when it was clear, but automatically he pulled into the driveway. As he stepped off the bike and removed his helmet, he saw that the neighbor was watching him. When Phillip also turned around, he sensed they were talking about him. Nicky stood by his bike for a moment, unsure of what to do. He wondered if he should just go in the house or if he should walk over and pretend he was just a guest visiting.

The situation was resolved when Emily barked for him and pulled on her leash toward the house. Phillip hugged the neighbor and then walked across the lawn to Nicky.

"Hey there," Phillip said as he rolled his eyes at the neighbor behind him.

Nicky responded with a smile and then followed him and Emily into the house.

"That was Jen; she lives two houses down. She and her husband bought their house a month after I moved in, so we're kind of buddies by default. Her husband, Jake, passed away last year, so she's a little lonely these days," Phillip said as he took Emily's leash off her.

"How did he die?"

"Heart attack. He was in his early fifties. I always thought he was in good shape by looking at him. He was one of those outdoor, rock-climbing, hiker kind of guys. They used to go kayaking, mountain biking, all that shit. She was at work one day and came home and found him dead in the garage."

"Wow, that's horrible."

Phillip started to walk down the hall when Nicky jumped on his back, swinging one arm around Phillip's upper chest. "Hold on, buddy. I need a kiss before you hole up in the bathroom for the next thirty…"

Without warning, Phillip let out a scream as he went down to the floor, taking Nicky with him. Phillip groaned in pain as he rocked his body side to side on the floor. Nicky had no idea what happened, and he stared at Phillip, who had lost all color in his face and looked to be on the verge of tears.

"What happened?" Nicky begged.

"It's my back… just let me be!" Phillip's tone was sharp.

Nicky hovered over Phillip, not knowing what to do. After about ten minutes, Nicky begged Phillip to let him call an ambulance.

"No. Just help me up." Phillip was dead weight as Nicky got him up.

Using the wall on one side and Nicky on the other, Nicky was able to get Phillip into bed. "What can I get you?" Nicky asked.

"Just a glass of water."

By the time Nicky had returned, Phillip had several pills in his hand and an open pill bottle sitting on the edge of his nightstand. Nicky handed him the glass of water and watched as Phillip took a handful of pills.

Sleeping for two days, Phillip woke up only long enough to take more meds. Seeing Phillip completely down on his back, Nicky couldn't believe what he had done. He was only trying to be silly, and now look. He begged Phillip for forgiveness whenever he saw that he was awake.

Nicky stayed close, only leaving the house to take Emily out on a very short walk. He quietly checked in on Phillip, peeking into the dark bedroom at least once an hour, finding him sound asleep more times than not. Several times, Nicky came close to calling Tyler for help on what to do. Nervous that it was more serious than Phillip was letting on, he hoped Tyler would know what to do, but Nicky also understood that would mean revealing their relationship. He had already caused enough damage.

By mid-week, Nicky knew that Phillip had had enough of him when he told him to return to Hayden Hall as there was nothing for him to do there. After losing the argument as to why he couldn't leave, Nicky returned to campus only to find that Hayden Hall was now chaotic with new students arriving in preparation for the fall semester. The small parking lot was full of trucks and vans as well as beat-up compact cars stuffed with furnishings. Parents were everywhere, ready to move their child into their new residence, and baby brothers and sisters were running everywhere out of control.

Nicky waited at the elevator for what seemed like an eternity before it arrived, packed with fathers with empty suitcases ready to retrieve their next load. Once the elevator emptied out, Nicky stepped in, followed by three men loaded down with boxes and a young girl carrying two large trash bags full of something.

"Three please," Nicky politely asked as he was forced to the back of the elevator. With the door closed, the loud elevator made its way to the second floor. The scent of dirt penetrated Nicky's nose. He didn't remember the elevator stinking this bad and wondered if it was just because of the high traffic. When they arrived on the second floor, the door sprang open, and one of the men exited, replaced by two men who joked about not wanting to wait for it to come back down.

When Nicky exited onto his floor, the long corridor was littered with packing material and empty boxes that had been shoved out of newly occupied rooms. Nicky made his way down the hall, passing several doors that had been propped open. He could see moms and dads packed in the rooms, not ready just yet to say goodbye to their children.

Unlocking the door to his room and seeing that he was alone brought mixed emotions; he missed his friend, yet he didn't want to explain where he had been. Turning on the TV, Nicky was thankful for Tyler's addition to the room as he channel surfed and listened to the sounds of loud footsteps running up and down the hall. In the room, the noise sounded as if buffalo were making their way from one end of the hall to the other. Hayden Hall was living up to the name as the noisiest building of the three dorms. Nicky remembered now that this went on until at least midnight and then picked back up again in the morning. He laughed to himself now, remembering the little inconveniences of dorm living.

When Tyler came in the room around eleven, there was little doubt Nicky was happy to see his friend, long past bored of the mindless TV programs without any kind of cable. Initially, Nicky thought he was sensing something was wrong. Tyler was not his usual lively self. He barely got a hello from him when he came in. Nicky watched for a few minutes before saying anything. "So what's up? What happened to you this morning at practice?" Nicky asked.

"Oh, so you get to ask me where I've been, but I can't ask you. Hardly seems fair, but if you must know, I met this guy from Russia in the club last night."

There it was. Tyler was definitely mad over something; his tone said it all. Watching Tyler move about the room, Nicky knew he had to humor his friend for a moment. He was like a puppy: Give him a little attention, and he'd forget he was mad. "From Russia? Are you kidding me? Come on, you have to tell me everything!" Nicky begged, trying to seem interested.

Without skipping a beat, Tyler took the hook, "He works for Set Sail Cruise Line, and their ship came into port yesterday morning. He's cute. I saw, I marched, and I conquered," Tyler joked as he stripped his clothes off. "I can still smell him, sweet and spicy. I have to take a shower." Tyler paused for a second, "What are you doing here tonight, anyway?"

"I have some stuff to work on, and I need my computer," Nicky replied. "So did you go on the ship?"

"No, don't be silly. He was on his day off while the ship was in port, so he had a hotel. We went there." Now down to his black boxer-briefs, Tyler made no bones of freeing himself from those as well.

"You know, you can use my laptop any time. Take it with you...wherever you are going."

Ignoring Tyler's little dig, Nicky asked, "So were you with him all day?"

"Yeah, it was hot. We had sex like three times," Tyler said as he brushed through his drawers looking for a clean towel. "God, was he hung. You got to love those Russians."

"Are you kidding me? Tell me you're joking!" Nicky said, slightly embarrassed by Tyler's frankness.

"Check my phone; see for yourself. Unlike you, I don't keep secrets," Tyler said as he wrapped the towel around his waist and headed for the shower down the hall.

Tyler's comment stung a little. *After all, he's right,* Nicky thought as he looked at the first picture on Tyler's phone, which took his breath away. He was shocked—shocked that people took those types of personal pictures. Nicky wondered if the Russian had the same type of pictures of Tyler on his phone.

Through phone calls and text messages, Phillip reassured Nicky that he was feeling better every day. Nicky hadn't seen Phillip in over a week, since Phillip insisted he return to the dorm. It ate at him every day that he caused so much pain in someone he loved.

With just over a week until the new semester started, followed by swim season officially starting the following week, Nicky was glad that their practices had been moved from the city pool back to the aquatic center on campus.

He and Phillip had discussed the issue of them being in public together and the complications that accompanied it. Nicky sensed that Phillip was more nervous than he was. For Nicky it was a plus: more time with him and not having go all day without seeing him.

That morning, Nicky and Tyler headed over to the campus bookstore to purchase some of their books and supplies for the upcoming semester. Running into J. B. inside, Tyler goosed him in his crotch. "What happened to you this morning? We missed you at the pool."

J. B. ignored Tyler's little stunt. "Yeah, I had to stay home and watch my little sister Penny. She woke up throwing up, and mom had to go to work. Did I miss anything?"

"Naw, same shit," Nicky reported.

The three gathered their books and headed to the checkout stand, where Tyler tried to move them over to the line with the male checker. "Come on, get in his line," Tyler whispered.

"Dude, it's twice as long," J. B. replied.

"So? I want to see if this guy is gay. He's a little hottie," Tyler responded.

"Are you serious? We're going to wait in line all day so you can check out some guy?" Nicky whispered.

"Come on, I would do the same for you if you asked," Tyler whined.

"That's just it. We wouldn't ask because it's stupid," Nicky answered. "I'm not doing that."

Standing their ground in the shortest of the three lines, all Tyler could do was stare at the clerk, waiting to make eye contact. "Damn, he's cute," Tyler whispered to no one in particular.

When they made it to the front of the register, Nicky watched their clerk as she rang up J. B.'s books. The total continued to climb fast with every book she scanned, and when done, Nicky saw that J. B.'s total was over seven hundred dollars.

"Shit, I can't believe the prices of these books!" Tyler shouted.

Nicky shook his head, amazed at the prices as well. Watching as J. B. pulled out a check card and pay it, Nicky noticed that he never batted an eye at the total.

"Must be nice to be rich!" Tyler declared.

"Dude, keep out of my fucking business," J. B. shot back as he picked up his purchases and walked out of the store.

Standing there trying to figure out what just happened, Nicky felt his phone buzz in his right front pocket. Hoping it was Phillip, his suspicion was confirmed when he looked at the newly received text: *Feeling much better and missing you :) come over :).*

⚕

Surprised by the unexpected text earlier in the day inviting him over, Nicky was excited to be back at Phillip's. It had been the longest they had been apart since getting together a month and a half ago, and Nicky was about to go crazy if he had to spend another day separated.

Sitting in the living room, Nicky watched as Phillip carried a large platter, a bottle of champagne, and two wine glasses into the room. Signaling for Nicky to take the champagne and glasses, he placed the platter on the coffee table in front of them.

"What all do we have here?" Nicky asked, looking over the assortment of appetizers on the plate. The fact Phillip had brought two champagne glasses instead of just one indicated something special.

Phillip pointed to each item on the platter starting closest to Nicky, "This is goat cheese, Brie, Danish Blue, fresh mozzarella, and a Manchego." Skipping over the grapes and sliced apple wedges, Phillip smiled at Nicky as he pointed at the liver pate, figs, and a ramekin filled with honey. "You can put the pate on the crackers, the honey over the Brie. Do whatever you like. And of course, you know what these are," he said as he pointed to the Totino's Pizza Rolls.

Receiving a light kiss from Phillip, Nicky gently licked his lips, tasting the salt from what was likely a cracker. Brushing Phillip's arm, Nicky stared at the pizza rolls and then over at the assortment of cheeses. Pointing over the cheeses, Nicky asked, "Which is your favorite?" The only one he had ever heard of was the mozzarella.

"Well, probably the goat, although it is not even close to my mother's. She makes the best goat cheese. I can't wait for you to try it someday." Phillip spooned a little bit of goat cheese on a cracker and fed it to Nicky.

As Phillip fed him the cracker, Nicky was thinking about Phillip's choice of words. *"I can't wait for you to try it." Does that mean I will meet his mother someday?*

No sooner did the cracker hit Nicky's mouth did his brain shriek "no," as he fought unsuccessfully not to frown. Showing Phillip the mushed-up cheese and cracker on his tongue, Nicky grumbled, "I don't like it."

Laughing hysterically, Phillip watched his silly lover as he held his tongue out like a three-year-old. "You have to eat it!"

Spitting the cheese out into his hand, Nicky's eyes watered. "There is no way!"

"Here." Phillip passed a half a glass of champagne to Nicky. "We're celebrating tonight."

"Celebrating what?" Nicky asked as he took a drink of his champagne, trying to get the bad taste out of his mouth.

"'Fifty-four days together." Phillip held up his glass to toast.

Nicky was confused as he thought about the number fifty-four. "I don't get it?" he asked.

Phillip chuckled as he took a sip of his champagne. "It is how many days we have been together. It is also the total of our two ages. Get it? Thirty-five plus nineteen equals fifty-four."

Nicky smiled back, not knowing what to make of it, or if it was something people really celebrated. He liked the champagne as he popped a hot pizza roll into his mouth. "These are more my speed." Realizing they were too hot, he rolled the bite around in his mouth, trying to cool it off before it burnt his tongue.

Clearing his mouth of food, Nicky hesitated as he looked over the platter for something he could trust. "This is so sweet. What's our next celebration?" he said, taking a handful of grapes from the tray. Nicky picked one off its stem and fed it to Phillip before he picked one for himself.

"Thanks. If I get to be with you, every day will be a celebration." Phillip leaned in and took a gentle kiss from Nicky.

After swallowing a mouthful of grapes, Nicky asked, "So did you meet Tyler's parents when you were recruiting him?" His roommate was like no other person he had ever met, so sure of himself and outspoken. Nicky wondered where someone got that. It was certainly nothing he ever saw in anyone else he knew growing up.

"What?" Phillip asked as he cut his eyes over at Nicky and then back at the platter. "What are you talking about?" asked the coach.

"Tyler said he was adopted, but he never talks about his parents or anything about his home life," Nicky said.

"Well, from what I can remember, his adoptive parents were quite old. I mean, like in their seventies."

"Really!"

"Yeah, apparently it was their daughter who originally adopted Tyler when he was seven. She was killed in a drunk driving accident when he was around ten, and her parents took him in and raised him."

"So what was the house like? Could you tell anything about them?"

Phillip smiled, "Yeah, I could tell a lot about them. They were filthy rich… mansion, staff, private nurse, the works. His father was sharp. I noticed on some of his school forms that they were listed as his legal parents and not guardians. I met his mother briefly when she came into his father's office to bring us coffee. She introduced herself and then left. It was much like a business meeting instead of a recruiting weekend. When I met his father, Tyler was not even in the room. I didn't meet Tyler until the end of the weekend. The whole thing was weird."

Nicky and Phillip continued making their way through the platter, Nicky mostly sticking to the pizza rolls and fruit. Catching Phillip staring at him, he got the sense that something was off with the coach—he appeared restless and kind of nervous suddenly.

"What?" Nicky stopped eating, thinking he had done something wrong.

"Well. I've been thinking—" Phillip stated and then went quiet.

"And?" Nicky asked.

"I want you here in the morning—every morning. I have been thinking, what do you think about moving in?" Phillip paused as he stared at Nicky. "I want you all the time, here, next to me. I've missed you so much this last week."

Nicky waited, unsure where Phillip was going with his speech.

"I'm just going to say it. I love you," Phillip murmured.

Nicky couldn't believe Phillip had just asked him to move in with him. For a split second, he even questioned if he heard it right. He loved Phillip as well, and this week had been just as hard on him. Did it mean they were going public? Nicky wondered, feeling a rush of emotions sweep over him.

"Say something," Phillip asked.

Nicky got that he was supposed to say yes, although in his head he had already said it. He wanted to say to Phillip, "*And l loved you from the first day that I met you. When you were sitting in our dining room, I knew I loved you. It was crazy, I didn't even know you, but I knew I loved you and one day you would love me too,*" but none of that came out. He remained silent. Nicky had never told anyone that he loved them, not even his parents. To say it now sounded to him as if he was only repeating it back to Phillip because he said it.

"Come on, say something. 'You're moving too fast.' 'Fuck off,' or even better, 'Yes, I'll move in,'" Phillip stammered out.

Nicky looked into Phillip's brown eyes as they madly darted back and forth, waiting for an answer.

"No...I mean yes, I want to be here too. I...I...I want to move in. I *like* you a lot." *What was so hard about saying "I love you?" You love him. Just say it.* Nicky leaned in to kiss Phillip to accompany this answer and then opted for a controlled hug, not wanting to reinjure his lover.

The coach was so excited that he didn't hear what Nicky had failed to say. "Great! How about tomorrow? I can't wait a moment longer."

Nicky sat still, stunned and silent that Phillip had asked him to move in. "You know I have to tell my parents and Tyler something. What do I do?" Nicky asked as the questions started to flood his brain.

"I think you should hold off doing anything official. If we make it official, the school would want a forwarding address."

"So we're still keeping it quiet?" Nicky asked, unsure what this meant.

"I guess you'll have to tell Tyler the truth, but please, ask him not to say anything. Do you think we can trust him?"

Nicky saw the concern in Phillip's eyes as he asked the question. "If I make him swear, I don't think he'll say anything." Nicky wasn't sure he even believed it. Not wanting to admit his lack of trust in Tyler, Nicky didn't know what else to say.

"Okay," Phillip responded.

Nicky released a heavy sigh. "I guess I don't have to say anything to my parents. How would they know? They call me on my cell phone anyways." Nicky was thinking out loud to himself as if they were hatching a secret plan.

"Don't move out; leave some of your stuff in the dorm just in case," Phillip told him.

"Just in case what?" Nicky again heard red flags but was unsure what they meant.

"You know, just in case they check your room. Or suppose your parents visit." Phillip gave Nicky a light kiss before grabbing a piece of cheese from the near-empty platter.

"Trust me; they're not going to surprise me, popping up unannounced. My parents don't do anything spontaneous."

After thinking about it, Nicky laughed. He knew this would also allow Tyler to have the room all to himself for the whole year. Oh, what will Tyler do with a room to himself? What were the challenges of keeping their relationship a secret until they were ready to go public? Publicly, they only saw each other at the pool for practice. If he wasn't at the dorm, who would miss him? The only other swimmers that lived in the dorm besides Tyler were the three new freshmen that the coach recruited, and Nicky hadn't even met them yet. Nicky's brain was on overload.

That weekend, Nicky texted Tyler to ensure he was in the room before he headed over. The sooner he told Tyler, the sooner he could move his essentials out of his room and into Phillip's home. Although Nicky had been spending almost every waking hour over there, moving in and not having to ask to come over cemented that they were a couple.

When Nicky showed up early that afternoon, Tyler was napping in bed. Hearing him come in, Tyler looked at his phone to see what time it was. "Hey, what's up?"

Nicky tried to act causal, like he was there because he lived there. "Did you get into all your classes?" Nicky checked inside their mini refrigerator for nothing in particular as a sense of nervousness set in.

"Yeah, I got into my freedom of speech, French two, calculus, and sociology classes. I have to walk in to see if there is room for my nineteenth-century philosophy class, though." Tyler let out a loud sigh, trying to shake his nap off as he stood up in front of his bunk.

Nicky repeated "nineteenth-century philosophy" in his head, unsure of exactly what it even was. "Do you think you'll have any problems getting in?"

"Naw, not from what I was told." Tyler finished the last of the water from a bottle sitting on his desk.

"I don't know how you do it all." Nicky thought about the four classes he was taking and knew it was going to be a struggle to keep up with those.

The two had been in the room for about an hour together when Nicky worked up the courage to tell Tyler the real reason he was there. "Tyler," Nicky mumbled.

Nicky's tone clearly caught Tyler's attention as he looked up from his laptop. Turning to face his friend, Tyler waited for Nicky to say something.

"I have something to tell you. You have to promise not to tell a soul. No one!" Nicky ordered.

Tyler continued to stare. "'Kay, what?"

"Do you swear?"

"Yes, I swear!" Tyler agreed.

"The guy that I have been seeing is," Nicky's throat, swelled forcing him to take a big swallow, "Phillip."

"Phillip who?" Tyler's eyebrows had folded inward over the bridge of his nose.

"The coach. Coach Silva," Nicky added, not expecting the need for clarification.

Jumping to his feet, Tyler grabbed Nicky by his waist, "Oh my God! Not the coach! Are you lying to me? No way!"

Concern that the neighbors would hear, Nicky tried to break free from Tyler's grip as he repeatedly shushed him. "Now you have to promise to keep the secret." Nicky tried to get out of the way as he watched Tyler jump about the room screaming.

"Tyler, Tyler. Calm down! You can't tell anybody!" Nicky begged.

Tyler stopped for a minute as he grabbed Nicky by the arm. "Now if anybody would be in a scandalous relationship... You know them bitches would've said it would be me." Tyler broke out into laughter.

"There's more," Nicky announced.

"Good lord, you're pregnant?" Tyler continued to laugh as he wiped the tears from his eyes.

"Ah...no. I'm moving in with him."

Tyler stopped in his tracks, "He asked you to move in! Damn, you two move faster than lesbians."

Nicky didn't know what in the hell Tyler was referring to, but he was pretty sure it wasn't important.

"So you say it's a secret, okay, Honest Abe, I can't wait to see how you're going to pull off this big fat lie. You little harlot, you."

"We're not going to lie; we're just not coming out announcing it to the world. Everyone doesn't need to know my business," Nicky retorted, even surprising himself at his harsh tone.

"That's called a lie by omission; it's the same thing. Don't be so naïve."

A ping jolted in Nicky's gut; the word *naïve* stung. He wished he would have never brought it up. His reaction to Tyler had little to do with what his friend said and everything to do with Cowboy Mike.

17

With his junior year now under way, J. B. thanked Jesus for the anonymous donor who once again had paid the year's tuition in full. Over the summer, J. B. had received a letter from the school advising him of the anonymous donation, just as they had done his freshman and sophomore year. All J. B. knew about this donor was they required him to never talk about his finances to anyone and to carry at least a C average in his studies. J. B. took those two stipulations seriously, not chancing anything and doing one better with a 4.0 GPA.

J. B. remembered the night he graduated high school—his mother had thrown him a summer BBQ in their backyard. That evening, he and Desiree were standing by the grill, talking with J. B.'s big brother Maurice. The two brothers were arguing over the readiness of the coals when their little sister Tina yelled from inside the house that someone was at the door. When he and Maurice went to investigate, there was an elderly white man in a black suit asking for J. B.

Seeing the man, J. B. knew it had to be bad news of some sort. White men just didn't show up in his neighborhood unless it was bad news. Cautiously opening the door, J. B. asked the man who he was looking for.

"I am looking for a Mr. Jeremy Ronald Breedlove," the elderly man asked, his eyes darting between J. B. and Maurice.

"Whatcha want with him?" Maurice barked as he stepped in front of J. B. in protective mode. The elderly man took a step back.

"I'm Jeremy," J. B. said as he moved into the doorway. "Whatcha need?" J. B. glanced up seeing a white Toyota Prius parked along the curb. *Ain't no police drive a Prius.*

The man removed a white envelope from the inside of his suit coat and handed it to J. B. "Have a good day," the man said as he took another step back, spun on his heels, and made a hasty retreat to his car.

J. B. and Maurice stood there looking at the envelope as Desiree and his mother approached from behind.

"What is it?" Momma B. asked. "Who was that?"

"I ain't never seen him before; he just gave me this envelope," J. B. replied, shaking the white envelope.

"Are you being sued?" Desiree asked.

"Some chick out there claiming you her baby's daddy?" Maurice interrupted.

"I don't know," J. B. said.

"Better not be no child support paperwork," Desiree snarled.

"Well, we'll never know if you don't open it. Come on, child, what's in the envelope?" Momma B. snapped.

J. B. warily tore the top of the envelope off as if it was going to blow up in his face. His heart raced as he thought about what his brother had just said. Pulling out four sheets of paper, J. B. scanned the first sheet. "It's a letter."

"What kind of letter?" Desiree's eyes were focused on J. B. and not the letter.

J. B. was silent as he took a moment to read the first page, his family standing impatiently around him.

"I can't tell from who, but I think it's saying that I was accepted to Tampa Bay University and tuition has been paid in full for my freshman year."

"What? From the school?" Momma B. asked, crossing her arms over her large breasts.

"I can't tell... It looks like a scholarship or something. I can't tell from whom."

J. B.'s hands shook as he continued reading the letter.

"I thought..." Momma B. sounded a little suspicious. "Didn't you tell them you can't afford it?"

"Yeah, but..." J. B. removed his ball cap and scratched the front of his hairline as he processed what was going on. He remembered the day he realized that, even with grants and scholarships, he still couldn't afford books and the four-thousand-dollar balance that the grants and scholarship didn't cover. He knew he couldn't ask his momma to help, and between school, swimming, watching his sisters, and being required to carry a full load, there was no time for a job. "I was planning on going to community with Des."

"Did you call Bill Gates or write to Oprah or something?" Desiree asked.

"Would you guys be quiet for a minute so I can read this?" J. B. yelled.

Desiree snatched the papers from him, "You reading too slow." After several minutes, Desiree looked up at them. "It looks like you have been either selected or chosen, it's not clear, to attend TBU, and your tuition has been paid in full. It looks like you're supposed to contact a Rebecca Thomas at TBU on Monday. This letter is not from the school, but from the donor, who is trying to remain anonymous... I think."

"That sounds a little fishy," Momma B. grumbled, staring at Desiree as if she was making it up.

That Monday, when J. B. went to see Ms. Thomas in Admissions as instructed, he learned that the donor was indeed anonymous. J. B. spent hours in her office, completing admission forms and taking note of all the things he had to return to her before his enrollment would be official. Initially, J. B. thought it was his brother Clifford, but Clifford denied any knowledge of it during their visit to the penitentiary that following Sunday.

As he walked over to the aquatic center in the early morning, J. B. couldn't believe that was over two years ago. At this time in the morning, the campus was dark and quiet, but within a few hours, once the sun rose, it would be littered with lost students running around, trying to find their way to their classes. For J. B., it was this time in the morning, before the sun came up, that he did his quiet thinking.

Taking in the campus as he cut across the lawn, J. B. thought about how this place commanded his respect; it was the place that held the key to his future. Two years away from graduating and having that degree in his hand, this meant everything to J. B.

The team was gathering for their first official practice, where it was confirmed that Dutch was not returning for his junior year. He and Peggy had gotten married over the summer, and he had gone to work at his father's insurance agency.

The three new freshman recruits, Austin and Andrew Quintero—identical twins from California—and Braden, a local boy, appeared to be all strong swimmers. Nicky knew of the Quintero brothers and knew that Austin was the faster of the twins. On a national level, Nicky had swum against Austin twice, but he had never heard of this Braden, reminding himself to Google him later.

Nicky believed he was faster than Austin, although Austin was faster on the jump and his turns were amazing. Coach Silva was clearly excited to see what the three added to his team.

After a brief introduction to the newbies, the team hit the water just as the sun rose over the center. J. B. took lane one. Next to him was Nicky, followed by Tyler in lane three. Coach Silva came at them hard, quietly assessing who kept their training up over the summer. With most of the team taking more time off than they confessed to, Nicky, Connor, and Austin took a strong lead out in front of the rest of the team.

Halfway through the warm up, J. B. had dropped back from the pack more than usual. Nicky remained focused, gliding through the water with ease, leaving a wake of water behind his feet like a boat cutting across the bay. Connor and Austin stayed close to him with every stroke.

With the first practice out of the way, the team retreated to the locker rooms, breathless and hurting. Beaten down, the guys were quiet as they filed into their respective rows of lockers. Within time, the joking and taunting among the guys returned to normal.

Hearing screaming and scuffling coming from the showers, Nicky sat on a bench in front of his open locker. He knew his teammates had most likely waited until the newbies were soaped up and then dogpiled them to shave their heads. Nicky smiled as he remembered Tyler last year coming out of his initiation with a full erection and then chasing some of the guys with it. As Nicky threw his wet Speedo and towel in his bag, he overheard Coach Dean summon J. B. to his office. Nicky cautiously watched as J. B. stepped in and closed the door behind him.

Later that morning, several of the guys met up at IHOP for lunch. As they sat on the patio eating, J. B.'s absence was noticed by everyone, and the conversation swirled around his inability to improve as a swimmer.

The conversation made Nicky uncomfortable. J. B. was his friend, and he assumed everyone else felt the same until now. Changing the conversation, Nicky started talking about their first upcoming meet with Orlando. "Coach Silva said we should be able to rip these guys a new one, even with our legs tied together."

Squirrel, now also jumping into the conversation, leaned forward. "According to the coach, Orlando is at the bottom of the conference."

"Orlando is my old stomping grounds. I used to use that pool to practice in during the summer," Braden shared. Tall, with a broad chest and shoulders, Braden could easily double for a younger version of Michael Phelps. The chlorine had damaged most of his hair that hung down over his eyes like an old sheepdog. He was constantly brushing it back so he could see, and only then could you see his big beautiful grey eyes. It was also impossible to not notice how white his teeth were, since he was a babbler.

"Oh yeah? I didn't know you were from Orlando," Tyler said as he stared at Braden.

"Well, not really. When my parents divorced a couple of years ago, my mom and I moved to Orlando to be close to my grandparents. Before that we lived in Texas," Braden said.

"Which do you like better?" Squirrel asked.

"I do miss my big dumb Texas, but I think I've discovered a new love for ya'll Cuban boys. I think I might have a thing for chocolate," Braden smirked.

Nicky's eyes zipped back and forth between Braden and Tyler at the openness with which Braden laid his fondness for men on the table.

"They're more Mexican than black," Andrew interjected. "They're of Spanish descent. I think."

"You might be right, because they definitely got smaller tools in their belt," Braden replied as he licked his lips.

"You guys are getting gross. Let's change the subject," Squirrel demanded.

That night, Nicky and Phillip took up their usual places on the couch, where they ate dinner. Between two practices and his classes, Nicky hadn't adjusted to the demanding routine and was spent. In between classes, he tried to do as much of his school work as he could, hoping to have at least part of the evening free to spend with Phillip.

"How's your back?" Nicky asked, now completely aware of Phillip's constant pain. "I saw you on the pool deck during practice this afternoon. You looked a little tight." Nicky rubbed Phillip's back, brushing his hand up and down the broad back.

"Yeah, a little. I need a hot tub," Phillip said, chuckling.

"We should get one!"

"And put it where?" Phillip smiled at Nicky as he flicked the end of his nose.

Thinking about Austin and Andrew and what they brought to the team, Nicky remembered J. B. going into the office after this morning's practice. He also realized that J. B. hadn't shown up for the afternoon practice. "So, what's goin on with J. B.?" Nicky tried to ask casually.

"What do you mean?"

"Well, I heard Coach Dean call for him. Did you guys have a meeting? He wasn't at practice this afternoon either." Nicky knew he was prying, but J. B. was his friend.

Phillip looked up from his plate. "He's got to be able to hold his own. Orlando will be an easy win for us, but I'm not sure if I can put him in the water with Durham State next week." Phillip removed his plate from his lap, placing it on the coffee table.

"He's still on the team though, right?" Nicky hated the thought of the answer he was going to get as Phillip obviously looked uncomfortable. "I know he wasn't that good. Other than being a nice guy, I don't see what made you recruit him. What was it about him?" Nicky realized that he was talking about J. B. in past tense already, as if he was cut.

Phillip took a long pause. "I didn't recruit him. I got a call from the chancellor, who told me J. B. was trying out, and the chancellor doesn't make those types of calls for no reason. I read between the lines, and after watching him swim, I thought maybe I could work with him, improve his time a little. He wasn't anything I would have picked if it wasn't for the chancellor's call."

Nicky thought about what Phillip had just revealed, wondering who J. B. knew for a call like that to be made. "But he's still on the team, right?"

"Yeah, he is." Phillip ran his hand through Nicky's hair, tossing it about. "Stop worrying. We didn't remove him from the roster."

Nicky sighed with relief, not realizing that his heart rate had accelerated just thinking of J. B. being cut. Other than Tyler, J. B. had become one of his closest friends.

18

After their first week of practice, several of the guys' girl-friends organized a "Welcome to the Team" bonfire party for the new teammates down on Clearwater Beach. Nicky had to be persuaded by Phillip to go, if for no other reason than keeping up appearances with the team. What Nicky wanted was to simply be with Phillip. He saw no need in spending the evening with a bunch of random people when he had the chance to spend it with someone that he really wanted to be with.

Down on the beach that night, the air was slightly cooler than in the city, with a breeze coming in from the water. The tide was low, which gave the girls plenty of sandy beach to set up their spot for the evening. Around the fire, Nicky sat digging his feet into the sand as he talked with Austin, J. B., and Squirrel. Sipping beer out of red plastic cups, Nicky just listened as the others talked about their classes and instructors. Austin had just come in from the ocean and was standing with his butt to the fire, trying to take the chill of the ocean water off. Sitting eye level with Austin's crotch, Nicky glanced several times at the silhouette of Austin's dick as the soaked material clung to his body. Nicky was trying not to stare at Austin's crotch, but his board shorts hung low on his hip bone, revealing the tops of his pubic hairs. Nicky placed his cup over his own crotch as his body responded to his imagination.

"So when is the coach going to give us the lineup for Orlando?" Austin asked.

"We should know something by Wednesday," Squirrel responded. "It pretty much stays the same, with minor changes. You and Braden look to be strong off the block, although Braden has to watch that kick when he comes up; he's catching a drag from the guy to his left almost every time."

Squirrel threw his red cup into the fire. "Damn cup has a leak! I knew I wasn't dribbling." Squirrel got up and walked over to the keg for another cup. Standing next to the keg, Squirrel looked up at Austin and Andrew, holding off pouring his beer. "This will be my third year swimming for Silva, and he's good at giving you whatever you hate to swim. At least for most of your first year. He's testing you, and you've got to give it to him. The sooner he sees it, the sooner he'll back off of you."

"You got that right!" J. B. chimed in. "When he ain't looking, Coach Dean is."

Nicky sat quietly as he listened to the guys engage in their usual shit talk, which increased with each beer they drank.

Hearing female laughter across from him, Nicky looked over the fire at several of the girls, including Desiree. They were laughing and whispering to one another a few feet back from the fire. The girls had complained earlier that the fire was too hot for them to sit as close as the guys were, but really it was so they could have their girl talk.

Down the beach, about fifty yards, Nicky watched the shadows of Tyler and Braden as they stripped naked under the half-moon and made their way out into the water. Although the two bodies disappeared into the ocean, Tyler's high-pitched squeal and Braden's laugh were carried to shore with the waves. Nicky chuckled each time he heard Tyler squeal, as it was clear they were out there having a party just for two.

When Squirrel walked back to the fire, he looked out over the water in the direction of the squeals and cackles. "I talked to Dutch yesterday. He and super-tramp are living with her parents now. He hates selling insurance, but the money is good."

Over the squeals coming from the water, small talk made its way around the fire, mostly Austin and Andrew asking questions about their new team.

"Is that Tyler and Braden over there on the rocks?" J. B. blurted out.

Nicky stood up to get a better look and saw that Tyler was still naked, holding Braden's hand just before they disappeared over the rocks.

"What the heck?" J. B. shouted, "Did you guys see that?"

Nicky shook his head without commenting. The bravery of Tyler continued to amaze Nicky as he waited for more reactions from the guys. When nothing else was said regarding what they all undoubtedly witnessed, Nicky questioned the secrecy of his own relationship.

J. B. walked over to Desiree and sat down next to her. Nicky watched as J. B. put his arm around his girlfriend and gave her a peck on the cheek. Desiree turned and gave him a warm smile, and the two kissed again. On the other side of Desiree was a friend of hers named Raquel. Nicky had met Raquel a couple of times, but now she had caught the attention of Andrew, who was attempting to charm her with corny one-liners. Watching the whole mating and wooing in action made him think of where he really wanted to be, and this was not it. Remembering that Tyler was his ride out of here, Nicky glanced out toward the rocks.

The moon was high above their heads now, and the tide was coming in. Squirrel had left about an hour ago, and Nicky sat talking with Austin, the only other person around the fire.

"So why did you pick TBU?" Nicky asked, trying to make conversation.

"Well, my dad and his girlfriend live here, and we knew we wanted to be as far away from our mother as possible. She's psycho. We liked the program they have here, and we heard good things about Coach

Silva and Coach Dean," Austin responded. "And you?" Austin stared deep into the fire, focused as the flames flickered.

Nicky thought it was funny how Austin answered everything with "we." *It must be something twins do.* "Full ride. I couldn't pass it up. Plus, this is where Disney World and Lego Land are," Nicky joked as he avoided the truth.

Austin and Nicky sat mostly quiet as Andrew and Raquel were whispering to each other a few feet behind them. Nicky had been long ready to go, but Tyler and Braden hadn't come back yet. Nicky thought about asking the twins for a lift back to campus, but then he remembered his motorcycle was at the house where Tyler had picked him up. The house wasn't that far from campus. He could walk it in ten or fifteen minutes, he told himself. Tyler would know that he caught a ride with someone, surely. Letting out a heavy sigh, Nicky put his head down between his knees.

"Oh right, we're out of here," J. B. announced as he and Desiree stood up to leave.

"Can we drop you off?" Desiree asked as she pulled up her light jacket over her shoulders.

"No, I'm good, Tyler should be coming back any minute." Knowing J. B. would naturally assume he would need a lift back to the dorms, that would be a bad idea.

Down to the four of them, Andrew and Raquel moved closer to Nicky and Austin, trying to get warm from a dying fire that was mostly a pile of red glowing coals.

"Do you go by Nick or Nicolas?" Andrew asked as he stoked the ambers down between two glowing logs.

"Nicky's fine." *No one calls me Nick but my dad. My grandmother calls me Nicolas still.* Truth be told, Nicky didn't have a preference what name people used.

Andrew was able to get the fire going again as several smaller pieces of wood ignited. Taking a seat between his brother and Raquel, Andrew seemed satisfied with his work.

They really are identical, Nicky thought, as he searched for something to tell them apart.

Austin made eye contact with Nicky, and then looked way, "So… are you going out with anyone?" Austin looked back at Nicky.

Feeling like he had something lodged in his throat, Nicky took a deep swallow to catch his breath. He didn't know what to say. He wasn't a liar, but even more so, his relationship with their coach was not up for discussion, and he knew it.

He thought about just saying yes and then referencing to the coach as *her.* Say he met her somewhere outside of school. At least he'd have a girlfriend that he could share. But that seemed like a lot of work, something he knew he didn't want to start. Pushing that idea aside, he realized that he also didn't want them thinking he was straight. "No," Nicky murmured, wondering if they thought he was straight. Tyler and Braden, being naked, going over the rocks, holding hands, it wasn't like everybody didn't know what they were doing over there, and no one cared.

Thinking about it, Nicky also didn't care that everybody knew he was gay either, but he was certainly a lot more private than Tyler. Not being able to tell anyone about him and the coach made his stomach quiver, as if they were doing something dirty or wrong. "Well… I'm kind of seeing someone," Nicky mumbled before he could stop himself.

"Who?" Austin asked.

Damn it. Now what? Nicky wished he could take it back. "Well. I don't want to say. We just started going out. You know how it is." Nicky wondered if Austin believed him or if the whole thing sounded stupid.

"Cool, man, I get it. If she drops you, no one has to know," Austin joked as he stood up and brushed the sand off of his ass. "Well, dude, I hate to say it, but we got to go. Are you sure we can't give you a lift back to campus? I'm not sure when Tyler and Braden are coming back. I wouldn't suggest going over the rocks looking for them either."

Nicky thought about taking the offer and just calling Phillip to pick him up in front of Hayden Hall. After some processing, the lie of getting dropped off at the dorm and then finding a way to Phillip's just seemed too concocted. "No, I'm fine."

Soon after the three drove off, Tyler and Braden emerged from the dark. "Where's everyone?" Braden asked.

"Did they take the keg?" Tyler asked as he looked around for it.

"Yeah, it was Squirrel's. He didn't trust that we would return it. Austin and Andrew just left. Raquel caught a ride with them. Are you ready?" Nicky asked as he stood up, more than ready to get the hell off the beach.

By the time Tyler dropped Nicky off at the coach's house, Nicky was still stewing over why Phillip didn't want anyone to know about them. Initially, Nicky got it, accepted it at face value when the coach said it. *But who would care?* Nicky asked himself over and over.

Phillip was sitting on one end of the couch, and Emily was on the other. With no room for him, Nicky took a seat in the smaller loveseat facing Phillip. Nicky glanced at the empty bottle of wine that was sitting on the coffee table. "How's your back tonight?"

"I didn't sleep that well last night, and it's been hurting all day. I just took something. What's wrong?" Phillip asked.

"Nothing." *How would Phillip know anything was wrong?* Nicky let out a heavy sigh.

Phillip leaned forward, stretching out his back. "How was the bonfire?"

"It was all right," Nicky muttered as he watched Emily's chest go up and down as she slept.

"Spill it. Something's wrong. What happened?" Phillip asked as he sat up and turned the TV off. As the universal sign that they were going to bed, Emily's ears twitched at the sound of the TV going off.

Sliding off the couch, she took a long stretch before heading down the hall, leaving Phillip behind.

Nicky let out another heavy sigh.

"Come on, Nicky. If we're going to be together, then you have to talk to me. We have to communicate."

Not knowing where to start, Nicky just opened his mouth. "So tell me again why we're a secret. How come I can't say anything to anybody?" Nicky held eye contact, his stomach in knots for even bringing it up.

Phillip broke eye contact first, looking to see where Emily went. "I work at the school, you're on the team, and I'm the coach. I'm not sure how people will take that."

"Well, I know of other professors who are dating girls on campus. They don't get fired. Nobody cares about them." Nicky's tone was strained.

"Nicky...it's different. They're straight, and with a little more than a wink of the eye, most people don't care. But then, other professors and staff also don't respect them much, either." Phillip moved over onto the loveseat and squeezed down in next to Nicky.

"So why do we care what they think about us?" Nicky stared deep into Phillip's eyes as if he could find the answer there.

"It's not that simple. Some people, especially older people, don't look at two guys dating as the same. Because you're nineteen," Phillip paused as he rubbed his hands over his face. "Professors have tenure. It's a little harder to get rid of them. I'm not a teacher; they can fire me at will."

Nicky felt as if he wanted to die. Never having been in love before, Phillip was who he thought about every waking moment of the day. It was killing him to not be able to share with his friends the one thing that made him happier than swimming.

Phillip laid a gentle kiss on Nicky's bottom lip. "Maybe it's unfair for me to even be asking you for this. To keep a part of your life a secret just because of me."

Their faces were so close that Nicky felt the warmth of Phillip's breath, yet there were a million miles between them filled with self-doubt. Nicky had never before thought his attraction to the same sex was that complicated.

"If there is any doubt in your mind, know that I love you." Phillip leaned into Nicky and wrapped him in his arms as he squeezed. "I love you so much."

19

During that first month of the new fall semester, the campus was still busy with the vendors and clubs reaching out to the many freshmen who poured onto the university grounds. Nicky had just walked out of his history class when he bumped into his old roommate, Juan.

"Hey, Juan, good to see you," Nicky said with a smile, then innocently looked him up and down, resting on his long black eyelashes. Nicky remembered how he would stare at them, not just the eyelashes, but at his pupils, which were a dead giveaway for when he was high. Standing about three inches taller than Nicky, Juan crossed his arms, forming a barrier between them, and then took a step back.

"Oh, hey there, Nick. So you came back for another year. You swimming again?"

Nicky watched as Juan fidgeted, folding and unfolding his arms several times. "Yeah, and we have a couple of new swimmers on the team this year that are pretty damn good. It should be a good season for us. How about you? You playing soccer?"

"Naw, my parents put an end to that after last year's grades. My dad went crazy when the school almost didn't let me return because of them. Just hanging out this year. I don't care though." Juan unfolded his arms and cracked his knuckles. "I haven't seen you around the dorm; are you living on campus this year?"

"Yeah, I'm there," Nicky replied. He tried not to look away as the lie came out. Although their relationship never moved past roommate into the friend zone, he did like Juan.

"Oh yeah, what room?"

"Tyler and I are rooming this year," Nicky responded without directly answering Juan's question.

Juan's facial expression changed as he shifted his weight to his other leg. "Oh, yeah. I remember that guy. The tall blond guy, right?" Juan asked.

Since there was no doubt in anybody's mind that Tyler was gay, Nicky wondered if Juan was putting them together as a couple. *I wonder if he even knows I'm gay.*

Juan pulled out his phone and looked at it. "Look, I have to get across campus to lab. It was nice running into you."

Never being a convincing liar, Nicky felt as if Juan saw right through his bullshit and that was why he was acting weird. Seeing that he had about a half hour before his business management class, Nicky decided to walk over to the bookstore for a soda and a protein bar. He loved the campus in the fall and remembered when it was all new to him just last year. Now it was his life. Between practices and classes, he was here an average of ten hours a day.

Cutting across the lawn and under the old dogwood trees, Nicky breathed in the scent of the freshly cut grass, which made him think of home. It was always his responsibility to cut the lawn on Saturdays.

Walking into the store, he heard a voice greet him. Looking up, Nicky saw that it was that clerk that Tyler was hot for. "How's it going?" he asked as he smiled at Nicky.

"What's up?" Nicky replied, continuing to walk toward the back of the store. *He's kind of cute,* Nicky thought as he rummaged through the different flavors of protein bars on the shelf.

"So how's it going?" Said the same voice, now to the right of him. Nicky turned around and saw the clerk on his right side.

"Stuart." Extending his hand, the clerk smiled into Nicky's eyes, holding his gaze.

"Huh? Oh, how are you? I'm Nicky." He took Stuart's hand, his eye contact making Nicky uncomfortable.

"If you're looking for a good bar to try, I love the mint chocolate chip one. It's as good as candy," Stuart said as he continued to stare at Nicky.

Nicky broke the eye contact, turning his focus back to the shelf of protein bars. "Thanks, I'll try it," Nicky said as he reached for the bar that Stuart just recommended.

"I'm off at five; you wanna grab a coffee or something?"

Every time Nicky went to look at him, Stuart's green eyes were locked onto him. "I just live around the corner," Stuart added suggestively. When Nicky looked down at Stuart's hands, Stuart was rubbing one of his hands across his crotch and then gently squeezed it. "I'm sure you like coffee, don't you?"

As naïve as Nicky was, even he picked up that Stuart was coming on to him. "I have class. Then swim practice tonight. Sorry," Nicky muttered. Nicky grabbed the protein bar from the shelf. "See you around."

Not taking any chances that Stuart would return to his register up front, Nicky took his purchase all the way to the south entrance of the store.

When Nicky made it outside, he smirked at what Tyler was going to say when he told him what happened. He would inflate the story just a little, maybe put Stuart in some baggy sweatpants with no underwear. Add a raging woody that stuck up over his bellybutton. Tyler would scream like a fat woman in a Baptist church when he was done with his story. He could give Tyler a little dose of his own medicine.

When Nicky made it to the aquatic center that evening, he was physically exhausted. A morning practice, two classes, and now another practice, he questioned how he was going to get through the next two hours. Just thinking about all the work his history professor had

doled out this morning and the required reading he had to do tonight made him feel sick. At the moment, this whole college experience his family told him to enjoy was anything but fun.

Walking into the locker room, he had forgotten that the coaches
had announced during their morning practice that there was a mandatory team meeting this evening. Scanning the room, Nicky looked
to see who all was already here. *No J. B. or Braden.*

Nicky slipped on his Speedo and grabbed his goggles to clean
them while he waited for the coaches.

As other swimmers arrived, everyone gathered into one row of
the lockers just outside the coaches' office. Within a couple of minutes, Coach Silva and Coach Dean both walked out. Looking off to
the corner, Nicky watched as J. B. blended in with his teammates.

"Listen up, guys." Coach Dean cleared his throat. "This week we
swim against Orlando. They'll be here Thursday night, so we are
moving practice up one hour to allow them time in the pool that
night. This should be an easy win for us," Coach Dean barked.

"So that means everyone needs to take a piss in it before we get
out right?" Connor laughed.

"You're such a dumbass. We'll be in that same water the next
morning," Austin responded. "I don't know about the rest of you, but
I prefer not to drink your piss."

"If you two are done, I'll finish?" Coach Dean's tone told them he
was obviously annoyed at the interruption. "I'm posting the lineup
for Friday's meet. You can check it after practice tonight."

"Let's hit the water. Freestyle. We go until the whistle," Coach Silva
added as he slapped his hand on his clipboard, making a loud smack.

As they all filed out to the pool, Tyler tapped Nicky on his side.
"What am I swimming this Friday? I know you know."

Nicky chuckled. "It's the same thing you always swim, but he also
put me and Austin in that race," Nicky mumbled under his breath as
he slowed his walk. Not wanting to be overheard, Nicky lowered his
voice to a whisper, "He wants me to push Austin. He knows Austin
wants to beat me."

Tyler stopped in his tracks. "So me swimming in this race doesn't matter? What makes you guys so sure I won't take it?" Tyler snipped. "You do know that I can swim, don't you?"

"Hey, if you can beat us, have at it. It's anybody's race," Nicky said. "So, what's between you and Braden the other night, and where is he?" Nicky started walking again.

Tyler laughed, "What do you think happened?" Tyler stepped ahead of him, cutting him off as they made their way through the gate.

"No way! Behind the rocks?" Nicky tried to whisper. "Why didn't you say anything in the car when you dropped me off?" This time, it was Nicky who stopped.

"Hello! As soon as you got in the car, you were all pissy," Tyler replied with a bitchy tone.

"Sorry about that. What did you guys do?" Nicky couldn't image that Braden would let Tyler fuck him with other people so close by.

"I jacked him off first, behind the rocks. Then after I dropped you off, he came over to our dorm and we..."

"When you two love birds have time to swim, you're welcome to join us in the pool!" Coach Dean's voice echoed with a boom.

Seeing that everyone else was already in the pool, and Coach Dean was staring right at them, Nicky double-checked his drawstring. "You're telling me the rest later!"

"I just love not having you there," Tyler said as he adjusted his cap, tucking his ears under it as he took his lane.

Wondering what happened in his old room, Nicky hurriedly jumped into the pool before Coach Dean became unglued. *He's lying,* Nicky thought before he turned his complete focus on swimming.

They swam one lap after the next, with Coach Dean yelling from the side of the pool as he walked each lap alongside of them. "Come on, Andrew! Let's look like you are at least trying to keep up! Let's go, ladies!"

Connor was in the lane next to Nicky, slightly behind him. Nicky knew he was drafting off of him, so he moved to the rope on his opposite side to shake him. Coach Dean yelled, "Watch your stroke length, Nicky. Pull it out!"

"Are we going to kick Orlando's ass this week?" Coach Paul could be heard shouting. "You're not a fish, J. B., you need to breathe. One, two three, breathe. This is basic swimming 101!"

They had been in the pool for over an hour moving through the various strokes before Coach Dean blew the whistle, signaling they were done. Nicky glided into the wall and then dipped down under his rope, crossing three lanes over to Tyler and J. B.

Blowing the water out of his nose, Tyler was fighting to catch his breath. "Damn, that was rough."

Breathing heavy as well, Nicky glanced over and saw that Braden had shown up at some point and was staring in their direction. "So are you crushing on Braden?" Nicky asked Tyler as he peeped over at him. "He's hot."

"Oh, hell no." Tyler took a swig of water in and sprayed it back out of his mouth. "He's a hot mess. Worse than me. I had to cut that shit loose."

"You're not right," J. B. murmured as they all climbed out of the pool.

Loving the feel of his abs after a workout, Nicky poked at them as he counted all eight of them. They were tight and drawn in, showing every muscle in his stomach. For one of the shortest swimmers on the team, he got his strength from his shorter muscular legs. He saw so many swimmers with skinny legs and arms and wondered where their power came from.

Back in the locker room, Austin caught Nicky as he was opening his locker. "Hey, Nicky, anything going on tonight?" he asked.

"Not sure. I'm heading home. I have a ton of studying to do," Nicky replied.

"Austin! I told you we're heading to the Harbor to shoot pool," Austin's twin shouted from three lockers down. "Nicky, you can ride with us if you want to go," he added in a friendlier tone.

Austin tore off his wet Speedo and walked over to the table of clean towels. "I was just asking if anything else was going on." Austin scurried off into the shower where four teammates were teasing Squirrel about his faux Mohawk.

By the time everyone was showered and dressed, Coach Dean and Coach Paul had already left. Declining Andrew's offer, Nicky finished dressing and headed out. Passing the coaches' office, he saw Phillip studying video footage. Nicky continued on outside toward his motorcycle.

The fresh air was welcoming after working up a sweat in the pool and then being stuck in the musty locker room with the hot showers running. As he jumped on his bike, feeling horny, he hoped Phillip wouldn't be too long.

That Friday morning, when Phillip and Nicky woke up, Nicky was charged and feeling good about that day's meet against Orlando State. Rolling over, he was surprised Phillip was gone already. Hearing the shower running, he realized he was still in the house. Nicky crawled out of bed, hoping he wasn't too late for a little shower sex as a relief from the tension growing about the meet.

With Phillip's back to him, Nicky eased past the shower curtain, slipping into the shower behind Phillip, who was rinsing soap from his hair and face. Nicky's dick instantly swelled as he stared at the soapy water running down Phillip's back and through the crack of his fuzzy butt. He loved Phillip's muscular butt, reaching out and cupping it with his hand.

At the touch of Nicky's hand, Phillip jumped, startled by another's presence. "Hey, what are you doing in here?" he asked.

Nicky pulled on Phillip's meaty tool and smiled. "Well, I was hoping to get a little of that this morning." Continuing to gently tug on Phillip's penis, Nicky smiled as Phillip took note of Nicky's hard-on pointing right at him.

As Nicky begged for it, he saw that Phillip was frowning. "Are you okay?" he asked.

"Not really," Phillip responded. "My back is killing me this morning."

"Oh, can I do anything?"

"No, just hoping the water loosens it up a bit," Phillip responded with a slight grunt.

"How often are you in pain?" Nicky took the shared loofah from Phillip and squeezed the excess soap out of it before running it under the water.

"Pretty much all the time. The doctors say this is only the beginning. As I get older, it will probably get worse. The medication isn't doing the trick."

"I'm sorry, honey," Nicky replied, forgetting about having sex. Nicky poured soap onto the loofah and started with his armpits. "Do you need me to do anything for you before I take off?"

"If you could load the car for me, that would be great. I'm heading over to the director's office this morning. I'll meet you at the pool at noon," Phillip grumbled to Nicky.

Nicky finished lathering up the rest of his body as he watched Phillip. Overcome with sadness at the sight of his boyfriend struggling to just finish his shower, Nicky didn't know what else to do but watch.

"Are you going to be able to make it today? Do you want me to call Coach Dean or Paul?" Nicky asked.

"Hopefully, the meds will kick in soon," Phillip said as he rinsed the last of the soap off his body and stepped out. "Before I forget, I invited Steven and his partner Martin over for dinner this Saturday. You'll love Martin. He's funny." Phillip patted the towel across his chest, drying himself off in front of the mirror.

When Nicky had finished loading Phillip's car, he ran back inside to kiss Phillip goodbye before heading out for his morning class. When he walked into the bedroom, he was surprised that Phillip was sitting on the edge of the bed still naked.

"Are you okay?" Nicky asked as he kneeled down in front of Phillip.

"Yeah, I'm fine. I just need a minute for the painkillers to kick in."

Nicky grabbed the little box that was lying next to Phillip's thigh and read the label. "What's a Fen-ta-nyl patch?" he asked.

"It's just pain medication on a patch that gets absorbed through the skin. It's easier to take it that way," Phillip told him, taking the box back. "Go to class. I'll be all right."

Concerned and a little surprised, as he never realized what the patch was for, Nicky stared at his lover before tenderly kissing him on the top of his head and then heading out to campus.

Nicky was pleased with his performance at the Orlando meet that evening. He swam his fastest time in the 400 freestyle, taking the win from Austin in the last twenty yards of the pool. Nicky knew at the beginning of the race that Austin's pace was too fast in his first 100 yards. Nicky dropped back to third until he knew that Austin was feeling the burn. He knew Austin wouldn't be able to hold that pace. At 300 yards, Nicky pushed Austin and then backed off a couple of times. Playing the whole cat-and-mouse game would mess with Austin's mind. When Austin had nothing left, Nicky overtook him, touching the wall in just less than four minutes.

As Nicky sat on the sidelines regaining his breath, he overheard two of his teammates talking about the upcoming 1,000-yard race.

"Did you say that I was added to the race?" Nicky asked, thinking he must have heard them wrong.

"Yeah. Coach Dean pulled me and added you. I'm swimming your 100 backstroke instead," one of the swimmers replied.

Nicky couldn't believe what he was hearing. "I can't swim the 1,000. I just got done swimming the 400. That would kill me." Nicky rose to his feet, looking for Phillip to verify if this was true.

When Nicky approached Phillip, he interrupted the conversation he was having with two other swimmers. "I'm really swimming the

1,000 next? I just got done with the 400. I'm *not* swimming the 1,000 on top of that!"

Phillip turned, looking at Nicky as if he didn't know who he was. "What? What are you talking about? Can you not see that I'm having a conversation?" Phillip snapped.

Nicky heard in Phillip's tone that he had overstepped and that he was angry, but Nicky was mad, too. As he waited off to the side to talk to Phillip, he heard the whistle for the call of the 1,000. Phillip was ignoring him, and Nicky was baffled as to what he should do. When he heard the whistle a second time, he knew he had to take his place on the block or be disqualified.

"Nicky! They called your race; let's go! Get into position!" Coach Dean bellowed out.

Nicky blew out a large sigh as he stripped his cover shorts off. Taking his place on the block between Connor and the favorite to win, Rusty Ferreira, the junior from Orlando, Nicky thought about the forty laps he had to do, hoping his arms would hold up.

By the end of the race, every muscle in Nicky's body was on fire. Sinking just below the surface of the water, he needed a moment to catch his breath before trying to climb onto the deck. He pulled his body up out of the water; he was pissed about having to swim that race. His stomach flexing as his lungs fought for air, Nicky stared up at his time on the board, seeing that he got it done, placing third. As expected, Connor took second, and Rusty Ferreira came in a one one-hundredth of a second faster than Connor.

Looking over at Phillip, the coach's face was cold. Making eye contact for a brief second, the coach turned his back to him. Nicky didn't care; he was just as mad.

After the meet, Nicky walked out of the aquatic center with every muscle in his body hurting. He had no idea how he was going to ride his motorcycle in the shape he was in. When he looked across the parking lot, he saw someone standing next to Phillip's car. When he looked closer, he saw that Phillip was sitting in his car with the window down, talking to the person. Nicky didn't recognize who it was, taking a closer look at the thin male who was leaning into the window. Nicky took one more look, making sure he didn't know who the guy was, before putting on his helmet and driving out of the parking lot.

When Nicky arrived home, he first fed Emily and then rehydrated his body, drinking copious amounts of water. He anticipated Phillip couldn't have been that far behind him. His body still hurting, Nicky lay down on the couch under the ceiling fan in hopes that would do the trick. "That was such bullshit," he mumbled to himself.

Twenty minutes later when Phillip came in, Nicky was still lying under the ceiling fan, replaying the way Phillip had yelled at him in front of everyone. Phillip walked passed him without speaking into the kitchen. Rolling his eyes, Nicky hesitated but got up and followed him into the kitchen.

"So I take it you're mad at me?" Nicky asked softly.

Phillip poured himself a glass of wine. Staring at Nicky, Phillip took a sip before speaking. "No, I'm not mad at you, and I'm sorry that I snapped at you. I was as completely caught off guard as you were about you being switched, but I was right in the middle of some other bullshit that Dean was trying to pull. I'm sorry."

Nicky took a seat at the bar. "So what happened?"

"I don't know yet, but despite whatever he was doing, it should have gone through me first."

"What does *despite* mean?" Nicky asked.

Phillip cracked a smile and let out a slight snicker. Crossing his arms in front of him, he shook his head. Nicky stood there as the muscles in Phillip's jaw relaxed and a smile overtook his frown. "Come here," Phillip stated, opening his arms to Nicky.

Standing in the kitchen, the two held one another for several minutes, Nicky's face against Phillip's chest. "I love you so much," Phillip whispered before placing a gentle kiss on the top of Nicky's head. "I haven't had a chance to talk to Dean about what happened today, but I will."

By mid-morning the next day, all had returned to normal between them as they prepared for their guests that evening. Just after six o'clock that night, Nicky had just come out of the shower and could hear Phillip in the kitchen.

"Is there anything I can do to help?" Nicky stood at the entry of the kitchen with just a towel wrapped around his waist. His abs and biceps were still hard from the workout they received yesterday. "Damn, it smells good in here," Nicky added as he came up behind Phillip and placed a kiss on his back shoulder.

"No, just make sure we have ice in the bar in the living room. And you may want to put on a shirt, although Martin would like it if you didn't."

"So tell me again which one is Steven and which one is Martin?" Although he didn't say so, Nicky was nervous about meeting Phillip's friends and wondered if they would like him.

"Steven is the younger one, and Martin is the little fat one. Just remember *Steven the stick* because he's skinny and *Martin the marble* because he's round." With Phillip's little laugh, Nicky felt just a little more relaxed.

Within minutes, Nicky saw Steven and Martin's black BMW as they pulled up in front of the house. "Honey, they're here," Nicky called out.

Phillip was in the middle of stuffing the pork tenderloin, and his hands were covered in olive oil. "Can you let them in? I'll be right there."

"But I don't know them," Nicky replied as he ran into the kitchen.

"All you have to do is let them in. I'll be right there," Phillip snapped as he hurried to get the meat in the oven.

Hearing the doorbell ring twice in rapid succession, Nicky sluggishly made his way to the entryway and opened the door. Nervously, he smiled at the two men. "Hello." Nicky said, "Come in. Phillip's in the kitchen."

Martin stepped in first, handing off a warm tray wrapped in foil to Nicky. "Cuban Bacardi rum cake, my mother's recipe. She used to say if you can't be sweet, then bring something sweet." Martin did the sign of the cross, ending with a kiss to his fingers.

The warm, sweet aroma of sugar and rum quickly invaded Nicky's nose, causing instant hunger pains in his belly. Looking at both Steven and Martin, Nicky noticed they appeared to be his parents' age, which took him by surprise. Martin was short and wearing a bright purple shirt and yellow pants that did nothing for his round shape. Steven appeared a bit more normal in his appearance, giving Nicky a warm smile as he extended his hand to greet him.

By the time their guests stepped inside, Phillip had arrived in the entryway. "Hey, guys, how are you?"

The men stood in the entryway, briefly hugging and exchanging pleasantries. Nicky was standing just slightly behind them when Martin took a step closer to him. "So this must be the Nicolas I've been hearing so much about."

Nicky felt that he was being checked out from head to toe as Martin's eyes inappropriately moved up and down him.

"Aren't you delicious?" Martin said as he turned to Phillip. "I've stolen a mother's child from her, but never her baby... Good job, Trixie."

Nicky was taken aback by Martin's brassiness, not knowing how to take him and wondering who Trixie was. Uncertain if Martin was making fun of him, Nicky sensed they were laughing at him, and he didn't know why. Either way, he knew he didn't like it. Nicky lingered slightly behind as the group moved into the living room, still talking about him as if he wasn't in the room.

"What can I get you to drink?" Phillip asked the two of them as he took their jackets.

Steven asked for a gin and tonic as he followed Phillip over to the corner where the bar was.

"I'll take a glass of champagne if you have any chilled," Martin asked.

"I do as a matter of fact, just not out here. Nicky, can you look in the fridge and grab the champagne?" Phillip walked over to the bar to make cocktails.

When Nicky returned with the champagne, he asked, "Is this the right one?" holding up a 2009 black bottle of Laurent-Perrier.

"I'm not sure it's even legal for you to drink, but I do hope you'll join me in a glass of bubbly, princess." Martin smiled as he took the bottle from Nicky.

Nicky knew he didn't want anything that Martin was offering, sub-consciously moving closer to Phillip for protection. Nicky stood at the end of the bar, watching Phillip as he mixed a drink for Steven and himself. "Baby, what can I get you to drink?" Nicky was surprised that Phillip was directing the question to him.

"I think I'll just have a soda," Nicky answered as he watched the monster that had positioned itself at the other end of the bar. Although they looked nothing alike, Martin made him think of Tyler. Was it his laugh, the loud voice, or how he could be bitchy and make it sound nice? Tyler was a "Martin" in the making, with the exception of the hair on Martin's head, which looked like a dead rat laying up there.

Listening to the three of them talk, Nicky drank his soda and wondered whether it was still okay to have something a little stronger than a soda.

"So Steven told me that you guys are getting a new priest at Holy Trinity?" Phillip was directing his question at Martin, although he was watching Nicky, who was scratching Emily behind her ears.

"Oh dear, yes. This interim priest we've been suffering through for the last year is going to get the boot. Our permanent priest is coming on the first." Martin shook his head as if he had pity on the old soul.

"The priest who's coming is supposedly out, and even has a part-ner," Steven interjected.

"He's gay?" Nicky asked, thinking he said the priest was gay. This was the first time Nicky had taken part in their conversation since they arrived.

"Yes," Steven and Martin said simultaneously.

Nicky knew little about any churches other than the tiny Catholic Church he and his family would visit on Christmas Eve and Easter Sunday. But what he did know was that a gay priest and the Church were like oil and water. Glancing at Martin, Nicky thought it was a little weird that Steven and Martin even went to church, being gay and all. "So how can a priest be gay?"

Martin adjusted his napkin in his lap before resting his champagne glass on it. "Child, I take it you've never spent a lot of time around a priest, have you? We attend the Episcopal Church. It's like a Catholic Church, but modern. Think of it as Catholic 2.0. They're for full legal equality of gays and lesbians, and they allow gays and women to serve as priests."

Nicky stared at Martin, unsure that he was telling him the truth. Looking at Phillip, who smiled and gave him a little wink, reassured Nicky they weren't bullshitting him.

"Father Morales and his partner will be here in two weeks. I Googled him, and he's cute. I guess at one time he was a Catholic priest in Colorado. I think Denver."

"I can't believe you Googled him," Phillip joked as Steven rolled his eyes at his husband.

"I Googled you too," Martin said as he pointed one of his fat little fingers at Phillip.

As the conversation turned to people Nicky didn't know, he grew bored again. Trying not to stare, Nicky watched both Steven and Martin. They were probably a lot older than his parents. He thought about those times when his parents had friends over for dinner and he couldn't wait to be excused to his room until dinner was ready. Again, he sat waiting to be excused, but knew it wasn't going to happen tonight.

"So how do you like Florida?" Steven directed his question to Nicky.

It was a second before Nicky realized that Steven was addressing him. "Oh, huh? Me? Yeah, I like it," Nicky responded.

"So what was it about Tampa that made you choose us?" Martin asked.

Nicky thought about being honest and telling them he just wanted Phillip to fuck his brains out. "It was the aquatics program the school was investing in. Me and my parents liked Coach Silva. I mean, Phillip." Stumbling over his words, Nicky took a breath. "Plus it was far away from home," he added as he nodded.

"Have you had a chance to go to Disney World yet?" Martin asked.

Nicky picked up on Martin's tone as if he was addressing a child. He so wished he could have said no, but he had gone at least four different times with various campus groups since he had been here and loved it each time.

"Yeah, I have. Have you been?" Nicky directed the backhanded insult back to Martin.

The night didn't get any better for Nicky. By the end, he was feeling like a fish out of water as the three dominated the conversation. He couldn't look at Martin without thinking how much he wanted to punch the old man in his mouth just for breathing.

When Steven and Martin prepared to leave just after eleven o'clock, the four of them stood at the doorway exchanging polite hugs and kisses as if they would never see each other again. Nicky was exhausted and just wanted to go to bed as Martin reached for a hug from him.

As Martin hugged him, Nicky felt his hands rub down his back and then slide down across his ass before Martin let go. Martin tapped Nicky in the middle of his chest three times. "Steven, we must go see this one in the pool."

Once the door was closed, the two started turning off all the lights in the house. "So what did you think of them?" Phillip asked as he felt under the lampshade for the off switch.

Not sure how to answer the question, Nicky gathered several of the glasses that were left on the coffee table before speaking. "Is Steven younger than Martin?"

"Yes, maybe ten or twelve years. I think Steven is around forty, so Martin is around fifty or so, I think," Phillip responded.

Fifty sounded really old to Nicky, as he picked up the dessert plates from the end of the bar and followed Phillip into the kitchen.

"Let's just put it all in the sink and take care of them of the morning," Phillip told him, putting what little food was still out into the refrigerator and turning off the kitchen light. "Come on, babe, let's go to bed; it's late." Phillip extended his arm and wrapped it around Nicky's neck.

❧

That Sunday morning, Nicky and Phillip lay in bed while Emily was curled up in her own bed, an old loveseat that she commandeered as her own. Since Nicky moved in, she was no longer permitted to sleep in the bed, so she took to the loveseat on Phillip's side of the bed.

"Are you awake?" Nicky asked as he moved his hands over Phillip's nipples.

"Yeah, I'm just laying here."

"How's your back? You looked like you were doing better yesterday," Nicky said.

"It comes and goes. I'm always in pain. I just mask it." Phillip turned and gave Nicky a gentle kiss.

"Do you feel like messing around?" Nicky sheepishly asked as he pressed his hard dick against Phillip's thighs. "I'll do all the work, I promise," Nicky added as he stared into Phillip's brown eyes and then back at his protruding nipples.

Phillip knew Nicky wasn't going to take no for an answer, as much as he wanted to say it. He lifted the covers up, revealing his naked body to Nicky, inviting him to fire up the equipment necessary for him to give Nicky what he was really asking for.

20

F all having turned into winter, Nicky still could not get used to the lack of a real change in the weather. Christmas was not Christmas without snow, but that was never going to happen in the Sunshine State.

Nicky sang Christmas carols as he rinsed the remaining soap off his body and then towel-dried himself in front of the large vanity mirror. He loved this bathroom, larger than his whole dorm room; it was open to the master suite with a separate tub and shower. He had never seen a house that had both; it was always a combination of the two. Hanging his towel up, he first applied lotion to his entire body in attempt to prevent the dry skin caused by always being in the water.

Looking at the time on the alarm clock on Phillip's side of the bed, he knew he only had a couple of minutes before Phillip would be coming in. Slipping on his jeans and a red TBU hoodie, he wanted to be ready to go when Phillip came in from a last-minute meeting with his boss.

Tonight, the plan was to go Christmas tree shopping and decorate the inside of the house. The fall classes were even harder than last year's, and he didn't even want to think about the upcoming spring semester.

Nicky had told his parents that because of how the swim meets fell in December, he had to stay in training but would be able to fly home on the twenty-fourth and could stay until the twenty-sixth. The real plan was that he and Phillip were going to have their Christmas together on the night of the twenty-third, which was three days from now.

That evening, when they arrived at the Christmas tree lot, Nicky could smell the sweet scent of pine; they walked the lot, looking for the perfect tree for the house. Earlier in the week, Phillip had given Nicky one of his credit cards and told him to buy the decorations for the tree. Phillip had made the mistake of saying that his mother had always handled the decorating around the house. Only after Nicky jokingly called him a pig did Phillip see the error in his thinking. It wasn't until they got the tree home that night that they realized Nicky had bought enough decorations and lights for three or four trees.

Late into the night, they laughed and played as they decorated the tree and Emily watched, baffled as to what they were doing with a tree in the house. "I can't believe you never decorated a Christmas tree," Nicky stated.

"I can't believe you've never had a *real* Christmas tree," Phillip joked.

"My parents are way too cheap to get a real tree when they can reuse that same plastic tree that we've had all my life. I never heard of a real tree until probably my senior year in high school, I think. So your family always had real trees?" Nicky asked.

"Yeah. It was a big thing in Texas. We always went shopping for it on a Saturday morning. We went to a Christmas tree farm just outside of Imperial and cut one down. Then my dad would have to shape the bottom, and my mom would hose it down before he could bring it in the house, so it wouldn't get decorated until Sunday night. The whole weekend was about decorating the house; it was my mother's favorite holiday. Not the gift part of it, but just the spirit of the holiday."

"My mom too! Christmas and Easter were the only times my parents were religious." Nicky had to pause for another kiss from Phillip. The game they played was anytime they put something on the tree that began with a vowel, they had to kiss. As the night continued, the kisses got longer and more heated.

The night before Nicky was to fly home, Phillip put together a small Christmas meal for the two of them. After dinner, Nicky told Phillip to wait for him in the living room next to the Christmas tree. Nicky slipped into the bedroom and changed into a pair of red socks that came up to his knees, a red jockstrap, and a Santa hat. When he emerged, Phillip smiled from ear to ear at the sight of his half-naked elf.

Nicky loved being sexy for Phillip, as he knew how much it drove him crazy. He teased Phillip as he brushed his bare bottom against him and then moved away. Each time Phillip went to put his hands on Nicky's ass, Nicky would wave his fingers at him and remind him that he had to be good. If Phillip had his way, Nicky knew he would have had him naked within two minutes. Nicky hummed "Silent Night" as he purposefully exposed his ass and pretended to look under the tree for a specific gift he had gotten him.

"Oh, here it is," Nicky said, handing Phillip the first of many presents he had bought for him. When Phillip had given Nicky his Visa, he had told him to use it for the decorations, presents, and his flight home.

Phillip smiled as he took the present. "Thank you, sir. What is it?" Phillip asked.

"Open it, silly." Nicky watched Philip, who was undoubtedly more interested in unwrapping him than the present.

Phillip unwrapped the bow and then gently peeled the paper off around the box. "How did you know I wanted one?" Phillip held up the newest version of the iPhone.

"Because your phone sucks? Because it's is so old and your screen is all jacked up?"

Phillip then reached under the tree and grabbed a gift for Nicky. "Here you go, sexy man."

Nicky tore into the box, only to find a smaller box inside it. After tearing into the second box, he had to open three more before he got to the final box, which was a jewelry box. Staring at Phillip, Nicky opened the box and found a large Burberry watch.

"Turn it over."

Nicky turned the watch over and read the engraving: *You have a way of making time stand still. I love you – P.S.*

"I love it; thank you so much," Nicky said as he first put the watch on and then flung his half-naked body into Phillip's arms.

Immediately, their kiss went into overdrive due to the surge of sexual tension that had been building all night. Phillip laid Nicky's body down on the carpet next to the Christmas tree. Finally within arm's reach, Phillip went to peel off the jock strap from Nicky's slender waist.

"Not so fast, mister," Nicky murmured into Phillip's ear, redirecting him to his lips.

"Please." Phillip's sanity was on the fringe, and he didn't know how long he would last. Phillip rolled his hand across the front of the jockstrap, feeling how full it had become. "Please," he begged.

Nicky went in for another kiss, sealing their mouths as one, not giving in to his lover's desire.

Phillip melted, slowly lowering his weight over Nicky, allowing his erection to push against him. "You're maddening."

"You've got all night to play with your gift." Nicky grabbed Phillip's face again, this time nibbling on his ear as he let out a light moan.

Under the twinkling lights, the two bodies ignited into a sea of pleasure, soaring higher than they ever had before.

21

J. B. sat behind the steering wheel of Desiree's car as he drove his mother through the front gates of Marshall County State Penitentiary. He never got past the eerie feeling of being on prison grounds, the grey building, and the men above him in the guard towers holding rifles. The smell of body odor, bad food, and shit all rolled into one was distinctive only to prison grounds.

As he circled around looking for a parking space close to the visiting processing center, his cell phone rang. J. B. looked at the screen and saw that it was Nicky. "Hey, what up, man," J. B. said.

After a moment, J. B. responded, "Man, I wish I could, but I'm out of town right now. I'll be back tonight; call me around ten." J. B. hung up the phone and put it in the glove box, out of sight of anyone wandering around in the parking lot. "That was my boy, Nicky. You know that white dude I told you about—the one I swim with. He wanted me to take a look at his bike and play some pool later."

Out of respect, J. B. felt the need to explain to his mother who was calling him. He knew she worried he would end up like his brothers, even though he promised time and time again that he wouldn't.

J. B. and Momma B. sat in the car, emptying their pockets and ensuring they only had the things they could take in with them. He had made the mistake once before of having his cell phone on him. One of the guards accused him of attempting to smuggle it inside.

They revoked his visiting privileges for three months because of it. Since Momma B. didn't drive, the punishment impacted her as well.

He and his mother entered the visiting processing center, which was full of other family members being processed. The line was long, and J. B. knew it would take at least two hours before they were inside and visiting with Clifford. He couldn't understand why they couldn't have a better system in place that did not take valuable time away from the family's actual visit.

He remembered one time last year, when they arrived late; by the time they were inside, they only had forty-five minutes left before visiting hours were over. He learned that, if he had his mother there first thing in the morning, they would be in by ten o'clock and could visit with Clifford most of the day.

As usual, Saturdays were full of visitors, all showing up at the same time, bright and early. Once inside the visiting room, J. B. found a table for him and his mother as they waited for Clifford to be processed in from the other side. The visiting area was full of mothers and fathers, women with children, and the usual hookers and hoes visiting their pimps. The large room was full of tables, chairs, and vending machines. It was divided into four squares by an imaginary wall. The blacks took one corner, the Mexicans took the next, and the whites were on the other side of the room, next to the Asians. Although the room was not designed that way, it was Prison 101 to never mix with the other races, so the visiting families followed that unwritten rule as well.

When Clifford came through the door, J. B. thought he looked good. J. B. noticed he was a little heavier than the last time they saw him, and he had shaved his head bald. He wore the standard prison clothes: black boots, denim pants, and a white shirt with his prison number sewn on the front. The guard buzzed him through the final door into the visiting room, and Clifford smiled when he saw his waiting family.

They exchanged a quick hug before a guard could intervene, reminding them of the prison's rule of no body contact. They took their seats at one of the many metal tables inside the visiting room. J. B.'s mother caught him up on everything that was going on in the neighborhood, in church, and at work. Clifford had never been much of a talker, so he sat and listened to Momma B. go on about nothing and everything.

J. B. sat and listened as well while he watched the interactions between other prisoners and their families. It was all the same; whether on the black, white, Mexican, or Asian side, they all looked sad and lifeless as they went through the motions.

J. B. was off in his own world when his mother spoke to him. "Boy, Clifford axed you a question."

"I'm sorry, man. I was checking out this ho behind you with that dude. What up?" J. B. responded. No sooner than the word "ho" had come out of his mouth, J. B. saw the look on his mother's face and knew he shouldn't have been so crude.

"I asked you how school was going. What classes are you taking this semester?" Clifford repeated with a fatherly tone.

"I got philosophy, Spanish II, accounting, and world history this semester," J. B. replied.

"Money's good? Got enough for books and the things you need?" Clifford asked as he looked at J. B., who sat glaring back.

"I'm good. I don't need your money. I got this," J. B. answered in an unsteady voice. J. B. knew that Clifford had never held a job a day in his life and any money he was offering was drug money.

"Boy, don't be a fool. Take the money if you need it. You think these white folks you hang out with are going to help you if you need money? Go on, take the damn money if you need it!" Clifford snapped. "Don't let pride be the thing that stops you from gettin' yo' education."

"I said I'm good!" J. B. shot back in a low, intensified tone.

"Boys, relax. Clifford, I'm sure Jeremy would take the money, just as I would if we needed it, but we're managing. Thank you for the offer." Momma B. had a way of bringing a subject to a halt. "Now, Clifford, are you still going to church on Sundays? Sister Bertha from our church was talking about gettin' the choir together and comin' up and singing for ya'll. Can they do that?" she asked.

"Not sure, Momma, I guess they would have to contact the warden or somebody for permission," Clifford answered.

It was a long day for J. B. as he sat at the table listening to his mother talk while his brother ate up everything they bought him from the vending machines. After about an hour, he was usually ready to go. He squirmed in the hard plastic chair trying to get comfortable—to sit there for five hours was torture for him. Occasionally, Clifford would throw him a question, asking about Desiree, sports, and the homeboys across the street. By the end of the day, his mother had the best day of her life, and J. B. was ready to punch the wall.

When J. B. and his mother arrived back at the house, the sun was setting, and the "thugs" were coming out to play. J. B. pulled the car up to the curb and turned the ignition off. His mother shot him a look and then exited the car, walking into the house with no concern about what those boys were doing across the street.

"What up J. B.!" Ray-Ray shouted out to him. "Been up to Marshall to see my boy?" he asked.

"Yeah, he's doing all right," J. B. replied as he strolled across the street and shook each of their hands, street style. "What up, Tiny, Lil' Kev," he said as he nodded to the other two. "He said he'll be in touch with you, Ray-Ray."

"Yeah, that's yo' bro, runnin' shit from inside the pen. Ain't no runnin' from him," Tiny chirped in as he grabbed the front of his pants, trying to hold them up.

J. B. stayed out with the boys for just a couple of minutes, knowing Desiree was in the house watching the girls while he and his mother were gone all day.

When J. B. walked into the house, he could smell sweet potato pie. "Damn, who's cooking that pie?" J. B. hollered out. "What ya'll have for dinner?"

Desiree appeared from the kitchen. "Who you think is cooking that pie? We had spaghetti and catfish. Got some left in the fridge for you."

"What's the occasion for the pie?" J. B. asked as he took off his cap, throwing it on the back of the couch.

"There's no occasion; Tina and Dee-Dee wanted to know how to cook one, so we walked to the store and got what we needed. They did well." Desiree said as J. B. pulled her up into his arms.

"Damn, baby, I love you," he told her, moving in for a kiss.

After dinner, Desiree, J. B., and his baby sister Penny sat on the couch, watching TV. When Momma B. emerged from her room, she had changed into her red and black 7-11 shirt. "Ya'll, I got to run. J. B., I'll see you in the morning."

After about an hour, J. B. picked up Penny's sleepy, limp body and carried her into his mother's room, which they shared. He thought about waking her up to brush her teeth and change her into her pajamas. Tired himself, though, he tucked her into his mother's bed and walked out, leaving the door cracked enough that a little light shined into the room for her.

When he returned to the living room, Desiree was up and putting on her coat. "Where you going?" J. B. asked.

"I got to get home. I have church in the morning, and I haven't had a chance to study all day," she responded as she kissed J. B. on his beautifully shaped lips.

"Really? I was hoping you could stay just a little while longer, if you know what I mean?" J. B. lowered his head and made a pouty face.

"Yeah, I do know what you mean—that's why I'm jumping up out of here. Not tonight, baby," Desiree told him as she kissed him again before walking out the door.

22

That Monday night, as Rory sat in the student lounge waiting for his math tutor, he couldn't believe that he was back in school. After being thrown out of TBU and having to get a job, Tampa Community College was the only school left in the area that would take him.

Rory was from the Bronx, and although gay, he was known on his block to be a fighter. As he was one of the only white kids in the neighborhood, his father used to tell him to punch or be punched. Rory's shoulder length hair was the color of black coal, masking a good portion of his long, narrow face. His lips were full, which made him appear to be pouting. Although he lacked charm, there was something about him that was exotic and sexy.

There were only a couple students in the lounge during the evening, which made it easier for his tutor to pick him out in the room. As she approached him, her face lit up with a warm smile. "You must be Rory? I'm Desiree." She extended her hand to him. "Thanks for calling me; it's so nice to finally meet you." Desiree dropped her backpack on the table and emptied her books, laying them in front of Rory.

"So tell me again what math class you have," she said.

"Math AB109," he responded.

"Do you want to learn it, or just pass the class? That will make a difference in how much time we spend on this book. Some people just have better math skills. It's really about what side of your brain is dominant," Desiree explained as she searched for the right book among the many she had packed.

"I don't know. I guess I just want to get through this class."

Desiree flashed him another warm smile, revealing the tiny gap between her two front teeth. "Let's get started."

From that day, Rory and Desiree met twice a week in the lounge. On occasion, they would change locations and meet at the Chicago Coffee House, which was closer to her house. Desiree was an excellent math tutor, and as they worked together, the two also became friends. She had a warm quality that Rory found non-threatening when it came to him learning and not being judged.

Halfway through the semester, Rory lowered the protective wall that he often had with straight people. Feeling comfortable around her, he shared that he was gay as well as HIV positive. This didn't worry Desiree; she had been around plenty of HIV-positive patients during her time volunteering at the hospital. What she wanted to ask him was why two gay men would have unprotected sex in today's world.

One day, as the two were taking a break from the math, they were having a casual conversation when Rory mentioned attending TBU.

"Really? You went to TBU. When? How come you didn't finish?" Desiree asked.

"Girl, slow down. That's too many questions at once."

"I'm sorry." Desiree noticed that as Rory grew more comfortable with her, his animation grew as well.

"It was two years ago. I was a freshman and in love with this guy at the school. We hooked up and were sleeping together for a couple of months. He was hooked on painkillers and would take them like crazy—totally addicted." Rory leaned back in his chair, ready to gossip.

"Are you serious? No way," Desiree said, enthralled by his story.

"I use to keep a whole mess of his pills in my gym locker at TBU. He was buying them by the boatload down in China Town, and I would pick them up for him. One day, maintenance came to cut a lock off a locker, and girl, they cut my lock by mistake. When they cut my lock, the pills fell out like a vending machine. The police came to my class and arrested me in front of everyone. It was the first time I had ever been to jail. That place is no joke. The food was horrible… but the sex was free." Fanning himself, Rory took a breath.

Desiree giggled and then felt bad for laughing at such a sad story. "Why didn't you just say they weren't yours?" she asked.

Rory shook his head and laughed. "Really? Are you serious? Who they gonna believe, me or their golden new coach?"

"A coach?" Desiree shrieked.

Rory smashed his fist on the table as he leaned in. "Girl, he was the swim coach!"

"Shut up!" Desiree shrieked again.

"So I'm sitting in jail, where he left my ass." Rory was on fire now as he told his story. "I found out later that he was on some sort of probation already or had been fired from somewhere else for this same thing. Then my attorney told me that they screwed up the case when they forgot to Mirandize me, and they had to release me." Rory's eyes were as big as baseballs as he shook his head.

"That man had the nerve to plead with me not to say anything. Even though I was mad at him, there was no reason to get him fired, so I kept my mouth shut. I still see him from time to time."

Driving home that night, Desiree was in disbelief at what she had learned. Wanting to call J. B., she looked at her phone and saw that it was almost dead. With no car charger, she didn't want to risk it going dead and having something happen on the way home. She hadn't laughed so much in one night in a long time. She felt bad about laughing at parts of his story, but Rory was so funny. Although she was sure Rory was talking about Coach Silva, she didn't let on that her boyfriend was swimming for him. She had never seen or heard rumors that the coach was ever high, and she couldn't believe that part of the story could be true.

When Desiree made it home, she called J. B. at his house. She couldn't wait to tell him what Rory had said. After telling him everything, J. B. was in disbelief at the juicy gossip they had stumbled on.

"Des, you can't tell nobody 'bout this shit. If this shit gets out, coach would be fired." After making her swear to not tell a soul, they sealed their secret with a phone kiss.

Later that week, Desiree showed up at the aquatic center to pick J. B. up from practice. Arriving early, she took a seat on the bleachers next to Squirrel's new girlfriend, Ginger. Ginger had been seeing Squirrel for about a month, and they were becoming serious. Ginger was a fitting name for her, as she was a redhead with pale freckled skin, and she was petite like Squirrel.

"So how long have you and J. B. been seeing each other?" Ginger asked.

Desiree smiled as she thought about her answer. "Oh my gosh, since we were in high school. I've known him since third grade. We grew up together." Desiree looked at Ginger's open-toed sandals, noticing that her toenails were well manicured and painted. "Are you coming to the swim meet this Friday against South Carolina? It's right here at four o'clock," Desiree asked as she caught Coach Silva out of the corner of her eye.

"Oh, I didn't know anything about it. Well, maybe if I can get off work early that day. Fridays are tough," Ginger replied.

"Where do you work?"

"I do bookkeeping for my dad's trucking company. Fridays I do payroll."

As the girls sat on the bleachers talking, Coach Dean blew the whistle, signaling that practice was over. Within a couple of minutes, both J. B. and Squirrel walked up to the bleachers and gave their girls dripping kisses.

"I see you two met," Squirrel said to Desiree as he turned to J. B. "Hey, man, this here's my girl Ginger. Ginger, this is J. B." Squirrel was grinning as he introduced his new girlfriend to his friends.

"Nice to meet you. Do you go here too?" J. B. asked.

Ginger smiled as she brushed her long hair back out of her face, tucking it behind her ears. "No. I work for my dad's trucking business. Bookkeeping."

"We're going to hit the showers," Squirrel announced to the girls. After giving Ginger a second kiss, he trailed J. B. into the locker room.

After the guys left, Desiree turned to Ginger. "So how did you and Squirrel meet?"

"We met at our church," Ginger said.

Desiree wasn't sure she heard her right; she repeated, "At church?"

"Yes, I've seen him there over the last year or so, but was too shy to say anything to him. Then last month we both signed up to help with the breakfast club on Sunday morning, and he asked me out."

Squirrel in church, Desiree thought to herself. She had no idea.

Nicky, Tyler, and Braden came out of the locker room first. The three said hello to Desiree as they passed her on their way out to the parking lot. Andrew and J. B. could be heard laughing and clowning around as they came out the door, followed by Austin. Desiree met them halfway, and after kissing J. B., she waved goodbye to Ginger.

On the drive home, Desiree asked what the plans were for the weekend. She had learned that, if she didn't ask, J. B. would forget to tell her, and she hated surprises.

"Yeah, Momma's got a catering job at Crestwood Lake. A wedding. She hasn't had a job this big in over a year. Me and the girls are going to help."

"What day?" Desiree asked.

"Saturday, in the afternoon. Dinner's at three."

"What's she cooking?"

"I'm not sure. It's for some lady that she works with at Sears. She's probably doing her chicken or ribs, potato salad, greens, and cornbread, but I ain't for sure."

"Is she doing her amazing catfish nuggets?"

"For sure; shit, that's what they love the most," J. B. said. "It's coming up at the right time, too. I talked to the landlord the other day. He came by the house looking for his money. Guess momma only paid him half the rent this month."

"Yeah, tough times are here for all of us," Desiree said as she reached over and touched J. B.'s hand.

After a brief pause, Desiree asked, "Did you know how Squirrel and Ginger met?"

"No."

"At church!" she announced as if letting go of another secret.

"So?"

"I didn't know he even went to church. What kind is it?"

"I don't know. I guess he's Mormon or something like that," J. B. answered as he stared out the window.

"I think they're a cute couple. They kind of look like brother and sister though. She's pretty." Desiree said.

Desiree knew by J. B.'s silence that he was in deep thought and not really listening to her—most likely thinking about the rent that they didn't have. She wished she could make it all better for him. She hated that he worried about taking care of his family. She knew he felt the pressure of being the man of the house, believing that both Maurice and Clifford had failed at it.

J. B. had told her several times about feeling like less of a man because he wasn't bringing any money into the house and had to watch his mother struggle to make ends meet. Although Desiree never asked because it was none of her business, she knew that from time to time Momma B. accepted money from Ray-Ray, Tiny, and Lil' Kev, who worked for Clifford. She hated the fact that it was Clifford and his boys that ran the dope in the neighborhood, but in her heart, she knew those three clowns were also watching over the house while Clifford was doing his time.

Desiree remembered one of her and J. B.'s biggest fights was over Clifford. It was a turning point in their relationship, learning that J. B. worked so hard in school to get his family out of the hood while Clifford, his ass in prison, was still the protector of the family.

23

With another swim season ending, the TBU swim team managed to finish in their conference one spot higher than the previous year. The efforts of Coach Silva in creating a team that would one day dominate the league was coming together much faster than he or his superiors ever expected.

Earning invitations to state championships, Connor placed first, Nicky third, with Austin securing a fourth place finish in several races. The three went on to the conference championships, where all three again seized a spot in the top ten. Putting TBU on the short list of schools to watch, there was talk, for the first time, of TBU having three Olympic hopefuls.

With radio interviews, local talk show appearances, and the many invites the three were receiving for special guest appearances, Nicky dropped two of his classes, and he continued to struggle at his four remaining ones. At the suggestion of his advisor, Nicky changed his major from business management to sports management, where the workload of the classes was greatly reduced.

One day after class, Nicky and Tyler were strolling through the supermarket, picking up groceries for the evening. Nicky had planned to cook Tyler and Phillip one of his mother's casseroles that evening. He had called his mother the night before and gotten the recipe over the phone. Nicky paid for the groceries with Phillip's debit card, which he had been told to keep.

Seeing the grand total and the card that Nicky used, Tyler commented, "Is that his card?"

Nicky inserted the card back in his wallet and tucked it in his back pocket. "Yeah, why?"

"Really? He gave you his bank card?"

"He didn't *give* it to me. I usually do most of the grocery shopping these days. It makes things easier." Nicky didn't tell him that Phillip had given it to him before Christmas last year, telling Nicky to use it for anything he wanted.

Nicky and Tyler carried the plastic bags of groceries the two blocks back to the house. Walking past a little neighborhood bakery, Nicky stopped to look at the pastries and cakes on display in the window.

"Can I ask you something?" Tyler continued, not waiting for approval. "How do you think the coach can afford a house down in Old Hyde Park?"

"I don't know. Is that a nice part of town or something?" Nicky asked.

"Hello! Some of those are million-dollar homes in that neighborhood," Tyler shot back.

Nicky shrugged, not having an answer to Tyler's question. In fact, he had never given any thought to the price tag on the houses in the neighborhood. All he saw was that it was a nice neighborhood.

"So, do you love him? "Tyler asked.

"Who?" Nicky's voice trembled as the question echoed in his head.

Tyler grabbed Nicky's shoulder and spun him around toward him. "You know who I'm talking about. Don't play dumb."

"I don't know. Why do you ask?" The question was too direct for Nicky. It was such a black-and-white question. "I know I've never felt this way about anybody. I think about him in class; I think about him while waiting in line at the bank, when I'm watching TV."

"Yeah, go on," Tyler encouraged.

"He's in every thought I have. I ache when we're apart. The sex is amazing! I know that he loves me because he says it all the time," Nicky said. A rush of emotions flooded his soul, and his throat thickened, signaling the onset of tears.

"Sounds like you love him," Tyler said as he grabbed both sides of Nicky's shoulders and shook him. "You need to wake up!"

"Really?" This made Nicky wonder as he brushed a tear from his eye that had not yet fallen. He had never told anyone that he loved them, not even his parents. Of course he loved his parents, and they loved him. There was no need to say something they already knew. There was no value in that; that was how he was brought up.

"I've never told anyone that I loved them. Is that weird?"

Tyler broke eye contact, looking back at the pastries. "It's not as unusual as you think. But if you're blessed with someone you love, you need to tell them. Say the actual words to him so he can hear them. Not for you, but for him."

Not for you, but for him. Nicky let out a heavy sigh. "Tonight?"

"Yeah, tonight. Tomorrow may never come. You're a beautiful person, Nicky, and the coach should get all of you." Tyler turned back to his friend, grabbing him up. He squeezed Nicky, hugging him tightly for a moment.

"Tell you what," Tyler announced as he let Nicky go. "I'll take a rain check on tonight's dinner. You two need to be alone… And you need to say it." Tyler thumped Nicky on his forehead as he smiled at his buddy.

That evening when Phillip came in, Nicky had flowers on the table, candles burning, and a casserole in the oven. He'd bathed and applied scented lotion to his hairless skin. This was one of the perks of being a swimmer, shaving your body and no one questioning it. He fumbled through his side of the dresser and then their closet before he found the perfect outfit.

When Phillip walked into the kitchen, he found Nicky wearing nothing but one of his nice ties tied around his neck. "Wow, what is all this? Come here."

Phillip reached out his arms and pulled Nicky's naked body up into his arms and chest. As he kissed Nicky, his hands moved down, reaching around and resting on Nicky's smooth ass.

For a split second, Nicky almost gave into his advances as his face pressed against Phillip's chest, but remembering dinner, he squirmed out of Phillip's grip. "No, not yet. After dinner. Go get cleaned up; dinner's almost ready."

"God, it smells good in here. What are you cooking? I thought we were having dinner with Tyler?" Phillip asked as he adjusted himself in his jeans.

"Tyler had something that came up at the last minute." Peeking in the oven, Nicky stuck a fork in the middle of his casserole, ensuring it was done. "I don't know what you call it. My mom cooks it all the time. It has chicken, string beans, and a bunch of other stuff in it, and you mix it all together with cream of chicken soup and cook it."

"I didn't think you knew how to cook," Phillip snickered as he rubbed his hand down Nicky's back, stopping on his ass.

Nicky turned around and jabbed the fork at Phillip, pushing him back. "I called my mom yesterday, and she walked me through it."

"Did she ask you where or why you were cooking it?" Phillip asked as his eyes dropped down Nicky's tight abs and V-cut waist. Phillip reached for Nicky's cock.

"No, no, no. After dinner!" Nicky laughed as he grabbed Phillip's hand, stopping him within inches of getting what he wanted. "I told her I was giving it to one of my professors."

After dinner, the two laid on the floor on big oversized pillows in the living room. When the time felt right, Nicky readjusted himself, propping himself up on to one side. "I want to say something... Well, no, I want to tell you something." Feeling anxious, Nicky took a breath.

"What is it?" Phillip gently stroked Nicky's arm.

Nicky's voice cracked as he spoke. *Just say, "I love you. I loved you from the first day I met you."* Stopping, Nicky felt the tears welling up in his eyes as he fought not to cry. *Why are you crying, you big baby?* Nicky gasped for air as he cleared his throat. "When you were sitting in our dining room talking to my parents, I knew I loved you. I didn't even know you, but I loved you. I didn't know I was coming here, but I knew I would be with you. I saw it as if it was a dream. No worries, no plan as to how or when, because I just knew it. I have always been yours. I figured it all out thanks to a conversation today with Tyler." Nicky had managed to fight back the tears and get it all out.

"Did any of that make sense?" Nicky asked insecurely as he looked for a sign that he had fucked up the moment.

Phillip's eyes didn't blink as they burned into Nicky. They were like liquid as they watered up. Phillip gently took the hair that had fallen across Nicky's face, moving it to one side. With Phillip's touch, Nicky's body tingled, and his heart skipped a beat as it pounded in his chest.

The silence felt like minutes, and then it was finally broken by Phillip. "I love you, Nicolas."

Nicky watched as Phillip moistened his lips with his tongue. Bracing for the kiss that was coming, Nicky turned his head slightly just as Phillip's lips touched his. With the weight of Phillip's body, Nicky laid onto his back. His back on the carpet and head sustained by the large pillows, Nicky let out a light moan as Phillip took his breath away. They kissed for several minutes as things heated up rapidly.

Nicky felt Phillip pull away from him. He looked up at his lover, who stood up and offered his hand to him. Taking it, he was led down the hall to their bedroom. Nicky lay across the bed with Phillip's thin neck tie as his only covering, his erection fully on display. "Can you believe I've never told anyone that I love them? I'm not sure why my parents never said it. I didn't realize we never used the word until the day you told me that you loved me, and for some reason, I couldn't say it back to you. I'm sorry I suck at saying the L word."

Phillip's body hovered over Nicky's, with just a couple of inches between them. Staring deep into Nicky's eyes, he ran a finger lightly around Nicky's nipple. "Shh. Did I ever tell you that you talk too much?" Smiling, Phillip leaned in and lightly kissed the nipple he had just touched.

Nicky's upper body jolted as if he was just shocked by electricity. "I love you, I love you, I love you," Nicky moaned as he searched for Phillip's mouth, longing for a kiss. That night, Nicky wanted Phillip more than ever before. To feel his partner, to be consumed into the arms of the man he loved.

When Phillip laid Nicky down, the two came together as one, igniting a fire within Nicky that swept through his entire body as he received his lover fully. Nicky took Phillip in with a hunger he had not experienced before, making love and not just having sex.

24

It was 2:45 am when Nicky was awakened with the urge to go pee. After coming out of the bathroom and realizing he was wide awake, he grabbed his robe and made his way out to the living room, where he found Emily sleeping by the front door.

"Do you need to go pee too?" he whispered to her. He watched as Emily raised her head at the sound of his voice and then lowered it back down, tucking it into the side of her stomach.

Nicky tossed the couch pillows around, looking for the lost remote control, and then rumbled through the top drawer of the entertainment center in hopes of finding it there. As he was moving things around, he came across a photo of the coach and another guy. They appeared to be at a party of some sort. Staring at the picture, he couldn't help but notice that he looked familiar, though Nicky couldn't place him. He dropped the picture back into the drawer and moved on to the next drawer, which was full of papers.

Without really looking, his eyes scanned a stack of bank records. It was the large figures in the accounts that caught his eye. He then looked at the dates and saw that they were all recent statements. Knowing it was none of his business, but the figures having grabbed his attention, he continued to scan the personal financial records. Shuffling through the papers, he realized there were numerous banks and accounts, all containing thousands of dollars in each of them. He knew he was invading Phillip's personal space, and listening to his conscience, he put the papers back as he found them and closed the drawer.

Nicky, without thinking, went back to the first drawer and grabbed the picture again. Instantly it hit him: it was the guy he saw Phillip talking to after the Orlando meet. His hair was longer now, but he was sure it was the same person.

Nicky sat on the couch, wondering who the guy was. Feeling guilty for looking at the bank statements, Nicky couldn't believe how much money Phillip had in those accounts. His mind bouncing between the photo of the mystery guy—*Is this an ex-boyfriend?*—and the bank statements—*Just how much does a college coach make a year?*— there was no chance of Nicky going back to bed now that his brain was fully engaged.

The next day, with no swim practice, Nicky got to sleep in a little longer, but was out of the house before Phillip woke up. Sitting in his Spanish class, Nicky received a text from Phillip saying good morning. Texting back, Nicky yawned as he sat waiting for the instructor to return the quizzes from last week. Now regretting not grabbing that coffee when he passed by the student café, he fought to stay awake.

Though he wasn't expecting to do that well on the quiz, Nicky was still stunned when he saw that he had failed it, which now required him to attend lab this weekend. Attending Saturday lab was going to cause him to miss the boot camp training that Coach Dean provided during the off-season. Missing this pissed him off more than failing the actual test.

Nicky scanned the quiz, looking at his paper and the English paragraph they were given to translate into Spanish. Nicky re-read the first sentence: *Jose was born on March 6, 1985, in the city of Guadalajara, Mexico,* and then he looked at his translation and saw that not only did he transpose the date, he failed to use the proper conjugation. As he continued scanning the entire paragraph, he saw it was full of simple and stupid mistakes he had made. Knowing he was barely passing the class, his hope was to get in more study time now that the swim season was over. He shook his head as he looked at the paper once more before tucking it away in his backpack. Looking around the large classroom, it was the last place on earth he wanted to be this morning.

If it wasn't for swimming, Nicky would not have chosen college. Last year was tough, but this year, his classes were really challenging him. Phillip told him that if his grade point average dropped anymore, his scholarship would be in jeopardy. Studying hard was never Nicky's thing and never would be.

Embarrassed about flunking out, Nicky wondered what his parents would do if he told them he was dropping out to train full-time. He imagined himself on an Olympic podium. Naturally, he was receiving the gold medal. *If Phillip could get there, he could surely train me. I could do it.*

Off in his head, the instructor had moved on, and now Nicky was lost as to what he was talking about. Not that concerned that he was even lost, Nicky's thoughts wandered off.

"Do you have a pen I can borrow?" the girl to his right whispered to him. "Mine just stopped working."

Nicky looked over and saw that it was the Thai girl who had been sitting in that same seat since the semester started. He had no idea what her name was, even though he had been sitting next to her for nearly a month. "Yeah, I've got one," he answered as he dug down into his backpack. "Here you go; you can keep it," he whispered to her as he handed her the pen.

"Aren't you on our swim team?" she asked.

"Yeah, I'm Nicky," he told her as he smiled at her.

"Hi, I'm Leigh," she said as she smiled and took the pen. Nicky watched as Leigh turned back to her book and began scribbling fast, making up for everything she missed during that thirty seconds of conversation with him. Nicky smiled, thinking it was cool that she recognized him.

After class, Nicky was one of the first out the door as he bolted for his motorcycle, wishing he was already in the pool. Within minutes, he was out of the parking lot, racing across town to the city pool.

When he arrived, the parking lot was empty, which meant he didn't have to wait for a lane to open up. He was in and out of the locker room within minutes and scanning the pool for which open lane he wanted.

Seeing Austin and Andrew in lanes four and five, Nicky noticed the lanes on either side of them were vacant. As he walked over toward the lanes, he kicked his flip flops off and threw his towel over a chair. Dipping his goggles in the water to clean them, Nicky watched as Austin approached the wall and stopped.

"Hey man, what's up?" Austin said as he pulled up his goggles and balanced his weight on the lane rope.

"How's the water?" Nicky asked.

"Nice. Is this your normal time?" Austin asked.

"Yeah, kind of. My classes are jacked up, so it changes on Tuesdays and Thursdays. You?" Nicky adjusted his goggles on his head.

"Naw, I try to maintain the same time as during the season, but I couldn't get up this morning, so I said the hell with it. Talk to you later," Austin said as he kicked off the wall, resuming his workout.

Nicky jumped in the pool and within seconds was gliding through the water and falling into his rhythm.

At the halfway point of Nicky's workout, he stopped when he saw that Austin and Andrew were getting out of the pool. "Are you leaving?" Nicky asked.

"Yeah, we're done," Austin replied as he fought to catch his breath.

"Question for you," Nicky said as he removed his goggles. "You're taking Spanish 4, aren't you?"

"Yeah," Austin replied.

"Can you tutor, or do you know anyone who can? I think I'm failing my Spanish class, and I can't afford to let my GPA drop anymore." Nicky was slightly embarrassed about asking, but it was better than failing the class.

"Yeah, I think I got someone who can hook you up. I'll check and text his name and number," Austin said as he wrapped a towel around him and then slipped off his wet Speedo. Grabbing his sweats, Austin then slipped those on before releasing the towel. "We're out of here," he told Nicky as he shoved his wet Speedo and towel down into his bag and walked toward Andrew.

By the time finals week hit, Nicky had been working with his Spanish tutor for a couple of weeks and was confident he had pulled his grade up enough to pass the class. He and Phillip had also had a heart-to-heart talk about his lack of studying since moving in and established a set time for when this was to be done. When Phillip first approached the subject, the conversation did not go well. The coach had been tipped off by one of Nicky's instructors that he was failing and that his GPA had fallen to a 1.6. Phillip initially came across like he was Nicky's father, and Nicky had pushed back more out of embarrassment than anything else.

In working with Nicky, Phillip realized that academics weren't Nicky's strong suit and they were going to have to solicit more help than just one tutor. Nicky wanted to recruit Desiree to help, but J. B. told him she was buried in her own schoolwork. Now that her pre-req classes were done, she was starting the actual nursing program.

Nicky had worked harder than he had ever worked before, studying and reading into the late hours of the night. Phillip at times had to pull Nicky away when his brain became so saturated that he wasn't processing any more information.

By the end of finals week, Nicky had taken his written finals and one lab final and was emotionally exhausted. They hadn't had sex in over a week, and Nicky had stopped training for three weeks just trying to save his GPA.

Nicky knew he passed his lab final and did well on his Spanish and human behavior finals, but it was his economics class that he struggled in the most. During the final, he was the second to the last student to leave the class, with eight minutes to spare before the instructor called time.

Waiting for two weeks for the grades to be posted on-line, Nicky had all but worried himself sick. He had received passing grades on all of his classes thus far; however, he was still waiting for his grade from his economics professor. The day that grade was finally posted, it was a quarter to five when Nicky checked the website and saw that the PIN to access his grade had been posted. With J. B. and Tyler bullshitting, Nicky silently pulled up the site and entered his name, social, and PIN. He waited while the site connected and his name appeared. Nicky was afraid to look as he scanned the screen, holding his breath. He passed. At the bottom of the screen, he saw that he had passed the final with a seventy-three percent and an overall grade of a C. Nicky smiled as he exhaled the air he had been subconsciously holding in.

"What? What are you smiling at?" Tyler asked as he looked over at Nicky.

"I passed. A seventy-three percent on the test! I got a C! I can't believe it, I passed!" Nicky hollered as he jumped up out of his seat, letting the moment take over. He grabbed Tyler and hugged him as he continued to repeat, "I can't believe I passed, I passed economics!"

J. B. stood next to them as he congratulated Nicky, happy that he was able to pull it off.

Nicky raced home and was glad to see Phillip's Audi in the garage. As he ran in the house, he screamed, "Honey, I passed economics. I did it!" Nicky ran from the kitchen to the bedroom, looking for Phillip as he continued to scream for him.

Phillip almost hit him with the door as he and Emily came in from the backyard to see what all the hollering was about. Nicky was on the other side of the door about to open it when it flung open, narrowly missing his face. Oblivious to the door almost knocking him out, he screamed, "I passed economics!"

Emily barked due to the excitement, as Phillip grabbed Nicky's waist. "I knew you would do it. I knew it was going to be okay," Phillip said.

"Oh, my God, I'm not doing this again. Next year, I'm not going to get this far behind. Even with swim season, I have to stay on top of it!" Nicky said.

"Well, this calls for a toast," Phillip said as he walked into the kitchen and grabbed a bottle of champagne from the refrigerator. After pouring two glasses, Phillip held up his glass. "To Nicky, the hardest-working student at Tampa Bay...and to Greece!"

Nicky looked at Phillip funny when he heard the toast. "Why are we toasting to Greece?" he asked.

"Because that's where I'm taking you this summer for vacation. I already booked it because I knew you were going to be just fine," Phillip told him.

"Are you kidding? I'm going to Greece!"

"No, *we're* going to Greece. Baby, you deserve it. You worked hard for it."

Nicky screamed as he leaped into Phillip's arms. He started to wrap his legs around Phillip's waist but thought he'd better not. Phillip tried to move his ear away from Nicky's piercing screams while Emily continued to bark at the two of them.

That night, as the two of them crawled into bed, Nicky leaned over and kissed Phillip. "You know, I was thinking while you were in the shower, I'm going to have to tell my parents something, why I'm not coming home this summer."

"How about the truth?" Phillip asked as he smiled into Nicky's beautiful green eyes.

"Really? It would be okay with you that they know about us?" Nicky sat up against the headboard as he also realized he would be coming out to them.

"Baby, I love you and want to spend forever with you. You're an adult; you're not a child anymore. From all I heard about your parents, I think things will be fine." Phillip was still lying down with one arm propping his head up on his pillow.

"Hmm, but what about the school finding out?" Nicky kicked the covers off of him as he voiced his concern. "You said you could lose your job. I don't want that." Nicky's voice had lost all of the enthusiasm of the evening as it took on a more serious tone.

Phillip brushed the hair away from Nicky's eyes, "Honey, everything I've heard about your parents, they sound like nice people; we'll figure the next part out when and if that day comes."

Conflicted, Nicky let out a big sigh. "Oh, my God, they won't believe I'm going to Greece," Nicky said as he snuggled up close to Phillip's naked body under the sheets. Phillip welcomed the closeness as he seductively grinned at Nicky and then reached over to turn out his light.

25

When their plane landed in Athens, the first thing Nicky noticed was the hot, stale air that surrounded the airport, even at eleven o'clock at night. They had been traveling for almost sixteen hours, and now that Nicky was fully awake, he was starting to panic with everything he saw just in the airport. The heaviness of the air, the people, the different language he was hearing, even the smells were all different as Nicky tried to take it all in. Uncertain about everything, on their way down to baggage claim, Nicky stared cautiously at the tiny gift shops and food vendors. He felt as if everything was a danger and hung close to Phillip.

After picking up their suitcases, Nicky and Phillip made their way out of the airport, where the taxis were parked. Immediately, several men ran up to them, surrounding them and trying to pull their suitcases out of their hands. Defensively, Nicky grabbed his suitcase up tight as he moved in closer to Phillip.

"No, no. No thank you!" Phillip told them as he brushed them back, continuing toward the taxis. When they reached the taxis, Phillip held out a piece of paper. "English?"

"Yes, sir," the little grey-headed man replied as he stared at the paper.

"Hotel Astro. How much?" Phillip made the universal sign for money by holding up his hand and rubbing his fingers together.

"Americano dollars…eleven dollars." The man smiled, revealing several large gaps between his dirty teeth.

As soon as Phillip agreed, the petite man started stuffing the large suitcases into his tiny trunk. Within minutes, they were off and heading into the great city of Athens.

"Wow, that was freaking bizarre. I thought they were attacking us." Nicky's heart was racing as he tried to relax within the safety of the taxi. The car was small, with little room for anything other than just them. "What did all those guys want when we came outside?"

Phillip scanned the city of Athens as they approached it. "They were trying to get us in their taxis is all." Phillip rested his hand on Nicky's leg as he smiled at him. "You okay?"

"Yeah. I mean," Nicky paused as the men flashed in his mind, "If they were muggers, I was ready to fight."

"You didn't exactly look like you were ready to fight." Phillip laughed as he rocked Nicky's knee, trying to relax him.

Within ten minutes, the Acropolis came into sight, and their driver exited the freeway, dropping down into thick traffic heading toward their hotel.

After checking into the hotel and being shown to their room, Nicky and Phillip closed the door behind the young Greek boy who had escorted them up. Phillip and Nicky took off their clothes, which they had been wearing since the day before. Stripping down to their underwear, they tried to cool off from the sweltering midnight air.

Phillip had just taken more pain meds and stretched across the bed, trying to undo what sixteen hours of sitting in an airplane seat had done to him. Nicky, astonished with everything he saw, stared out the window down into the city. From their room, they had a picturesque view of the remains of the Acropolis, the ancient citadel, located high on top of the mountain, lit up in all its glory. Watching the people and cars move about the city in the middle of the night, he wanted to be down there, too.

The next morning, Nicky rose with the sun after only sleeping five hours. He ordered coffee to be brought to the room as Phillip continued to sleep. Nicky took his coffee out onto their sixth-floor balcony so he could resume watching the city as it moved about under him. Seeing the Acropolis in daylight was even more extraordinary than seeing it last night. He was so excited that, while he tried to sit and drink his coffee, he kept popping up to look over the grand balcony at everything that moved. Listening to the cars and scooters blowing their horns below him, Nicky could not believe this was his life. He wished his mother was there to see all of it.

Nicky thought about the phone call when he told his mother that he wasn't coming home for the summer but instead was going to Greece with Phillip. He purposefully called when his dad wasn't home yet; otherwise, both his parents would have been on the phone at the same time. He knew she was disappointed that she wasn't going to get to see him, but once she realized it was just the two of them and not a school trip, she went silent. Nicky pushed on through the conversation, knowing he also had to tell her that they were also going to be living together without using the words "boyfriend," "lover," or "sex." This had been the way their family communicated, saying something without actually saying whatever it was they were trying to say.

She said little more, not even asking about his grades before getting off the phone. He wondered if and how she was going to say anything to his dad. Growing up in a small town such as Brandy, there were no Pride parades, gay bars, or to his knowledge, gay people. Good or bad, he couldn't recall ever hearing his parents speak about their views of homosexuality. They were simple folks with no strong opinions about anything that didn't directly affect them.

After taking several photos of everything he could from the balcony, he realized that he was leaning against the railing in nothing but his pajama bottoms, in plain view of everyone. Hearing a commotion below him, Nicky looked down and spotted four young guys whistling and calling up at him, one even blowing kisses to him. "Americano! Americano! Sexi Americano!" Embarrassed, Nicky waved and promptly took a step back out of their vision. He couldn't believe what just happened as he giggled to himself.

"Americano, Americano! Come back!" the voices cried out to him.

After about an hour on the balcony, Nicky heard the sliding glass from their room open as Phillip flung the drapes open.

"Good morning," Phillip said to him, standing in the door frame naked, revealing his morning wood.

"Well, good morning it is," Nicky answered. He looked at Phillip's furry but bulky chest and pearly white teeth before licking his lips at Phillip's manhood pointing right at him.

Phillip moved his hand down over his chest and stomach as he gently brushed past his erection. "Do you want to come inside and play for a little while?" he asked, grinning at Nicky.

Nicky's body reacted to the mere suggestion of sex as he stared at Phillip, still standing in the doorway. "Oh yeah!" Nicky answered, and he stepped inside the room with a partial hard-on already in his PJs. Phillip grabbed him, backed him toward the unmade bed, and then gently pushed him down across it.

Phillip laid on top of Nicky, and the two kissed. With the curtains and sliding glass door still open, the two made love in the tiny hotel room as their moans echoed down over the balcony and onto the streets.

As Phillip brought Nicky to climax, he too released everything he had, quivering as he gasped and moaned at the top of his lungs. Nicky's body twitched under Phillip as he too gasped for air. The nerves in their bodies sent spasms throughout them as they struggled to return their breathing to normal.

After breakfast, the two headed out into the streets of the city, ready for a day of adventure. "Wow, the sidewalks are made of marble—look!" Nicky said with excitement in his voice.

"It's unbelievable that they used marble hundreds of years ago to make these sidewalks and buildings," Phillip responded.

"I feel like we're on a different planet or something; look over there!" Nicky said as he pointed across the street to the Olympic Stadium.

They crossed the busy street and made their way into the Olympic Stadium. "I think this is where some of the first Olympic Games were held," Phillip said.

They stopped to read the plaque inside the stadium:

> *The Olympic Games were held here from 776 BC to 393 AD. This stadium was a holy place for the ancient Greeks and is where sporting activities dedicated to Zeus were held.*

Nicky and Phillip stood in silence as they both took in the marble slabs used for seating around the ancient track. There were people meandering around the two-thousand-year-old Greek statues and sitting in the legendary stadium like it was just another city park.

"This is just incredible. I can't believe how old this place is, and they let people just walk all around." Nicky took out his phone and starting clicking, making sure to get plenty of Phillip.

That week, they also made their way to the Acropolis to visit the Parthenon, and they visited the Temple of Apollo. They slept in until noon on some days, having lunch at two o'clock and dinner in the late hours of the night. They watched as young lovers crossed their paths every day, both gay and straight, holding hands, fully engulfed in each other. Within days, Nicky and Phillip let down their guards and fully embraced the ancient city of love as well.

On their last night in Athens, they enjoyed a candlelit dinner in a small restaurant they had walked by several times during the week. Along the sidewalk, the tiny restaurant had several outdoor tables covered with white linen set up under a wooden pergola. Purple wisteria draped from the pergola, with its gentle fragrance permeating the air. The aroma coming from the kitchen made their bellies growl as they relaxed back in their chairs.

When the young waiter arrived, he welcomed them with a bottle of Pellegrino and bread. The waiter, who spoke with a thick accent, carefully described in English what would be served this evening. There was no choosing; the chef had prepared one dinner that was served in four courses over the next hour and a half. They drank a bottle of wine as they laughed and flirted with one another in full view of the public, who paid them no attention.

"Can you believe it's been a year?" Nicky asked as his eyes drank in his surroundings. From where Nicky sat, he eyed the massive full moon as it lit up the sky in shades of blue. Dipping his bread in a tiny bowl of olive oil, Nicky smiled at the man who had shown him a whole new world—not just Greece, but love.

Often on the trip, he felt as if his heart was going to explode; hypersensitive to Phillip's light touches throughout the day and the way he gazed at him, it physically left him breathless.

"No, but also I feel like we've been together for years. The love I feel for you can't be possible in just one year. I can't imagine my life without you in it," Phillip said, his leg brushing against Nicky's under the table.

Nicky took in a big breath and exhaled. "I love you so much. Thank you for everything."

"I love you more," Phillip responded.

When the waiter approached the table, he cleared several of the empty plates as he smiled at both of them. Earlier in the meal, they had decided that he must be the son, and his father was in the back kitchen, creating the amazing meal. They laughed and debated about the young woman who sat them at their table—was she the sister or the mother? She was beautiful and spoke no English.

"Are you excited to travel to Mykonos in the morning?" Phillip asked as he watched the flicker of the candle in his young lover's green eyes.

"I guess so. This place is so fantastic. I don't want to leave, but I want to see Mykonos too." Nicky leaned back, allowing for the young waiter to set two small dishes in front of each of them.

"*Diples*," the waiter said, explaining the Greek pastry as best he could before leaving them.

"Well, you can't have both sweetheart, so you have to choose."

"Then I want to go to Mykonos!" Nicky replied as he stared at the fried wonton-looking pastry that was covered with powdered sugar and drizzled with honey. At the same time, they each picked their diples up, and with honey all over their hands, devoured the light but sweet pastry.

After dinner, the two walked down the marble street toward the hotel. When they arrived, Nicky thought they were returning to their room and was ready to make love when Phillip announced that he had a surprise for him. Phillip put Nicky in a cab and told the driver to wait one minute as he ran into the lobby of their small boutique hotel. Moments later, Phillip returned with a picnic basket in hand and jumped in the taxi. Phillip gave the driver their destination and off into the country hillside high above the city they drove.

When the taxi stopped, Nicky looked out the window and saw nothing but vineyards along both sides of the narrow road.

"We're here," Phillip told him as he nudged Nicky to get out.

Nicky looked at him and then again out the window. "Here where? It's dark out there!"

"Just get out. It's a surprise!"

Nicky watched as Phillip paid the driver, and the taxi drove off, leaving them on the side of the dirt road in the middle of nowhere. "Are you ready?" asked Phillip.

"For what?" Nick asked. Even with the moon high above them, it was blackness all around.

Phillip grabbed Nicky's hand and led him toward the silhouette of grape vineyards. They walked under the light from the moon for several hundred feet until they reached the end of the row of vines.

Before them was a grassy slope that overlooked the Acropolis, the Plaka, and the entire city of Athens. Lit with only the full moon above their heads, Nicky watched as Phillip removed a blanket from the basket, then a bottle of wine. They drank their wine and made love on the hillside under the moon, just as young lovers did five hundred years ago.

26

The trip to Greece was as amazing as it was rejuvenating for both Nicky and Phillip, especially on the island of Mykonos. Nicky noticed that Phillip was not taking near the amount of pills for his back as he did at home. After they arrived home, Nicky was finding it difficult to return to their secretive life together as moments of their vacation replayed in his mind.

Entering his junior year, with the new swim season starting, Nicky knew it was time to get back to real life. Nicky sat with J. B. and Tyler as they reconvened at their usual table at Java Express, a small coffee shop two blocks from the campus.

"So are you ready?" J. B. asked Nicky as he removed the lid to his coffee and blew on the steaming fluid.

"Yeah, this semester I'm feeling better about my classes," Nicky answered. After his summer vacation, Nicky felt as if he was ready for anything. "Are you on track to graduate this year?" Nicky asked J. B.

"God willing; this summer was a bitch taking those summer courses. Desiree was in school all summer, too."

"Does she want to work at Tampa Medical Center?" Tyler asked.

"Yes. Her aunt is a nurse there, and she likes it," J. B. explained. "After I graduate, we're probably going to look at buying a house over by my momma's."

"Yeah so you can get off her couch at night," Nicky said.

There was a pause in the conversation as the three sat enjoying their coffee. It was J. B. who was the first to break the silence. "I heard that Connor was thinking about trying to train for the Olympics after he graduates this year."

"No way. I don't see it happening for him," Nicky said. "I can beat him any day of the week. I think he's a better water polo player."

"I don't know. He's good," Tyler interjected.

Out of the corner of his eye, Nicky saw Coach Dean's truck as it passed the café. Seated in the passenger seat was Connor.

"There goes the asshole now," Nicky said as he pointed to a white pick-up truck that was stopped at the light.

"Wonder what they're up to?" Tyler asked. "I hate them both."

"Hey, did you get your apartment?" J. B. asked Tyler.

"Yeah; it's going to be me, Andrew, and Austin this year. They're going to share one bedroom and split their half of the rent," Tyler replied.

J. B. turned and looked at Nicky. "You staying in the dorms again this year?"

Caught off guard with the question, he had to lie, "Um, yeah." Nicky mumbled. "Have you seen the apartment yet?" Nicky asked Tyler, attempting to deflect the conversation back on him.

"Not yet. Next Tuesday, but I've been to a couple of parties in that building so I know what they look like."

On the first day of swim practice the following week, Coach Silva and Coach Dean called a meeting on the pool deck. Steam rose from the water, and they had about thirty minutes before sunrise. Coach Silva introduced the newest members of the team and lectured all of them about what to expect this season. It was the same speech they gave the last two years.

Nicky watched Tyler, who was taking his first look at one of the newest swimmers, Eduardo Dias. Eduardo was a six-five slender

Brazilian with bright emerald eyes and dark hair. His broad back was completely covered in a massive dragon tattoo that curved around to his left side. Coach Phillip had recruited him away from a college up north when he heard he was unhappy and looking for a new team. As a sophomore, Eduardo was known for putting up some staggering, record-breaking times.

Once practice was under way, it was all work as the coaches hammered them, assessing who trained over the summer and who didn't. For Nicky, it was business as usual as he paced himself, cutting through the water like a dolphin on crack. The water was Nicky's world, and with every lap thrown at him, he welcomed the challenge of taking on his own body, pushing it further and harder than his mind could even conceive. This was going to be his year, with plans on taking both the NCAA and SEC Championships; Nicky was hoping that would get him an invitation to the Pan American Games being hosted in Boston in July. If successful there, he would be eligible to participate in the World Championship trials next year.

After practice, as they all gathered in the locker room, Nicky overheard Austin talking to Connor about their summer training schedule. It caught Nicky by surprise when Austin asked Connor if he went to any of Coach Dean's boot camps and Connor said he hadn't seen him until just today. Nicky had seen them together last week in Coach Dean's truck and wondered why he was lying.

Nicky stripped his wet swimsuit off and wrapped a towel around his waist. When he looked at Tyler, he was just sitting there. "What are you doing? Why are you just sitting there?" Nicky asked.

"Shush, I'm waiting for Eduardo to go in the shower. Did you see the front of his suit?" Tyler whispered.

"Are you kidding? You're a freak." Nicky couldn't believe that Tyler would even think about making a move on him in the showers with everyone around.

"Yeah, a freak who wants to be Eddie's teddy," Tyler explained.

Nicky shook his head as he closed his locker and walked toward the showers behind Ron and J. B. While in the shower Nicky, Ron, J.

B., and Austin laughed and teased one another as they showered, one by one leaving the shower.

When Nicky was done, he grabbed the towel he hung on a hook outside the shower and walked back toward his locker. When he looked up, he saw Eduardo heading to the showers, and unbeknownst to Eduardo, Tyler was moving fast right behind him. Nicky smiled and winked at Tyler as the two passed each other. He could hardly wait to get the full scoop later.

That night, Nicky and Phillip took up their usual spots in the house: Phillip at his desk studying video and Nicky in his sweat bottoms and no shirt sitting on the daybed with his laptop, studying. The two were silent for several minutes until Nicky broke the silence. "I talked to my mom today. She and my dad want to come out sometime during the season to a meet."

"Huh, what?" Phillip's leaned up in his chair. "Do tell: How did this come up?"

"I called her after I left the gym. I just wanted to talk to my mom. Hearing her voice, I was missing them so much, and before I realized it, I asked her if she and dad were ever going to come out to see me swim." Nicky closed his laptop, knowing he was done for the evening.

"What did she say?"

"At first, she was quiet. I think she heard it in my voice that I was in a bad space. I do miss them," Nicky added. "So then she agreed to come. Of course, she had to talk to my dad to see when, but at least she said yes."

"Wow. That's great. We have Miami this week, and then we're away for the Alabama Trojans meet—that would be a good one for them. If you want, you can invite them to stay here with us after we return from the meet," Phillip said.

"I hadn't thought about it. I just assumed they would get a hotel."

"Well, if you want, invite them. Even if they don't choose to stay here, you at least invited them." Phillip took a sip of the last of the wine in his glass. "I missed Steven's call last night. I haven't talked to him in a couple of days." Standing up, he walked over to Nicky and bent over for a hug. "I need to go call him. I'll call him from the bedroom." Picking up his empty wine glass, Phillip walked out of the room.

Settling on his bed, Phillip scrolled through his phone, looking for Steven's number. After pressing the call button, Steven picked up on the fourth ring. "Hey, Phillip. "

"You wouldn't believe the week I've had," Phillip vented. "Between these kids fighting and some shady shit that Coach Dean has been pulling, I'm ready to call it quits."

"More drama?" Steven asked.

Phillip unleashed on him. "Well, to start, Dean has been challenging me on the littlest things recently. I'm not sure what it's all about."

"Have you talked to him about it?"

"We've been so busy, I was just hoping it was a passing thing."

"So how are things going with *Nicolas*?"

Phillip laughed and then paused long enough to take a sip from his second glass of wine. "Oh, my God, I forgot how horny we were in our twenties. At first, I loved it; now it's killing me to keep up with the little shit," Phillip snickered.

"Well, we should all be so lucky to have that problem. Sorry if I'm unsympathetic toward your current situation. Martin is pretty much all talk these days. When he hits the bed, he's snoring within seconds."

Phillip lowered his voice. "Can I ask you something? I trust that you'll tell me the truth."

"What? What is it? It sounds serious."

"I'm thinking about cutting one of my swimmers from the team. The kid is good, but he's aggressive to several of the other swimmers. It's becoming a real problem."

"Aggressive? How so? Like bullying?" Steven asked.

"Well, yeah, kind of. Definitely a racist; he's made several racial remarks toward my one African-American swimmer."

"So why would you stand for that shit? You're better than that to stand by and let someone go through that—why?" Steven questioned.

"You're right, but the problem is, he's a senior, a promising swimmer, and is looking to go to the Olympics. If he's kicked off the team, he would most likely lose a huge portion of his financial support and would have to leave school. It could affect his ability to get sponsorship."

Interrupting Phillip, Steven asked, "So how is any of that your problem? He should have thought about that before being a bully."

"Yeah," Phillip replied, "but it does weigh on me as the one who would pull the trigger."

"No, he pulled the trigger. This is his doing, not yours. You're just the one revealing the consequence of his actions. Let's see it for what it is, Phillip." Steven's tone was persuasive as Phillip listened to him.

Phillip knew what Steven was saying was right, but it didn't make it any easier. "Maybe I'll have a talk with him first," Phillip added.

"Are you kidding? You haven't even had a conversation with him yet? That should have happened as soon as this shit started." Steven's voice escalated. "And now you're ready to flush him. I hate to take his side now, but that's not fair, either. You never gave him a chance to clean it up." Steven sounded annoyed.

After Phillip hung up the phone, he was no closer to figuring out an answer to his problem than before his conversation with Steven. Disciplining his swimmers for poor behavior out of the water was a lot harder than for swimming poorly. He would rather sit in meetings all day than handle conflict.

That week during the Miami meet, the guys found they had swum harder during some of their practices. The majority of the meet, TBU's competition was with each other.

In the 400 freestyle, Connor asked to be put in the race with Nicky and Austin. It was rumored that he had a potential trainer there looking at him, and Connor wanted to show his best. Nicky was a little surprised when he saw the lineup and that Phillip hadn't said anything about him swimming against Connor.

Prior to the 400, Nicky watched as it appeared Phillip and Coach Dean were having a heated discussion about something right out in the open. Creating some distance between them, Nicky walked to the other end of the pool, telling himself that he had to ask later what it was all about.

The small crowd that had come to watch the meet was booing at the current swimmers in the pool just finishing the 200 butterfly. TBU had a one–two finish again, making it five wins in a row. When the whistle blew for the next swimmers to take the block for the 400, Nicky took to lane four, with Austin on his right and Connor to his left. Nicky shook his head and arms as he worked out the tension that was building within him.

When the starting gun went off, Connor sprang from his block, getting a slight jump on both Austin and Nicky. Dead even, Nicky and Austin's bodies entered the water milliseconds after Connor. Nicky had gotten a good feel for the water in his earlier race and knew he had to adjust his stroke to grab more water.

As Nicky narrowed in on a good pace that would sustain him for the next sixteen laps, he saw Austin was even with him and Connor was just ahead of them. Nicky knew Connor had just swum the 100-yard race three races ago, which warmed him up and gave him a fresh feel for the water.

After their first flip, Nicky and Austin remained even during their next twenty-five yards. Nicky kept an eye on Connor, noticing him lengthening his lead by half a body length. Austin remained even with Nicky, holding the pace behind Connor as they were now entering their third lap. As Connor held his lead, Nicky pushed him, increasing his pace slightly, with Austin adjusting his stroke accordingly. Nicky knew Connor felt the push and dug in, grabbing even more water. Nicky moved closer to the rope between him and Connor and drafted off his wake, decreasing his effort but holding his pace.

Using Connor's wake, Nicky pushed him again, increasing his pace slightly. When Connor realized that Nicky was drafting him, he moved to the other side of his lane, now within an inch of the rope. It didn't matter to Nicky; he had a lot left in him. He pushed him again, carefully not wanting to take the lead.

When Nicky looked over to his right, he saw that Austin had pushed too, had overtaken him, and was challenging Connor for the lead. As all three swimmers entered their fifteenth lap, Connor and Austin were dead even, with Nicky slightly behind them. Nicky pushed again, seeing that Connor had nothing left as he approached the wall and made their final flip.

Nicky had less than twenty-five yards to finish this up, and he increased his stroke rate, propelling his body past both Connor and Austin. Seeing this, both Connor and Austin attempted to dig in as well, but Connor had nothing left. Nicky felt the vibration of the crowd as they stomped their feet in the bleachers as the swimmers all hit the wall.

Nicky removed his goggles to look up at his time, and he saw that both he and Austin had broken the conference record and that Connor had not finished third but had slipped to fourth, coming in a half-second behind third.

The crowd was on their feet, shouting from the bleachers, "NICKY! NICKY! NICKY!" They chanted and screamed at him. Nicky looked over at Austin and smiled, knowing Austin was proud of his time.

Nicky and Austin stood on the deck, both being interviewed by reporters as the crowd continued to go crazy. Nicky looked over the reporter's shoulder and saw Connor leaving the pool area, heading toward the locker rooms.

When it was over, Miami quietly boarded their bus and were gone within an hour. It was a night of celebration for the home team, as this was their best win this season—they were ready to party that evening.

ॐ

The entire team reconvened down at the pool hall on the harbor several hours later. With just about the entire team there, Nicky and Austin were in the hallway talking when suddenly, they heard Connor's voice getting loud. They ran into the main room, where Connor and J. B. were in each other's face in a heated argument.

"Damn nigger!" Connor shouted at J. B. as he spat in J. B.'s face.

J. B. leaped toward Connor, knocking over Squirrel's girlfriend in the process. "Come on! Let's do this! I'll kill you!" J. B. roared.

Eduardo, Andrew, and Austin grabbed J. B. seconds before he reached Connor. Several guys were also holding Connor as more people entered the room.

"Get him out of here!" Nicky shouted to Desiree and the boys who were holding J. B. back. "Go on," Nicky pleaded, "Get him out of here!" By this time, Desiree was behind J. B., pulling on his arm to back him away and toward the door.

After helping Ginger to her feet, Nicky went to J. B. "Come on, J. B., that piece of shit isn't worth it; go with Desiree," Nicky command-ed, and then again repeated more forcibly, "I said, go with Desiree!"

Nicky followed J. B. and Eduardo out the back door and toward Desiree's car. "Man, what the hell was that about? You were about to kill him. I've never seen you like that. Dude, you were crazed," Nicky asked as he trailed behind J. B.

"One day, I'm going to beat his ass. I'm going to kill that redneck son of a bitch," J. B. roared.

"What happened?" Nicky asked again, realizing he hadn't gotten a straight answer.

J. B. refused to look at him as he got in the car. "That dude just doesn't know that I'm not playing with him. He better stop coming at me like I'm some bitch!"

After J. B. and Desiree left, Nicky returned to the pool hall to find Connor in the middle of the room, talking to Squirrel and Ginger. As Nicky approached them, Connor saw him and yelled, "Don't bring your punk ass over here. Go with your nigger friend!"

Hearing Connor's comment, Nicky leaped toward Connor, ready to finish the job J. B. had started. Squirrel, who was standing between the two of them, caught Nicky just as Nicky had grabbed Connor's shirt.

"What the hell is that supposed to mean?" Nicky yelled as Squirrel and Austin fought to pull Nicky off of Connor. "You're a fucking bigot!" Nicky screamed.

Nicky's teammates encircled Nicky as he fought to catch his breath. For two years, Nicky had listened to Connor's racist comments about blacks, Jews, Mexicans, and gay people. If he could have gotten to him, he would have ripped his head off. It was bullshit that everyone just let him get away with it, and Nicky couldn't understand why.

Knowing Connor wasn't worth his time, Nicky broke loose from Squirrel's grip. "I'm all right. Let me go." Grabbing his things, Nicky turned around and left the pool hall.

When Nicky arrived home, Phillip was sitting up in bed, reading. Nicky told Phillip what had happened at the pool hall as he took his clothes off and climbed into bed.

"I'll take care of it," Phillip told him as he reached around Nicky's neck, bringing him in under his arm.

Just as Phillip kissed the top of Nicky's head, Nicky jerked up. "Oh, what were you and Dean fighting about before the 400 today?"

"Did it look bad?" Phillip asked, sounding surprised that Nicky witnessed it. "Without saying anything to me, Dean had changed the swim lineup, adding Connor in the 100 and then the 400 and taking him out of the two races I had him assigned to. Connor had two potential trainers there tonight looking at him."

"So it's true: Connor's looking to train for the Games in London?" Nicky asked.

"Yes, but I'm not sure it's going to happen after today's race. At least not with those two trainers. Dean had given him the most perfect setup for that 400. He should have taken that race."

The next morning, when Nicky went to use his phone, he realized that it wasn't his phone. He saw that the screen saver was of Ginger and knew he must have picked up the wrong phone from the table last night after the fight. Nicky called his phone, and Squirrel answered.

With a sigh of relief, Nicky exhaled. "Hey man, you know you have my phone. I must have picked yours up by mistake," Nicky said.

"Really, I didn't even notice. I'll bring it this morning to the pool."

"That's cool. So how was the rest of the night? Did anything happen after I left?"

"No, I drove Connor home and crashed at his place."

"So what was the fight over? J. B. wouldn't tell me," Nicky asked.

Squirrel's voice lowered to a whisper. "Man, I'll tell you later."

Nicky envisioned that Squirrel probably slept on the couch and was still over there. "Yeah, no problem. I was just wondering."

After Nicky hung up the phone, he thought about the ton of texts from Phillip that clearly revealed their intimacy, as well as texts from Phillip about a meeting he had with the head of the athletic department about having Connor removed from the team. He prayed that Squirrel hadn't looked at them. *How could I have been so stupid not to erase them? Should I say something to Phillip?*

When he met Squirrel for practice that morning, everything seemed normal as the two exchanged phones. Nicky had told himself that Squirrel wouldn't snoop; how Christian would that be? The moment his phone was back in his possession, he deleted all of the messages from Phillip.

27

The next week, as the team loaded onto the bus for the long ride to Alabama U, they took their normal seats: Austin and Andrew, followed by Nicky, Tyler, and J. B. in the middle of the bus, and Squirrel and Connor in the last row with Eduardo. The bus was packed, as they had a few extra staff members with them who wanted to avoid making the drive themselves.

Preparing for a long bus ride, Nicky sat back in his seat, adjusting his music when he looked over and saw the guy from the photo in Phillip's house just as he disappeared around the side of the building. Nicky looked for Phillip on the bus and saw that he hadn't boarded yet. Nicky stood up, thinking he would get off and see if Phillip was in the office, concerned that he was with the stranger in the picture.

Why would he be here on campus? Nicky wondered to himself as he realized he wouldn't be able to get off the bus. There were too many people in the aisle and still standing in line, waiting to board. As he watched, he saw Phillip exit the building with his briefcase and gym bag in hand and walk toward the bus. Nicky continued to watch for any sign of the other guy.

As the bus pulled out of the parking lot and their trip began, everyone was talking among themselves. Although the thought of Phillip with that guy weighed heavily on Nicky's mind, he was excited about seeing his parents at the meet. The plan was, they would join up with them at the meet and then return with them back to Florida for a week.

All week, he and Phillip prepared for their visit, shopping, cleaning, and removing the nude artwork that hung in the living room. They hid the pictures that were on their nightstands and ensured the dirty magazines were picked up and hidden in the closet.

Midway during the drive, the team had stopped for lunch, giving everyone a chance to stretch their legs. Pulling into a large strip mall, the guys had lots of options and split up in different directions to eat. After lunch, they boarded the bus again, this time fully energized and smiling. Immediately the joking and teasing started, with everyone taking a turn at someone. Both Nicky and Tyler sunk their bodies down into their seats, hoping to escape the one-liners that were being flung back and forth.

Making his way to the front of the bus, Austin grabbed himself a Mountain Dew from the cooler and then raised one up, offering it to Squirrel.

"You think you're funny?" Squirrel replied.

"What, you don't do the Dew?" Austin asked as he kept the offer out in front of Squirrel.

"He's Mormon, you moron; it has caffeine in it," Connor interjected.

"Oh, I didn't know," Austin said as he sat back down across from Nicky and Tyler. "I don't get it. He drinks beer, has premarital sex, and curses, but he can't have a Dew?" Austin whispered across the aisle to Tyler.

Tyler let out a light laugh. "Jezebel on Friday and Saturday night, Mormon on Sunday morning; what's new about that?"

Andrew, who was sitting in front of them, turned around in his seat, leaned in, and whispered, "I thought it was hot drinks like tea and coffee that they couldn't have."

"Who cares?" Tyler said as he stared at the fullness of Andrew's lips. "You know you have beautiful lips. That's how I can tell you and your brother apart; yours are a little larger than his."

Austin turned to Tyler. "What, you don't like my lips?" pretending to attempt to kiss him.

Nicky sat listening to the banter going on next to him, trying not to laugh when he heard Connor shouting to J. B.

"Hey J. B., you know Squirrel's dad is a guard up at the Marshall County State Penitentiary?" Connor's voice was booming. "He says there's a nigger on his cellblock that looks just like you. The funny thing is, he got the same last name as you, too."

The bus fell deathly quiet. Nicky looked for J. B., who was sitting three seats in front of him. His head never moved, making Nicky unsure whether J. B. even heard him. There was a chance that, if he had his earphones in, he didn't hear the asshole's comment.

"Now, that's enough. Shut the hell up, Connor, or I'll shut you up! That's bullshit," a voice roared somewhere behind Nicky.

Turning to identify the voice, Nicky saw that it was Bryson, who was sitting directly in front of Connor. Now standing, Bryson looked like he was about to fight. As more people jumped to their feet, Coach Paul rose as well. "Everyone, sit down. Calm down!"

Nicky looked back at J. B. He was still sitting there, but now two of their teammates were standing in the aisle next to him. It appeared they had it under control, as J. B. was just nodding his head.

"Connor, you're out of line," Coach Silva shouted. "When we stop, you need to come with me. Understand?"

Coach Silva made his way over to J. B. and leaned into his seat. "You all right? I'll take care of this. I promise."

J. B. remained focused on the seat in front of him. His face was stern and tight, not saying a word as he gave Coach Silva a simple, slight nod.

When the bus pulled into the hotel parking lot, the bus was still quiet, with everyone whispering among themselves. As they gathered up their gear and exited the bus, they trailed into the hotel lobby single file.

Nicky was just about to walk through the doors when he heard the commotion behind him. He turned around and saw everyone in a big pile, yelling and arms moving everywhere. He could tell it was a fight, but he couldn't see who.

Throwing his duffle bag down to the ground, Nicky ran toward the fight, realizing who it most likely was. He pushed his way in and found J. B. pounding Connor's face with his fist. Connor was covered with blood and barely moving as J. B. repeatedly struck him full force with everything he had. It took five of them to pull J. B. off of what was left of Connor.

When they had J. B. restrained, Nicky remained straddled across J. B.'s chest. "Buddy, you're all right. Just breathe. That's it, just relax. I'm here for you." Nicky's voice was low as he spoke softly to J. B. J. B.'s eyes were blank as they stared up at Nicky. In unison, J. B.'s nostrils flared in and out, and his chest heaved up and down, his lungs fighting for air.

When the police arrived, Nicky was asked to step away. He and his teammates watched as J. B. was handcuffed and placed into the back-seat of a nearby patrol car. Concurrently, the paramedics were preparing to transport Connor to the hospital. Nicky watched as Coach Silva climbed into the back of the ambulance prior to them shutting the doors and driving off.

Time had become a blur for Nicky as he looked down and saw blood on his knuckles and shirt. *It has to be Connor's,* Nicky thought to himself as he was being ordered into the hotel by Coach Paul and a couple of hotel security staff. Nicky wanted to stay, but Coach Paul was stern in his orders as the team trudged into the lobby.

That night, at the team dinner, the only coach at the table was Coach Paul. Refusing to answer any questions about J. B.'s whereabouts, Coach Paul did let the team know that Connor had been admitted into the local hospital due to his injuries and that both Coach Silva and Coach Dean were with him. The team was sent to their rooms after dinner, where they were quarantined for the remainder of the evening.

Nicky and Tyler lay in the room they were sharing. Nicky hadn't spent this much time in a room with Tyler since he moved out of their dorm room. The two lay on their beds watching TV while they talked about the brewing feud between Connor and J. B.

In an abrupt change in conversation, Tyler questioned Nicky on how it was to live with the coach and pushed for the dirty details regarding sex with him. Tyler wanted all the details, even though Nicky was attempting to be as vague as possible.

The room was quiet for a moment when Tyler asked, "What do you know about the coach's past relationships?"

Nicky silently lay on his bed, thinking about Tyler's question and the photo he had found, seeing Phillip with that person.

Tyler spoke again. "I heard that a couple of years ago the coach was involved with one of his freshmen swimmers. I think it was the coach's first year here. So what was that, four years ago? Anyway, the guy ended up being a drug dealer. He was caught with drugs in his locker and was kicked out of school."

Not knowing who Tyler was talking about, Nicky laughed, trying to brush it off. "Where do you hear this shit?"

"J. B. told me. His girl Desiree tutors the guy. He's over at Tampa Community now. For real, you can ask him. She also said he was HIV positive."

Nicky had heard enough. "How about I just ask Phillip?" Nicky snapped.

The room went silent again as Nicky lay there, thinking about what Tyler had just said. Nicky had never thought to ask about Phillip's past relationships, but now was feeling threatened by the presence of this other guy he had seen Phillip with.

The next day, the team was in the lobby by nine o'clock in the morning. There was no sign of either Connor or J. B. On the bus ride from the hotel to the pool, Nicky sent several text messages to Phillip, looking for him and asking about J. B. The rumor on the bus was that Connor had a concussion and J. B. had been arrested. When they reached the university, Nicky still had not received a reply from Phillip.

Nicky looked for his parents in the bleachers. He first saw his mother wearing her green shirt with the big four-leaf clover. In the middle of the clover was a picture of Nicky that had been taken almost five years ago, with his name printed on the back of the shirt. Sitting next to her was his father, wearing his grey windbreaker he got for Christmas when Nicky was just a baby. Nicky loved his parents and smiled when he saw them standing and cheering as the team entered the pool area.

Even with his parents in the bleachers, Nicky's mind was racing with the fight between J. B. and Connor, where Phillip was, and the guy Tyler was talking about last night. It was a long meet, and by 3:30 that afternoon, Tampa Bay had lost miserably to Alabama U.

When the bus left the parking lot for Tampa, Nicky was surprised that J. B., Connor, Coach Dean, and Phillip weren't on it. The original plan, that Nicky was going to ride back with his parents, was scrubbed after the meet. Coach Paul had ordered the entire team on the bus. Between the loss and the fight, the team was withdrawn for most of the trip. The guys had taken their usual seats, leaving both J. B.'s and Connor's seats empty.

"Hey, are you asleep?" Tyler nudged Nicky awake.

"No, not now," Nicky fumbled with the volume switch on his phone to lower his music. "What's up?"

"Have you heard anything about J. B.?" Tyler asked before lowering his voice even more. "Has coach texted you anything?"

Not wanting to verbalize his answer in case someone could hear them, Nicky shook his head no. Wondering just where Phillip was, Nicky sent him a text to see if he could get a response. Within seconds, his phone buzzed: *Leaving now. Get your parents settled in and I should be home shortly after you.*

Leaving from where?

Car rental.

Love u. Nicky smiled as he hit send. Nicky thought better than to communicate any of this to Tyler with so many ears around them. Seeing that Tyler was rapidly pounding out a text to someone, it was clear he had already moved on.

Wondering if J. B. was in jail, Nicky thought about asking Tyler if he could send a fancy lawyer to help. At least get him out of there, if that was in fact where he was. Connor deserved that beatdown, and it should have happened a long time ago. Nicky shook his head, questioning why everyone was scared of Connor.

Once back on campus, Nicky wasted little time exchanging good-byes as he raced to his dad's car, which was parked off to the side of the bus. Glad for the short drive, they pulled up in front of the house shortly before ten. He could tell that his mother was worn out, so he wasted no time in showing them the spare bedroom. After his parents washed up, Nicky was surprised when his parents reconvened in the kitchen where he was fixing himself a sandwich.

"I thought you guys were going to bed?" Nicky asked as he closed up the loaf of bread.

His mother stepped up and placed one hand on Nicky's shoulder. "Honey, there's no sheets on the bed. Dad pulled the comforter back—"

"Oh, shoot, Phillip asked me to put them on before we left, and I forgot." Nicky put his sandwich down and was about to go hunt up the sheets when his mother stopped him.

"Just tell me where they are, and I'll fix it up. Eat your sandwich." Nicky's mother wrapped one arm around Nicky's waist and brought her son in close.

Mr. O'Hare stepped up as well, resting his hands on the counter. "Well, since you have the stuff out, I might as well make me a sandwich too."

Nicky's dad had been eyeing the cold cuts and cheese since they came in. "Do you have any tomatoes?"

Nicky pulled away from his mother and went to retrieve a tomato from the refrigerator for his dad. When Nicky came up out of the refrigerator with a tomato, his mother had moved Mr. O'Hare out of the way and was laying the thin lunchmeat onto the bread.

"Dad, can I get you a soda? I know it's too late for you, Mom, so I won't even ask." Nicky pulled two Cokes and a bag of BBQ chips from the pantry and set them next to his mother.

"I'm fine, honey, but I will take a glass for the bathroom."

Nicky remembered that his mother always kept a water glass in the bathroom in case she got thirsty in the middle of the night.

The three sat at the kitchen bar for about thirty minutes before the garage door to the house opened and Phillip walked in.

Usually, the first thing Phillip did when he walked in was kiss him. *Surely he wouldn't,* Nicky thought as he watched Phillip re-introduce himself to Mrs. O'Hare first, before shaking his dad's hand.

Nicky was about to ask Phillip where J. B. was, but Phillip started talking to his dad.

"Sorry we're not getting together after a win, but they gave all they had today," Phillip said.

"It was just nice to see Nicky again in the water. He looked good," Mrs. O'Hare said as she turned and smiled at her son.

"Yes, he's really filling out; you've been able to put a little muscle on him. He looks good," Mr. O'Hare added.

Nicky, embarrassed by his parents, stood off to the side watching as Phillip, looking stressed and in pain, engaged with his parents. "We could have had them in a couple of those races, but I think they were still mad at us for whipping them last year," Phillip said.

You weren't even there; how do you know? Nicky wondered, thinking he must have gotten it from Coach Paul at some point. Nicky knew the truth about their loss. They lost because their head was not in the game and their leader wasn't there to make it right.

"I love your home. Did you have it professionally decorated?" Mrs. O'Hare asked as her eyes moved about the room.

"No, I did it myself. It took a while, but it's all me." After fixing himself a glass of wine, Phillip moved everyone into the living room so they could sit and be comfortable.

It was well past midnight as they all talked. Nicky sat to the side, rubbing Emily behind her ears as his parents and Phillip did most of the talking.

That night, after everyone had gone to bed, Nicky finally had the chance to ask, "So what happened to J. B.? Where did he go after the fight?"

Phillip's facial expression darkened as he rubbed his nose. Nicky saw the tiredness in Phillip's eyes. "I stayed at the hospital until we could reach Connor's parents and they were able to fly out. Because Connor's injuries are so bad, the police got involved."

"What happened to him?" Nicky whispered, not wanting his parents to hear them.

"J. B. fractured Connor's jaw and broke his nose. They were going to do surgery today on it to try to set it. Most likely, he'll need some major dental work when this is all said and done."

"Where's J. B.?" Nicky needed to know where his friend was.

"Coach Dean followed J. B. over to the station, where he had to give a statement. Lucky for him, they let him go, and Dean rented a car and brought him home last night."

"So he didn't get arrested?"

"Not yet. They were going to forward the report to the district attorney's office, and they will make the call if he is charged or not. But Nicky, I can't see them not charging him. J. B. really hurt Connor and could face some real jail time for what he did." With the back of his hand, Phillip gently slid them over Nicky's cheeks. "Connor probably had it coming, but you can't go around kicking the shit out of people. If he's arrested, he's likely to be kicked off the team and possibly even expelled from campus."

"Can you do anything?" Nicky pleaded as he sat up in bed.

"I don't know what I can do."

Nicky paused for a minute before leaning back on the headboard. What Tyler had told him in the hotel room the other night had also been weighing on him. "Have you ever been involved with another swimmer?"

Phillip sat up. "What are you talking about?" he asked, his eyes wide as they stared at Nicky.

"It's just a question. Have you?"

Phillip looked down into his lap and cleared his throat. "Well, I don't know what you heard, but yeah, I have. A couple of years ago. His name was Rory. He was a freshman. It was my first year here. We dated a couple of months, and then it was over."

Nicky continued to stare at Phillip, even though Phillip wouldn't keep eye contact. He thought about everything Tyler had told him. "I heard there were drugs involved."

"Who have you been talking to? Where are you getting all of this?" Phillip questioned.

"Tyler told me. He said the guy was a drug dealer or something. Is that true?"

"No, it's not true! He was found with a bunch of pills in his locker, and the school expelled him. But that didn't have anything to do with me or why we broke up."

"I was in the cabinet in the living room. I ran across a picture of you and another guy. Who is that? Is that him?" Nicky asked.

Phillip knew exactly what picture Nicky was talking about. He had forgotten the picture was in there. "Yes."

"I saw you with him last year after a meet, and then you were with him again the other day, weren't you?" Nicky asked.

Phillip shook his head. "It was nothing, baby. It's not what you think. I run into him all the time; he still lives in town and occasionally shows up at a meet. When I was seeing him, it was a couple of months of bad sex. We weren't even a couple."

"Is he HIV positive?" Nicky asked.

Phillip was again shocked at the question and paused for a minute.

"Is he?" Nicky pressed.

"Yeah. Why are you asking?"

"Are you?" Lifting a single eyebrow, Nicky looked straight at Phillip.

"No. Of course not."

"We haven't used a condom since I moved in here. Did you use one with him?" Nicky's voice escalated as he also thought about Cowboy Mike fucking him without a condom his freshman year. Cowboy Mike didn't look like he was infected with the disease. But then, neither did Rory, or Phillip, for that matter. Nicky felt like an idiot. He was stupid and irresponsible for having unprotected sex, and it might cost him his life.

"Shh, keep it down; your parents will hear you," Phillip pleaded.

"I don't care about my parents. Did you use a goddamn condom? Yes or no?" Nicky repeated.

Phillip rubbed his eyes with his hand as he slid his other hand across his mouth. "No, we didn't."

Nicky reasoned with himself that what he did with Cowboy Mike was different. Not the same. It was one time. "Have you ever even been tested? Why would you do that if you knew he was positive?" Nicky asked as he removed himself from the bed.

"Nicky, come on, you'll wake your parents."

"How do you know you're not positive if you've never been tested?" Nicky shouted.

"Nicolas, really. Calm down. I'm not positive; you're not positive. We're okay. You're blowing this way out of proportion. What's going on? What are you really upset about?"

"You weren't honest with me. Why didn't you tell me any of this?" Nicky cried as he fought to understand his own anger. He too was a liar. Not only had he never told Phillip about not being a virgin, he too had unprotected sex with someone. Now here he was, mad with Phillip for not telling him the truth. How silly was that?

"Tell you what? About Rory or sleeping with someone who was HIV positive?"

Nicky didn't answer. He felt rushed with emotions of guilt and shame. If he was mad at anything, it should be himself, not Phillip. It wasn't right. Nicky knew it, yet it didn't change the fact that he was mad. Nicky gathered up the comforter from the bed and wrapped it around him.

"What are you doing? Where are you going?" Phillip asked as his posture slumped.

"I'm going to sleep in the living room."

As Nicky shut the door behind him, Phillip fell back onto the bed. He wanted to chase Nicky, but he knew better than to take the argument into the living room. His back was throbbing from the long drive, his mind and body had hit the wall, and he was done. Getting up, Phillip made his way over to his briefcase. Pulling out the bottle containing the Oxycodone that Rory had given him, he poured out two pills and popped them into his mouth before returning to bed. Phillip told himself that this had to have been the worst day of his life. It was not how he had envisioned the night, wanting so much to impress Nicky's parents, his future in-laws, with a special evening—and now this.

28

The next morning when Phillip awoke, the house was quiet. Embarrassed and ashamed, he made his way down the hall listening for the sound of voices. Making it to the kitchen, the house was empty. Seeing a note next to the coffee machine, Phillip didn't want to read it but did: *Gone out for breakfast – Nicky.*

Feeling relieved that he had a little time before he had to face Nicky's parents, Phillip turned and poured himself a much-needed cup of coffee. Phillip waited for hours for them to return as he nervously paced the house, not knowing what to expect when they did come back. The sickening feeling in his gut over the possibility of losing Nicky was more than he could bear.

That afternoon, Phillip heard the key unlocking the front door. Phillip's stomach tightened, knowing it was Nicky. Maybe his parents wouldn't be with him. Maybe they heard and headed home so they wouldn't be a part of whatever was going on. *Not so lucky*, he thought as he caught a glimpse of Mr. and Mrs. O'Hare come in and go straight to their room, shopping bags in hand.

"So I see you took them to the mall?" Phillip tried to joke as Nicky stepped into the kitchen. Phillip looked over Nicky's shoulder for his parents. "Nicky, can we talk?" Phillip softly asked as he moved in close to Nicky.

Nicky nodded in agreement. "I think my mom and dad are in their room. Let's go out back."

As they stepped outside, Phillip shut the door behind them. "Do they know?" Phillip asked as he leaned against the wall.

"Yes, they heard the whole fight. Apparently, you have cheap insulation in these walls," Nicky answered.

"Look, Nicky, I'm sorry for not coming clean about my relationship with Rory. I would be willing to go and take an HIV test for you. Just so you know that I'm not positive, that you're okay. I love you, and I hate fighting with you," Phillip spoke softly as he watched Nicky's body language for signs that he was willing to forgive him. "I love you so much," Phillip repeated as he clasped Nicky's hands. Phillip had lost so much in his life, but losing Nicky would truly be losing everything.

Nicky moved in and laid his head against Phillip's chest, tucking his head in the crevasse of his chest muscles. The two stood in silence for several minutes as Phillip gently rubbed the back of Nicky's head. "I am so sorry for hurting you," Phillip whispered down into Nicky's hair.

Nicky pulled away from him. "I have something I need to tell you."

Phillip's heart sunk at Nicky's sorrowful tone.

"I lied, too. I had sex once. Before you. I wasn't a virgin like you thought." Nicky took a seat in one of the patio chairs. "And I had unprotected sex that night." Nicky looked down at the table as if the words he was searching for were there for him to read. "Last night, I think I was madder at myself for lying to you and being the hypocrite than I was for not being able to tell you the truth."

Phillip took a seat next to him and took his hands. "I guess that makes both of us liars." Smiling at Nicky, he wasn't the least bit mad at Nicky's confession. "We were both stupid, and lucky. You know, Nicky, there comes a point in our life when we have to choose between ego and honesty. No matter how old you are, it never gets easier to do."

"Do you want to know with who?" Nicky asked.

"Do I know him?" Phillip cocked his head slightly.

"No."

"Then it doesn't matter. It's your past, and we should leave it there, where it belongs." Phillip leaned across the table and lightly kissed Nicky's dry lips.

After two more passionate kisses, Nicky pulled away, stood up, and adjusted his crotch. "We need to go inside in case my mom and dad are looking for us. They might think you killed me or something." For the first time in two days, Nicky laughed.

"I have to say, I'm embarrassed to look at your mom and dad right now," Phillip said as he stood up and took Nicky's hand.

Nicky snickered. "Don't be. You already made up with them by paying for their whole shopping trip today. They're all good!"

Grinning, Phillip asked, "Excuse me? What are you talking about?"

"I'm just kidding." Nicky rolled his head into Phillip's chest.

"I still need to say something to them. I'm looking like a fucking schmuck at the moment, I'm sure," Phillip muttered, more to himself than to Nicky.

That evening, after Nicky's parents got up from their nap, Nicky spoke to his parents first, assuring them that everything was okay. After an awkward and brief apology, Phillip suggested dinner at Terra Bella's Steak House in an attempt to make up for the previous night. After a discussion on how that wasn't necessary, his parents agreed to dinner.

At dinner, after being seated, the mood was subdued as everyone stared at their menus in silence. Mrs. O'Hare broke the silence, surprising Nicky when she asked him to pass her the wine list.

"Why?" Nicky jokingly asked.

"I think I'll have a glass of wine with my dinner. Is that okay with you?" she replied.

"Really? You never drink, never!" Nicky couldn't recall a time in his life that he had ever seen his mom take a drink of alcohol. On rare occasions, his dad was known to have a beer or two, but that was the extent of it.

"Well, sometimes. On special occasions, and tonight is a special occasion."

With no one else taking the bait, Nicky asked her, "And what is the special occasion?"

"It's not every day that we get to meet and know your boyfriend. In fact, we've never met anyone you have ever dated, right?" Mrs. O'Hare said to Nicky's father.

"I think I'll have one too!" Mr. O'Hare added.

Nicky's stomach churned at the unexpected word *boyfriend* coming from his mother's lips. He had spent all morning with them, and they hadn't said anything about his relationship other than admitting to hearing them arguing and asking if everything was all right. When he didn't have an answer for them, the subject was dropped. "Oh, my God! What is going on with you two? You guys never drink!" Nicky laughed nervously.

After placing their dinner orders with the waiter, Phillip took a sip of his wine and cleared his throat. "I would like to take a minute and just welcome you guys to Florida. I know that what happened last night was awkward, and I know that I probably made the two of you uncomfortable, and for that, I'm truly sorry."

Nicky watched as his parents turned their attention to Phillip. He could tell by his dad's expression that he was uncomfortable sitting there.

Over the next hour, the O'Hares shared stories with Phillip of Nicky as a child, school stories, grandma stories, and early swim meet stories, some of which Nicky was hearing for the first time as well. Nicky was glad to see that the mood had changed over to laughter and storytelling and that he was a part of the conversation, correcting his parents when they had their facts wrong in the story they were telling.

When the bill came, Mr. O'Hare attempted to pick up the tab when the waiter presented it, but Phillip was quick. "I'll take care of that," Phillip said as he grabbed the bill off the table.

After dinner, they drove to the harbor and walked the street along the water as the sun set. Prior to leaving the harbor area, Nicky took them by his favorite pastry shop, where they shared a colossal slice of chocolate cake until they couldn't eat anymore. When they arrived back at the house, it was going on nine o'clock. Phillip excused himself and grabbed Emily's leash to get the 120-pound baby out for her evening walk.

After Phillip left the house, Nicky waited for his dad to go into the bathroom and then asked his mom what she thought of Phillip. Nicky knew his dad would retreat to the bathroom after a large rich meal, giving him at least twenty minutes with his mom.

"I like him. I know your father was nervous about coming." Mrs. O'Hare removed her light shawl and took a seat on the couch.

"He looked nervous at dinner." Nicky's hunch about his dad was right, which was no surprise.

"When I told him that you were living here, he never said anything. You know that, when your dad gets quiet, it's because he doesn't know how to deal with something. Under normal circumstances, he's a man of few words, and this shut him down for days."

Hearing this, Nicky regretted bringing up the subject, but he also had a driving need to hear that everything was okay. "Did he ever say anything?" Nicky delicately asked, his stomach in knots.

"No…not really, but every once in a while, he would ask a question about you or Phillip, so I knew he was thinking about it." Nicky watched as his mother twisted and played with her wedding ring as she talked.

"Like what kind of questions?" Nicky asked.

Nicky's mother was silent for a moment. "It was little things. I remember one night we had just finished dinner and I was about to clear the table. Out of nowhere, he asked if I knew how old Phillip was. Then one day he asked if I knew that you were gay."

"Really?" Nicky responded, surprised at hearing his mother using the word *gay* for the first time ever.

"Oh, yeah, I think we both knew, but we never said anything. You were such a sweet boy. You were sensitive to everyone's feelings and needs, even as a kid. The world can be cruel at times, and we worried it would steal that sweet quality from you, that part of you that everyone adored in you." Mrs. O'Hare paused, taking a look toward the hall. "You know, your Uncle Kenny was gay."

Nicky tried not to smile as a long-time suspicion about his uncle was confirmed. "I thought so! I remember before he died—when I was little—that man that he lived with. Was that his lover?"

Glancing towards the hallway, Nicky's mother nodded. "We all assumed he was, but it was never discussed. They lived together for almost thirty years until your Uncle Kenny died."

"What ever happened to him? His name was Roger, right?"

"Roger…yes, it was Roger. After your Uncle Kenny died, Roger sold the house and moved closer to his daughter. I think it was Missouri. She called me a couple of years ago when Roger died. She had some things that belonged to your Uncle Kenny and wanted to know if we wanted them."

"Wow. So you like him?" Nicky asked.

"Who?" his mother's eyes narrowed, telling Nicky she was confused.

"Phillip!" he squawked.

"Yes. He seems like a nice man, and you look happy. That makes me happy. You know your father and I don't care about who you're sleeping with. To tell you the truth, my concern was if it was a healthy relationship, being that he is your coach. What if it didn't work? How would it affect your schooling? But after meeting him, I'm not as concerned. I liked him from the first day we met him. When he came to Brandy and we sat and talked at the kitchen table, we liked him then, and we like him now."

"He loves me," Nicky told her, knowing the impact the word would have on her. "You know he went to the Olympics when he was twenty. He never got to swim because of that accident with the van and the polo players. Do you remember that?" Nicky asked.

"I do. He was in the van *too*? I thought everyone was killed in that accident!"

"All the polo players were. He was thrown out and was the only survivor."

Nicky sat in the living room talking to his mother for about a half hour. It was Phillip and Emily who were first to return, followed by his father, returning from the bathroom with the newspaper under his armpit.

Over the next three days, they took Nicky's parents on a tour of the campus, a sunset boat cruise, and several outings around the town. The night before Nicky's parents left, Phillip and Nicky made plans for Nicky to skip the morning practice to ensure they got off okay. Since Phillip would be gone before sunrise, he was going to say his goodbyes this evening.

With the ten o'clock news wrapping up, Phillip knew it was his bedtime. "Well, you guys, I'm off to bed. Since I won't see you in the morning, I want to tell you goodbye now."

Nicky's mom stepped around Nicky and his dad to give Phillip a hug. "Thank you for having us. I am sure you're dying to have your house back."

Although Nicky couldn't answer for Phillip, he knew he was. Having quiet sex was not his forte, and he was tired of Phillip cupping his hand over his mouth while telling him to shush.

"Yes, thank you for letting us stay here," Mr. O'Hare added, finally picking up on what was happening.

"I know I'm not what you had in mind for your son. But I promise you, I love him." Phillip took a step back. "He's the rainbow in my life, bringing color and depth into it. I couldn't imagine a life without him."

"Thank you for saying that," Mrs. O'Hare replied. "He is the rainbow in our lives as well." She turned to smile at Nicky as she extended her arms for a hug.

Nicky hugged his mom, holding onto her tight. He could see his dad standing off to the side, taking it all in. The one thing Nicky knew for sure was that if his dad wasn't alright, his mom would have never been as relaxed and pleasant as she was to Phillip. Although he was a quiet man, his mother catered to his father, and often when she spoke, she was speaking for the both of them.

Phillip shook Mr. O'Hare's hand as the two men smiled at one another. "Come back anytime. We would love to have you."

"We will. Thank you," Mr. O'Hare responded as he released Phillip's hand.

The next morning, Nicky helped his dad load the bags in the car as his mother finished up the breakfast dishes. Standing next to the car, Nicky watched as his dad reorganized the bags Nicky had just put in there.

"Dad, can I ask you something?" Nicky's throat tightened at what he was about to do.

"Yeah. What is it, son?" Mr. O'Hare answered with a hint of caution in his voice.

"I need you to trust me on this. What me and Phillip feel," Nicky watched as his dad's face tightened, "well, it feels like what I imagine how you and mom feel about each other. I've never had a girlfriend, and no, I've never had a boyfriend either, in case you're wondering. Anyways, what I want to say is that it feels right. Phillip is a good man, and I love him. I know he loves me because he tells me so every day. There is not a day that goes by that he doesn't tell me that he loves me."

Mr. O'Hare fiddled with something in the trunk, clearly avoiding eye contact. "Son, I just don't understand it." Raising his head out of the trunk, he put his hand on Nicky's shoulder. "Is there something your mother or I didn't give you as a child? I like Mr. Silva and all, but how do you know you're in love with him if you've never been with a woman?"

Nicky felt the tears coming, and he didn't want to cry in front of his dad like a big baby. He wanted to be man, standing on equal ground with his father for the first time. Fighting back the tears, Nicky continued. "I know he's a lot older than me, and I know you worry about that. Who I'm dating will never change the fact that I'm gay. I can't change that. But trust me, dad, you don't want me dating people my own age. They're a hot mess, and I probably would get my heart broken because I love like mom does, freely."

Pausing for a minute, Nicky fought to regain his emotions. "Dad, I know your ability to love and accept me is separate from your ability to understand this, and that's okay."

Mr. O'Hare's shoulders relaxed, and the muscles in his face softened as he looked at his son. A slow smile formed on his father's face as he pulled Nicky in, hugging him as tight as he could. "I do love you, son."

⤵

A week had passed since they had their first official big fight. When Phillip came into the house that evening, he handed Nicky a white envelope. Nicky was lying on the floor in the living room studying, feeling a little tense about the amount of work he had to do and that it was piling up on him again. As he took the envelope from Phillip, he asked, "What is this?"

"Open it," Phillip told him.

Nicky opened the envelope, seeing that it was lab results. "What is it?" Nicky asked.

"It's my lab results, from my test."

Nicky studied it, still not knowing what he was looking at on the form. He scanned the document until he saw the words *NEGATIVE* to the right and HIV to the left. He knew what Phillip was showing him, but Nicky continued scanning the document, picking up more and more information. As his eyes rolled down the paper, he saw Phillip had the HIV test the day his parents had left. The blood sample was drawn at 1:45 pm. Sample results negative. Sample tested by M. Bishop.

Seeing the results in writing and knowing that Phillip did this for him, Nicky felt guilty again. He should have done the same for Phillip. It was surprisingly freeing knowing that Phillip was negative, although he never truly had thought differently.

"You didn't even tell me that you were going to get tested?" Nicky said as he looked up.

"I told you I would. I promised you that I was okay."

Nicky thought about Cowboy Mike. What if Mike was positive and gave the disease to him? He knew there was that possibility that he could be a carrier and not get sick. He had to be tested, too.

"Why did you practice safe sex with me, but not with Rory?" Nicky asked.

Phillip sighed. "That's a very good question. The truth is, that with Rory, I acted irresponsibly. We should have used condoms, but the first time it happened so unexpectedly that neither of us was prepared. Then after that, it just seemed like a moot point. I thought about it, but since he wasn't pressing the issue, I figured he was okay with it."

"Did you know Rory was HIV positive when you two were sleeping together?"

"No. I'm not even sure that he was HIV positive at that time; that was three years ago. I know for a fact that he learned that he was positive after we were no longer seeing each other. How long he'd been positive, I honestly don't know."

Phillip thought about the years past, the countless times he had sex in that dirty alley in New Mexico. Nobody ever asked him to suit up before he fucked them. At the time, because he had no desire to bottom, he assumed his risk of infection was much less. He knew better now. Truth be told, with all the stupid decisions he had made in his past, why he wasn't dead by now escaped him.

29

Two months into the next semester, the team was having an impressive season, despite having lost J. B., and Connor. It was rumored that Connor's doctors were going to take him out of the water for the rest of the season.

After Connor returned to campus for his academics, the school moved to protect themselves from further liabilities and expelled J. B. They stated they had received notification that the district attorney was filing charges and they had a moral and legal obligation to protect their students from harm.

When the news broke about J. B., Nicky and Tyler rushed to his house since he wasn't responding to any of their text messages. Reaching J. B.'s house, Tyler pulled his Range Rover against the curb of the quiet neighborhood. There was no one around, not a soul on the street.

"It doesn't look so bad. Not what I thought it would look like," Tyler said, shutting the ignition off.

Nicky looked at the numbers on the front of the house. "This is it," he muttered as he stared at J. B.'s house. Although it was the middle of the afternoon, Nicky knew they were in a neighborhood they didn't belong in. Two white boys in a Range Rover—it wasn't long before trouble found them.

"Hey, hey, what we got here? You white boys looking for something!" Ray-Ray asked as he came stepping out of the house across the street. Mimicking smoking a joint, he asked again, "Whatcha looking for?" It wasn't long before Tiny and Lil' Kev both followed out the front door as well.

Both Nicky and Tyler froze in the car as the three black dudes, all wearing various colors of wife beaters, approached the driver's side window. Just as Ray-Ray used his knuckles to tap on the window, Nicky heard J. B.'s voice.

"Leave 'em alone. They ain't looking for no weed!" J. B. was standing in the archway of his door with the screen door wide open. "They cool, Ray-Ray. They my homies."

Nicky let out a big sigh, trying to catch his breath, realizing he must have been holding it. He was never so glad to see J. B. in his life. Nicky looked over through Tyler's window and saw that the guys were backing up just enough for Tyler to get out. With little remorse for Tyler, Nicky was glad that he didn't have to exit on that side of the car. Nicky opened his door and made his way up the path to the house, never looking to see how Tyler fared. Making it to the porch and standing next to J. B., Nicky turned around to check on Tyler. Tyler had made it out of the car, Nicky saw, and he was standing at the rear of the car talking to one of the thugs. Nicky watched as Tyler spun around and set out toward the porch, slipping his phone into his back pocket.

"Whatcha doin' here?" J. B. asked as he smiled at them. "Ya'll look like you seen a ghost." J. B. laughed and invited them into the house.

"Is my car going to be safe parked there?" Tyler murmured to J. B. as he made his way inside the house.

"We tried texting you, but you never responded," Nicky said, interrupting Tyler, as he was not concerned about the car. Looking around the house, it was even smaller than his house in South Dakota. The front room was dark, with the lavender-colored shades drawn.

"Yeah, I lost my phone," J. B. mumbled. "So, what up, homies? Sit down. The girls are still in school, and I was just kickin' it."

"We heard the news about you being kicked out. Just wanted to know if you were all right," Nicky stated, taking a seat on the smaller of the two couches.

J. B. nodded to Tyler to take a seat as well. "I was wondering how long it was going to take before the news broke."

"Yeah, Coach Dean told us that it was pending and that's why you weren't practicing," Tyler added.

"Well, don't believe everything that bastard says. They sent me a letter the other day saying that I was barred from the campus. Connor got a restraining order." J. B. nodded his head toward a stack of papers on the wooden end table. Nicky and Tyler both looked at the pile of papers, but neither made any move for them.

Right after the fight, several of the swimmers met with J. B. at the coffee house off campus, but no one had seen him after that. Since they were all there when it happened, there wasn't much of a need to rehash the events of that day. They just wanted to ensure their friend was okay.

"Do you need a lawyer?" Tyler asked. "I can make some calls to see what I can do."

"Nah, they gave me a public defender. She seems all right. Ya'll want something to drink?" J. B. made little eye contact as he spoke.

"No, I'm good." Nicky was the first to decline the offer.

"I'm fine too," Tyler responded.

The three sat and talked about nothing for about an hour. J. B. asked how everyone was dealing with it all. Nicky did the best job he could trying to assure J. B. that mostly everyone was on his side and he had the support of the team.

When it was time for them to leave, J. B. walked them out to the car.

"When you find your phone, shoot me a text so I know I can reach your ass when I need to," Nicky told him. Not knowing if it was okay to hug him, Nicky was relieved when J. B. opened his arms first and came in for a hug.

The two headed back to campus. They had about two hours before their afternoon practice, and since Tyler had to pick up Austin and Andrew at their apartment, Nicky agreed to hang out with them. Out of the neighborhood and on the freeway, they only had a couple of miles to travel. Both quiet, Nicky could only feel sad for his friend who didn't deserve to be kicked out of school as well as off the team.

"You know, I was thinking. How come the coach didn't tell you that J. B. got expelled?" Tyler asked.

Nicky shrugged. "I dunno; maybe he doesn't know either." Surely Phillip would have said something had he known. Tyler would have been surprised at how much Phillip told him.

"I was scared out my ass when we first got there and those dudes came up to the car," Nicky admitted as he adjusted the temperature for the passenger side.

Tyler first smiled, and then a slight snicker came out.

"What?" Nicky asked, when he heard Tyler laugh at him.

"You're such a little white boy." Tyler pulled out his phone and showed Nicky his screen: *Lil Kev 407-555-6171.*

Nicky stared at the screen, not sure what to make of it. "They gave you their phone number? Why?"

Tyler smiled. "First I wasn't sure until the one that put it in my phone smirked at me. It was an '*I want to eat you smirk.*'" Tyler glanced over his shoulder as he changed lanes and accelerated around a large truck.

"I can't believe you. Can't I take you anywhere without you turning it into the *Dating Game*?" Nicky laughed.

When they arrived at the apartment, Austin was standing shirtless in the kitchen fixing a PB&J sandwich.

"What up?" Austin said when Nicky and Tyler entered the room.

"What's going on?" Nicky replied as they fist bumped.

"Ah, so what's this I hear about you living with the coach this year? I thought you were in the dorms."

"What?" Nicky's heart sank as his legs went weak. Looking over at Tyler, Tyler was wide-eyed and appeared just as shocked.

"Yeah, Squirrel was talking about it this morning. After practice." Austin tossed the knife in the sink and then folded the two pieces of bread together before taking a massive bite out of it. "Are you renting a room or something?" Austin managed to get out with a mouth full of peanut butter.

"Um…" Nicky stumbled for something to say.

"It's got to be better than living with Tyler and my brother. How much is he charging you? Maybe I can get in on that deal too. How many rooms he got in that house?"

He doesn't know anything. Just relax. Play it cool. Nicky smiled and replied, "Four hundred a month." He couldn't deny living there. Whoever it was that said something obviously knew that he was there. Nicky looked at Tyler again, as he was the only person to know.

"That's cool, man. I got to wake Andrew up." Austin licked a dribble of jelly that had run down his arm before walking out of the kitchen.

"I swear, before you yell at me, I didn't say a word to anybody!" Tyler whispered. Holding his hands up, Tyler's eyes were still wide as he looked at Nicky.

Nicky didn't know what to think. He knew Tyler had a big mouth, yet if he had said something to Austin, why would he ask if he was renting a room? That part didn't make sense. He continued thinking it over as Tyler pleaded with him. *Shit, if Squirrel and Austin know, then who else knows? I have to tell Phillip.* Nicky pulled out his phone to text him the news when he remembered Squirrel had his phone at one time. Maybe he did read the messages after all.

A minute or two after sending the text, he received a reply from Phillip: *Yeah, I know. Coach Dean asked me about it this morning. I told him u were renting a room from me. That I needed the cash. Talk later k.*

Nicky felt sick, like he was going to throw up. Where did the information come from? Tyler was the only one who knew.

Walking into the locker room, everything seemed normal. Nicky didn't know what he expected, but it was normal. Eduardo was walking right towards him. As the two passed, Eduardo nodded. "What's up?"

"Nothing. Hey, have you seen Squirrel. Is he here?" Nicky had to find Squirrel.

"Nope. Haven't see him." Eduardo kept walking toward his row of lockers. Nicky looked through the windows into the coach's office and saw Phillip and Coach Paul each sitting at their desk, talking to one another. No Coach Dean, Nicky noticed.

Nicky had just changed into his Speedo when the whistle blew and Phillip and Coach Paul came out of their office. "Guys, let's hit the pool. Varsity, you're swimming with Coach Paul after the warm up. JV, you're with me today," Phillip announced in his big coaching voice.

Making their way out to the pool, Nicky spotted Connor sitting on the bleachers with several members of the dive team. The good news was that his jaw was still wired shut so he couldn't talk. When Connor spotted him, his eyes locked and followed him across the deck until Nicky's back was to him.

This day was too much for him. He was panicking, and he knew it. He wanted to talk to Phillip. He could calm him, tell him that this wasn't a big deal. But right now, something didn't feel right; his gut told him so. Where were Squirrel and Coach Dean?

Practice was all but a blur for Nicky as he raced home and waited for Phillip. Nicky was taken aback when Phillip walked in the house and greeted him as if nothing were wrong.

"Well, so, what happened?" Nicky needed to know exactly what was said between him and Coach Dean.

"What, what do you mean? Phillip asked as he moved in for a kiss.

"About me living here. How did Coach Dean bring it up? What did he say?" Nicky couldn't understand why Phillip was acting so normal, like nothing had happened.

"Baby, it wasn't that big of a deal." Phillip motioned for Nicky to follow him into the kitchen. Once in the kitchen, Phillip poured himself a glass of wine and then exited to the back patio. Nicky trailed him, not believing what he was seeing. Phillip sat in one of the lounge chairs and then motioned for him to sit on his lap.

"No, I don't want to sit there. I know what you want. What did he say?" Nicky rested his butt on the corner of the lounge chair.

Seeing that Nicky wasn't going to let up, Phillip reclined back in the chair. "Let's see. We were in the office, and Paul had just walked out." Phillip paused for a second. "Dean said something to the effect that he heard you were renting a room from me. Initially, I was caught off guard by it but the fact that he had said it the way he did, I played right into it. We're both grown adults; it isn't that big of a deal. I'm your coach, not your English professor. We probably spend more time with you guys than your friends do."

"Did he say it like he was fishing or it was no big deal?" Nicky asked, wanting details.

"I think your making this into something that it's not. Relax."

Nicky took a deep breath. "So where were he and Squirrel for practice this afternoon?"

"Squirrel texted me that his grandmother was in the hospital, and Dean flew out this afternoon on a scout. I sent him to check on someone we're looking at."

Nicky rolled his eyes, not ready to believe that this wasn't a big deal to anyone. "Why did you send Coach Dean? You never send anyone."

Phillip grabbed Nicky by his waist and forced him up onto his lap. "Because I didn't feel like being away from you for the next four days, that's why. Now quit worrying, you little water rat."

30

With Tyler confirming that Nicky and Phillip were not the center of gossip, Nicky took Phillip's advice and put his paranoia to rest, concentrating on the issues he could control: his studies and his swimming.

By mid-December, Nicky and Phillip were surprised when the coach received a call from J. B.'s mother. Momma B. was extending a Christmas dinner invite to a few members of the team who were not going home for the holidays.

J.B. had been distraught and doing little around the house other than sleeping and tending to his sisters. She asked that they come and enjoy a home-cooked meal and spend some time with her boy, hoping it would cheer him up.

When Coach Silva put the word out to the team, Austin and Andrew snapped up the offer. Not wanting to be left out, Tyler opted to join them as well, saying that he would fly home Christmas Eve night, intentionally trying to minimize his time with his own family.

With just days before Christmas, the Breedlove house couldn't have been less cheerful when the gang arrived. An artificial Christmas tree standing at about five feet was set up in the corner of the room. The tree was covered with African-American angels, cherubs, and gold bows. There were several strands of multi-colored lights that flashed and twinkled in no particular order. At the top of the tree sat a larger African-American angel in a fuchsia dress. At the base were maybe ten presents. Other than the tree, there were a few holiday decorations scattered around the living room, and a dried-up mistletoe hung above the doorway leading into the kitchen.

"Here you go," Penny said to everyone as she sat down a bowl of nuts and another bowl of Chex-Mix on the coffee table in front of them. "Momma said dinner will be ready in an hour." Penny was dressed in a lime-green holiday dress laced with black netting over the lower part. To complete her outfit, Momma B. had purchased her a pair of black patent leather shoes and black knee-highs—of course, only when they'd been on sale, plus her employee discount.

"Thanks, Penny," J. B. told her as he grabbed a handful of the nuts out of the bowl. After Penny returned to the kitchen to finish helping Momma B. and Desiree, everyone else jumped into the bowls, devouring both.

With the elephant in the room, Tyler was the first to ask, "Have you heard anything from the D. A. on your case?"

"Nah, nothin'. My attorney left, and they had to assign me a new one." J. B.'s face was drawn and shrouded, with sadness in his eyes. Everything about him seemed different as Nicky sat and listened to J. B. talk about how he was the victim of deep-rooted racism, not only by Connor, but the university, with their decision to expel him, and now by the police and the courts in how they were treating him.

"Have you ever thought about writing Connor a letter saying you're sorry?" Tyler asked.

"Why should he have to?" Austin answered before anyone else could. "It was Connor who caused his own ass whippin'. That's such bullshit, that he should have to say sorry to him. If anything, Connor should see the damage that his words caused and say sorry to J. B.!" Austin's posture was stiff, his jaw muscles clenched as he sat up in his chair.

"It's better than going to jail," Tyler stated as he leaned forward to take on Austin.

"So you're saying he should say he is sorry for something he didn't cause, just so he doesn't have to go to jail? That is so 1950s. So when a gay guy gets bullied, he should tell the bully he is sorry for being feminine? Is that what you mean?" Tyler's suggestion had clearly struck a nerve with Austin.

"Austin, that's not the same, and you know it," Andrew said, coming to Tyler's defense.

"It don't matter. I couldn't anyways. I have a restraining order, so I can't have any contact with him," J. B. spoke up.

"That's not the point," Austin shrieked as he stared at Tyler and Andrew.

Drawing in a breath before speaking, J. B.'s voice was shaky. "Truth is, I shouldn't have done what I did to him. Doesn't matter what he said or did to me. He's white; I'm black. The law's on his side, and I'm the one going to jail. The funny thing is, I've seen both him and Coach Dean driving through the hood. They're the ones stalking my ass."

"Oh, come on, don't play the race card," Tyler said. "You kicked his ass!"

Nicky had heard enough. "What the fuck are you talking about? It's about race! He called him the 'N' word how many times in front of us, and what did we all do?" Nicky jumped into the conversation. He didn't agree that it was as simple as J. B. made it out to be, but he did know that nobody under a hundred years old used the "N" word without understanding the implications of its use. Looking at Phillip, Nicky treaded a delicate line.

It was a relief when Penny interrupted the heated conversation, calling everyone to the table to eat. The guys took to their seats around the table quietly as the girls filled everyone's glasses with ice followed by iced tea. Momma B. had cooked turkey, catfish nuggets, mac and cheese, candied yams, collard greens, and black-eyed peas and rice. The meal drew their attention, as they passed around bowl after bowl, spooning out large portions of everything onto their plates.

The stereo played Christmas carols from Natalie Cole, Patti Labelle, and Lionel Richie, the rich aromas filled Nicky's nose, and the guys laughed and listened to stories about J. B. and his siblings growing up. The food was plentiful, taking up most of the table.

Three years ago, Nicky would have never imagined he would be living with a partner, having dinner with an African-American family, eating soul food, and listening to R&B Christmas carols. Without a doubt, he knew what he was thankful for. Smiling, Nicky looked across the table at Phillip. The coach smiled back, then looked away, trying to avoid notice. They had planned on opening their gifts from one another when they returned home that evening, and Nicky was looking forward to *unwrapping* the sexy one across from him. Nicky felt the front of his pants tighten at just the thought of Phillip being naked. Nicky looked at Desiree's breasts to get his nasty thoughts under control.

Austin and Andrew, sitting side by side, had taken to silence as they devoured all the food they had piled onto their plates. The two Canadian boys ate so much food that their skinny bellies had started to bulge.

"This is great, Momma B," Andrew told her as he reached for a third helping of her collard greens. "What are these again?"

"Child, they're greens. Ain't nothing new. Black folks have been eating them for years." Momma B. shook her head as she watched the meal she had spent all afternoon cooking vanish before her eyes.

"Can we have the recipe for our mom?" Austin asked.

"No," Desiree responded in laughter. "If white folks bought them, they'd jack up the price, and they'd become high-class veggies for the rich. Ya'll just leave them alone."

After dinner, J. B.'s three sisters carried over a peach cobbler, sweet potato pie, and bread pudding that Momma B. had made for dessert. Never having to move, the guys continued for hours, laughing and talking at the table.

Stomachs full and plates empty, it now felt like Christmas. J. B. and Desiree sat close to one another, holding hands—Nicky wishing he, too, could hold his lover's hand like that. So ordinary, it most likely went unnoticed to everyone at the table but him.

♉

The next morning, with Phillip already gone and no morning practice, Nicky dozed on and off in bed. Having a lazy Sunday, he thought about the great food at J. B.'s followed by the terrific sex he and Phillip had once they returned. Nicky's morning wood reflected that he could easily go again if Phillip were still there.

It was almost one when Nicky crawled out of bed and made his way over to the campus library to meet some of the guys for a study group. When Nicky walked in, he saw Connor standing over with several other swimmers in the corner.

Walking up behind Connor, Connor turned to him. "You're just in time to hear this. You know J. B.'s going to jail for what he did to my face. He'll be right next to his brother, where he belongs."

Nicky wished he could rewire the asshole's jaw again as he shook his head at what Connor was saying.

Connor continued, "Come to find out, his brother shot some dude and stole a quarter of a million dollars' worth of drugs from him. Even though he went to prison for the murder, they ain't never found the dope. That's who's been paying that darkie's tuition. It's blood money from that dope."

Connor had just cracked a smile at his little announcement when Nicky jumped in his face. "That's such bullshit!" Nicky shouted as he pushed his chest into Connor's. "Your ass got the beatdown your big racist mouth deserved! You're lucky you didn't get killed for your ignorance and hatred. J. B. shouldn't get anything but a medal for shutting you up!"

Squirrel managed to position himself between Nicky and Connor as the entire library turned their focus on the escalating confrontation in the corner. Gently pushing Nicky back, Squirrel tried to calm his friend down. Nicky continued to shout around Squirrel, "I can't believe you motherfuckers aren't saying anything! Fuck him!" Nicky shouted as he pointed his finger at Connor.

Ron stepped up. "Come on, Connor. Even if it was true, that doesn't mean that's where the money's coming from."

"Well, where else do you think it's coming from? It isn't like he's got a job, and nobody is going to pay him for swimming like that," Connor barked, staring at Nicky.

Nicky threw his backpack on the table and yanked a chair out. Sitting down, Nicky's face had flushed, red spots surfacing on his neck and cheeks. Feeling his heart pounding in his chest, he knew he wanted to rip Connor's head off and that he had to calm down. Unpacking his bag, Nicky's hands were shaking. "Are you guys ready to study?" he asked as he turned his back to Connor. Over the next hour, there was an unnatural silence as the group studied, going over material and aiding one another.

"Can I talk to you?" Squirrel leaned over and whispered to Nicky.

"Sure, what's up?"

"No...privately, outside." Squirrel motioned toward the door.

Nicky could tell by the look in Squirrel's eyes that it was serious. Hoping it was some insight into Connor's behavior, Nicky agreed and pulled out his chair to get up. Squirrel rose too and headed out the front door ahead of Nicky.

When Nicky caught up to him outside, he noticed Squirrel was pacing. Squirrel shared the news that Ginger was pregnant and how they weren't ready to be parents. Initially, due to their faith, an abortion was not an option, Squirrel told him, but now, they were both rethinking it. Nicky listened as Squirrel justified his reasoning for thinking about an abortion, sounding as if his mind was already made up. Seeing the frightened look in Squirrel's eyes, Nicky couldn't help but wonder why Squirrel had chosen him to confide in and not his best friend, Connor.

Realizing there was nothing for him to say, Nicky listened as Squirrel negotiated his crisis aloud, sometimes pausing for long periods of silence before starting up again. Nicky offered no judgement or admonishment to Squirrel's actions as he continued to lay out his case for an abortion. After about forty minutes, Squirrel had come to a decision and was no longer in such an emotional dark place. Nicky watched as Squirrel ran off to talk to Ginger.

As presumed, it was made official that Connor's injuries would be keeping him out of the pool for the remainder of the season, forcing Nicky, Tyler, Austin, and Eduardo to fill the hole.

Even without Connor, Coach Silva's young men continued to set state and conference records, challenging every record they could, but the big win was Nicky setting a national record in the 200 Freestyle.

It was before the Missouri meet in February that Squirrel told him in a panic that he had to talk to him after the meet. Seeing the fluster in his face, Nicky sensed it was most likely an update on their conversation several weeks ago.

After the meet, when it was apparent Squirrel wasn't coming to him, Nicky swung his gym bag over his shoulders and set out toward Squirrel's locker. Finding him sitting alone on the bench in front of his open locker, Squirrel was mumbling as he read from the Book of Mormon that he held in his hand.

"What's going on, Squirrel? Is everything okay?" Nicky asked as he took a seat next to him. He saw that Squirrel's eyes were red, like he had been crying. "Are you okay?" Nicky asked.

"Ginger lost the baby the other day. We were at her house when she started cramping. She knew something was wrong, as the pain kept getting worse. I called the doctor's office, and they told us to come in. By this time, she was bleeding and could hardly stand up. I knew she was losing the baby; I just knew it." Squirrel wiped his eyes with the back of his hand as he cried.

Just as Nicky was about to extend his arm to hug Squirrel, there was a loud click, and the lights went off. If not for the light on in the coach's office, they would have been in total darkness. Nicky continued, wrapping Squirrel in a hug, shoulder to chest as Squirrel tried to continue talking through his tears.

"They say she lost the baby at the house, probably when she was on the toilet; that's when the cramping and bleeding was really bad. Man, I thought she was going to die. I was so scared, Nicky. I thought she was dying," Squirrel cried.

"I'm so sorry. How is she?" Nicky murmured.

"Better. The first day was bad." Attempting to gain composure, Squirrel pulled away from Nicky and sat up. "The funny thing is, we were planning to tell our parents this weekend about the baby. We even talked about getting married before she was showing." Squirrel let out an awkward laugh. "Maybe people wouldn't put it all together, just thinking we work fast."

"So do they know now?" Nicky asked sympathetically.

"Yeah, the cat's out of the bag."

Within moments, the two began to laugh simultaneously at the bad analogy Squirrel had just made by accident.

Squirrel wiped his eyes again. "I had to call her mom once I got to the hospital. I was so scared she was going to die. I didn't know what else to do."

Nicky sat as Squirrel went on about how he thought that it was God's doing and he was giving them a second chance. He related that he and Ginger had both decided to not have sex anymore and that they were going to wait until they got married. Nicky tried not to roll his eyes as Squirrel talked about God. He hated where Squirrel was going with the whole idea that God would kill a baby so he could pretend he was a virgin again.

As they talked, Nicky was surprised when he heard voices coming from the coach's office. Thinking they were alone, Nicky listened to the voices as they grew louder, recognizing that it was Coach Dean and Phillip. Although Nicky had first-hand knowledge of the tension between them, it was growing apparent to the rest of the team as well in the recent months.

"You may have recruited this team, but it's because of me those kids swim as great as they do! I did that, not you. It was me!" Coach Dean could be heard yelling.

"Are you delusional or crazy? You think you made this team what it is?" Coach Silva bellowed. "You're good, but you're not that good!"

"Over the last year, between you being high on pills and screwing our new swimmers, I've been running this damn team!"

The hair lifted on the back of Nicky's neck, hearing Coach Dean's declaration. The conversation between him and Squirrel stopping, the two automatically tuned into the argument. They froze when they heard the office door open.

"This conversation's over. I'll deal with you in the morning!" they heard, followed by the slamming of the office door, then footsteps hastily walking in their direction. Nicky knew that they were hidden by darkness, sitting in the middle of the row, when he saw Coach Silva storm by. Although Phillip hadn't see them, Nicky knew it was Phillip as he hobbled past the row of lockers, his gait reflecting he was in a great deal of pain.

"Woo, what the heck was that about?" Squirrel asked.

"I'm not sure," Nicky responded as he jumped up. "I've got to go!"

Pulling his motorcycle up behind Phillip's car in the garage, the two arrived at the house at the same time. Waiting for the garage door to close, Nicky saw that Phillip didn't appear to be as mad as he sounded when he left the gym moments ago.

"Are you okay? Squirrel and I were in the locker room and heard you and Dean fighting." Nicky followed Phillip into the house, where they were met by Emily. Wanting to get to the bottom of the fight, Nicky opened the back door for Emily to go pee instead of reaching for her leash. "Are you going to tell me what happened?" Nicky asked again.

Phillip tightened his fists and then loosened them. "He's a liar. A couple of months ago, when I sent him on a scouting trip, it was a test. I knew the kid and his parents. In fact, they're good friends of mine, but Dean didn't know it. I had been suspecting he was undermining me with some of the things I was hearing." Phillip poured himself a glass of wine as Emily reentered the back door, now looking for dinner. "He met with the Powells and was supposed to offer an apology for me not being there but instead communicated to them that I was the current head coach in name only and that he had been doing all of the recruiting over the last three years."

Nicky watched as Phillip took a full-sized swig from his glass. "So today I confronted Dean about it. It took everything I had not to punch him right then and there."

Nicky's suspicions of Coach Dean resurfaced. "But you're the head coach; can't you fire him?"

"It's not as simple as that. He has a contract. The school will want more than this. Especially when he could easily say that it was me who was setting him up, that I knew this family and didn't tell him." Phillip took another drink from his glass, finishing it off before pouring another one.

Nicky wanted to again bring up the leak of him moving in, how his gut told him that Dean was dirty. Phillip took his glass of wine into his study, and Nicky heard the door close behind him.

31

Several weeks went by without any news on J. B.'s case moving forward in the courts, and the team externally seemed to have grown into two factions: Team Silva and Team Dean. The once close-knit swim team was peeling away at the seams as tension loomed over them.

With Art's Pool Hall being their refuge, Nicky and Tyler waited for J. B. and Eduardo to join them. Having the luxury of being twenty-one, Tyler ordered them a pitcher of beer, which had just arrived when Eduardo walked in.

Nicky, Tyler, and Eduardo were already shooting their first game and finishing up the pitcher of beer when J. B. walked in. Nicky could tell J. B. wasn't in a good mood because he was being unnaturally quiet. His face was long, and his jaw was clenched.

"What's up, J. B.?" Nicky asked.

J. B. mumbled something as he took a seat on one of the bar stools along the wall. Tyler looked at Nicky and rolled his eyes as he walked over to the table to take his shot.

"Are you okay?" Nicky asked.

"Just dealing with bullshit that never stops coming."

"What's going on?" Eduardo asked.

Tyler took his shot, dropping the green and white ball in the left corner pocket. It was clear to Nicky that Tyler was tuning J. B. out as he took another shot, slamming his pool stick into the white ball, propelling the red and white ball into the air and onto the floor.

J. B. paid Tyler no attention. "I didn't want to say anything, but I met with an attorney that my brother arranged for me to see. That public defender wasn't doing shit. He found out that Connor is trying to sue me as well."

"I think you're getting ahead of yourself," Tyler spoke up. "You haven't even lost a criminal case yet! What can he get from you, anyways?"

"So I'm supposed to sit around and wait for it all to happen before I do anything? Just sit back and hope for the best?" J. B. shot back, "Well, it don't work that way in my world; you shoot first or you'll get shot. I ain't talking to you anyways!" J. B. turned his body away from the direction of where Tyler was standing.

Tyler threw his pool stick onto the table and walked toward the door. "Hey, where're you going?" Nicky asked, puzzled that Tyler looked like he was leaving.

"I can't take any more of this bullshit, listening to him whine about how the whole world hates him just because he's black." Tyler turned and looked at J. B. "Dude, get over yourself already! You're not the only one on this planet that's been dealt a bad hand!"

J. B. chuckled as he stared down Tyler. "Yeah, but it's not the same. You can take one look at me and see that I'm black. So you're flamboyant. Trust me, nobody feels threatened by that."

"Hey, Tyler, he was just expressing how he feels. Relax," Eduardo said.

"I'm not talking about being gay!" Tyler shot back, "Try being the son of a crack-head whore. I feel my shit every day, knowing everyone around me is better than me!" Tyler stormed back toward J. B. "You know what, I'll tell you about a messed-up hand being dealt to someone. Try being born to a junkie who would bring her tricks home just so she could buy her shit. As a little boy, laying there sleeping and being woke up in the middle of the night and being told to go sleep in the living room so your mother could have some stranger fuck her in the only bed in the apartment!" Tyler screamed at both of them.

Nicky was in complete shock at what he was hearing as Tyler continued in a rage. "Oh, it gets better, Mr. I-Don't-Want-to-Be-Black-No-More. Try looking into an empty box of cereal only to find that's where your mother hides her needles, or being so hungry that you eat out of dumpsters when your mom has been gone for three days straight. You're not even sure she is coming back, because you know that if you were given the same opportunity, you wouldn't come back, either! At the age of seven, having your mother drop you off at stranger's house, and while she's pushing you toward that person, she is telling you that's your new mommy! Yeah, that's right. I wasn't adopted. I was given away!"

Tyler jumped in J. B.'s face even closer. "Let's trade, come on! Give me your shit, and you take mine! I'd rather be black, blue, or purple any day of the week than to have had a childhood where death would have been better. Come on, give me your shit, mister!" Tyler sniffled and then wiped his eyes.

The room was deathly silent as Eduardo, J. B., and Nicky sat there, and Tyler trembled in front of them. Nicky stood up. Attempting to hug Tyler, he was pushed back. "I don't need a damn hug... I feel nothing. What I need, you can't give me!"

J. B. stood up from his stool. Hanging up his pool stick, he grabbed Tyler with force and pulled him in close to his chest. "Yeah, you do need a hug. You need to know what it feels like when someone loves you. When someone says they're sorry, what that feels like."

Tyler made an ill attempt to break free from his friend. J. B. snickered, "No, I don't want your shit, and your shit is real. Why we've been given this path to walk, we may never know, but we own it. It'll make us what we'll become. Sometimes, it takes others to show us that."

Nicky watched as J. B. and Tyler connected, Tyler's shoulders relaxing as a whimper was heard. Then, as if a switch was turned, Tyler pulled away. His lips beginning to quiver as he shut his eyes and took in a big breath. Massaging his temple with his finger in a circular motion, he exhaled. "I'm done. I'll see you guys later." He said without giving them a chance to stop him this time.

Tyler stomped out of the room, leaving Nicky surprised at what all he had just heard. The desperation and look on Tyler's face, though—it was real and honest. Nicky felt his pain.

That night, when Nicky caught up with Tyler at his apartment, he had calmed down considerably.

"Hey, I am sorry about this afternoon. I didn't know any of that about your childhood, and I'm sure J. B. didn't, either. I know he meant no harm. After you left, he said he felt bad about stepping on you like that."

"Sometimes I just get tired of people playing the poor-me card."

"Yeah, we got that." Nicky tried not to laugh. "Can I ask you something, though? Phillip told me that your adoptive parents were wealthy and elderly, so your childhood got better then, right?"

Tyler scoffed. "That depends on your definition of *better*. Yeah, I had everything—everything but love, attention, or affection. After the woman who had taken me in was killed in a car accident, her parents took me in. They had no idea how she got me; there was no legal trace of me being adopted or even who my birth mom was."

"So you weren't adopted?" Nicky asked, sounding a little confused.

"Nobody knows. But the people I call my parents are really my grandparents per se. But the likelihood was that this lady probably bought me, paid my mother some cash, and she was never seen again. Since the Rogers had no idea where I came from, they couldn't just give me back, so they took me in and put me upstairs in this big room, where I grew up…"

Nicky saw by the look on Tyler's face that this was just as horrible as anything he had endured with his birth mother. "Were you kept in that room like *Children in the Attic?*"

"No, not actually, but I might as well have been. I had more inter-action with my nanny and the maid than with them. My nanny was a swimming instructor and a lifeguard prior to coming to us. She and I spent a lot of time in the pool—sometimes literally all day in the summer. My parents continued to travel, being gone for long peri-ods, like months. I had no friends and was homeschooled until high school. I remember when I asked my mother if I could go to a regular school, she never even looked up at me when she said, 'If that's what you want.'"

"Wow, that sucks. You think being rich that your life would have been awesome," Nicky said, looking into the sadness that lay beneath Tyler's eyes. He realized that his best friend wasn't the slut he thought he was. He was only looking to feel something from anybody. The only thing he knew was what he saw his mother do as a child, and that was a heartbreaking revelation.

After several minutes of silence, Nicky spoke up again. "Can I ask you something else?"

"What?" Tyler replied sounding a little edgy again.

"Why are you here? I need this degree to make it in the world. I struggle with a 2.0 GPA. But you, you're carrying a 4.0. You're rich. What's a piece of paper going to do for you? You're a great swimmer, but you're not a serious swimmer...so why?"

Tyler paused for a long time—so long, Nicky wondered for a sec-ond if he was going to answer.

Tyler released a heavy sigh. "Maybe because I want a life I choose... not a set of circumstances that are bestowed upon me or circum-stances I've survived. This degree will be the first step toward the life I choose. Is that so wrong of me to want?"

32

Nicky and Phillip drove an hour outside the city in an attempt to have a discreet but romantic dinner to celebrate Valentine's Day. During dinner, Nicky shared with Phillip the big blowup at the library he had with Connor.

Phillip was furious. "Are you kidding me? Why am I just now hearing about this? I'm trying to get this idiot off my team, and you're holding information back that I could use. I should have kicked him off the team months ago, long before all of this mess."

Feeling as if he had just been scolded by Phillip, Nicky held his tongue. He had been talking about Connor's shady behavior for months, long before it was "this mess," as Phillip put it. He'd never asked a single question or wanted details whenever he bitched and moaned about the guy, but Nicky didn't want to fight, not tonight.

"Speaking of telling you things," Nicky wiped his mouth with his hand as he swallowed the food in his mouth. "A couple of months ago, when I was in the cabinet in the living room, I also saw bank statements. Do you make that kind of money?" Nicky's eyebrows squished together as he wrinkled his nose.

Phillip chuckled as he mimicked Nicky, wiping his mouth, but with his napkin. "No, I wish I made that kind of money coaching you knuckleheads. That is money from my accident. The Olympic Body, the transport company that owned the van, the truck that hit us, everybody just wanted to settle the case. The payout to the families that lost someone was in the millions. The lawyers who had the case explained to me that, because I survived, my settlement was substantially larger than the grieving family members. There's probably close to four million dollars in those accounts."

Nicky's eyebrows raised in disbelief as he leaned in closer to the table. "Are you shitting me? If you have that kind of money, why the hell are you working and not laying on some beach in the Bahamas?" Nicky whispered as if they were talking about a bank heist.

"It's not about the money, Nicolas, it's the need to be by the pool, to feel like I'm doing something..." Phillip's words trailed off as he reached for his wine glass.

The next morning, Phillip was leaning against the counter waiting for the coffee pot to generate enough for his first cup when the phone rang. His back was killing him, and neither the Oxycodone nor the Fentanyl patch were doing anything for him. He wheezed as he answered the phone.

"Good morning, Coach Silva? This is Ms. Graves, Chancellor Carroll's secretary. The chancellor would like to see you this morning in his office. Would eight-thirty work for you?"

By the tone of her voice, he knew she was not asking for his input on the time. "Yes, I can make it. May I ask what this is regarding?" As the pain surged up through his body, Phillip bit his lip, trying not to make any noise.

"The chancellor can explain it when you arrive. We'll see you then."

Hearing the dial tone, the coach played scenarios in his head as to what the meeting could be about. Hoping it was a follow up to some of his discussions with his boss about Coach Dean and Connor, Phillip attempted to stand straight up, the first step to making it to the shower.

When Phillip arrived at the chancellor's office, he was escorted inside by Ms. Graves. When he entered the room, he saw that Chancellor Carroll was standing behind his desk. To the right of him were Executive Vice Chancellor George Wilton and the Administration and Finance Officer John Gilbert.

"Good morning, Phillip. Come in. Take a seat. You know Mr. Wilton and Mr. Gilbert." Chancellor Carroll pointed to the woman sitting next to the door. "And this is Deanna Graham. She is in charge of public relations and legal affairs."

Phillip's eyes moved about the room as he took his seat. "May I ask what this is about? You're making me nervous," he said, directing his question to the chancellor.

Mrs. Graham took charge of the room as she rose and walked over to Phillip. "Coach Silva, the university has uncovered some rather disturbing news. We expelled a student three years ago for possessing illegal drugs on campus. Rory Gossett? Surely you remember him."

Phillip leaned back in his chair, crossing his arms.

"Well, information has come to our attention that the drugs that were found may, in fact, have been yours. Based on your past problems with prescription drugs and all, it seems very coincidental." Mrs. Graham stared down at him, offering an artificial half-smile.

Phillip was frozen. His throat closed up as he gripped the chair. What all did they know? he asked himself over and over as he waited for her to finish. He stared as the short, plump woman held her eyes on him. Her tone was cold and accusatory as she addressed him.

Mrs. Graham's voice dropped a note as her speech slowed. "Now, I'll be honest with you; we don't have hard evidence that they were indeed yours, but what we do have is three years of records from the Cedar Woods apartment complex where Rory Gossett resides. They reflect that Mr. Gossett's rent has been paid by you for the last three years. Why is that?"

Phillip took a deep swallow, feeling that his mouth had gone dry. His chest was tightening as he fought for something to say.

"You don't have to answer." Mrs. Graham told him.

"Payment to the Cedar Woods apartments over the last three years. This is a rather large sum of money, wouldn't you say, Phillip?" Chancellor Carroll added as he cleared his throat.

The chancellor handed the coach detailed records reflecting every cent he had given Rory. "We believe this was a payoff in exchange for him keeping his mouth shut about the drugs. Were you not in fact sleeping with him at the time?"

"Um…" Phillip released a loud sigh as he slumped deeper in his chair.

"Do we also need to discuss your current relationship with Mr. Nicolas O'Hare?" the chancellor added harshly.

"Do I need a lawyer?" Phillip was able to mumble. He didn't want to say something that could be used against him later. Wherever this was going, it was bad.

Mrs. Graham came from behind the couch. "That is up to you, Coach Silva. The university is prepared to accept your resignation today. We are not offering a severance package but are willing to bury this whole story in exchange for your resignation. We don't need this negative attention, and based on your past, neither do you. So the decision is yours."

Phillip didn't like this woman. He stared at her cold, unsympathetic face; her muscles were tight in her face as she stared back. He knew this was the only offer she was prepared to make. "Do I have a minute to think about this?"

"No, we need an answer from you, and I believe you already have it."

"Well, I guess I'm resigning." Phillip shifted his weight in his chair as he took in a deep breath.

"Good. Why don't you come by my office in an hour, and we can finish this matter up there," Mrs. Graham told him as she turned and looked at the chancellor.

As Phillip sat in his car in front of Mrs. Graham's office, he was overwhelmed with emotions. He felt wrecked. He couldn't think of anything other than what had just happened.

He was in her office for less than ten minutes. He signed several papers, including a gag order, a pre-typed resignation, and confidential agreements to the terms of the resignation, as well as several papers he still was not sure of what they were. It didn't matter. His career was over. He turned over his employee ID card and his set of keys and walked out of her office in a daze. He checked the time on his watch; he wanted a drink. Visibly shaking, he tried to put the car in reverse as he stepped on the gas pedal. He hadn't even put the key in the ignition switch.

Phillip didn't remember the drive home or pulling into the garage. He sat in his car inside the dark garage after the automatic light went out. He wasn't sure how long he had been sitting there when he heard Nicky's voice. "What are you doing? Why are you just sitting here? Is something wrong? Honey? Honey, hello?"

When Phillip turned toward Nicky, he saw that he was still in his pajama bottoms and hadn't combed his hair yet. Unable to hide the devastation on his face, Phillip didn't make eye contact.

"What's wrong? Why are you home already?" Nicky asked as he rubbed Phillip's arm.

Barely audible, Phillip muttered, "I've been fired."

Nicky tried to squeeze in the car next to him, positioning himself on the edge of the seat. "What! What happened?"

Nicky unhooked his seatbelt and nudged Phillip to get out of the car. Walking into the house, he didn't care what time it was or what Nicky might think. He needed a drink. Phillip poured himself a glass of gin as he looked at Nicky.

"What happened? Talk to me," Nicky pleaded.

Phillip didn't say a word as he walked into the living room. Stopping short of the couch, he turned towards Nicky. "You want the truth?"

Phillip retrieved Rory's picture from the entertainment center. His eyes were bloodshot as he mumbled something, his speech initially inaudible. "I haven't told you the whole truth. I've been lying to you."

33

Phillip knew he was on the edge of losing it all, and by the end of the day, there was a good chance Nicky would be gone as well. He had spun a life of lies, to the point he too was lost as to where the line that separated reality and invention laid.

Somehow from the kitchen to the living room, he had downed the glass of gin he just poured for himself. Taking a seat, he contemplated going for a refill before attempting to open up to the only person that mattered.

Since revealing to Nicky moments before that he was a liar, Phillip noticed that Nicky had been silent, his eyes following every move he was making. He saw in Nicky's eyes uneasiness, tension, and concern. That sweet, naïve expression told Phillip that Nicky was going to be hurt—deeply hurt. How could he hurt someone who looked at him the way Nicky did? He couldn't.

Clearing his throat, Phillip's right leg rapidly bounced up and down. "Oh, where do I start?" Phillip had no idea what he had to tackle first. It didn't matter; it was all a lie. "I was fired." Phillip's chest tightened, and his breathing accelerated. "I was fired because of drugs." That was the truth. He had said it, and no matter what came after, it had to follow the truth.

"Drugs? What are you taking about?" Nicky's expression told Phillip he required a full explanation.

"Not what you think." Phillip released a sigh, trying to control his breathing. "The medicine I take, I have a prescription for it, but some of it is bought illegally…off the street." Phillip thought about his conversation he had with Nicky several months ago, when Nicky outright asked about Rory and the drugs and he lied, saying it had nothing to do with him. "I get them from Rory, my ex."

Nicky's body pulled back slightly. "I don't get it. If you have a prescription, why would you get it from him?"

Phillip was embarrassed and ashamed. He couldn't even put it into words what he needed to say to the man who trusted and loved him unconditionally. He wanted another drink. "Nicky, I take way more than what my prescription calls for. My pain, it never goes away. So I run through my prescription fast."

"So?" Nicky brushed his hair out of his eyes. "Why don't you ask the doctor for more?"

Phillip had to say the words, admitting it to Nicky as well as himself. "I am addicted." Phillip's stomach churned at the words coming off his lips. Unaware of his restless leg bouncing, he wiped his sweaty palms on his pants and took in a deep breath, "To Oxycodone and Fentanyl. I take *way* more than what a doctor would ever give me… or anybody. What I take would probably kill the average person. I'm surprised it hasn't killed me some days…although that wouldn't necessarily be a bad thing." Phillip saw Nicky's body jerk as a reaction to what he just said. "I probably drink too much as well."

Phillip looked at the empty glass, wishing it wasn't. His mouth had gone dry. "I get my medicine from Rory. In exchange for what he gives me, I take care of his rent. I have been for the last three years."

"You called him your ex. You told me that you two only dated a few times. Is that a lie too?" Nicky's eyes burned into Phillip. "Are you still sleeping with him?" Nicky shifted his weight away from Phillip.

"No, baby. I have never cheated on you. I love you. Rory only gets me my medicine. The reason he was kicked out of TBU was because of me. He had just purchased some stuff for me and was waiting to give it to me when campus security accidentally found it."

"So you let him go to jail and get kicked out of school instead of telling the truth?"

Phillip felt like a piece of shit, an enormous first-class loser. How could Nicky look past that? "I don't know. If the charges hadn't been dropped, I don't think I could have gone through with it. When the charges were dropped, neither of us saw a need for the truth to come out at that point. Rory hoped if he didn't say anything, we would continue, and I used that to my advantage."

"So what happened? Why didn't you stay with him?" Nicky scowled, his eyes bloodshot.

"I wasn't emotionally available after that." Phillip stared at the coffee table, really staring at nothing. "He moved on. I don't know where he gets the medicine. I've never asked. I pay him the money for the medicine as well as take care of his rent. I don't give him any extra money. Well, on occasion, but not regularly."

Nicky blew out a breath as he stood up. "I have to pee." He glanced over at Phillip before walking out of the room.

There was a short moment that Phillip wanted to take this opportunity to fix another drink. Fighting off the urge, he waited for Nicky to return.

When Nicky came back, he took a seat opposite Phillip. "So what? Do you get help? What do we do?"

It was clear to Phillip that Nicky had been crying. His nose and eyes were red; he had successfully hurt him. Phillip thought about his two failed attempts to get clean in rehab. Going back into rehab was not an option. He couldn't live with the pain. He couldn't live without the drugs.

"I can't even begin to understand any of this: your pain, the pills, the addiction to them," Nicky murmured. "I can't believe there is nothing you can do."

Phillip's heart raced as he waited for Nicky to tell him he couldn't do it, that he was ending it between them. It was coming; that, he knew. "Believe me, I wish I could figure it out myself."

They sat in silence for a long time, the sound of the clock echoing in Phillip's ear. After what felt like eternity, Nicky asked, "Do you believe Rory said something to the school? Is that how they found out?"

"I don't know. By coming forward, what does Rory gain?" The thought never even occurred to him to question where the information came from. That was the least of his concerns.

"If he knows about us, maybe revenge?" Nicky posed the question. "It's not likely they would prosecute him now. What else is there?"

"Nicky, I don't know." Phillip knew as it came out that his tone was harsh.

"There's more," Phillip said, "I lied to you about J. B." Phillip watched as Nicky cocked his head to the side, waiting for it. "Do you remember when I told you that Chancellor Carroll called me about him? Calling in a favor. That was a lie. I never got any call from the chancellor. J. B. doesn't even know, but I've been the person responsible for his tuition."

"Why? Why would you do that?" Nicky asked. "Why would you hide that from me?" Nicky crossed his arms in front of his chest as he leaned back in his chair.

"I don't know why I never told you the truth about that. I can't explain that part. I was sitting at home watching TV, and J. B.'s brother's trial was going on. It was a big case in this area, and it was on every channel, every night. I saw his family at the court house, in the background, every day. They were there for him every day, despite the kind of a person he was. I remember thinking, *Why would you show up for someone who's guilty? He's a killer.* I saw they didn't have much. The news showed their house, the neighborhood, and at the time I was hating everything I had, guilty for having it, and throwing it all away, being an addict. One day, I don't even know why, but I was Googling his family and saw that J. B. was a swimmer. Looking up his stats, I saw that his times sucked, but I didn't care, I wanted to do something for them. Now his grades, they were a different story. The kid is smart. His SAT scores were off the chart. TBU already had an application on file, but I saw that he had turned down the partial scholarship that was offered. I wanted to be a part of something good—anything. So I made up the grant and offered it to the only person that would qualify for it, and that was J. B."

"I don't get why you would lie about that." Nicky stared at Phillip. His eyes were cold, and for the first time, Phillip couldn't read him. *I get it if you're mad; you have a right to be.* Phillip let out a long sigh as his stomach churned at what he was about to say.

"I'm not well." Fighting off the feeling that he was about to cry, he continued, "I have…" Phillip felt as if he was having a heart attack. "I want a drink. I want a drink real bad. I want to take my meds, have a drink, and go to bed." Phillip's tone was straightforward. "I'm an alcoholic. I'm addicted to painkillers. I'm fucked up, and you should run as fast as you can from me."

"Are you telling me to leave? What are you saying?" Nicky asked.

"I'm saying if you leave, I can't hurt you any more than I have. That I can't do this and not continue to hurt you."

The only thing Nicky said to Tyler when he called him asking if he could stay at the apartment for the night was that he and Phillip had a fight. When Tyler attempted to press for details, Nicky shut him down, stating he wasn't in the mood to talk about it. Luckily, Andrew and Austin were away until Sunday, so Nicky wouldn't have to explain anything to them.

When Nicky arrived at the apartment, Tyler told him that he could use the twins' bedroom. Though he wasn't able to guarantee how clean the sheets would be, at least he would have some privacy.

Nicky looked around the room, which brought back his freshman year in the dorms. The twins had, of course, twin beds with matching sheets. Both beds were unmade, with a single sheet crumpled across the mattress. Nicky knew it didn't matter which bed he chose as he tossed his body across Austin's bed and buried his head into his pillow. *Really, no pillowcase?* Nicky sniffed the pillow, instantly regretting doing so as the stench penetrated his nostrils.

Phillip was a neat freak and would be having a cow if saw this. The sheets were changed every time they had sex on them, and Phillip insisted that dirty clothes go in the hamper and wet towels go into the dryer before being tossed in the hamper to avoid mildew.

Nicky rolled over onto his back and grabbed his phone to check the time. Stunned that it was four in the afternoon, he hadn't taken a shower, had missed both his classes, and hadn't eaten a single thing all day. With his stomach in knots, the last thing he wanted was anything to eat. In the year and half he had been with Phillip, he had grown accustomed to eating regular meals and having a clean house. It seemed so normal now to have clean sheets. Removing his t-shirt, Nicky wrapped it around the stained pillow before laying his head on it.

He wasn't sleepy, and his only thought was of what Phillip was doing at the house. *Why did I have to leave the house? Is Phillip going to break up with me? What did I do? Who told the school about us?* And then the distorted thinking set in: *Is Rory there? Is Phillip lying about them not having sex still? Is Phillip at Rory's apartment now? How many times has he been to Rory's apartment since we've been together? How sick is Phillip?* Nicky couldn't turn it off as the questions kept pounding into his brain. Nicky lay for what seemed like hours until there was a knock on the door.

"Hey, you going to practice? You want a ride?" Tyler asked on the other side of the door. "Are you awake?"

"Yeah. I'm awake." Nicky hoped he wouldn't open the door, rolling over to face the wall in case he did. "No. Go without me. I'm not feeling good. Tell them that I'm not coming." Nicky pictured this afternoon's practice; Phillip wouldn't be there.

"'Kay, I'm leaving. Text me if you need anything."

"'Kay." Nicky lay listening as Tyler made his way through the front door and could be heard running down the concrete steps leading down from the apartment.

Not realizing that he must have dozed off, the feeling of his phone buzzing startled him. Nicky searched for his phone, which had been in his hand, realizing by the pulsation it was now under his body. Seizing it, he looked at his screen, seeing a new text from Phillip: *I love u.*

Nicky read the message again and then looked at the time displayed in the lower corner of his phone; it was three in the morning. He didn't know what to make of the simple message as his mind processed what had happened. There was that pit in his belly; he wanted to vomit. Why was he here instead of at home with Phillip?

Nicky typed back: *I love u more. I am at Tyler's. Can I come home?* How long was he supposed to stay here, away from his own house? What was Phillip doing? There was no plan. Phillip had told Nicky he needed space to think, and so he had left. Nicky stared at his phone, waiting for a reply.

The apartment was quiet. Wondering if Tyler was home, Nicky slipped out into the hall bathroom to pee. Exiting the bathroom, Nicky saw that Tyler's bedroom door was shut. *He must be home.*

Returning to his room, Nicky checked to see if Phillip had replied. Nothing. His eyes adjusting to the dark room, Nicky sat up against the headboard, bringing his knees up into his chest to rest his head on them. He had practice in two hours, and he was exhausted. There was no way it was going to happen, he told himself, when he felt his phone buzz: *Get some sleep love bug. See u at 9.*

Why nine o'clock? Nicky wondered as he tossed the phone toward the foot of the bed. Within seconds, Nicky reached for his phone again and went to his Facebook account. He hadn't been on Facebook in weeks and had two hundred and seventy notifications. First checking to see if he could find this Rory guy, Nicky hunted but found no one that fit the bill. Clicking through the notifications and private messages, Nicky ticked off the hours until he couldn't take it anymore. Grabbing his shirt, he rinsed out his mouth with a bottle of mouthwash that was sitting there. With several swishes, Nicky spit down into the sink and then bolted from the apartment.

When he arrived home, the street was tranquil, sprinklers were going, and a few women were out doing their power walking. It felt as if he was gone for a week. Entering the house, he saw Phillip sitting in the living room. The house was still closed up as Nicky made his way to Phillip.

"Good morning," Nicky whispered, unsure if Phillip was awake, seeing that his body was not moving. "Hey, baby. Are you okay?" Nicky called out as he got closer.

Just as he got to the couch, Phillip lifted his head and smiled. Standing up, Phillip reached out and embraced Nicky, wrapping his arms tightly around him. Feeling Phillip's body tremble, he knew Phillip was crying. He had never seen his lover cry. Even on the worst days, when his pain was unmanageable, he didn't cry. His man was not a crier. Phillip held him tight, Nicky melting in the folds of his arms. It had been the longest night of his life without Phillip, and he never wanted to leave again.

"Sit down. We need to talk," Phillip's eyes were swollen, as if he had been up all night. His beard was rough, with a day's growth. But it was the tone in Phillip's voice that alarmed Nicky more than his appearance.

Phillip dropped his head as he scratched his hair and then lowered his hand across his face. His voice was deep as his bloodshot eyes bolted from the floor to Nicky to the ceiling fan that spun above them. "I have to get help." Phillip paused for a second and released a breath. "I can't do this on my own."

Nicky didn't understand—of course, he wouldn't have to do it on his own. He was here for him; they would do it together.

"After you left yesterday, I made some calls. I found a treatment center that specializes in pain management and addiction. I have stuff I need to work on. The drinking, for one."

Nicky glanced around the room to locate a wine glass or an empty bottle, the signs that he had been drinking. There was nothing. Phillip coughed as he started to say something. "There's a place in California. They can get me in the day after tomorrow. I have to do a detox; I'll start methadone." Phillip stopped. "I'm saying too much. I know you don't get it all, and you don't have to. But know that I want help. Anyway, I have to leave tomorrow."

Nicky had seen people in detox on the TV and in movies; they were not his Phillip. They were crackheads, junkies, and hookers, not Phillip. "There is nothing you can do here? So I can help you?"

"Sweetheart, you can't help me." Phillip took Nicky's hands and clasped them. "I have to do this on my own."

Nicky took his hands back. "What does that mean?" He knew what it sounded like.

"I'll understand if you can't do this, if you want out." Phillip took Nicky's hands back, this time holding them tighter. "I love you. It's you on the other side that I'll be fighting to get to. I love you." Phillip leaned in, and the two embraced until Nicky felt Phillip's hand lift his chin. "Look at me, baby," Phillip said as the two looked into the other's eyes. "I've chosen darkness for so long. But there is light, and for the first time in a long time, I choose light."

Nicky fought the tears unsuccessfully. "Do you remember telling me that you were so depressed after your accident? You were back home in a wheelchair, and your coach, Marcus, came in and surprised you."

Phillip's eyes prickled with tears. "Yeah?"

"You were surprised to see Marcus; do you remember? You asked him what he was doing there. Do you remember what he said to you?"

Subdued laughter was freed from Phillip. "He told me to get up."

"That's right." Nicky placed his hand over Phillip's heart. "I'm here for you now, and I'll be here for you tomorrow, and the next day, and the day after that."

Phillip hugged Nicky tightly as he rubbed his hand up and down Nicky's small frame. "I love you so much."

"I love you more," Nicky murmured back.

"It's weird. You remember when you asked me why I coach when I didn't have to work? I thought by being close to the pool, to swimmers, I could find myself. I really thought this until I met you and fell in love." Phillip gently placed a kiss on Nicky's bottom lip. "I realize now that I was wrong. You can't go home again. I was chasing a bogus dream to avoid reality, and the drugs and alcohol helped me do this. They're a problem for me, a real problem. When I fell in love with you, you became the reason to get up in the morning, to want to live a better existence, but like an addict, I wanted both. Before you, I truly thought that I lost it all in that accident, that my dreams and my life were gone. But now I know, the accident was my real journey, my real life."

34

Tampa Bay University put out a press release that Coach Silva had resigned from his position and was moving on to new opportunities. They named Coach Dean as his replacement as the university's new head coach of the swim team, followed by a short bio of the coach's accomplishments that made him qualified for the position.

The next day, Phillip's phone rang non-stop from reporters wanting the exclusive real story. Phillip was not ready to talk to anyone, so they unplugged the phone in the house for the remainder of their time together. Tyler was the only person that Nicky confided in, telling him everything, venting to his best friend about all of it. The rest of the world was told that Phillip was tired of coaching and had a business proposal in the works.

In silence, Nicky pondered just how this information became known to the school. The logical answer was Rory, but that didn't make sense. What was he gaining by telling? Nicky needed to know who was behind destroying the coach and why. Three people knew of Rory and the drugs: Tyler, J. B., and Desiree. Did they know about the rent situation as well and use that for their advantage? What motive could they have to destroy the coach? Nicky began to regret that he had confided everything to Tyler.

As Nicky sat on a stool in J. B.'s garage watching J. B. change out the spark plugs in his mother's new used car, he waited for the right time to confront J. B. about what he knew about the coach and Rory. Could he have sold out the coach for money? None of it made sense. When J. B. asked how the coach was, Nicky used this as his in. "I don't know. I guess he's got other plans."

J. B. smirked. "Come on man, let's be honest. Since he's not there anymore, let's keep it real. We know ya'll were fucking. Whatever you do in your private life is your business. I don't care, you know that. I got a cousin who's queer."

Nicky was taken aback that J. B. was so forthcoming with knowing about them. "Who told you?" he asked, suspecting it had to have been Tyler.

"Shit, I don't know. The whole team knew. The only secret was that you guys didn't know we knew. It probably came from your boy Tyler. You know he can't keep a secret."

Tyler? He couldn't believe it was Tyler, but then again, he knew his inability to keep secrets. *Why would he do it, though?* "Did he ever say anything to you?" Nicky asked.

"No."

"Well, since we're talking about Tyler, he told me that you knew something about Phillip's ex-boyfriend," Nicky stated.

"Yeah," J. B. paused for a minute, stopping what he was doing under the hood. Wiping his hands clean with a rag, he walked over to Nicky. "Yeah, last year Des was tutoring some dude over at Tampa Community. At the time, I didn't know anything about you two. She said this guy claimed he was the coach's boyfriend, or whatever you call it. Anyway, he told her that he went to jail for some drugs that were supposedly the coach's and that the coach was hooked on drugs. I don't know if any of it was true. I see the coach every day, and he don't look like an addict to me. This cat didn't know that Des was dating me, and she never told him either."

Nicky pretended to look surprised at what J. B. was saying. "Did you tell anyone what Des told you?"

J. B. nodded as he stared at Nicky. "Yeah, I think I told Tyler. Shit, that was last year."

Nicky knew J. B. was telling the truth, as his story matched Tyler's. He felt the sincerity in J. B.'s voice and was comfortable believing he was not the source. He also knew that if Rory was talking and telling random people about what happened, the information could have come from anyone.

In an effort to not look like he was fishing for information, Nicky changed the subject. "So what's up? What are you going to do about finishing up school? That was bullshit that they kicked you out and nothing happened to Connor."

J. B. smiled as he shook his head. "Connor never did like me and wanted me out, and he got what he wanted."

"Well, you're not alone. I suspect he hates me too."

"You're probably right." J. B. laughed. "Mom is talking about wanting to open up her restaurant. She wants to call it Catfish Corner. She said her catering is doing well and has dreams of opening up her own place. She was talking about Maurice and me helping her out. With my schooling, she figures I could manage the place, the business end of things, and Maurice could be the muscle. Can't do anything without no money though, and ain't no bank going to loan us no cash. She was talking about asking some of her white friends about investing. They're always asking her to cook them something for their parties. They love her soul food and have more money than they know what to do with."

Nicky looked at J. B., thinking that he had just the person who might want to invest in J. B. and his dream of Catfish Corner.

That day, there was one more person Nicky wanted to talk to, and that was Squirrel, Connor's best friend. Coming around the corner, Nicky spotted Squirrel out in the front yard, washing his car in the driveway.

"Hey, what are you doing here?" Squirrel asked, surprised to see Nicky.

"I was just driving by and saw you and remembered there was something I wanted to ask you."

"Oh yeah, what's that?" Squirrel asked apprehensively.

"A couple of weeks ago, when you and I were talking, and the coach walked past us, you asked me about his back and how he was doing. Why did you ask me?"

"Did I? I don't remember asking you that. Are you sure it was me?" Squirrel dipped his rag in the soap bucket before starting on the driver's side, splashing soap everywhere.

"Squirrel, don't lie to me." Looking Squirrel straight in the eye, Nicky asked, "You knew we were together didn't you? That's why you asked *me*. It was a slip because you were genuinely concerned for him." Knowing just how religious Squirrel was, Nicky knew he wouldn't be able to lie if he stared at him. "You told the administration about us, didn't you!" Nicky snapped.

"No, I didn't say anything. I swear!" Squirrel stopped washing his car and looked up at Nicky.

"You pretended to be my friend and came to me when you were in trouble, and then you turned around and got the coach fired!" Nicky yelled as he jumped in Squirrel's face, grabbing him up by the collar.

It was all too much for Squirrel, who tried to cover his face so Nicky couldn't hit him. "It wasn't me; it was Connor and Coach Dean. They went to the school. They were the ones who told! I swear it wasn't me!" Squirrel cried out.

Knowing he had taken the bait, Nicky didn't let up. "You liar! Jesus, what about your faith? Since when is it okay to lie?" Nicky shouted.

"Let me explain. It was all by accident," Squirrel cried. "Ginger and I were looking at moving in together when we thought we were going to have the baby. She went to her apartment manager and asked about putting me on her lease."

"I'm listening," Nicky said as he let go of his shirt and watched as Squirrel fell to the ground.

"When the manager found out that I swam for Tampa, she brought up Rory. He lives in the same complex, and she told Ginger that the school was paying his rent. She thought he was still swimming for the team. At first, I asked Connor if he knew anything about the school helping us with our rent so I could get a break too. Connor denied knowing about any program, but a couple of days later, he told me to tell Coach Dean about what I heard. I didn't understand why." Squirrel was in tears at this point as he took a pause for air.

"Go on," Nicky said.

"About a week later, Connor came to me and told me that Coach Dean found out it was Coach Silva who was paying his rent, not the school. I don't know how he found out; he didn't tell me!"

"So then who went to the school and told?" Nicky demanded.

"I don't know! I guess the coach," Squirrel suggested.

Nicky got what he came for, as he shook his head in disgust. "Well, just know that your so-called friends played you! They used you to destroy the lives of others."

Navigating his motorcycle in and out of traffic, Nicky couldn't believe what Squirrel had told him. Trembling, Nicky couldn't wait to share it with Phillip. As he came to the red light, he inched his motorcycle through the cars to the front of traffic. He waited for the light to change, playing Squirrel's confession over and over in his head. When he glanced over to his right, he saw Coach Dean and Connor sitting at a table, having lunch on the front patio of a cafe.

Nicky stared at them, sitting there laughing and talking. Seeing them somehow validated what Squirrel had just told him, making his heart race even more. He remembered that J. B. said the whole team knew about his and Phillip's relationship. Finding out about Rory was the last piece they needed to get rid of Phillip. They were the masterminds behind this whole mess. Connor, the bigot, got what he wanted; he got rid of J. B. and Phillip. It was the perfect plan, which included Dean getting a promotion.

When the light turned green, Nicky initially thought about pulling the throttle back as far as he could and crashing his motorcycle right into them at full speed. He wasn't concerned if it would kill him as he revved up the engine.

Parking the bike at the curb next to them, Nicky removed his helmet and casually walked over to their table.

"What's up, guys?" Nicky called out as he approached the table. Seeing him, both Connor and the coach had a look of surprise on their faces. "I know what you did!" Nicky pointed his finger at Dean. "You're a snake, and you're going to get yours."

Coach Dean popped up out of his chair as if ready to fight. "Hold on, O'Hare! You better reel it in, and real fast. Don't you ever talk to me like that. I don't know what you're mad about, but you better fix it!"

"Fuck you!" Nicky snapped, "I know what the two of you are all about!" Staring at Connor, Nicky whacked a glass of water off the table, splashing it all over Connor's shirt and lap. "You're going to get yours too. Start looking over your shoulder, because I'm coming for you! You'll never be shit because I'll be there every time to take it from you. You will die being second to me!" His whole body quivered as he stared them both down.

With the coach entering rehab, Nicky knew his days of swimming with Coach Dean were numbered, anyway. He had no desire to swim for him. Nor could he face Squirrel or Connor and their righteous little group ever again.

Storming back to his motorcycle, Nicky popped the clutch, and the front of the bike shot up as the back tire screeched, leaving a trail of white smoke in its wake.

Trying to get his emotions under control, Nicky propelled the bike through the streets toward home. He had no idea what he was going to do about school or swimming. Looking at Dean and Connor in his rearview mirror, Nicky did know he would never get in another pool with them.

☙

When Nicky walked in the door, he was on fire, slamming the door behind him. Phillip, hearing him come in, met him in the hallway. "What's going on? You're in a snit."

"Yeah, I don't know what a snit is, but I just had it out with Connor and Coach Dean. I've got to go pee, and then I'll tell you everything."

Coming out of the bathroom, Nicky found Phillip in his office, talking to someone on the phone. From what Nicky could gather, it sounded like instructions or a to-do list for someone in his absence.

"So what's going on?" Phillip asked as he turned his cell phone back off. Giving his full attention to Nicky, he reclined his chair. Over the next hour, Nicky filled him in on every detail of his conversations with J. B. and Squirrel, followed by the fight with Coach Dean. He shared with Phillip his gut feelings on Coach Dean, Connor, and Squirrel, starting on his first day on the team.

Hearing the depth of deception by those closest to him, Phillip drew inward, growing quieter and quieter. By the time Nicky was done and came up for air, Phillip had little to say. Taking in a big breath, Phillip exhaled the air from his lungs, pushing it out until there was no more. "Their day will come."

"That's what I told them—" Nicky shrieked.

"No, hear me out." Phillip held up his hand, trying to quiet Nicky. "Their day will come, and that is not up to us to decide when that is. I can only take on the part that I did, that I have control over. What they did only brought to light the wrongs that I was doing. I own that."

"But—" Nicky tried to interrupt.

"What they did, it was wrong. They need to own that themselves, not me. I've got more on my plate then I can already handle. I'm not looking to take on anyone else's shit. I've got enough to last me the rest of life. I need you to be here for me, in the present. I leave in the morning, and this is not how I intend on spending my last couple of hours with you."

That night, the two went to bed early, under the pretense that they had to be at the airport early. Their naked bodies brushed one another as they talked about everything, from the first day they saw each other to children and death. Instead of making love that night, Phillip held Nicky tightly as Nicky talked. It wasn't until Nicky heard the light snore emanating from his lover that he knew he had fallen asleep. Secure in his arms, Nicky snuggled in, and when he found that perfect position, closed his eyes as well.

Three days later, keeping a close eye on Nicky, Tyler had been calling, checking to see if he was okay and asking for any updates on Phillip. This morning, though, Nicky didn't feel like talking to anybody. After letting Tyler's call go to voice mail and not responding to his texts, Nicky wasn't that surprised when Tyler showed up at the house. Like a storm, Tyler huffed at him for ignoring him as he trailed Nicky into the kitchen.

"What are you wearing?" Tyler asked, staring at Nicky's ass under the only garment he had on: a white dress shirt. "Do you have underwear on?"

"No," Nicky answered. "It's one of Phillip's dress shirts. He had it on the day before he left. I can smell him on it."

"Let me see your ass!" Tyler teased.

"Tyler. Go away." Nicky pulled out a stool at the kitchen bar. "Get me some orange juice?" Nicky pointed to the cabinet that contained the glasses.

"The things you miss, by not living with me and not returning my texts. Do you remember Lil' Kev?" Tyler asked as he retrieved the orange juice from the refrigerator and poured himself a glass of juice first.

"No. I don't. Nicky shook his head, not knowing where this was going.

"He was the guy when we went over to J. B.'s house that gave me his phone number. Well, I called him, and it turns out Lil' Kev ain't so little."

Nicky let his head collapse onto the counter. "Really? I'm not in the mood to hear about your sexual expeditions right now. Maybe later."

"No, hear me out," Tyler bellowed. "I've been listening to you cry since the coach left. Now it's your turn." Tyler pulled up a stool close to Nicky. "Like I was saying, so I called this dude, looking for a little Mandingo. Turns out he isn't even on the down low. There's this new super breed of gays called *Thug Gay*. Gay gangsters, inmates, bikers, dudes all tatted up. Who knew?"

Nicky let out a sigh as he tried to follow his friend.

Ignoring him, Tyler continued, "One night, after Lil' Kev had his little sugar cube, we were laying there in bed when he asked me about testosterone and why swimmers are doping. I said, 'What? What are you talking about?', as my ass was still twitching from the workout he had just put it through."

"Tyler, come on," Nicky begged him to stop.

"Hold on, I'm getting there. So I asked him why he was asking. Sidebar—you know he runs his own business, right?"

"Meaning he sells dope. Yeah, I got that memo." Nicky was checking out from the conversation as Phillip drifted into his thoughts.

"So you got that," Tyler continued. "He tells me that he's been supplying one of the coaches at the U testosterone. I mean, not just a little for weekend parties, he's talking a shitload."

"Phillip isn't using testosterone!" Nicky angrily put Tyler on notice to stop.

"No, I'm not talking about your boo. I told him to describe the person to me, and he described Connor to a T. He said that Connor was buying the shit for about eight months, then one day he showed up with this other dude." Tyler paused, taking a drink of his orange juice and then cleared his throat. "So I showed Lil' Kev a photo of both Connor and Coach Dean, and he confirmed that it was them. He said that the second dude was the one buying a shitload of the stuff."

Nicky let out a sigh as he thought about what Tyler was telling him. "What if Connor is doping? Why would Coach Dean be buying it too? Who else on the team would be doping?" Nicky scrambled to come up with someone on the team who would be doping. He couldn't believe what he was hearing. How he wanted it to be true, but he knew better than to take Tyler's word.

"The T is not for us, you idiot; it's for Dean's water polo boys. Look at them. They're massive. All of those motherfuckers are doping!" Tyler slapped his hand down on the counter for effect.

"I'm listening. But we can't go to the school, and say, 'Hey, they're doping.' We don't even know who on the team is taking the stuff. Does J. B. know about this?"

"No, J. B. don't know shit. That boy is too square to even know what to do with T. He isn't involved in the business at all, according to Lil' Kev."

"So is this Kevin dude willing to testify against them to prove it?"

"Are you stupid? Lil' Kev isn't going to the police with this. We did one better." Tyler reached down into his messenger bag and pulled out a photo.

Staring down at the photo, Nicky saw Coach Dean facing the camera with the back of Lil' Kev's head. Sure as hell, he appeared to be counting money, and the other dude was holding a box between his arm and his body.

"Look what the box says. Here on the side." Tyler pointed to something that appeared to be writing.

"I can't read that. It's too small."

"Yeah, in this picture it is, but if you blow it up, it's easy to read. It says, 'Depo-Testosterone 200 mg/ml (10 ml vial).' We don't take this to the school. We leak it to the media and let them do the work for us. And our hands are clean."

"Who took this picture?"

Tyler just smiled. "Don't ask so many questions. This isn't CSI."

Less than a week later, Nicky picked up the paper after Emily's morn-ing walk and saw the headline "New Head Coach at TBU Suspended." Under it was that same photo of Coach Dean that Tyler had shown him in the kitchen last week. Nicky smiled as he took the paper inside to read the full article with his morning coffee.

Reading the article, he discovered that not only was Coach Dean suspended, but Connor and several of the water polo players were, including subjects in the investigation. Nicky chuckled, wondering who it was giving up names so fast. It was karma working at its finest.

Nicky made no plans that morning other than walking Emily first thing in the morning. Today was the first day that Phillip might be able to make his first call to the outside world. If he was going to call, Nicky sure as hell wasn't going to miss it. Since the call would be a collect call, they were told that it had to be placed to a landline, so Nicky sat and waited. When the call never came, with each passing day, Nicky grew more and more discouraged and ventured out more to pass the days.

Each night since Phillip had left, Nicky played a song called "Blank Page," a song Phillip had told him to download and listen to the morning he had left. When Nicky looked up the song to down-load it, he was surprised it was by Christina Aguilera and immediately fell in love with the lyrics. Each time he listened to the song, although it was Christina's words, he could only hear Phillip's voice, "How do I say I'm sorry? How do I say I'm sorry?" It brought tears to his eyes, knowing just how much he loved him.

It had been a total of two weeks since Phillip had entered treat-ment. Keeping the house going and taking care of Emily was about the only thing Nicky was capable of doing. He hadn't been to class or practice since his showdown with Coach Dean and Connor. If he had to repeat the semester, he really didn't care. His heart wasn't there.

He had just stepped into the shower when the house phone rang. It was music to his ears, and he raced to the phone, located on the nightstand next to the bed. Soaking wet, Nicky flung his naked body over the mattress before the answering machine could pick up. "Hello." *This has to be him.*

"You have a collect call from Debbie's House. Push one to accept, two to decline." Nicky knew that was the name of Phillip's treatment center. He liked that name; it didn't sound so grim or extreme.

Unsure he heard the directions right, Nicky pushed the number one key and then heard his lover's voice, "Hello?"

"I'm here! How are you?" Nicky was about to jump out of his wet skin; he was so excited.

"I've been better." Phillip's voice was weak and deeper than normal. "I only have a few minutes, but I was missing you so much. I couldn't do another day without talking to you. The staff thought it might help me to hear your voice. How are you?" Phillip's voice cracked as he cleared his throat in the receiver.

Initially, Nicky wanted to fill him in on everything, tell him about Lil' Kev, Coach Dean, and the suspension, but hearing Phillip's frail voice, none of that mattered. He just wanted to hear his baby's voice. "Me and Emily are missing you like crazy. You do what you have to do to come home to us. We will take care of everything here. Don't worry about any of it. We got it." Nicky fought back the tears that were forming in his eyes. "Just work on yourself, and we'll figure the rest out later."

"I love you." Phillip's voice cracked.

"I love you more," Nicky replied, meaning every word of it.

"You're an amazing man." Phillip's voice sounded normal again. "I don't deserve you, but I do cherish you. I can't wait to come home. To hold you. I miss your smell."

Nicky smiled, thinking of what Phillip just said. His heart ached in the absence of his lover as well.

The call was short, but bigger than anything Nicky could have ever asked for. He knew they were going to make it. Just like that pastor in Iowa once told him, God works in extraordinary ways.

∿

Within weeks of the doping scandal breaking, the national news as well as ESPN picked up the story. As anticipated, Nicky's mother immediately called, and with mixed emotions, he answered the phone. Her disbelief was apparent as Nicky quickly clarified that neither he nor Phillip were involved. But it was also a time to come clean about Phillip and his addiction. Drawing from the strength that Phillip had shown him in the days prior to leaving, Nicky told her everything. Not completely thinking of all the details, he forgot one.

"So how are your studies coming with all of this going on?" she asked.

Nicky was speechless and was all too ready to lie, but he couldn't. "Well," he stuttered, "I'm kind of taking a little break."

There was silence on the other end, so he continued to talk to fill in the silence. "Mom, this is hard, harder than anything I've ever done, and I'm not sure it's right for me. I want to swim; it's the only thing I want. It's what I live for, and school, my studies, they take me away from what I love." Just saying those few words empowered him to continue, "Mom, I'm not like Dad. I'm not a brainiac. I'm miserable trying to do this, and I'm tired of failing at it." Nicky stopped to gain a sense of how she was taking it, whether he was going to be in for a fight. "Mom, are you there?"

He heard a sniffle; she was crying. He hated when she cried, and although she cried at everything, it still stabbed him in the heart each and every time.

"Yeah...I'm here." Her voice was weak as she forced herself to pronounce each word.

"Mom, don't cry. It's not that I won't ever go back. But right now, it's my time to swim. I can't do this when I'm old, but it doesn't matter if I get my degree when I'm forty." Nicky knew she heard him, but even more, he was proud of himself for standing up and telling her the truth. He also knew this would not be the end of their discussion—she'd be back.

35

Phillip had been in California for just over four months—a lifetime for Nicky. A simple telephone call was a luxury for them, with sometimes just two calls in a week. Phillip was eventually moved out of detox onto the rehab side of the facility and eventually from there into a sober living recovery house. His new schedule of N. A. and A. A. meetings, appointments with his psychologist, and mandatory house group therapy left little time for anything else.

During this excruciatingly long period, one morning, while sitting on the couch sharing his Cocoa Puffs with Emily, Nicky was mindlessly surfing the internet when he stumbled across a website for the local *Icy Waters* swim club. Seeing their Olympic-sized pool, the thought hit him like a ton of bricks what it was he wanted.

That evening, Nicky was down at the swim club's facility, signing up to join. Just in time for their practice, he swam for hours with his new team. Although Nicky was undoubtedly the youngest in the organization, he could outswim all of them.

Nicky left the house each day for practice, releasing the day's tension and doing what he loved to do, swim. He set out to improve his times to be fast enough to earn him a spot at the U.S. Nationals, with sights set on the World Championships. Being out of the house for several hours a day also worked to relieve some of the stress of living in this world without the man that he loved.

During the late evenings, missing his Phillip, Nicky took to Phillip's office, where he studied every swimming video the coach had in his files.

The night before Phillip was scheduled to fly home, Phillip made his final call home to let Nicky know how late his flight would be getting in. During the conversation, Nicky insisted on picking Phillip up from Tampa International. Initially, Phillip poo-pooed the idea, saying that he was coming in too late.

"No, I wanna pick you up," Nicky's voice was stern. "I don't care how late your flight gets in. I want to see you the minute your feet touch this state." Sitting in the home office, Nicky glanced around, zeroing in on his favorite photo of Phillip, the one of the two of them taken last summer in Greece. That first night they were having dinner, the waiter in his broken English offered to take a picture of them with Phillip's camera. Sitting side by side, both leaning in towards the other, they were unware that their hairlines were touching. Phillip's smile was radiant; his eyes were bright with a sparkle, something Nicky had not seen in a long time.

"Nicky, it's too much trouble. I can catch a cab to the house." Phillip pushed back.

Phillip finally caved in; Nicky had won. Nicky would meet him down in the baggage claim area. Trying to be funny, Phillip made Nicky promise not to bring the motorcycle.

The next day, Nicky was beside himself, cleaning the house, grocery shopping, doing laundry, giving Emily a long-overdue bath, and doing a little special grooming for himself as well. Nicky even got on the gardener's last nerve micromanaging the trimming of the rose bushes in the back yard, but he didn't care. Everything had to be just right. By evening, with just one load left in the dryer, he was ready.

He watched the clock, going over a million times how long it would take to drive to the airport, find parking, and then get to the baggage claim area. Nicky guessed that Highway 60 would be clear at that time in the evening, so traffic wouldn't be an issue.

Backing Phillip's Audi out of the carport, Nicky noticed the gas tank was near empty. *Shit, I forgot to get gas yesterday. I told myself to remember. If I stop for gas, I might be late. I think I have enough to make it.*

At the end of the driveway, Nicky stopped, looking both ways down the dimly lit street for traffic. As he was about to enter the street, his phone buzzed. Checking his phone, there was a text from Tyler—*Is Phillip home yet?*

Nicky hesitated for a moment, debating on if to respond to the text or continue backing out the driveway.

No I am on my way to pick him up now—Nicky tapped out before setting the phone down on the seat next to him and pulling out onto the street.

Arriving at the airport at the exact time as Phillip's plane was scheduled to land, Nicky had just enough time before Phillip would disembark and get over to baggage claim. Using short-term parking, Nicky got lucky finding a prime parking spot just across the way from the baggage claim area. With lightning speed, he arrived at the baggage area as the passengers were arriving from their flight.

Looking around for Phillip, Nicky noticed a thin man in a navy-blue pea coat was walking towards him. *Was that Phillip?* How could he not recognize his own boyfriend? Surely not, this man was way too thin and his hair much shorter than Phillip would ever wear it. Drawing closer, the man smiled at Nicky, a soft warm smile, growing into a full grin. That smile belonged to his Phillip. His skin tone was a pale yellow, as if he was sick. There was sadness in his sunken eyes. His once-beautiful brown eyes with long lashes had been replaced with dark circles and sadness.

Nicky's heart pounded as he placed one hand over his mouth in an effort not to scream or cry. Tears were forming, and he was going to cry, no doubt about it. Nicky began crying, tears of joy of seeing his lover, but also at the physical evidence of all that Phillip had gone through. The void of his absence was replaced with overwhelming joy and relief to have him home.

They hugged, a hug that was much longer than simply two friends who hadn't seen each other in a while. Nicky completely lost his composure at the moment of impact. Phillip took him into his arms and gently rubbed his back up and down as Nicky buried his face into his chest and cried.

"It's all right, baby. I'm home now." Phillip murmured in his ear.

When Nicky finally pulled himself together enough to lift his head out of Phillip's chest, the eyes of strangers were upon him, pretending not to watch. Nicky didn't care, as he wiped his eyes dry, followed by a couple of light sniffles. These people no longer held any power over their relationship. They could show as much PDA as they wanted. They were free to be who they were, a couple who loved each other deeply.

In the car, the conversation was light, as Nicky poked fun of those watching them in the baggage area. "Did you see the look on some of their faces? I should have kissed you. That would have surely have gotten their eyes to pop out of the heads."

"Yeah, mine too. I'm not sure if I'm ready for full-on PDA in front of an audience." Phillip took Nicky's free hand and lightly massaged it.

"How was your flight? Are you hungry? We can stop if you want to pick something up to eat." Nicky glanced back and forth between the traffic and his lover as he merged onto the freeway.

"No. I'm good. Just tired. It's been a long day. I was up early trying to get everything settled, doctors and medication prescriptions transferred, as well as making contact with my new sponsor here. I'm supposed to meet him tomorrow. Hit the ground running, as they say."

Once in the house, met at the door by Emily, Phillip showed more energy than he had all night as he rubbed and massaged Emily all over her body. Happy her daddy was home, she fell on her back, kicking her long skinny legs up into the air.

Standing in the foyer, instinctively, Nicky waited for Phillip to head to the kitchen and pour himself a glass of wine—normally in the past, the first of many for the night.

Almost as if he sensed it, Phillip stood up and placed a gentle re-assuring kiss on Nicky's bottom lip, tugging ever so slightly. Releasing a moan, Phillip's kiss was a drug all to itself, sending Nicky into ec-stasy, his head going light-headed from a single kiss. "Damn, I miss those kisses. I can't wait to get you into bed and get more of those." A charge surged down in the crotch of Nicky's pants at what was about to come.

"Well. About that. It's been a really long day. My head is killing me. Can I take a rain check on that? At least until morning?" Phillip brushed his hand over Nicky's growing bulge, disappointed that he didn't have the strength to give him what he wanted.

"Sure." Nicky's heart sunk a million feet. "I understand." He didn't. "I like morning sex better anyways." Something was definitely wrong, Nicky thought.

The next morning, Phillip's body was still on West Coast time. At a lit-tle after eleven in the morning, he was just waking up. Usually by this time, he would have had breakfast, showered, and attended either his first meeting or therapy session. Rolling over, Nicky's side of the bed was empty, cold. Listening, he could hear that the house was quiet.

Dragging himself out of bed, Phillip had to contact Adam, his new sponsor that he was connected with through the program. They had talked a few days ago, but today, they were going to meet for the first time. The plan was to meet at Hope Lutheran Church down on sixth, where Phillip would attend his very first local A. A. meet-ing. Concerned with who he would see there, of bigger concern to Phillip was who was going to see him. His sponsor in California had been telling him several times that ownership was part of his recov-ery, owning up to who you are, an addict.

Making his way into his bathroom, the medicine cabinet com-manded his attention. Phillip stared at the mirror past his reflec-tion. Anxiety and fear accompanied Phillip's desire to open up the medicine cabinet to see if any of his drugs were still there. He didn't want any of the pain pills, he told himself as he continued to stare at himself in the mirror. His mouth dry as a bone, he bit at his bottom lip. He wanted to back out the room, run as fast as he could, back to California if he could.

Phillip felt as if he was having a heart attack as his chest tightened and he lost control of his breathing, hyperventilating, sweat beading across his hairline. Snapping open the cabinet door, the loud pop of the spring hinges startled him. Did Nicky hear the noise? Phillip thought before remembering he was likely alone in the house.

Empty. The cabinet was completely empty. Nicky had to have moved them. A moment of panic struck him, realizing that Nicky must have seen everything. Bottles and bottles, different labels, but all containing the same thing, his Oxy. They were all gone. Did he throw them out or just hide them? Where would he hide them?

Anger washed over Phillip. Where could Nicky have hidden his pills? He didn't want any, at least that's what he was telling himself, but—. He stopped in mid-thought. That was bullshit. He was an addict. Phillip's breathing accelerated even more as the walls of the bathroom closed in on him.

His doctors and fellow addicts had been telling him in his daily meetings that his first time back in old familiar places was going to be a bitch, and they were right. He wanted to punch the shit out of the mirror, smash the glass into a thousand pieces. Or was it the reflection in the mirror that was provoking such rage? He could kill someone right now. Thank God Nicky wasn't here. He had to get his emotions under control. With a quick shower, he was out the door in less than twenty minutes. Leaving the house was like a weight being lifted off his chest. He could breathe again.

He couldn't get to Hope Lutheran Church fast enough, with just one stop at the Bay Shore Pain Management Institute for his morning dose of methadone. Seeing Adam standing in the parking lot, he recognized him from his Facebook profile picture. Short, dumpy, with a scruffy salt-and-pepper beard and mustache. Adam's face down in his phone, he didn't see Phillip as he drove past him and down a row of parked cars looking for a parking space.

Parking the car, Phillip hurried back towards the entrance where Adam was standing. "Hey, you must be Adam." Phillip offered his hand to exchange handshakes just as he reached Adam.

"Oh, hey there." Adam tucked his phone in his pocket. "You must be Phillip. Nice to finally meet you."

After exchanging pleasantries, Adam led Phillip into a small room where the meeting was going to be held. Phillip had already learned quite a bit about Adam over their telephone conversations, and now he had to listen as he laid down the rules of staying sober, according to Adam prior to the meeting starting.

The meeting was nowhere as encouraging as what Phillip had come to know in California, like the guys in there were just putting in their time, getting a time stamp. After the hour was up, Phillip was never so glad to get out of there. He had a two o'clock meeting with his new physical therapist, and then he could head home. Hoping that Nicky would be there, he just wanted to hold his baby. This recovery was like no other he attempted to do in the past. He really wanted it, more than anything.

By the time Phillip arrived home, Nicky had walked Emily and was standing in the kitchen putting the final touches on two salads. Off to the side, Phillip noticed two large nicely browned chicken breasts.

"Good Lord, you really weren't lying when you said you were learning to cook." Phillip walked around the breakfast counter towards Nicky. Taking Nicky into his arms, he scooped him up slightly onto his toes. "I've been thinking about you all day. I missed you this morning." Phillip laid another kiss on Nicky's lips, this time, stretching the kiss into several small, light nibbles.

Nicky licked his lips as he struggled to pull away from Phillip. "I actually went to the pool early today so I could skip training tonight. I want as much time as I can get with you." Adjusting his bulge in the crotch of his pants, Nicky smiled. "Don't start nothing you're not ready to finish." Nicky kissed him again, this time pressing his erection into Phillip's thigh.

"Didn't I promise you last night? You were the one who skipped out early, mister." Phillip gently massaged Nicky's growing cock. "No underwear...why don't we take this into my boudoir?"

"I'm not sure what your boudoir is, but I'm game."

Phillip gently pulled on Nicky's drawstring as he led him through the house and into their bedroom.

Laying Nicky down on the bed, Phillip smiled. "God, did I miss you. You little sexy stud." The day had been long for Phillip, and he was ready for some sense of normalcy. To make love to the one man who occupied so much of his thoughts while he was away was all he wanted. Gradually, the two slipped out of clothing one piece at a time in between kisses. Phillip lay on top of Nicky's now-naked body, gently kissing at his slim smooth neck as he took in the intoxicating mixture of chlorine and soap. The heat in the room rose as Phillip's senses engulfed him.

"I won't last long," Nicky cried as he thrust his hips up. "I missed you so much."

Mapping Nicky's body with small kisses, Phillip took in again the scent of his lover. "I love you, baby. I will do whatever I need to do to never leave you again. You're the air to my lungs." Phillip wouldn't last longer either. "You're so beautiful."

Their bodies shifting back and forth against one another, the friction tempered his sanity. Within minutes, Phillip grabbed both of Nicky's wrists and yanked them against the headboard. Stretching Nicky's slender body across the sheets, Phillip cried out as he thrusted, one, two, three times, "Oh God, Nicky!" In unison, Nicky cried out in ecstasy as well, his legs wrapping completely around Phillip, holding him close.

It took several moments for their breathing to come somewhat under control. Nicky reaching out and stroking Phillip's hair, their breathing was somehow now in sync. Still short of breath, Phillip rolled over and drew Nicky up into his arms, holding him close to his heart. The whole interlude took less than ten minutes.

Stroking Nicky's soft, creamy skin, Phillip felt the well-developed muscles in Nicky's back and arms. "Damn, you feel good." Phillip lightly squeezed Nicky's bicep. "You're doing some major swimming."

"Yeah, I can't wait to show you some of the times that I posted just last week." Nicky was in the best shape of his life. His finishing times were record setting, and even he couldn't believe them when he looked at them.

Lightly brushing the hair from Nicky's eyes, Phillip smiled. "Do you know how much I love you?"

"Yeah, but tell me anyways." Nicky rubbed his nose against Phillip armpit. "Will you go to the pool with me tomorrow?"

Nicky gazed into Phillip's eyes, and Phillip could only say yes to those eyes. "Yes. What time? I have to take my methadone before noon and then an N. A. meeting afterwards. What time is practice?"

"Five-thirty. Most of the guys work during the day. You can show up anytime that you want, though. I just want you there. I miss you yelling at me."

Phillip released a little snicker as he lightly traced the outline of Nicky's face with his finger. "I have an appointment at four with my regular doctor. She wants to see me. Follow up, just to see how I'm doing."

Nicky sat up. "Can she do anything about your weight? I don't like you this skinny. I want the meat back on my man."

"You should have seen me coming out of detox. I was even lighter than this. When they first started my methadone, of course, I had to suffer every side effect of it. I was vomiting and had diarrhea at the same time. It wasn't pretty."

"Yeah, that might be too much information for me."

"Then the insomnia set in. The doctors said right from the start that the high levels of narcotics that I had been abusing, that I was lucky to be alive. My addiction was about as serious as addictions got for the clinic and staff. Initially, for every good day, I had three or four bad days of intense pain and setbacks."

"Yeah, I remember that first call. When you called me, you sounded so sick. You were out of it."

"I don't even remember that call." Phillip's voice cracked as he closed his eyes thinking about four months ago. "I was really out of it..." his voice trailed off.

The conversation coming to an end, Nicky leaned in towards Phillip for a kiss and then shuffled his body into a position that he could lay his head across Phillip's chest.

After a couple of minutes of just silence, Phillip asked the question he had been holding off asking for the last month. "So what's going on with school?"

When Phillip first picked up that Nicky was no longer attending classes, not only was he disappointed, but he also blamed himself for wrecking both of their lives. But in the state he was in, he had to stay focused on himself. His counselors in rehab told him that he couldn't control what Nicky was doing two thousand miles away.

Nicky sighed. "College isn't for me. If school was the only thing that I had to focus on, that would be one thing, but it's the least important—"

"No, it's very important," Phillip interrupted.

"I know it's important. Just hear me out," Nicky cut back in. "My swimming, that's what I want. I'm knocking out some of the greatest times I have ever had. I have a chance next year of going to the U.S. National Championships in Illinois if I continue on this pace. I posted a 1:59 in the 200 Backstroke the other day. That's two seconds faster than anyone out there is swimming in a college pool."

"Are you kidding me? Are you sure about that time?" Phillip sat up. He couldn't believe his time could be that fast. In four months, results like that were impossible.

"Come see me. I'm a monster. I can't do that if I'm sitting up in a classroom all day. I hate school. It's not me." Nicky said, "I'm not interested in returning to school. I want to swim. Would you have let anything stop you?" Nicky's mind was made up and there was no changing it. "I've been thinking. I really think I can make the

Olympic team. I feel it! I just need the right coach!" Nicky pinched Phillip's right nipple as he gave Phillip a naughty grin.

"Oh, baby, I know you can... But right now, I'm in no shape to be anyone's full-time coach. I have to work on my own self—daily."

Nicky could hear the sorrowfulness in Phillip's voice. "Okay." Nicky shook his head trying to come up with something. "What about part-time? I need you! Not only as my lover and friend, but as my coach. I can't do it without you. There's no way," Nicky pleaded.

Phillip propped his head back against the headboard, pausing for a second. "I need you too. I love you so much." Phillip leaned in, gently kissing Nicky's forehead as he brushed his bangs back. I'm in."

"We're going to the Olympics, baby!" Nicky smiled as he threw himself on top of Phillip.

Phillip knew Nicky wasn't joking. There was no doubt they were heading to the Olympics.

EPILOGUE

One year later

They had been working so hard over the last year, Phillip attending A. A. and N. A. meetings daily still, facing his pain head on. He had transitioned from a physical therapist to a chiropractor. Phillip had been researching some of the results on pain management that some of the younger chiropractors were doing. He was enthusiastic about the possibilities of what he read and located one of the most highly talked about chiropractors who was just an hour away from Tampa.

Nicky accomplished his goal of earning an invitation to the U.S. Nationals as well as some national coverage when one of the top sports magazine ran a story about young Olympic hopefuls. After that article ran, the local media started calling him the Dark Horse because he came out of nowhere.

Phillip's recovery was not an easy feat for either of them. To celebrate his one year of sober living, a well-deserved vacation was in order—a getaway, a time to reconnect. They planned a trip to Hawaii, this time to the island of Oahu, the place known for its volcanoes and beaches with warm bathwater.

It was one morning on their third day, during one of their hikes in the countryside, that they stumbled upon a tattered old gate that was partially open. On the front of the gate, barely hanging on, was an old *For Sale* sign. Entering the gate, their eyes widened as if they had discovered Oz, both thinking the same thing at the same time.

"We should buy this place," Nicky was the first to say.

The old farm-style house sat on five acres, filled with rolling hills and mango trees. Walking the property, they discovered towards the back three old farm buildings barely standing.

"Are you kidding me? Look at all this great barn wood?" Phillip shouted as his eyes darted around the scenery.

Nicky's eyes lit up, knowing exactly what he was looking at. "Yes, my new pool. Right here!"

Laughing, Phillip shook his head. "Do you know how much money I would have to sink into this place for this to work?"

"So how much am I worth?" Nicky could barely contain himself, thinking that he could have his own training facility right here on their property.

The two moved at rapid pace on the purchase on the property with the idea of completing their move within three months. The fact that Phillip was not working played in their favor. When not attending one of his sober living meetings back at home, he Skyped daily with the local general contractor they hired to make the house move-in ready. In addition, by clearing an acre of trees, he also promised to have Nicky's four-lane, fifty-meter pool completed before their return.

JUST BEFORE SUNRISE, Nicky sat outside at the small bistro table overlooking the tops of the mango trees and ocean. The morning air was cool, and his hair had not yet dried from his morning workout. Phillip was somewhere, most likely engaged in conversation with one of the locals. As the warmth of the rising sun smiled down on Nicky's face, the front door of the house opened. Knowing the sound could only be Phillip, he called out to him, letting him know he was out back with Emily.

Phillip appeared at the back door with a radiant smile and then strolled across the grass toward Nicky.

"Don't you ever get tired of watching the sunrise?" Phillip asked as he neared where Nicky and Emily were sitting.

"No, not at all, "Nicky replied, noticing that Phillip had a spark about him this morning. "Seeing the sunrise is a gift. How can you grow tired of a gift?"

Phillip smiled. "You're right. Every day we get is a gift."

"How's the love of my life doing this morning?" Phillip asked as he kissed Nicky on the forehead and then took a sip from his glass of water. Emily rose, wagging her tail, and trotted over to Phillip for her welcome.

"Yeah, I love you too, Emily." Phillip scratched behind her ears and then down her neck, giving her a good rubdown. Within seconds, Emily did her usual, lying down and rolling onto her back so Phillip could rub her belly. "You like that, don't you, girl? Yeah, you like your belly rubbed."

Nicky pointed out past the acres of mango tree. "Look, another cruise ship is coming into port this morning."

For the last hour, Nicky had been watching the large cruise ship in the distance heading towards their island. Soon, Waikiki would be bombarded with a thousand people ready to get off the ship to explore the island.

Phillip laid down a week's worth of mail he had just picked up from their box down the hill and softly kissed Nicky again, first just his bottom lip, then returning for a full kiss, the one that drove Nicky crazy.

"You have a letter from J. B.," Phillip announced as he took another sip from Nicky's glass. "Did you ever write him back?" Phillip asked, referring to the letter Nicky received last month.

"I did... I wish he would just call or just email. Using the computer would be so much easier than these letters. He's so old-fashioned."

Phillip had now turned his attention to the ship out in the distance, "Yeah, he is." The ship was within thirty minutes of reaching shore.

Phillip sat quietly, watching the ship as Nicky read the letter aloud.

> *Dear Nicky and Coach Silva,*
>
> *Life is good here in Tampa. Mom and Desiree both say hi and are doing well. We went to court again last week, and the district attorney offered us a plea deal. My attorney said that's the best offer he had ever seen them give on a battery charge. I am officially on formal probation for the next three years and have to attend a couple of anger management classes over at Tampa Community. I am just glad to have that mess behind me finally. Desiree is doing well at General. She is working in Labor and Delivery. She loves being with the babies and new moms. Maybe after we get married next year, we can start on our own family. The world could use a couple more J. B.s in it.*
>
> *Catfish Corner had another big write-up in the Tampa Tribune. Every time we are in the paper, we get a surge of new customers. I have enclosed the article with this letter. I still can't believe the place is ours and is doing so well. The days are long, but Mom is loving it.*
>
> *Tyler came by the other day and looks good. He hung around for over an hour—I can tell he is missing you, Nicky. Can you please call him so he will leave me alone? I think he thinks he is black now that he has eaten everything on our entire menu at least twice.*
>
> *I know I have told you guys before, but I will never stop saying it: Thank you for believing in me and loaning us the startup money for the restaurant. I promise to pay every cent back to you. Enclosed is another check towards the loan. You have shown and given me and my family way more than any*

degree ever could have. Maybe someday I will finish my educa-
tion, but for now, I'm just enjoying life.
    Your bro for life,
    Jeremy Breedlove

Folding the letter, Nicky stuffed the tan paper back into its envelope and then did a quick visual of where the cruise ship he'd been watching was. The day had just started, and Nicky's cup was already running over with joy and appreciation for all that he had. Never in a million years would he have guessed this was going to be his life—a boy from Brandy, South Dakota, had a life full of love, which was all he had ever wanted.

ABOUT THE AUTHOR

Bryan Thomas Clark is a boisterous extrovert who is a proud member of the LGBT community. After twenty-seven years in law enforcement, Bryan retired in 2015 to focus on his writing full-time. His first novel, *Ancient House of Cards,* published in 2014, pushed the boundaries with a brilliantly crafted story of a young priest coming to terms with his homosexuality and was nominated for GOODREADS M/M ROMANCE 2014 Best Debut book of the year. Bryan's readers come as far away as India, Australia, and Germany.

Behind his keyboard working on his next novel, Bryan writes gay fiction with an emphasis on moral dilemmas and M/M romance. His multicultural characters and riveting plots embody real life, filled with deception, personal growth, and of course, what we all desire—love.

When Bryan isn't writing, he enjoys traveling, lying by a body of water soaking up the sun, and watching a good movie while snuggled up with his husband on the couch.

Born in Boston, Massachusetts, Bryan has made his home and life in the Central Valley of California.

Please visit his website at http://www.btclark.com